WILD FURY

THE GATEKEEPER'S FATE: BOOK THREE

EMMA L. ADAMS

1

Never expect a faerie not to screw you over.

Given my years of experience in dealing with the Sidhe, you'd think I'd know what to expect by now, but after two weeks had passed since the god of death escaped into the mortal realm and the Unseelie Queen had yet to make an appearance, I couldn't help thinking that she cared more about screwing with me than she did about catching said death god before he wreaked havoc across two realms.

I'd given Winter's monarch an enticing offer, or so I'd thought, but weeks had passed since I'd sent Lord Lyle to tell her that I would willingly help her catch the escaped Wild Hunt warriors who'd caused her so much grief if she offered to give me the means of finding the elusive death god myself. While the time difference between the mortal realm and Faerie was as variable and inconsistent as the weather, I doubted that was the reason for her lack of response.

If the god of death had been roaming around Faerie, she might have been singing a different song altogether, but since he'd vanished in the mortal realm, she plainly wasn't in any hurry to agree to my deal. While the god, also known as the Scourge, had yet to return to the city of Edinburgh, any potential disturbance in the realm of the dead had everyone on high alert, which was how I'd found myself spending this morning helping some of the local necromancers handle complaints from the locals about a screaming spirit in the catacombs.

"They weren't more specific than that?" I asked my cousin Morgan, who also happened to be the older brother of the necromancer guild's Gatekeeper of Death.

"No," he replied. "The ghost is stuck in a wall, apparently. Are you finally joining the guild, then?"

"No." I dropped my voice as the rest of our patrol joined us: Jas, Keir, and Lloyd. The latter held the reins of Pepper the faerie puppy as he ran around barking excitedly, as if we'd taken him to the park and not a hole in the ground. The rest of us were less than enthused about combing the underground tunnels, especially me. It'd been my cousin Ilsa who'd actually invited me on this mission, but she'd been dragged into a guild meeting with her boyfriend River and left me to cobble together an excuse as to why I could suddenly use necromancy despite having had no aptitude for it in the past.

As it turned out, borrowing magic from the Morrigan, the soul-eating queen of the death fae, had some major side effects.

At the foot of the stone staircase, we found ourselves in a series of interconnected square rooms with stone walls which exuded a chill that reached the very marrow of my bones. The only decent source of light was the witch-made spell Jas wore on her wrist, which emitted a glow like a torch, while Morgan and Lloyd got out a couple of necromantic candles whose small bluish lights didn't do much to dispel the gloom.

Pepper ran in circles and happily sniffed every corner while Jas held the light spell in front of her. Since she was barely five feet tall, her light only showed a small area of the room and left the ceiling in shadow. "I can't sense any ghosts."

I'd have to take her word for it on that. She and the others had easy access to the spirit sight, while I could only use mine if I shape-shifted into a giant bird-woman, and I figured the others didn't need to see that mentally scarring sight in an already creepy set of catacombs. Besides, if I used my spirit sight to peek at the souls of living and dead beings, I became unable to see my real-world surroundings, as I'd learned the hard way through sustaining several injuries while exploring the extent of the powers the Morrigan had loaned me before her inconvenient disappearance.

"Where'd the reports say the wailing was coming from?" asked Lloyd.

"Inside the walls." Jas took a step back, the light casting eerie shadows across her pale features and glinting on the piercing in her lower lip. "Supposedly. These tombs have been here for, what, at least a century?"

"Ghosts don't last that long." Keir produced a torch and shone it around the smooth stone walls before walking into the neighbouring room.

"Hey, don't run off with the light," Morgan protested.

"You could have brought something more effective than a candle," the vampire said over his shoulder. "Isn't this place supposed to be a tourist trap? You'd think a screaming ghost would be good for business."

"The guild is obligated to investigate any spirit-related complaints from the public," Jas said. "However ridiculous they might be."

Keir made an irritated noise. Jas's boyfriend seemed to have been forced into the guild under duress, since he had zero interest in routine missions and was more likely to be found wandering off and getting into fights than actually banishing ghosts. Then again, Morgan's penchant for running headfirst into danger and Jas's tendency to blow holes in the walls with experimental witch magic didn't make them particularly reliable either.

Why did I come with them again? I shivered, digging my hands in my pockets to avoid the chill and wishing I'd thought to borrow one of the necromancers' long black cloaks, which formed the main part of their uniform. My tattered jeans and jacket had seen better days, and while it wasn't like I had to go to the Unseelie Court on a daily basis anymore, if I kept getting invited to meetings with the Council of Twelve, I needed to upgrade my wardrobe. Somewhat difficult since all my cash went on paying the bills.

Until recently, I'd scraped together a living doing odd jobs for the local mercenaries, hunting down troublesome rogue fae beasts. Since the one souvenir I'd kept from my days as the Winter Gatekeeper had been the Sight—the ability to see faeries—I'd been uniquely equipped to deal with any fae-related issues. Work had been in short supply lately, so I'd decided to put my newfound skills to use instead, but we didn't see a single ghost as we made our way through the catacombs. Neither did we hear any wailing, except from Pepper when Morgan accidentally tripped over him in the dark. The faerie dog recovered, ran ahead into the next room, and then began barking frantically.

"Calm down." Morgan followed him, the candle in his hands making his tall, skinny frame resemble a wandering reaper. "Pepper, what are you doing?"

The puppy barked again, striking the wall with his front paws. As the rest of us entered the room, a faint sound echoed within, like the whistle of wind in the treetops.

"What's that?" asked Lloyd.

"Shh." Jas caught his arm. "Keep quiet, everyone. I heard something."

Gradually, the sound resolved into a voice, muffled as if trapped behind a wall. "Hello?"

"Someone *is* in there." Lloyd drew to a halt next to his boyfriend, who dropped his candle in surprise at the sudden voice. While Morgan scrambled to retrieve it, Jas hurried over to join the puppy beside the wall.

"Is anyone in there?" she called out. "D'you think there's a hidden room or passageway behind there?"

Keir rapped on the wall with his knuckles. "No, that's solid rock."

Silence spread throughout the room, but no further greetings followed from the disembodied voice. Ghosts usually haunted somewhere they'd spent time while they were alive or where they'd died, but these tombs had been mostly frequented by tourists since the twentieth century, as far as I was aware. How had a wandering spirit possibly ended up trapped all the way down here?

"There can't be a ghost inside the wall," Lloyd said.

"Try telling him that," said Keir.

"There's no room for a living person," said Jas. "Maybe the spirit doesn't realise he isn't solid and that he can float straight through the wall and escape."

Morgan peered at the solid surface. "Oi, ghost. Fly towards the light."

No reply came. Jas knocked on the wall with her knuckles. "Can you hear us?"

"Hello?" the disembodied voice called back. "Who's there?"

"Necromancers," Jas replied. "Are you inside the wall?"

"I don't know, but it's dark." The ghost's voice echoed faintly. "Can you help me get out of here?"

"Was the ghost's body buried under the wall?" Lloyd asked.

"Hope not," said Morgan. "Listen, you should be able to fly out. Should I come and get you?"

"I'm not dragging your disembodied form out of the wall if you get yourself stuck, Lynn," Keir said.

"Shut up, Langford." Morgan rapped his knuckles on the wall. "Better than leaving him in there."

"Keir, be nice," Jas said to her boyfriend.

The vampire shook his head. "Look, if I'd known we were dealing with a spirit this dense, I'd have asked the guild to send some novices instead."

"You *are* a novice," Lloyd pointed out. "If you want to

be pedantic. Anyway, the ghost might be part of something more."

"Aside from the wall?" Keir faced the solid surface. "Listen, mate, how long have you been in there?"

"Since they built this place in the nineteenth century?" said Morgan.

Not likely. Usually, spirits returned shortly after their death and didn't last for more than a few days.

"Don't give him ideas," Keir said. "He doesn't talk like a two-hundred-year-old ghost. I think he's bullshitting us."

"I dunno. The veil has been screwed up recently." Morgan gave the wall another firm knock with his fist. "I can definitely see *something* in there."

"Fine, I'll look." Keir's eyes glowed faintly grey-blue as he studied the wall. Without my own spirit sight turned on, it was harder to tell when a necromancer disconnected from their body to wander the spirit realm, but from the way the vampire's body went completely still as though the Unseelie Queen had turned him into an ice statue, I suspected he'd floated straight through the wall to take a look for himself.

"Hey—are you seriously rescuing the ghost yourself?" Morgan said to the vampire's statue-like body. "You bloody hypocrite. You're not supposed to go drifting off without using candles, anyway."

"Oh, come on, Morgan," said Lloyd. "You never follow the regulations yourself. Maybe the vampire can see what's going on over there."

Keir stirred, his eyes opening wide as he returned to his corporeal form. "Something is blocking me from reaching the ghost. A barrier of some sort."

"You mean the wall?" said Lloyd.

"No, something else." Keir paced along the wall, while Jas crouched down near the spot where he'd been standing.

"Hey," she said. "Check this out."

Everyone gathered around her to look at the underside of the wall, where a half-concealed opening was visible. It was barely big enough for a child to fit into, but Jas shone her glowing wrist into the hole and then stuck her head in to look around.

"Jas, don't get buried under the wall," Lloyd said. "*Is there an invisible barrier under there?*"

"I can't see one, but the tunnel passes underneath the wall," she said. "I can crawl in, I think. Unless someone else wants to volunteer."

Given that Jas was the smallest member of our group, she was the only person likely to be able to crawl through the tunnel without getting stuck.

"No," Keir said. "You might get trapped in there."

"I have this." Jas indicated the light spell, which overlapped with several other bracelets on her wrists. "I also have more spells to protect myself if the wall collapses on my head."

"Don't tempt fate," said Morgan. "Rather you than me, then."

"It's no big deal." Jas lay flat on her stomach and wriggled headfirst into the hole, disappearing inch by inch. It wasn't until her feet were barely visible that she exclaimed, "Hey, I found something."

"What is it?" I asked.

Shuffling noises came from inside the wall. "There's some kind of marks on the floor."

"Witch marks?" I crouched down in an attempt to see

past her, but I hadn't a hope in hell of fitting into that narrow tunnel, and besides, Jas's feet entirely blocked the view.

There came a loud scraping noise, followed by indistinct laughter from somewhere within the wall. Then a flash lit up the room from somewhere behind us, and a half-dozen transparent figures filled the space around us. *Ghosts.*

All of us spun around as the ghosts' hands ignited with blue energy. Kinetic power blasted off the walls, forcing us to drop to the stone floor. Morgan and Lloyd scrambled to retrieve more candles from their pockets, while shadows swept across my hands, turning them into curved black claws. I grabbed at the nearest ghost before it could corner the others, and it shrieked in surprise when the curved end of my claw hooked straight into its transparent form.

"Go to hell." I flung the ghost aside and into the path of a blast of necromantic power from Lloyd's hands. The ghost vanished in a flash, while a second took its place. They weren't powerful spirits, despite claiming the element of surprise, and each took only a couple of hits before vanishing into the afterlife.

Keir grappled with another ghost, a glowing light spreading from its transparent form to his hands before the spirit vanished. Up close, his vampire's draining ability didn't look that different from the magic I'd borrowed from the Morrigan, though I didn't know if he'd appreciate me pointing that out. Come to think of it, though, a vampire's ability to drain someone's spirit essence worked on living people as well as dead ones. Did the Morrigan's magic too? I doubted anyone would line up to act as a guinea pig, so I pushed the question to the back of my mind for the time being.

As the last two ghosts launched into an attack, Morgan and Lloyd stood back-to-back with glowing candles in their hands and yelled, "I banish you!"

The two ghosts flashed into nothingness, while Keir crouched down beside the tunnel opening. "Jas? Everything okay?"

"Yes," came her muffled reply. "I scrubbed out the marks on the floor, but I'm not sure what the spell was. Maybe some kind of ghost-attracting signal."

"The ghost is gone?" Keir asked.

"Yeah… I might need a hand to get out of here, though." A thud and a curse followed. "I can't turn around."

"Hang on." He took hold of her ankles, tugging hard. Jas's swearing echoed off the walls when she emerged in a rush and crashed straight into Keir. The vampire recovered, catching his balance against the wall, while Jas sprang to her feet.

"The ghost was a decoy," said Jas. "Can't say I know who crawled into that tunnel to draw the marks, though."

"Must have been a really short witch," said Lloyd. "Or maybe a goblin."

Jas elbowed him in the ribs. "Oi. We can't all be six-foot giants."

Morgan snickered at Jas's scowl. Even the vampire looked amused, though his expression darkened when he looked at the hole in the wall. "Those were weak spirits, but whoever led them here intended to draw us into a trap. We'd better make sure the person responsible isn't still lurking around."

I hoped the marks had simply been witch magic, but only Jas had seen them up close, and no living individuals appeared in the catacombs. After a thorough search, we left via the same stone staircase we'd used to enter. When we reached daylight, I took the lead and let the others' chatter fade into the background, wishing I'd stayed at home instead. I'd gone on this mission as a favour, but I hadn't even needed to fully access the Morrigan's powers to handle the ghosts.

Then again, devouring the souls of the dead would be classified as weird even by necromancer standards. So would devouring souls of the living, come to that. Every day seemed to bring new surprises from the magic I'd borrowed, and it was no wonder the Unseelie Queen had changed her mind about simply killing me outright. My ability to heal would-be-fatal injuries was useful enough for her to request my help to find the Wild Hunt and return them to jail in Winter, but maybe I'd gone too far in requesting the Scourge's name in return.

The complicating factor was the fact that the Wild Hunt had initially summoned the god of death in order to slaughter him and use his blood to remake the cauldron of resurrection, the former instrument of the Sidhe's immortality before its destruction at the hands of the once-leader of the Wild Hunt. The Sidhe weren't taking their newfound mortality well, and part of me wondered if the Unseelie Queen had other reasons for delaying the god's banishment than her reluctance to sign a deal with a mortal.

As for the humans? Their own plans remained to be seen, including those of the leaders of Edinburgh's necromancer guild. The guild was solid brick inside and out, with shimmering wards built into the walls, which glowed faintly when our group entered via the twin oak doors. Silence pursued us across the lobby and through the draughty corridors and worn staircases to the upper level. Most of the novices must have been out on missions, though I doubted even the senior necromancers were pursuing the escaped god themselves.

The Scourge was a relatively unknown entity here in Edinburgh, but a few centuries back, he'd been the beast to whom the Sidhe sacrificed the souls of unfortunate humans every seven years. My ancestor had escaped that fate by inadvertently dooming generations of Lynns to enslavement to the Sidhe, and while my cousin Hazel had broken the curse and set us free, she hadn't guessed the god might one day return to this realm.

As if conjured up by my thoughts, my cousin's loud voice echoed down the corridor like a particularly persistent ghost. When Morgan pushed open the door to the archives, it was to reveal both Hazel and her twin sister, Ilsa, standing among the shelves of ancient tomes. The two couldn't have been more different at first glance. Hazel sported hints of blond in her hair where her sister's was dark brown, her strong frame muscled from her Gatekeeper's training and her worn jeans and jacket similar to my own. Ilsa was curvier and dressed in the dark cloak of the guild's uniform, but having seen her talisman in action, I was pretty sure she'd come out on top in a fight between the pair of them.

"Hey, Holly," said Hazel. "Had fun on your mission?"

"Not especially, but Jas had it worse." I stood back against the wall to let Morgan and the others squeeze into the room. "She decided to crawl into a hole to find a ghost pretending to be stuck in the wall."

"Nobody else volunteered," Jas said. "Besides, if I hadn't crawled in there, I wouldn't have been able to get rid of the marks someone used as a ghost magnet."

"Witch marks," Keir added in explanation.

Ilsa shook her head at us. "You found a dodgy hole in the wall, and one of you decided to climb into it? I expected it to be you, Morgan, but honestly."

"Hey," Morgan said indignantly. "I thought it was a bad idea."

"So did I," said Lloyd. "The ghosts were wimps, but the witch marks the person used to attract them were hidden away where most people wouldn't have thought to look."

"It wasn't a summoning, was it?" asked Ilsa.

"No," I said. "It was a trap for the guild. I'm guessing they assumed novices would show up, because they got a hell of a surprise when they found us instead."

They certainly hadn't expected my Morrigan's powers, but I wasn't on the guild's member list. Strictly speaking, I wasn't supposed to be in this room either. Then again, neither was Hazel. If I had to guess, she was helping Ilsa comb through the books they'd scavenged from their old house to find the identity of Janet Lynn, the person we'd all received an identical text message from a few weeks ago. Given that nearly every person I knew of with the surname Lynn was in this very room, we'd all been at a loss to figure out who Janet was, but since she'd also claimed to be able to help us deal with the Scourge, Ilsa had refused to dismiss her messages as a prank.

"Weird," said Ilsa. "By the way, the boss has finally got through the backlog of paperwork from all that ghost crap a few weeks ago, so now she's ready to move onto the latest emergency."

For some reason, she was looking at me. "Which means?"

"It means she wants to talk to you, Holly," Ilsa said. "Specifically, about the Morrigan's magic and the escaped death god."

Oh, boy.

2

There was no refusing a summons from the head of the guild, and so Ilsa led the way out of the archive and down the corridor towards Lady Montgomery's office. Considering how many times I'd come into the guild's headquarters without permission, it'd been a matter of time before word of my presence made its way to the boss, but that knowledge didn't make me less apprehensive about finally meeting the guild's head honcho.

Ilsa rapped on the oak wood door while I did my best to smooth out my expression. From what I'd heard, Lady Montgomery was widely respected and feared in equal measure, not because she exerted any Sidhe-style magical control but because she was damn good at her job. She'd presided over the guild for decades and seen her necromancers through crises ranging from the faerie invasion to the more recent fights with the Ancients and their kin.

She also happened to be River's mother. Ilsa's half-faerie boyfriend waited beside his mother's neat wooden desk when she called us into the office, and I recognised the resemblance between their serious, pointed features despite River clearly having inherited his curly blond hair and green eyes from his Sidhe parent. Lady Montgomery's face was lined with wrinkles, and she wore her greying hair tied back in a bun and sported a number of badges and pins on her long, sweeping black cloak. How she'd ended up having a relationship with a Sidhe which had resulted in a child was a question not even the other necromancers were brave enough to ask. While my encounters with the Unseelie Queen and the Morrigan ought to make this meeting tame by comparison, I found myself resisting the impulse to avert my gaze as Lady Montgomery looked me up and down. "So this is the other Lynn."

"I'm Holly," I said. "Ilsa and Morgan's cousin."

"I'm aware of who you are." She beckoned the others into the office behind me—Ilsa, Morgan, Jas, Keir, Lloyd, and Hazel. The latter looked as out of place as I did amid the neat shelves and pristine carpets, yet the entirety of the boss's attention was focused on me. "I'm also aware that you have the spirit sight, yet you have elected not to join the necromancer guild."

"I'm not a necromancer." That, at least, was the truth. "I borrowed these powers conditionally from Faerie, and I didn't expect to keep them permanently."

"Borrowed?" she echoed. "I'm not under the impression that the Sidhe like to lend out their magic to mortals."

"It was the Morrigan, not the Sidhe." I was sure she'd already heard the rumours, but she evidently wanted to hear the story from me. "I visited the Morrigan to request her help to fight the Wild Hunt. As a prisoner of the Winter Court, she wasn't able to help me directly, so she agreed to let me borrow her powers for the duration of the battle. When I went back to check on her afterwards, she'd disappeared, leaving me with her magic for the time being."

"Inconvenient, yet not entirely atypical of the fae," she said. "I'm told you used the Morrigan's powers to resolve the recent issues in Death, which stumped even our most senior members."

Worry clenched inside my chest. "I'm not trying to usurp your authority. I barely understand how her magic works, to be honest, but when I found out I might be able to stop the ghosts from being stuck in Death, I did what I could."

"You can travel through realms, including the spirit world, can you not?" she asked. "Like the beast which is currently on the loose in this realm."

"Yes, but I don't know how to find the god who calls himself the Scourge," I said. "If he's not in the city, then there's only one way I know of that might lead us to him."

"Is that so?" she said. "What is that method?"

"Summoning." Out of the corner of my eye, I glimpsed Hazel trying to get my attention, but I ignored her—my cousin's habit of running her mouth off would not help convince the guild's boss to agree to my request.

"That," she said, "is against the laws of the guild of necromancy and the Mage Lords."

My throat went dry. "If there's a better idea, then I'd gladly hear it. I don't intend to fall afoul of the mages or the guild."

"I said summoning was against the laws, not that there

aren't certain situations which are obvious exceptions," she said. "That said, it will not be a popular idea. I'm told you were in Faerie and therefore missed the events of several months ago, when we had to deal with a series of attacks from Ancients upon the necromancer guild itself, which almost brought about our destruction."

For a moment, her gaze travelled across the others. Jas inched closer to Keir, whose gaze was on the floor; Ilsa paled; and Lloyd and Morgan exchanged grim looks. Only Hazel seemed unaffected by her words. She'd been in Faerie at the time, too, as I recalled.

"Those Ancients aren't around anymore, right?" I asked. "How...?"

"If you want the specifics of how the other Ancients were killed, ask one of the witnesses," Lady Montgomery said. "The only way to be rid of an Ancient is to use one of their own weapons against them, or something of equal strength. But the death of an Ancient comes with other consequences."

"Their blood bestows immortality." Hence the Wild Hunt's plan. "Yeah... some of the Sidhe would take advantage of his death but not all of them. The Unseelie Queen implied that she might be willing to give me the name of the god in exchange for my help recapturing the Wild Hunt. The Hunt wanted to use the god's lifeblood, but if I ensure they're locked up again, there won't be any danger of them completing their plan."

"A dangerous assumption to make," she said.

"Is it more dangerous than letting the god continue to roam around this realm, though?" I asked. "A few centuries ago, he devoured the lives of mortals in exchange for granting favours to the outcast Sidhe. He's a lot more dangerous now his physical form is in this realm, rather than requiring a ritual to be contacted."

"Very true," said Lady Montgomery. "Yet having the name will not enable us to thwart him, and I will not put the guild in peril without a concrete plan of action."

"It doesn't help that we have yet to determine which abilities the Scourge has," River added. "From the previous incidents, some of the Ancients could communicate with psychics and possess them—"

"Fuck that," muttered Morgan.

"And most of them can shape-shift or otherwise change forms," River continued. "They can also travel from one realm to another, and some can even continue to exist after their physical forms are destroyed."

Like the Gatekeeper's god. Hazel had dealt directly with the god whose magic had fuelled the vow which bound the pair of us to the Court, but the god's lack of a physical form hadn't diminished the power of the binding that had kept our family tied to Faerie.

"We want to banish the god, not kill him," said Hazel. "The Sidhe can do both, I'm sure. They already did it once."

"They only banished the god because a rift into the other realm was already open at the time," I pointed out. "Which required seven lives to be sacrificed."

"No, the seven sacrifices are only required to summon the god from his own realm," Hazel said. "A rift can be opened without killing anyone."

"It's still blood magic." Tapping into the realm even the Sidhe feared on some level was not for the faint of heart. The Wild Hunt and Etaina of the Aes Sidhe might have been willing practitioners, but I wouldn't touch blood magic with a ten-foot pole.

"Some of us use blood magic for good and not evil," Jas ventured. "I don't know which realm the god came from, but opening the rift isn't likely to be as hard as closing it."

"Which is why we need the Sidhe involved," said Hazel, as if her statement would bring the Sidhe sailing into the room to offer her their support.

Ilsa cleared her throat. "And you're sure they'll agree? Some of them might have occasionally worked with the Council of Twelve, but they haven't deigned to show up to any meetings lately."

Huh. I hadn't even known there were meant to be Sidhe members of the Council, but it figured that they'd have no more respect for the leaders of the supernatural community than they did for the rest of us.

"The Council of Twelve will doubtless understand the need to use whatever means possible to rid this realm of the rogue god," said Lady Montgomery, "but I cannot say the same for the local Mage Lords. Their former leader was killed by one of the Ancients himself in a summoning gone wrong."

"The fucker deserved it," Keir said in a carrying whisper.

Lady Montgomery levelled a stern glance in the vampire's direction, but she didn't voice a disagreement with his comment. "The Council of Twelve has been briefed on the recent incidents as well as the previous attacks by the Ancients, and they plan on holding a summit tomorrow here at the guild."

"The mages will be here, then?" asked Ilsa.

"Yes, they will," said Lady Montgomery. "You had all

better present a strong case for proceeding with the summoning if you wish for them to grant you permission."

Typical. If the mages disagreed, they could ban us from going after the god altogether, and then we'd be breaking the law by default if we acted on our own. The rest of the Council of Twelve were keen to find a solution, but the Mage Lords had remained comfortably out of the action until they'd had their hands forced by the Council's arrival in the city. Even now, I wasn't convinced they understood the severity of the threat.

"I'll try my best," I said. "I wasn't here when the Ancients last attacked the city, but I know summoning is a contentious issue. I'll be careful what I say."

After a lifetime of dealing with the Sidhe's penchant for flying off the handle at the slightest provocation, I ought to be able to handle the mages. At least the chances of being turned into an ice statue were minimal, though the notion of asking the local mages for permission to break the laws was as appealing as convincing a troll to leave his hoard. Especially as I didn't *have* the god's name yet and therefore had no leverage.

"The summit is tomorrow at eight," said the boss. "I expect those of you who have been invited to arrive promptly. For now, you are dismissed."

I was all too glad to leave her office along with the others. When the door closed behind us, Hazel rolled her eyes. "Another council meeting. Great."

"You volunteered to help out," Ilsa pointed out.

"I assumed we'd be chasing the god across the Highlands, not arguing about blood magic in a stuffy meeting room."

I rotated to face Hazel. "How long have you known the Ancients have attacked the city more than once in the past? Because it's news to me."

"Ilsa told me," she said. "I didn't find out until weeks after, since the Sidhe made sure I missed all the action. What was that god called, the Shadow Fury?"

"That's the one," said Ilsa. "Nasty creature with claws that could yank out your soul like a fish on a hook."

"Excuse me?" Was this Shadow Fury some distant cousin or other of the Morrigan's? If the god in question was dead, I'd probably never know, but I still felt slightly put out that Hazel had remained up to date on the gossip while I'd heard virtually nothing from the mortal realm while I was the Winter Gatekeeper.

"That's right," said Hazel, as though I hadn't spoken. "Furies are death fae, right? I wonder why we don't find them in the Death Kingdom."

"Because Faerie kicked them out." Ilsa's gaze travelled over to me. "Holly, I'm guessing you've never run into a fury before?"

"No." How many other secrets had I missed out on in the years I'd spent ferrying messages between the Morrigan and the Unseelie Queen?

"Be glad you haven't," Ilsa said, as if she'd sensed my thoughts. "Furies are giant feathery monsters with hell-hound-like magic, but the Sidhe don't tend to let the gods' offspring run around their realm. Even in the Death Kingdom."

"By 'giant feathery monsters,' I assume you don't mean shapeshifter fae like the Morrigan?" I said. "Also, what do you mean by the gods' offspring? If those ghastly beasts procreated, it'd have been nice if someone had clued me in sooner."

"There's a resemblance between the furies and the Morrigan, now that you mention it," said Ilsa. "The furies got exiled from Faerie a long time ago. They used to be sealed in a rift between the realms, but nobody has seen any in months. No surprise, given how many of them Ivy alone has killed."

"Which god's offspring are they, then?" I asked

"The Shadow Fury's, of course," said Hazel. "Nasty creatures. I doubt anyone misses them."

"I assume they weren't as strong as the actual gods," I said. "How *did* you kill them in the last battle?" I addressed the last question to Ilsa.

"With difficulty," Ilsa replied. "And exceptional circumstances. The problem is that we don't know nearly enough about this particular god or his weaknesses. You're going home now?"

"Might as well." Roseanne would be waiting for an update on my mission, and it wouldn't surprise me if she'd come to the guild to look for me by this point. "See you later."

Hazel snagged my arm when I made to leave. "Word of advice? Don't start asking everyone in the guild about the last battle with the gods. Dozens of people were killed, so it's a touchy subject."

"I'll take that under advisement." Freeing my sleeve from her grip, I headed downstairs and across the lobby, leaving the guild for the cobbled streets of Edinburgh.

Outside, a crow sat perched on one of the old-fashioned lanterns affixed to the side of a stone edifice. Upon seeing me, it shifted into a gangly teenage girl with glossy dark hair. The half-fae offspring of the Morrigan gave me a frown. "You're late."

"I got an unexpected summons to meet the boss."

Roseanne had wanted to come along on the mission, too, but sixteen was the minimum age to join the necromancer guild. She was still a few months short, so she'd had to sit this one out. At my words, her eyes widened. "You aren't in trouble?"

"No, surprisingly," I said. "The boss wants me to talk to the Council of Twelve tomorrow and discuss how to find our missing god. Which I guess means telling them about the Unseelie Queen's offer."

"You're thinking of making a deal with her, then?"

"Assuming she ever responds." Which presented us with a conundrum if she didn't, considering that she was the only person I knew of who might have an inkling of the Scourge's true name. "There aren't many other options, unless the mages want me to fly around Death and find the god myself."

"Bet they're jealous of you," Roseanne commented, falling into step with me. "You saved the city when you got rid of that god in Death. Even the guild couldn't do a thing to stop it."

Her words strayed a little too close to hero worship for comfort, though they marked a change from being viewed as the villain. Roseanne had faced more than her fair share of derision from the other faeries because of her own relationship to the Morrigan, and if I could do anything to mitigate that, I was glad to. On the other hand, I didn't need to make the moment when I inevitably lost access to the Morrigan's powers any harder to bear. I hadn't intended or expected to keep it for this long, but despite the way I'd grown accustomed to the shadowy magic lurking beneath my skin, it wasn't mine to keep.

"What've you been up to, then?" I asked, changing the subject.

"Not much," she said. "Oh, Hawk invited us to dinner tonight."

"Did he now?" I'd expected as much, given that he did the same every other day. "Then we don't want to disappoint him."

Roseanne and I walked out of Edinburgh's Old Town until we reached the street corner marked by a sign that read The Goodfellow Detective Agency. While the name belonged to Faerie's most notorious prankster, it was Hawk who answered the door and led the way through the office to the back rooms where he and Puck lived. Hawk was half-Aes Sidhe on his fae side, which granted him the bright-green eyes of the Summer Court, while his medium-brown skin and dark hair came from his South Asian mortal mother, from whom he'd also inherited his impressive cooking skills. Several enticing-smelling dishes simmered on the stove in the kitchen, where the modern fittings contrasted the enchanted paintings that shimmered on the walls of the adjoining living room. Images of forests and fields draped in snow matched the cold December weather outside, and I didn't quite know how I felt about having visited their house enough times to notice the way the paintings changed with the shifting seasons.

"You're back later than I expected," Hawk commented. "Not trying to avoid us, are you?"

"No, I got delayed at the guild," I said. "Also, I'm wondering if Roseanne is trying to make a point about my culinary skills by inviting me here all the time instead of raiding the cupboards at home."

He grinned. "I'll accept the flattery."

"Don't do that. His ego won't fit in the doorway." Puck entered the room, his hands in his pockets and his smart-casual clothing fitted to his strong lean frame. Mischief lurked in his gold-flecked green eyes, while his hair flickered with the colour of autumn leaves or flames. Warmth threatened to creep up my neck when he caught me staring. Despite my many attempts to convince him it was a terrible idea for us to pursue a relationship with one another, my eyes saw what they wanted to, and the flutter in my chest when his gaze took me in with equal appreciation was hard to ignore.

"How was the mission?" Puck pulled out a chair at the kitchen table and lounged in his seat in the casual manner of a trickster fae. "You aren't covered in blood, so no zombies, I'm guessing."

"No zombies but a few ghosts," I said. "I also met Lady Montgomery, so it's been an eventful day."

"You met the guild's boss?" Hawk glanced over his shoulder at me as he dished out portions of rice between four plates. "I heard she's pretty hard-core."

"She is," I said. "I can see how she's carried the guild through so much upheaval with barely a scratch."

While we ate our meals, I gave a summary of the mission, followed by my unexpected introduction to the guild's leader.

"She wants you to summon the Ancient?" asked Puck.

"That was always the plan," I said. "Unless someone else comes up with a better idea. The Scourge hasn't been seen in weeks, and a flying monster with the ability to hop between realms might have gone anywhere."

"He might decide to settle in Antarctica," said Hawk.

"Are we likely to be that lucky?" I asked. "No, he'll come back. Edinburgh is a hotspot for the dead, and souls are the Scourge's meal of choice."

"Not at the dinner table, Holly," Hawk said. "I'd rather not think about soul-eating monsters while I'm eating."

"You're the one who brought it up." I jabbed my fork in his direction, trying to ignore the sinking sensation in my chest. The Morrigan's powers were nothing on the reputation which had pursued me all my life, but it was typical that as soon as I'd found some people who didn't judge me for my family history, the universe had seen fit to give me the creepiest magical ability known to humanity. Roseanne might be the Morrigan's daughter, but she didn't have the ability to tear out anyone's soul, and besides, she wasn't immortal. I didn't know whether the magic I'd taken had affected my life span, and frankly, I wasn't sure I wanted to find out.

Hawk shrugged. "Yeah, but it's my house, and souls are not on the menu."

"Hawk," Puck said. "Drop it. Also, it's my house, too, and I'm all for souls being an option for our incorporeal clients."

"We're not a restaurant; we're a detective agency," Hawk replied. "Lack of clients aside."

"We wouldn't lack clients if you spent more time looking for them rather than researching fancy recipes."

I tuned out their good-natured bickering and focused on my food instead. Sometimes I just wanted the Morrigan's magic gone but not while the Scourge remained at large with his own soul-devouring powers. Not to mention the Wild Hunt, who might come back to try to claim Roseanne again—but until the Unseelie Queen replied to my offer, I had no excuse to pursue them myself and risk angering the Winter Court in the process.

The rest of our meal passed in awkward silence, at least on my part, and when Ilsa texted me with the details of the council meeting tomorrow morning, I seized on the excuse to leave.

"I should go get an early night, since I have to meet with the council tomorrow," I told Puck.

"Sure," said Puck. "I hope the mages don't give you too much trouble."

"I'm well versed in diplomacy with touchy supernaturals," I said. "If nobody gets turned into an ice statue, I'll consider it a successful meeting."

After Hawk said goodbye and went to clear up the plates, Roseanne left the office first, while Puck tailed me to the door.

"Sorry," he said. "Hawk didn't mean to imply you're…"

"It doesn't matter," I cut him off. "He can call me a soul-eating monster if he feels like."

I'd heard far worse. Besides, the Morrigan *was* as bad as the rumours, and when I fully shifted into her, we were indistinguishable from one another. If the local mages had had unpleasant past experiences with other soul-eating gods, then I wouldn't do myself any favours by assuming they'd be happy to fight alongside me if they found out. They'd be more inclined to toss me into a cell and throw away the key instead.

"He won't," Puck said, "because I'll turn him into a toadstool first."

"I thought you could only turn people into animals."

"No, I can do other living things as well," he said. "Anything, except for humans."

"You're the definition of humble, you are."

A grin swept his mouth. "I try."

My heart skittered, while a brief glance at the road showed me that Roseanne had left us alone on the doorstep. She'd been doing her best to give the two of us space, but while Puck had made his interest in me clear, he seemed content to stand back and let me make the first move.

And so we remained poised on a threshold, while I grappled with the newness of being able to make the choice for myself. It was a new feeling for me, since until recently, I'd never even thought about sharing my life with another person. If you didn't count my first clumsy attempts at relationships as a teenager, when I'd crashed against the limits of my Gatekeeper's role and my mother's expectations, I'd long buried the notion that I'd be permitted to have a say in my own future. Much less that anyone else might want to stay involved in my life for the long haul.

"Holly." Puck's soft tone was inviting, not demanding, and a magnetic force urged me closer to him. An inch separated us, and I halved that distance until his lips ghosted over mine. The merest hint of his warmth dispelled the chill in my limbs, and the softest moan escaped him as the kiss deepened. Breathing became overrated; the last threads of my self-control threatened to give way and propel me into his arms.

"Are you going to close that door?" Hawk called out. "It's freezing in here."

Puck took a step back, a smile playing on his lips. "See you tomorrow?"

"Sure." I did my best to focus on his dazzling smile as he watched me leave and not on the voice in the back of my head whispering that my future might not entirely be within my own hands after all.

The magic of the queen of the death fae ran beneath my skin, and I'd crossed the void into the furthest reaches of the afterlife once already. If I had to do the same again to rid the world of the Scourge, then next time I might not be lucky enough to return to Puck's side.

3

The following morning, I said goodbye to Roseanne after breakfast before departing for the meeting with the Council of Twelve.

While the necromancer guild wasn't quite as fancy as the mages' headquarters, I was still underdressed in my jeans and jacket compared to the cloaked necromancers I met on the other side of the guild's door to head to the meeting. After I'd lost my Gatekeeper's magic, I could no longer use glamour to make my clothes faultless enough to compete with the Sidhe, while I hadn't been able to justify spending money on fancy clothes when I had enough trouble keeping up with rent. Unfortunately, my Morrigan's powers could only shift me into a giant bird, not give me a nice dress, so I had to make do with what I had.

Shivering in the draughty meeting room, I buried my hands in my pockets as I waited for everyone to take seats around the long wooden table in the centre. Since the local Mage Lords and the senior necromancers had joined forces with the Council of Twelve—I didn't know how they'd come by the name when they numbered far more than twelve—it was a challenge to fit everyone around the table. Few half-faeries were present, except for River, but every other supernatural group was represented.

Lord Colton, the head mage for the West Midlands when he wasn't fulfilling duties for the Council of Twelve, cleared his throat to silence the murmur of noise up and down the table. His commanding stance and six-foot-something muscular frame were formidable enough even without considering his mage powers, while like the other Mage Lords, he wore a knee-length dark cloak.

"Let us begin." He spoke in a posh English accent. "We are here to discuss the Ancient known as the Scourge, who is believed to be loose in this realm, and our plans to deal with him."

"We can't keep sitting around waiting to be attacked," said Lord Addison, Edinburgh's Head Mage. The thirty-something man looked much less imposing than the other Head Mage at the table, with angular features and a slight frame. His slick dark hair was wet with gel, which made his pasty skin look even paler. "We must send a team to hunt down this beast at once."

"I don't see you volunteering, mate," said a redheaded mage with a thin scar on his face who I'd never seen before. He spoke in an English accent, like Lord Colton, but his casual manner couldn't have been more different. "Have you done anything to find the god yourself?"

Several murmurs of disapproval from among the mages clashed with stifled laughter from the Council's side of the table, while the Head Mage flushed bright red.

"You have no authority here," Lord Addison told the newcomer. "Didn't you publicly quit working for the council yourself, Lord Tyson?"

The red-haired mage shrugged. "I came back because you're all hopeless without me around. Looks like I got here just in time too."

"Drake, that's enough," said Lord Colton. "Lord Addison, I'd advise you to have a course of action ready if the Scourge returns. Unlike the last time the city was attacked by an Ancient, you cannot pretend you haven't had any warning."

"We wouldn't need to prepare for an ambush if we hunted the beast down ourselves," insisted Lord Addison.

"You mean sent someone else to do it," said Drake. "This is an Ancient we're talking about, remember? He's not going to show his face without good reason."

"The Scourge can travel between realms," said Ivy Lane, who sat on Lord Colton's other side. "That includes Death, Faerie, and all the liminal spaces between. He can also fly to any location in this realm, so without a compass which will point us in the god's direction, we might as well be running in the dark."

Ivy was human herself, but she wielded a talisman containing the magic of an Ancient and possessed some of their abilities as a result. Ilsa did, too, but her talisman was more effective when used against ghosts rather than the living, and there was little the Gatekeeper's book could do to an Ancient with a corporeal form. I could only hope Ivy's talisman would fare better, because the local mages didn't have enough manpower to subdue the beast even if they did manage to track it down.

"This is supposed to be your responsibility, Lord

Colton," said Lord Addison. "The Council of Twelve was founded to protect this realm against otherworldly threats."

"It was," said Lord Colton. "However, the current Sidhe ambassadors have yet to share any information they have on the Scourge or to even respond to our invitations to discuss the matter."

"Well, that's just rude of them," Drake said.

"Is that so?" said Lord Addison. "The Sidhe exiled their gods from Faerie, so they have the means of ridding our realm of this beast if they choose to. If they refuse, then I'd consider your council experiment a failure."

"I'd like to see you negotiate with the fae," said Drake. "Yes, the Sidhe *can* fight the Ancients, but are you sure you want to stake the safety of your city on their whims?"

"Exactly," said Hazel. "Besides, there's no guarantee the Scourge won't strike the city anyway, just for the hell of it. You need to be prepared."

Unfortunately, she was right. Besides, if the Sidhe had taken to ignoring the council's requests for their help, that left us with one option… appeal to the Unseelie Queen and convince her to accept my bargain.

"Negotiating with the Sidhe was supposed to be the Gatekeepers' job, or so I was told," said a blond mage who sat on Lord Addison's right-hand side. "Whatever happened to them?"

"The Gatekeepers no longer work for Faerie." Lady Montgomery cast a glance in my direction, though it was beyond me to tell how much she knew of the events surrounding the breaking of the curse. Maybe everything, if Ilsa had told her the details.

"Exactly," Hazel said. "We gave up our magic in order to prevent this exact scenario a few months ago. You're welcome."

"Hazel," hissed Ilsa. Addressing the rest of the council, she added, "If you think it's worth the risk, we can send a team into Faerie itself to request the Sidhe's help."

"I'm more than happy to talk to the Summer King myself," Hazel said. "And Holly will talk to the Winter Queen."

Will I now? I shot her a glare, but when a dozen expectant stares turned in my direction, I smoothed out my expression. "I can't promise negotiating with Winter will yield any results, but the Unseelie Queen's main priority at the moment is recapturing the missing members of the Wild Hunt. They, too, are pursuing the Ancient."

Lord Addison's eyes gleamed with interest. "So finding these Wild Hunt soldiers will lead us straight to them?"

"Possibly," I answered, "but they aren't what I'd call typical faeries. The Wild Hunt outcasts are using a type of blood magic to enhance their fighting abilities, and they've even managed to evade Winter's forces. I believe they're hiding in the Grey Vale."

"You have spoken to the Unseelie Queen of this?" Lord Colton asked.

"Not directly," I said. "I offered to help her recapture the Wild Hunt, if she in turn helps us to track down the Ancient and subdue him. However, she has yet to respond to my offer."

"The nature of faerie vows means that she would be obligated to keep her word," said Lord Colton. "Correct?"

"Exactly," I said. "With faerie bargains, it's usually best

to ask for something concrete and unambiguous. Like… like the Scourge's true name."

"True name?" echoed Lord Addison.

"The Scourge's name in the gods' language," said Drake. "Keep up, won't you? Using a god's name is a shortcut to making him show up where you want him to."

"Not necessarily." I pushed on. "If he isn't already close by, then it'll take more than speaking his name to draw his attention."

"You mean a summoning," said the blond mage. "Lady Montgomery, you cannot possibly agree to this."

"I'm more than happy to listen to alternative ideas," said Lady Montgomery. "If you have any, that is."

Nobody spoke, so I said, "If we succeed in getting the Sidhe's support to subdue the Scourge, then summoning him would be far less risky. We'd draw him straight into a trap."

"How do you know?" asked Lord Addison, who'd gone noticeably pale. "If the Sidhe turned their backs on us and left us to the Ancient's wrath, what then? I will not allow any summoning to be conducted in my city."

"It doesn't have to be in Edinburgh," I said. "But if we want rid of the Scourge, we'll need the Sidhe's help to beat him."

"And we need his name," said Lady Montgomery.

"If the Unseelie Queen agrees to make a deal," I said. "It's that or let the Scourge hunt us down before we can do the same to him."

"She's right," Ivy said. "I don't like the idea of summoning an Ancient, either, but I've seen it work before. Just remember the god can't be contained in a regular summoning circle, and you might need to consult a map so that you don't accidentally summon him on top of any spirit lines."

"We are not incompetents," said Lord Addison.

"Could have fooled me," said Drake.

"That's enough," Lord Colton interjected. "The meeting is over. Anyone who wishes to speak to the Sidhe is to pass on their concerns to the ambassadors—that is, the former Gatekeepers."

I didn't volunteer for this. Not that anyone seemed keen to ask my opinion. When we'd all left the meeting room, I waited until the mages were at a suitable distance before rounding on Hazel. "What the hell was that?"

"What's the issue?" She arched one brow, her face the picture of innocence.

"Lord Lyle hasn't brought a response from the Winter Queen yet," I said. "If I walk into the Unseelie Court, I might get thrown in the dungeon for making assumptions about Her Highness's willingness to help me. Besides, I never agreed to be your sole Winter negotiator."

"If you wait for her, you might die of old age before she answers," she said. "Besides, Ivy is willing to go with you."

"Ivy doesn't strike me as someone who'd enjoy being an ice statue." The last time we'd faced a crisis, Ivy had decided to yank me out of my body to see if I could travel into Death using the Morrigan's powers. While she'd turned out to be right, that didn't mean I entirely trusted her not to land us both deep in the shit with the prickly Winter Queen.

"No thanks." Ivy approached us from behind. "I thought you already made a deal with the Unseelie Queen."

"I sent her the offer, but she didn't deign to respond," I said. "She won't make a deal with a human unless she's backed into a corner. Same as the Morrigan."

"That worked out in your favour, though," said Hazel. "Besides, the Unseelie Queen respects power. Ivy has plenty of that."

True, but while Ivy had bested a Sidhe and claimed his talisman, making her the equal to most of Faerie's warriors, there was a good chance the Unseelie Queen would hate her on principle based on her humanity.

"Last time we bargained, she threw me into the Vale and left me to die," I said. "Yes, I got out in the end, but if we're thrown out before we get the Ancient's name, then our whole visit will be pointless."

"We also need the Sidhe's help," said Ilsa. "We won't get very far if we summon the Scourge and then he goes on the rampage."

"Exactly," I said. "The Sidhe might easily wriggle out of the bargain or turn heel at the last minute and leave us to deal with the fallout."

Hazel scoffed. "Then we'll consult our friend Janet and see if she has any better ideas."

"This isn't funny." Janet Lynn probably wasn't even a real person. Her message made no sense, and besides, *finding* the Scourge wasn't the issue. Getting rid of him was our main concern. "You're welcome to address the Unseelie Queen yourself and see if you can appeal to her compassion."

"Does she have any?" Morgan asked, overhearing us on his way across the lobby.

"She murdered her own sister, so no."

Hazel gave a sly smile. "I don't know, I've been

tempted a few times… joking, joking," she added as Ilsa elbowed her in the ribs. "You're all such pessimists."

"Sometimes I wonder if you've actually spent the last few years dealing with the Sidhe at all." Regardless of my opinion on Hazel's methods, she had a point in that the Unseelie Queen would gladly string me along for the rest of my mortal days if she was inclined to. If I wanted answers, I'd have to risk her wrath and hope that her desire to use the Morrigan's magic outweighed her personal dislike of me. "If by some miracle the Winter Queen agrees to my bargain, then I'll have to hunt down the Wild Hunt in the Grey Vale to keep my word."

"You can travel between realms, can't you?" said Ivy. "That must include the Vale."

"Can't say I've had a ton of practise." The Vale wasn't somewhere even the Sidhe liked to visit, and besides, I'd half expected the warriors to hunt *me* down instead of the other way around.

"Then we'll give it a trial run." She strode towards the door. "Coming?"

Ilsa caught up to us outside the guild's door. "Ivy, don't yank Holly out of her body this time around."

"Hey, that was an emergency," said Ivy. "Besides, it shouldn't be necessary if she can fly between realms without leaving her body."

"I can, but I'd prefer to avoid any unwelcome surprises." I stifled a groan as Hazel emerged from the guild's headquarters behind her sister. "I also doubt I'll be able to carry any passengers."

Hazel gave a winning smile. "I'd still like to watch."

"Your funeral if anything nasty follows me out of the Vale."

I left the guild behind and headed down the cobbled street. Roseanne hadn't waited for me outside this time around, but I'd told her to sleep in while I was dealing with the council. Frankly, I'd rather go back to bed myself than visit the Grey Vale, especially in the company of Hazel, who insisted on tailing Ivy and me all the way through Edinburgh's Old Town to the Ley Line.

Picking out a suitable spot to cross over, I tried to ignore Hazel's presence nearby as Ivy and Ilsa sat down on a worn bench. Shadows folded over my arms, and my body shifted, hands becoming claws, wings sprouting from my back, shoulders hunching, black feathers coating my body. My vision altered, too, greyness filtering in as the spirit sight turned on and the bench vanished along with its occupants.

Glowing lights appeared like pinpricks in the darkness, each one indicating a nearby spirit. Ivy and Ilsa appeared more distinct, being closer, and Ivy's features came into sharp focus when she left her body behind to join me on the other side. The greyness of our surroundings made it difficult to see anything else, but I found myself glad I could feel my own solid form in the endless haze. When Ivy had yanked my spirit out of my body, it hadn't been a pleasant sensation in the slightest.

"Here we are," Ivy said. "I wonder if Hazel and Ilsa can still see you in the real world while we're here?"

"Not if it's this foggy on the other side," I said. "At least Hazel can't draw on my face if I don't leave my body."

While Ivy's faintly glowing form hovered above the ground, I stood on clawed feet and felt the wind ruffle my feathers as the gates of Death appeared as a shadow on the horizon. If Ivy got too close, she ran the risk of being sucked into the realm beyond, but thanks to the Morrigan's magic, I no longer had that concern. From this angle, the gates looked normal compared to the way they had a few weeks ago, and if the Scourge was in the area, I was fairly sure we'd know right away. Instead of the gates, I focused on the Ley Line's current of vibrant energy running beneath our feet.

"The Vale's that way." Ivy pointed behind the glowing line. "I need my talisman to cross between realms, but I bet you don't need a crutch. When you shift into the Morrigan, you take on her form and effectively become indistinguishable from her."

Didn't I know it. "When the Morrigan was fighting alongside Fionn and the Wild Hunt, how on earth did you take her down?"

"I killed her," she said. "She might be crafty and powerful, but a talisman can carve her up as efficiently as anyone else. When she was reborn into a new body, the Unseelie Queen put her in iron chains to prevent a repeat performance."

"I knew the last part, but damn." Ivy was no ordinary human, that was for sure. "Can your talisman kill an Ancient too?"

"Yes, but we don't know what kind of Ancient the Scourge is," she said. "If he's more incorporeal than corporeal, it might be hard to land a hit on him. I knew of one Ancient who survived through possessing other people and existed solely in spirit form. Not much a sword can do in that scenario."

"Shit, I hope he can't possess people." During our brief encounters, he'd appeared to have a physical form of sorts, but he hadn't entirely belonged to the same dimension as the rest of us either.

"You'll have to go through to the Vale by yourself." Ilsa's ghostly form appeared next to Ivy. "I'll keep an eye on this side of the Line."

Ilsa could theoretically travel between realms herself, but she'd explained that the backlash of using her talisman for that purpose had almost killed her when she'd dragged herself and the other Lynns out of the Vale after the former Seelie Queen had banished them there. Apparently, throwing anyone who annoyed them into the Vale was a common tactic among the Sidhe nobility.

I moved to Ivy's side as the winding paths of the Vale began to flicker into view above the Ley Line, transplanted over the grey light where the realms intersected. I beat my wings, focusing on the grey until I found my clawed feet touching down on a long, winding path. The indistinct shapes of trees bordered its edge, but it didn't have quite the same lifeless, frozen quality as the Grey Vale. The earthen path was flattened with the impact of countless hooves, while faint traces of fog lingered from the Ley Line.

Ivy whistled. "Nice going. You brought us to the Path of the Dead."

"Not the Vale." I'd been here beforehand—most recently, when searching for the Wild Hunt after they'd taken Roseanne—but I hadn't even considered that I might be able to use the Morrigan's powers to travel into Faerie itself as well as the Vale. "If I'd known I could get into Faerie this easily, I wouldn't have needed to keep borrowing the puppy or relying on Lord Lyle."

"The Path of the Dead isn't part of the Courts, though,"

she said. "I doubt you'd have an easy job getting into Summer or Winter, especially without an invitation."

"Still." At least I had a potential escape route if my plan went sideways. "How am I supposed to find the Vale, then?"

"The Vale was originally linked to this part of Faerie, I think." She looked down at the path, which wavered beneath our feet. "I think we can still get through."

I focused on the remnants of the fog drifting around the path, while several rippling paths appeared transplanted on top of one another as I sought out the semi-transparent Ley Line. I beat my wings, focusing on a familiar silvery path, until I landed in the Grey Vale.

Where the Path of the Dead was composed of hoof-trampled earth, the Vale's paths were covered in a coating of silvery leaves that never seemed to change, while the trees were preserved in an eerie state between life and death. Howls drifted through the bushes, the cries of something being torn to pieces, and shivers ran down my spine despite Ivy's presence at my side.

"Right, that's enough exploring for me," I whispered. "How do I get out?"

"Same way you got in."

A moment of panic seized me when I found I'd lost sight of the Ley Line's glowing current of light, but Ivy rotated on her heel and vanished in a flash.

"Wait." Too late. I floated to the spot where she'd disappeared, but Ivy had easily slipped out of the Vale back into the mortal realm while I remained in the dead forest, alone but for the sinister cries in the background. Despite my corporeal form, I had the odd sense of being as out of place as a ghost in the land of the living.

As though conjured up by my thoughts—which wasn't that far out of the realm of possibility in the Vale—a shadowy form appeared before my eyes, glowing with vibrant blue light amid the darkness.

"Go away." When the wraith turned its empty face towards me, I whipped out a claw, snagging its insubstantial form. Another swipe sent the wraith flying back and disappearing amongst the silvery trees. Furious with myself for fearing a mere spirit, I extended my clawed hand towards the invisible line I knew lay beneath this realm, connecting the realms like the layers of a spiderweb.

I closed my eyes and beat my wings, feeling my way through the layers, through the grey and into the fogginess of the mortals' Death.

When my feet hit solid ground, I released a breath. Walking from one realm to another might be second nature to the Morrigan, but my human nature rebelled against the notion of slipping through the cracks and getting lost somewhere in between.

"Holly." Ilsa studied my face. "You okay?"

"Yes." My voice came out steady. "Did you say some creatures *live* in the cracks between the realms? Because I can't imagine anything surviving in there."

"You'd be surprised," said Ivy. "The Morrigan's powers put even the furies to shame, though."

Furies. The word called to mind sharp talons and vicious beaks, jagged wings and claws designed to rip and tear. Perhaps I'd heard the name after all, in a long-buried memory of one of my mother's lessons about the beings too brutal even for Faerie's worst corners.

Furies, the word once given to all death fae. And the Morrigan, their queen, and master of all the realms.

Her magic ran in my veins. If I wanted to find the Scourge and bring down the god who'd terrorised my ancestors, I'd need to rein in my human instincts and give in to the fury within.

And hope that my mortal self would survive the fallout.

4

After our sojourn into the Vale, Ilsa and Ivy returned to the guild, while Hazel tagged along with me back to half-blood territory despite my pointedly telling her to go with the others.

"I want to make sure you don't take any detours," she said. "If we're to make it into Faerie by noon, then we should all assemble on the Ley Line within the hour."

I paused with my hand on the thorny gate leading to half-blood territory. "You want us to go into Faerie *today?*"

"Not my suggestion," she said. "The Council's. But they have a point. Faerie's time slippage means that every minute we spend there is potentially an hour or more in which the Scourge will have the chance to attack this realm."

"At the moment, the Scourge is paying zero attention to us," I said. "Look, I'd be all for it if Lord Lyle had actually brought me a response from Her Majesty, but he hasn't. No answer doesn't mean yes, and she's unlikely to suddenly change her mind if I show up on her doorstep."

"River, Ilsa, and I will be going to Summer," she said. "You're welcome to stay behind and wait, but what if Her Majesty *never* sends a reply? It's not unheard of."

It wasn't, unfortunately, but I wouldn't get anywhere by assuming she'd comply with my demands. The most I'd be able to do was seek out Lord Lyle and explain the Council's request in the hopes that it'd expedite the Unseelie Queen's decision.

"Fine." I pushed open the gate and entered the half-faeries' territory. "Let me tell Roseanne first."

Arguing with Hazel was usually a futile endeavour, but I'd have preferred to inform Roseanne and Puck of our upcoming visit to Faerie without her hovering over my shoulder.

"Right, you'll need a babysitter," she said.

"Don't say that in front of Roseanne," I said. "She's nearly sixteen, and she doesn't need supervising."

Hazel shot me a grin. "I can't believe you adopted a teenage half-faerie."

"I didn't adopt her, Hazel," I said. "I took her in because the other half-faeries would have abandoned her on the streets. Someone had already locked her in a cage in a redcap's den."

"Aww," she said. "I guess birds of a feather flock together."

I gave her a withering look. "Hazel."

"Come on, that was funny," she said. "You're such a killjoy."

I ignored her snickering as I approached the cottage I now called home. Half-blood territory had thoroughly embraced winter weather in recent weeks, with snow dusting the rooftops and frost stiffening the grass while the bare-branched trees swayed in the chill breeze. The ivy coating the front of the small cottage glittered with a dusting of snowflakes, and icicles adorned the windowsills. While losing my Winter magic had also taken away my immunity to the cold weather, part of me would probably always feel an affinity for the darkest season of the year.

Unlocking the door, I addressed Hazel. "I'll be one minute."

Not getting the message, she came into the hallway instead of waiting on the doorstep. I expected to find Roseanne in her room, but instead I found a note affixed to her bedroom door saying she'd gone to the Goodfellow Detectives' office. Had she suspected I'd end up getting dragged to Faerie, or had she just got bored of being home on her own?

I headed back downstairs to join Hazel. "She's gone to see Puck and Hawk."

"Ooh," Hazel said. "Excellent. I had a few questions I wanted to ask them."

"I thought you didn't want to waste any time." *Yeah, right.* She'd been trying to find an excuse to ingratiate herself with Puck for weeks, and she'd be happy to delay meeting the Sidhe if it meant satisfying her curiosity. "If you really want to pay them a visit, you can wait until after we're done in Faerie."

"I did wonder how many of the Aes Sidhe would settle in the mortal realm," she said in thoughtful tones. "Not many of them were half-blood, according to Darrow."

"He's half Aes Sidhe." I'd momentarily forgotten, probably because her boyfriend, Darrow, was so reclusive that

I'd never been properly introduced to him before. "Is *he* coming to Faerie?"

"He's not part of a Court, so no," she said.

"Then who does he belong to?" I hadn't thought much on the matter until now, but I'd yet to ask Hazel about her boyfriend's ties to the Aes Sidhe. "He doesn't live in Edinburgh."

In fact, if he'd been living in the Court of the Aes Sidhe when it'd fallen apart, he didn't necessarily have a permanent home any more than Hazel did.

"He's deciding," she said. "So am I. We might have picked somewhere nice to settle down if someone hadn't dragged us back up north."

"Blame the Wild Hunt, not me." After locking the door, I made for the back gate out of half-blood territory. "I seem to remember the rogue Aes Sidhe wanted the Gatekeepers dead because of what *you* did to their Queen, besides."

I'd killed Adria, their leader, but there was no telling how many other rogues might be at large. It wasn't necessarily fair to blame Hazel for their grudge against the Gatekeepers, given that Etaina had been attempting to take over the Summer Court when she'd met her end, but if Hazel insisted on holding a grudge against me for cutting her and Darrow's holiday short, then I'd pay her back in kind.

"The rogue Aes Sidhe were living in an alternate reality all of their own," she said. "Darrow told me that might happen. They worshiped their Queen and would accept no substitute. Given the literal brainwashing she used on them, it's kinda sad."

"I have no sympathy for them." The rogues had captured and tormented Puck and might have killed him if I hadn't intervened—not to mention their betrayal of their half-fae neighbours had led to over a dozen innocents being slaughtered by the Wild Hunt.

We reached the sign on the street's corner marking Puck and Hawk's office. Resigned to Hazel following me in, I pushed the door inward and found Hawk behind the front desk, chatting to Roseanne. A number of cardboard boxes lay piled on the wooden floor.

"Holly." Hawk's smile faltered when he spotted Hazel. "And… you're one of the other Lynns, aren't you?"

"I'm Hazel." She examined the landscape paintings on the walls with an appreciative eye, watching the glamoured snowflakes fall from the painted skies. "Did you paint these?"

"No, I have no artistic skill. I brought them from…"

"From the realm of the Aes Sidhe." Hazel sauntered over to the painting of a vibrant meadow which was now dusted with snow to match the world outside. Several frolicking deer scampered through the grass, while the water of the lake at the edge glimmered in sunlight from outside the frame. "What's with the boxes?"

"We're setting up a new computer," Hawk said.

"Good," I said. "Roseanne can help you with that while we're in Faerie."

Her head snapped up. "You're going to Faerie again? I thought you were waiting for an invitation first."

"Someone got impatient and decided to volunteer me to talk to Winter." I glanced over at Hazel. "No matter how we look at it, we need the Sidhe's assistance both to summon the Scourge and to get rid of him, so we'd better hope the Seelie King is more reasonable than the Unseelie Queen."

The door at the back of the office opened, and Puck walked in, his brows rising at the sight of Hazel. "Something you need?"

"Her, not me," said Hazel. "And boy, does she need it badly."

Hawk snorted with laughter, while Roseanne ducked her head behind a stack of boxes, no doubt to stop me from seeing her snickering as well. I levelled a glare on Hazel that made her take a step backwards as if I'd unleashed the Morrigan's infamous death stare on her, but it was too late to stop the heat creeping up my neck.

I swivelled back to Puck, whose eyes glinted with amusement. "Ignore her. We're going to Faerie to talk to both Courts and to request that they help the Council of Twelve rid this realm of the Scourge. Roseanne, Hawk, I'll be back as soon as I can. Puck—"

"I'll come with you," he said. "If any Aes Sidhe survived in the borderlands, I'd like to see them off personally."

"Then let's go." Hazel walked out of the office, while Hawk burst into laughter.

I flipped him off with one hand, waved to Roseanne with the other, and exited the office before I lost more of the remaining dignity I possessed.

Puck joined us a moment later. "I take it the meeting went well, then? I didn't know you were going back to Winter so soon."

"I wasn't until someone decided to tell the entire Council that the Unseelie Queen and I already made a deal." I jerked my head at Hazel. "So if we end up stuck in the Vale, it's on her."

"You can get out of the Vale, no problem," Hazel said.

"Not with another person," I replied. To Puck, I added, "Anyway, some of the others are going to negotiate with Summer while I talk to Winter. You want to go to the borderlands, right?"

Puck inclined his head. "The Aes Sidhe rogues might still be in the borderlands, since I can't be certain they were all killed in the battle. I want to ensure they haven't left any nasty surprises behind them."

He had a point. The battle with the Aes Sidhe had coincided with the upheaval in Death, so it'd been so foggy that we'd barely been able to see who we were fighting. We also hadn't scoured the borderlands of any stragglers, though I'd have thought the half-faeries would have ensured none of them had stayed behind to kill any more innocents.

"All right." I rounded the corner into the street where the Ley Line overlapped with the mortal realm. "Oh, for crying out loud."

Ahead of us, River and Ilsa stood beside Ivy and Morgan, with Pepper the faerie dog running in excitable circles around them.

"What?" said Hazel.

"This isn't a field trip." I knew a losing battle when I saw one, though. "Can you try *not* to get us all captured this time around?"

Given that Hazel was in one of her annoying moods, the odds were high that we'd come to blows, so I resolved to part ways as soon as possible.

"Chill out." Hazel walked to Morgan's side. "Ready, Pepper?"

The puppy barked and tugged on the lead, well practised at sensing the boundaries between realms. In one bound, he led our group onto the leaf-strewn path which linked the two Courts.

Ivy was the first to move, one hand resting on the hilt of her long sword as she surveyed our surroundings. "Where should we go first?"

"Summer," said River. "Have you ever met the Erlking?"

"No, but I'm acquainted with Lord Raivan, the ambassador to humans," said Ivy. "I've spoken to Lord Lyle of Winter before, too, but we're not close."

"I'll talk to the Erlking," said Hazel. "We know one another well. I helped him get crowned, in fact."

"Good for you." I faced Ilsa instead. "If we're going to split up, we'll need to arrange when to meet back here. Are the rest of you going to Summer?"

"I wanted to talk to the half-Sidhe in the borderlands first," said Ilsa. "Right, River?"

"You think they'll want to help us after the Aes Sidhe slaughtered a bunch of them?" asked Morgan. "They're more reliable than the Court Sidhe, but I wouldn't blame them for wanting to avoid the Wild Hunt."

"True," said River, "but we owe it to them to give them a warning in case the Scourge returns to this realm. They don't have the defences the Courts do."

"Good point," Ivy said. "I've met the leaders of Half-Blood Territory, so I'll come and talk to them as well."

"Excellent," said Hazel. "We're all heading for the borderlands first… except Holly."

"Holly and I are going to search the former home of the Aes Sidhe," Puck said. "To see if they left anyone behind."

"Exactly." In truth, I wanted to put off the moment when we had to face the Unseelie Queen, but I wouldn't be taking Puck with me to Winter. Besides, we'd never thoroughly cleared out the Aes Sidhe's former base since I'd killed their leader. "If they're plotting against Winter again, it might make negotiating easier."

"Sorted." Hazel took the lead as we headed down the winding path into the borderlands, where tangled undergrowth filled the gaps between tall oak trees that stretched long branches to form a canopy, creating a perpetual twilight effect on the world below.

Occasional howling noises drifted from amid the trees, but with Ivy and River wielding talismans, I wasn't too worried about running into anything nasty. The occasional fallen tree hinted at the devastation the Wild Hunt and the Aes Sidhe had left in their wake the last time we'd been here, but the magic of Faerie had already smothered the damage. It seemed unfair that the Wild Hunt had targeted the half-faeries who'd made their home in the borderlands after the warring Sidhe who'd once lived here had finally killed one another off, but I was surprised they'd lasted this long without being challenged. Granted, the Courts already had enough territory of their own, and the borderlands had always been a contested area.

If the Aes Sidhe had been willing to peacefully coexist with their new neighbours, things might have turned out differently. When we came to a clearing where a familiar tunnel entrance led deep into the earth, Puck and I parted ways with the others.

"Want to take the puppy?" Ilsa asked. "Or I can wait for you in the borderlands on the boundary with Summer, and you can meet me there when you're done here."

"Assuming they don't get *distracted*," Hazel said. "Or—*ouch*."

A branch tumbled out of a nearby tree and hit her on the head, eliciting a stream of curses. Puck stood at my side, a smile playing on his mouth, but he didn't own up to the prank.

"That's fine, Ilsa," I said. "See you in a bit."

To my intense relief, the Lynns, River, and Ivy went on towards the half-faeries' home, leaving Puck and me alone by the tunnel entrance.

"If you're going to ask how she survived being Summer Gatekeeper without one of the Sidhe throttling her, I have no idea," I said to Puck. "Our pact with the Courts made it inadvisable for them to do any permanent damage, but with her, they might have made an exception."

He arched a brow. "They weren't allowed to harm either of you?"

"Only in the interests of not accidentally giving the other Court an advantage," I explained. "If one of the Gatekeepers got killed, then there wasn't really a backup option. I was an only child, and Ilsa and Morgan both thought they had no magic for their entire childhoods."

In a way, it was fortunate that the curse had been broken when it had. If it hadn't, I might have ended up like my mother, ensnaring a mortal man solely to gain an heir to offer to Faerie as a sacrificial lamb. Bitterness and misery had consumed her long before she'd left her mortal body behind to become a wraith, and the same influences had seeped into me like water soaking into a sponge. Perhaps I'd never entirely rid myself of her taint.

I shoved the thought firmly out of mind as we entered

the tunnel leading to the Aes Sidhe's home. Last time, I'd had to ask Puck to use his glamouring ability to turn me into a crow so we could spy on the Aes Sidhe and learn of their alliance with the Wild Hunt. While the information we'd gained had been worth the inconvenience of being trapped in the form of a small bird, that didn't mean I was particularly keen to repeat the experience. The narrow earthen ceiling and walls were suffocating enough on their own, while several wooden doors led into cave-like rooms. Some held basic furniture, but the majority had no adornment, no decorations. This place had been constructed quickly, no doubt, but despite the resemblance to their old territory, the Aes Sidhe hadn't made it into a home.

After several minutes, Puck led the way to the office where we'd overheard the Aes Sidhe's plans and began to examine the large wooden desk in the centre.

"I wondered if they left any of their tools behind." He held up a pen-like contraption which shimmered with an odd bluish light.

I took a step back. "That's a blood magic tool, isn't it?"

"Yes," he said. "They must have a few, I imagine."

"Someone put the blood of one of the Ancients into that thing, you know." The Aes Sidhe must have brought the tools with them, but the fact that they'd left one behind suggested the survivors hadn't returned here after the battle.

"I know." He slipped the pen into his pocket. "I think it's safer with us, though."

Footsteps sounded nearby, and my body tensed. "Someone is in here."

I pulled out my knife and went out into the corridor

again. An instant later, a Winter Sidhe approached us, dressed in black and silver finery, his dark hair glossy and his eyes vibrant blue.

Lord Lyle. So he'd been keeping an eye out for me after all.

5

"Lord Lyle." I lowered the blade. "What are you doing in here?"

"I could ask you the same question." His gaze went to Puck. "Trickster."

"Can I help you with something?" Puck asked in carefully defensive yet restrained tones.

"I've heard about you," said Lord Lyle. "And the Aes Sidhe. Why are you here?"

"Looking for survivors," I said. "I didn't know you ever came to the borderlands."

"We'd be fools not to, given how recently the rogues attacked our territory," he said. "My queen is keen to avoid a repeat of the Aes Sidhe's treachery."

"Does that mean she has you looking for the Wild Hunt too?"

His expression darkened. "Those who would offer to venture into the Vale, yes. Not all would take that risk."

Reading between the lines, the Unseelie Queen's forces had yet to track down the missing Wild Hunt warriors.

Which struck me as a little odd, given how keen she'd been to recruit *me* to help her do so.

"I did tell you that I would be willing to aid her with the search," I said to him. "If the Unseelie Queen agreed to offer me something of equal value. Have you passed on my message?"

"Yes." His gaze darted to Puck. "What you asked for was not of equal value."

"The Scourge's name?" I frowned. "It's only a name, right?"

"The name of an Ancient is far more than a simple word," said Lord Lyle. "We value names considerably higher than you mortals do, and the true names of the gods are potent enough to allow anyone to contact an Ancient and therefore render the banishment obsolete."

"You think anyone would actually want to do that?" I asked incredulously. "Most humans can't even speak the Scourge's name aloud, except Ilsa and Ivy, and neither of them wants him roaming around our realm."

"Nevertheless," he said. "Her Majesty's answer is no."

Dammit. "Then what would she accept in exchange for the name? Isn't it enough for me to find the Wild Hunt and heal anyone who might be injured in the attempt? Nobody else in the Courts has that power."

"There are other ways in which you might be useful to the Winter Court, mortal."

Tension gripped me at the memory of the last time the Unseelie Queen had tried to force me to give up more than I was willing to. Namely, Roseanne.

"Does she want me to get rid of another ghost, then?" Last time, she'd tricked me into carrying the ghost in question into the Vale and then left me behind, but that was before I'd figured out how to travel between realms. "Or the Scourge? Because she knows what will happen if the Wild Hunt finds him first."

Lord Lyle's jaw twitched. "They plan to slaughter the god."

"And use his blood to reforge the cauldron." I doubted they'd let the Courts use it without a price, but perhaps the Winter Queen was desperate enough to take the risk. "I can find the Wild Hunt, but I'm not working for Winter on a permanent basis. Did the Unseelie Queen plan to ignore my request indefinitely?"

"I am not privy to her thoughts," he said. "However, I am sure she will be glad to bargain with you in person."

"It's not much of a bargain when one person can turn the other into an ice statue for an eternity if they wanted to."

At my side, Puck moved slightly as if anticipating a fight. Lord Lyle, however, studied me with a calm expression. "That would apply if you were negotiating as a regular human, Holly Lynn, but that is no longer the case."

Hang on. Was he implying that the Morrigan's magic might be able to prevent the Unseelie Queen from getting the upper hand on me? I'd never considered the possibility before, mostly because striking back against Her Majesty was a swift ticket to a grim death, but if it kept me alive, I'd hold that strategy in reserve.

"All right." I glanced at Puck. "I'll come and talk to her, but I hope she understands that my first offer is likely to be my only one."

"Then come." Lord Lyle beckoned me to follow him down the winding tunnel towards daylight.

Upon returning to the forest, we approached the

boundary between the Courts and followed the Sidhe until the ground hardened with frost and the trees shed their last leaves. The sun shone without warmth upon the snowy exterior of the grassy hill which housed the main part of the Winter Court. Sidhe dressed in Court finery walked in and out, while I looked self-consciously down at my battered jeans and jacket.

"Pity you can't glamour me into a dress," I whispered to Puck. "Or can you?"

"No, but I could turn you into a bear."

"I think I'll pass." My heartbeat accelerated as the Winter Court's centre loomed closer. "You should wait outside. And stay away from the ogres."

"I'll wait." He looked like he might have wanted to say more but not in front of the curious nobles who'd noticed our presence.

Puck vanished in a swirl of feathers, while I followed Lord Lyle up to the mound of snow-covered earth guarded by two hulking ogres.

Within, the wide cave's ceiling had been enchanted to resemble a starry sky, while stalagmites and stalactites cast glittering lights all over the cave. Noble Sidhe roamed throughout, while redcaps walked among them, serving drinks and snacks. The lilting tune of a harp played from the corner, and I resisted the impulse to look in that direction and see if the Unseelie Queen had captured some unfortunate humans to play for her again.

In the centre of the room, the leader of the Winter Court occupied her usual spot on her carved throne. She was as stunning as ever, with glossy dark hair, skin as pale as the snow, and vibrant blue eyes brimming with Winter magic that matched the blade resting against the side of her throne. She wore a black dress the same shade as the night sky above and dotted with gems which twinkled like stars.

"Mortal." The Unseelie Queen beckoned to me. "What a pleasant surprise."

Sidhe couldn't lie, so she clearly *was* pleased to see me… though not necessarily for reasons that *I'd* be pleased to hear. I walked to her throne, wariness prickling at my spine. It was hard to gauge her mood, given her mercurial tendency to leap from pleasant to murderous in the blink of an eye.

"What brings you here, mortal?" she asked.

"I came here because the authorities in the mortal realm are concerned about the Ancient which the Wild Hunt summoned and which is currently roaming around, unchecked," I said. "They wish for me to speak to the Winter Court and request your help with recapturing the beast."

"Oh?" A smile danced on her ruby-red lips. "And what would they wish for me to do for them?"

"To find the Scourge…" I faltered, my throat closing up when it struck me that the rest of the cave had gone quiet. The other Sidhe had retreated and left the pair of us alone, and I didn't dare glance behind me to see if Lord Lyle had left too. "To my knowledge, finding the Scourge requires us to summon him. I assume that his name isn't common knowledge even in the Courts."

"You would be correct in your assumption, mortal."

She didn't say more, so I pressed on. "Several weeks ago, you sent Lord Lyle to request that I aid you in finding the missing Wild Hunt warriors. I replied that I would be happy to do so in exchange for the Scourge's name."

"I am aware of your request, mortal," she said.

"Then do you have an answer for me yet?"

"No."

My heart missed a beat. "I thought you wanted me to find the missing Wild Hunt soldiers and to heal any Sidhe of injuries sustained in the process."

Her eyes narrowed a fraction. "What you offer is not sufficient to exchange for the name of an Ancient, mortal."

"Then what would be sufficient?" My hands curled into fists to hide the shadows which threatened to creep out at the hint of her mood shifting.

"You do not simply ask for the name of the Scourge," she said. "You desire the aid of my Court in recapturing and restraining the god, while your family members have taken that same request to Summer."

How on earth did she know? Had she been spying on the others while we were in the borderlands?

"There's no need to look at me like that, human," she said. "I have no desire to harm your allies. I simply wanted to keep an eye on the situation in the borderlands, and my curiosity was piqued when several humans decided to enter Faerie."

Her words weren't as reassuring as she probably thought. "Then what would you ask me to offer in exchange for helping us recapture the Scourge and sending him back to his own realm?"

"I want to talk to the trickster," she said.

I frowned. "He isn't here."

I hoped not, anyway. *Please tell me he kept his distance.*

"Isn't he?"

I swivelled around, dread clutching me as Puck

entered the cave, flanked by the ogres who guarded the tunnel. His expression was carefully nonchalant, almost bored, but he must know he was in one hell of a bind.

The Unseelie Queen's smile widened, while anger clenched a tight fist inside my chest. She must have had a trap ready to catch him at the first opportunity. She'd known he'd accompany me here.

Puck gave a bow that somehow managed to be both nonchalant and elegant at the same time. "Your Majesty, might I ask why you have had your delightful assistants escort me here?"

"You're the same as ever, I see, trickster." Her gaze travelled over to me. "Did you not know that your friend and I had met before? The trickster saw fit to break into my private quarters to spy for his leader, the false Queen known as the Lady of Light."

Holy crap. I knew Puck wasn't welcome in the Unseelie Court, but I assumed it was because he'd ticked off a noble or three, not that he'd done something to merit the fury of the Unseelie Queen herself.

Dammit. Why did he insist on coming with me?

"My actions were regrettable, but I was bound to serve the Lady," he said. "Now, I serve nobody at all, so I will not impose on your hospitality."

"I don't expect you will, yet I have wanted to talk to you for some time now."

The Unseelie Queen had planned this. She'd known he'd be close behind me, because she must have had people watching during our previous visits. Perhaps even Lord Lyle himself had told her. Whatever the case, I could hardly walk out of here and leave him behind, so I'd have to wait for her to say her piece.

"About what?" Puck asked. "I told you that my previous visits were at the request of the Lady to whom I was bound. Now…"

"You serve no one," she said. "How interesting. A trickster, however accomplished, is not a rare find. You must have been skilled for Etaina herself to personally pick you to work for her."

"Skilled in some ways, yes," he said. "In others, not so much."

"Nevertheless, I may have use of you," she said. "What would you say to joining my Court?"

What? Was she serious? Even if she did want him to join Winter, that didn't mean she wouldn't dispose of him if she changed her mind. And given her temperamental nature, that was a given.

"I will have to decline," he said.

"There is something your friend wants from me, is there not?" She turned towards me, her smile mocking. "You want the name of the god. I think your trickster is a fair exchange."

"Instead of finding the Wild Hunt?" I ignored the word "your," knowing she'd intended to get a rise out of me. "You don't need me to use the Morrigan's powers to help you?"

"You think yourself indispensable?" she asked. "You are mistaken."

"Then why ask for my help in the first place?" I asked. "Why drag Puck into this instead? I didn't think you'd ever think of employing a Summer fae, besides."

"He is not from Summer," she said. "He belongs—or belonged—to the Aes Sidhe."

"I thought it was Holly you wished to make a bargain

with, not me," Puck said. "She cannot give me to your Court as part of a vow. I must swear it myself."

Fair point. From the mere hint of a scowl on her face, she'd hoped he wouldn't come to that conclusion.

"Exactly," I said. "We aren't your pawns."

Despite the power radiating outward from her stare, my fury on behalf of Puck made me meet her gaze. Looking directly at a Sidhe was inadvisable, but despite my wavering vision, I refused to bend.

"You overstep, mortal," she said softly. "Perhaps I will see if your trickster is willing to change his mind of his own accord."

Ice crept from her fingertips, and Puck took a step back, alarm flickering in his eyes as his feet began to freeze into solid ice. Before my thoughts caught up with my reactions, claws replaced my hands, shadows sweeping up my arms, and I leapt between Puck and the Unseelie Queen. The ogres moved in unison to bar my path, despite their Queen being more than capable of striking me down on her own.

Yet she made no move to unleash her magic on me, her smile gaining a deadly edge. "So this is the result of the harbinger's magic residing in a mortal."

I glared at her, breathless with anger yet unable to speak without sealing Puck's fate. With difficulty, I forced the shadows to retreat. My hands shifted back to human ones, but her unblinking gaze never left me.

"So the harbinger's magic runs in your veins still," the Unseelie Queen said. "I wonder how long it will take for the power of the death fae to overcome your fragile human nature? I cannot imagine it will be pleasant when you lose that power. It might even destroy you."

My gut clenched. I'd wondered the same myself, but she couldn't possibly know the effects of the Morrigan's magic residing in a human. "Puck and I decline your offer. We will seek the Scourge's name elsewhere."

"Would you gamble on finding the name before the Ancient returns to slaughter your mortal friends?" she asked. "If you were wise, you would give me what I desire."

"Meaning my undying loyalty?" Puck said. "If you intend for me to aid in the search for the Wild Hunt, you should know that a vow I swore to the Court of the Aes Sidhe prevents me from harming any of them."

The Unseelie Queen rose to her feet. "*What* did Etaina have you swear?"

She hadn't known? Admittedly, even Hazel hadn't, and she'd *been* to the Aes Sidhe's home—but anything the Unseelie Queen was unaware of might be a loophole we could use.

"The Aes Sidhe and the Wild Hunt had an arrangement of sorts," said Puck. "Etaina's subjects were compelled not to harm any of the Hunt's members, and that vow holds even after her death."

"How devious of her," she said. "She must have asked for *quite* the favour in return from the Hunt."

I'd say she did. Blood magic, the tools to use the Ancients' powers, and direct contact with the gods. The Unseelie Queen must know of at least one of those things, but I'd rather not enlighten her on the rest. After all, it'd been the Aes Sidhe who'd sacrificed mortals to the god of death, and Thomas Lynn's escape had been aided by the Summer Court, not Winter.

"I was not close to Etaina," said Puck. "You mistake me

for someone who may offer you intelligence on your former enemy and the sorry remnants of her Court."

"The Aes Sidhe are dying out," she said. "I see, now, why they sought the favour of the Wild Hunt."

Was this *an attempt to gain information?* I couldn't help wondering if she'd already suspected ties had existed between the Hunt and the Aes Sidhe and had been attempting to trick Puck into confirming her own theories, and that she wasn't truly interested in recruiting him at all.

"Their home was abandoned," I told her. "If we were to find any remaining rogues, would it be suitable recompense for the name of the Scourge?"

"No," she said. "Their pitiful lives are not of equal value to an Ancient's true name."

What more could she possibly want? The Unseelie Queen valued power above all else, and nothing was more powerful than the name of an Ancient. "Is anything? Because if not, then I will respectfully take my leave."

"One thing may suffice." Her gaze lingered on the shadows creeping along my palms. "Show me the harbinger's magic again, mortal."

I didn't move. "You saw it for yourself, didn't you?"

"I did." Her mouth curled into a smile. "I wondered how large a fragment of her power she loaned you, but it is far more than I imagined."

Tension gripped my spine. I had an inkling I knew exactly what statement would follow, and sure enough… "I will give you the god's name if you agree to surrender the Morrigan's magic to me."

"No." Puck spoke before I could open my mouth. "That is not a bargain you want to make, Holly."

"The mortal can speak for herself, trickster," said the Unseelie Queen. "And I think it is a fair bargain. She never intended to keep the harbinger's magic, and it would serve me better than its original owner."

"You want to stick it in a talisman for your own use?" Puck said. "You think the Morrigan would be happy with that?"

"What the Morrigan desires is irrelevant." She straightened upright, the blue in her eyes brightening. "I will not have this insolence in my Court."

The ogres reached out, but Puck shifted into a bird, flying out of range of their grasping hands. As I wheeled around, Puck shifted into a bear and crashed on top of the ogres before they could seize me instead. The Unseelie Queen's magic whipped past my face, but Lord Lyle appeared between his Queen and me in a blur of movement. I took the chance to run for the cave entrance, while Puck flew ahead of me as a bird. The instant I sprinted outside, I let the Morrigan's magic flood me, and wings sprouted from my shoulders. I launched into flight then soared above the trees alongside Puck's crow form.

Behind us, the ogres barrelled through the undergrowth, but we easily left them behind, soaring over the forest until the snow-covered trees of Winter became the dense tangle of the borderlands.

Puck shifted into human form as he landed on the borderland path beside me. "That was a close call."

"What the hell, Puck?" I shifted back into my human form, the shadows retreating beneath my skin. "Did you want her to skewer us both?"

"You can't give her the Morrigan's magic," he said. "She intended to trick you."

"You don't say." I scowled. "You do realise they can follow us into the borderlands, don't you?"

"We're closer to Summer than Winter," he said. "In fact, we have company."

A fae with long, dark hair stepped out of the bushes. She didn't wear the attire of a typical Sidhe noble, so I hazarded a guess that she was one of the half-faeries who lived in the borderlands.

"Hey," she said. "I'm Viola. You must be Holly, right? Your cousins told me to look out for you."

"Did they?" I asked. "Where are they now?"

"They went to Summer." She pointed down a path on our right. "There's a shortcut that way."

I didn't move. "Neither of us is invited to Summer."

"Your cousins insisted that they'd wait for you." Her gaze travelled over the surrounding trees, and I noted the array of knives strapped to her belt. If any Aes Sidhe ambushed her in the borderlands, she was more than prepared to face them. "Good luck. Also, watch out for wraiths on the way."

6

We had no other way out of Faerie without risking running into the Unseelie Queen's followers, so Puck and I made for the path Viola had indicated. Not a minute had passed before I spotted the shadowy outline of a wraith ahead of me, a cloud of darkness lit by the sheen of blue Winter magic.

Shadows swept my hands, which shifted into claws, while Puck launched into flight as a bird and flew over the wraith's head as a distraction. While the last wraith I'd set eyes on had stirred a deep-seated fear within me, I struck this one down with ease, my claws hooking into the beast's insubstantial form, before I flung it aside.

"I banish you!" shouted a voice, and a blast of bright blue magic shot over my shoulder and crashed into the wraith.

As the wraith exploded into nothingness, Ilsa hurried over to us, clutching the Gatekeeper's book in her hand. "I figured you wouldn't find much in the Aes Sidhe's lair. Lord Hornbeam and Lady Whitefall rounded up all the surviving Aes Sidhe to stand trial on Half-Blood Territory for the crimes they committed."

Puck landed beside us and shifted to human form. "It's no more than they deserve."

"At least one of us has good news," I said.

Ilsa's eyes widened. "The Unseelie Queen refused to listen to you? Didn't you offer to help to find the Hunt?"

"We did, but she decided the Scourge's name was worth more than that," I said. "She wanted the Morrigan's magic in exchange. Nothing else."

"You didn't say yes?"

"Puck didn't give me the chance to refuse before he landed us both on her shit list again," I said. "I knew forcing her hand was a bad idea."

Puck shook his head. "She always intended for you to come to her."

"So she could tell me no to my face?" It wasn't out of character for her, but I'd thought her request for me to find the Wild Hunt was as genuine as when she'd asked Ilsa and me to get rid of the unwanted ghost haunting her Court. "Sounds like her, but our only remaining option is to ask another Sidhe for the name. Is anyone in Summer likely to know?"

"I honestly don't know," Ilsa said. "The old Erlking might have, but this new guy... he's not from the era of the Sidhe who dealt directly with the gods. Granted, not many of the Sidhe are, but I can't imagine they pass those names around easily."

Given the power inherent in the very language of the gods, I couldn't imagine they were commonly known. "Unless... wait, the Aes Sidhe must have known the name."

"Not all of them," she said. "Darrow didn't even know about their experiments with blood magic."

"Neither did I," said Puck. "I doubt Etaina would have kept a written record in case any fool decided to risk making a deal with the Scourge themselves."

"Agreed," said Ilsa. "The people who actually did the summoning are more likely to know the name than anyone else."

"The Wild Hunt." Wrangling the Scourge's name from them willingly would be almost as impossible as convincing the iron will of the Unseelie Queen to bend, but unless someone in the Seelie Court turned out to have in-depth knowledge of the gods, we might have no choice in the matter.

"Exactly," Ilsa said. "The others are talking to the River's father, Lord Torin. Except for Hazel, who went to see the Seelie King. We should join them."

"Puck and I have no invitation to Summer," I pointed out. "Who's to say we won't get kicked out of there too? Especially if Puck keeps up his habit of insulting every fae monarch he runs into."

"I only insult the ones who insist on sending their ogres to manhandle me," he said.

Something clenched inside me at the reminder of how the Unseelie Queen had toyed with him, pretending she desired her very own trickster in order to tease any useful information on the Aes Sidhe from him. While he'd been lucky to escape her clutches, I was still mildly annoyed with him for needling her. Not because I didn't understand why he'd chosen to avoid getting himself indebted to Winter and why he'd suspected duplicitousness in the Unseelie Queen's offer but because he'd been seconds from joining her Court as a permanent ice statue, and I wouldn't have been able to do anything to stop it.

"I didn't intend for you to end up trapped," I said. "I should have guessed she'd have her spies watching you."

"I was careless." He gave a nonchalant trickster shrug. "Summer has more cause to welcome me than Winter does."

"If the paths haven't moved by now." Ilsa led us a short distance through the woodland, where the sun brightened with every step and the temperature rose until my coat, which hadn't been nearly warm enough in Winter, felt stifling.

In Summer, the flowers were achingly bright and the trees thick and thriving. The sky sported not a single cloud. Yet the thick bushes might hide a thousand dangers, the fragrant earthy smells hinted at roots which yearned to suck the life from any trespassers, and the birdsong might turn from vibrant to threatening in a heartbeat. There was a thickness in the air that went beyond the heat. Life magic fuelled their territory, the antithesis to the darkness in my own borrowed magic, and I had to suppress the urge to turn heel and return to the shade of the borderlands.

Ilsa didn't appear to be bothered, but then again, she didn't have the power of the death fae buried in her skin like I did. Out in the brightness, paths wound between trees of a perpetual evergreen hue, while a meadow of vibrant yellow flowers stood on our right. Puck surveyed the field, a thoughtful expression on his face.

"I've been here before," he said. "There must be a shortcut nearby from the former home of the Aes Sidhe."

"I wouldn't talk about them here," I murmured to him.

"Sounds like they spurned the Erlking's offer of re-joining the Summer Court in favour of invading the borderlands."

"We'll start by seeing Lord Torin, not the Erlking." Ilsa turned down a path west of the meadow. "River's father isn't much of a fan of humans, but he's willing to tolerate the Gatekeepers."

She continued down the path until we came to a large, pleasant house shaded by tall oak trees and with a gate leading to an orchard nearby. Through the window, I glimpsed River, Morgan, and Pepper inside the house. The door opened before Ilsa could knock, revealing a tall male Sidhe with shoulder-length blond hair the same shade as River's. This must be Lord Torin, though it was disconcerting to think of him as River's father when they looked the same age.

"Ilsa Lynn." Lord Torin's gaze went towards Puck and me. "And you are?"

"This is my cousin Holly," Ilsa said.

His green eyes assessed me. "The former Winter Gatekeeper."

"Former," I emphasised. "I'm here to find my cousins. I'm not working for Winter."

His gaze flashed over me. "What power do you hide?"

The glow in his eyes brightened, and the suffocating sensation already present in the air pressed against me tenfold. Despite my best efforts, shadows crept to my fingertips, and I curled my hands in order to hide them.

"You carry the magic of the harbinger," he said. "You are not welcome here."

"Wait," said Ilsa. "She's not working against Summer."

"No," he said. "I will not be responsible for bringing war upon the Seelie Court."

The heat rose to an unbearable level. Instinct seized me, shadows overtaking my human nature and shifting my hands to claws and shoulders to wings.

Magic slapped at my heels as I took flight, past the meadow and down the path back towards the borderlands. I didn't stop until I veered around a corner, straight into the path of Lord Lyle.

"Whoa." I landed at a crouch in front of him, sharply conscious of the wings sprouting from my shoulders and the black feathers coating my skin. "Look, I was just leaving. You can forget you ever saw me."

"I have orders to rid Faerie of you, mortal," said Lord Lyle.

Puck swept out of the sky, landing at my side in a swirl of feathers and leaves. "You will not harm her."

Lord Lyle's expression was half anger, half regret. "The choice is not my own."

"She told you to kill me?" Damn her. Whether I fought back or not, the end result would be the same, and Puck would be vulnerable to the Unseelie Queen's wrath once more.

"No," he said. "Death is not as final a fate as she would prefer."

"So she wants to exile me to the Vale again?" The Vale... where the Wild Hunt's warriors roamed, searching for the Scourge. Now I'd lost my chance to question both Summer and Winter Sidhe, they might be my last remaining option. Assuming they hadn't already summoned and slaughtered the god according to their original plan, of course.

Lord Lyle took a step towards me. "I cannot disobey my queen's orders."

I glanced at Puck. "Go back and wait for the others. I'll be okay."

"No." He looked at Lord Lyle. "Where she goes, I go too."

Lord Lyle's jaw twitched. "Fine."

"Puck, you can't—"

A dazzling light flashed, and greyness blanked out the world as the path of the Vale appeared around us. The uniform appearance of its winding paths lined with silver-grey trees suggested the Vale had no beginning or end, which might well be true. Puck's autumnal-coloured hair formed a startling contrast against the drab scenery, and his gaze roved up and down the path.

"Puck, for crying out loud." I pressed a hand to my forehead. "I've never tried carrying another person out of the Vale before. I only recently figured out how to travel through realms myself."

"I can steal a horse, if need be," he said. "If we come to blows with the Wild Hunt, I rather think we'll have ample opportunity to borrow one of their steeds."

"You're..." I trailed off, hearing an indistinct noise somewhere in the background. "Insufferable. And we're walking targets here."

"Got a map?" His steps were light against the leaf-dappled path. "I see why this place doesn't get many tourists. I can't even sense my magic in here."

My heart lurched. "What, you can't shift?"

"I think I can, but the place feels weirdly lifeless, for Faerie," he said. "It must be worse for exiles who are stripped of their magic before being kicked out."

Frankly, I preferred the Vale's yawning emptiness to the suffocation of Summer, but then again, the Morrigan's death-centred magic fit in with the general creepiness in the empty paths. "I can control where the Vale leads us, but I need to ask the right question. The Morrigan has the same ability to influence the Vale as the Sidhe and the Ancients do."

"Is that how you found the Wild Hunt last time?" he asked.

"I asked for the paths to take me to the nearest way out of the Vale, and they led me straight to the Wild Hunt's horses," I explained. "Like I said, you have to be specific in what you ask, and the Vale is fond of trickery and leading people astray. Not all that different from the rest of Faerie, really."

His mouth pressed together. "This time we don't want to get out of the Vale, at least at first. We need to find the Wild Hunt, but I can't harm them directly myself. Would you be able to take on all three by yourself, or do you think you can corner one alone?"

"Not if they're travelling together," I said. "Besides, I don't want to kill or maim them, not before I get the Scourge's name." Which seemed a taller order than beating the three of them single-handedly. I'd hoped I might have the aid of the Winter Court at my back, but I should have known better than to expect the Sidhe to willingly offer me their help.

"I wonder why the Unseelie Queen had such difficulty finding them?"

"Precisely what I was wondering," I said. "Better hope I manage to get the upper hand. Otherwise, you're trapped in here for the duration."

Why had I counted on the Unseelie Queen agreeing to my bargain? Had I so easily forgotten her manipulative nature? Annoyance clouded my thoughts, and I willed myself to calm down before I walked on. I couldn't direct the paths of the Vale while I was too fixated on the shit show I'd left behind.

Puck tensed at the sound of footsteps on the path ahead of us. Shadows flowed over my hands, and I rounded the corner behind Puck as he ran at the person approaching us. Human, with long dark hair pulled into a ponytail, her blade wreathed in blue light and pointed straight at Puck's neck. *Ivy.*

"Whoa!" I ran to Puck's side. "Ivy? It *is* you, right?"

"Even Faerie can't make an illusion this good." Ivy lowered her gleaming talisman. "Be more careful. I might have taken your head off."

Ivy's leather-clad form looked rather out of place against the grey-lit backdrop, but I'd never thought I'd be so glad to see her grumpy face. "Fancy meeting you here."

"You're looking for the Wild Hunt too?" she guessed. "Lord Raivan told me the Winter Queen isn't even trying to find them, so I figured I'd take care of them myself."

"That's not the impression I got from Winter." I'd thought the Unseelie Queen *wanted* to hunt them down and lock them up again. "The Queen—"

"She's a liar," said Puck. "She's playing us, and so is Lord Lyle."

"What does she have to gain by letting them walk free?" I suspected he was right, but Lord Lyle wasn't the one pulling the strings. That honour went to his Queen. "Ivy, how did you plan to get out of here if you found them?"

"Didn't get that far." She glanced up and down the path. "The Vale has been leading me in circles for a while, but I'm glad it brought me to you. We stand more of a chance of taking down the Wild Hunt with three of us rather than just me."

"We need to get the Scourge's name first," I reminded her. "The Unseelie Queen refused to give it to me unless I gave her the Morrigan's magic in exchange."

Her brows shot up. "Can she just take the Morrigan's magic from you? I suppose if anyone can, it's her."

"Precisely my thinking." Unfortunately. "To top it off, Lord Torin kicked me out of Summer, so I'd better hope Hazel and the others have more luck with convincing the Erlking to send help."

"Hazel seems to know the Erlking well," said Ivy. "We can get the name, I'm sure of it."

"It'll be easier if we corner one of them alone," I added. "They're likely travelling together, so we'd either need to split them up or kill the others."

Ivy lifted her glowing blade. "No problem."

I wished I had half her confidence. I'd used the Morrigan's magic to scare the Wild Hunt off before, but even an iron blade to the eye hadn't been enough to kill one of them. They deserved worse for the murders they'd committed, but I didn't relish the idea of torturing them into spilling their secrets. I wasn't *that* much like my mother. Or so I told myself.

Ivy took the lead down the winding path while Puck and I walked behind her. I could only assume that Ivy's talisman gave her the same level of control over the Vale as me, though she walked without voicing any commands aloud.

"Slow down," I told her. "Where did you ask the Vale to take us?"

"Be ready," Ivy said over her shoulder. "I asked the paths to take us directly to the Wild Hunt."

"And not a giant snake pit to shove them into?" said Puck.

"Don't give the Vale ideas," I told him. "It's more likely to throw *us* into a snake pit."

Rustling leaves echoed in the background, followed by the faint pounding of hooves. Tension gripped my spine an instant before the three horsemen rode into view, their faces hooded in black, their armour spiked at the shoulders, their steeds' hooves beating against the path.

Ivy's blade gleamed as she leapt forward and slashed at the flank of one of the giant horses. Before her blow made contact, the beast smoothly glided out of her path along with its rider. Ivy certainly had the Sidhe matched for speed—another side effect of her talisman—but from the glowing symbols on the warriors' wrists, they were equipped with blood magic glyphs which made them even more unpredictable than usual.

The Wild Hunt's horse wheeled around, and its rider swung his blade at Ivy. She blocked him, the clash resounding in my ears as Puck transformed into a bird. He might not be able to harm the Wild Hunt warriors directly, but he could divert their attention and frighten their horses with ease, flitting from one form to the next.

Meanwhile, I flew into the air above the horses and directed every ounce of the death goddess's stare at them. The horses reared back in terror, but their riders somehow kept their balance even when Puck continued to fly in circles, shifting into leaping flames and fearsome beasts.

I lunged straight at one of the horses, causing it to bolt

into the undergrowth along with its rider. The second launched forward, his blade aimed at me, but I beat my wings and flew out of range before diving at him from above. The feathered coating on my skin cushioned me from the impact of his armour, while the horseman spat out a curse as the pair of us tumbled sideways off the horse. *Finally.*

I rolled on top of the horseman, trying to pin him down, but he flung me aside. I glimpsed the third horse fleeing in the wake of Puck's fire, and when the point of a blade struck the path at my side, I kicked out with my clawed feet and then flung an iron dagger at my attacker. The knife missed, his speed turning his armoured body into little more than a blur as he dodged Ivy's oncoming sword.

"Stay still, you bastard." Ivy's eyes bulged as her talisman clashed with his blade, glancing off the side of the fae-forged metal.

Puck appeared in the form of a bear, his huge paw swatting the warrior's sword out of his grip. As the horseman grabbed for the hilt, I kicked the blade spinning into the undergrowth, while Ivy's sword pressed against his neck.

"Don't move an inch, or I'll take your head off," she said.

The warrior ignored her, his gaze fixating on me. "You came back to find us, harbinger."

What is he talking about? "Are you honestly happy to see me? I thought you wanted me dead for killing your precious Etaina."

Ivy's blade bit into his neck, but the horseman continued to speak to me. "You might not be worthy of the magic you stole, mortal, but wielding the Morrigan's magic qualifies you to join the Wild Hunt."

Okay, this was not how I'd expected this conversation to go. "I think I'll pass. The Hunt doesn't exist any longer, besides."

"Our purpose was corrupted," growled the warrior. "But we will ride again on the longest night."

"What the hell have you been smoking?" Ivy wore an expression of bewilderment that mirrored my own. "I thought you planned to kill the god you summoned and reforge the cauldron of resurrection. Don't you want your immortality back?"

"Immortality is not for us," said the horseman. "Our purpose was to ferry the dead."

"If you don't stop talking in riddles, you'll join the dead yourself," Ivy said.

"Hang on." His words made no sense. Hadn't their plan always revolved around revenge on the Gatekeepers? "Have you seen the Ancient—the Scourge—at all? Are you hunting him?"

The warrior's face twitched, blood beading on his neck where Ivy's blade cut into the skin. "We will ride on the longest night."

"The solstice?" I could only assume he meant the humans' longest night, since regular markers of passing time didn't exist in the Vale. "Winter's magic is at its peak on that night. Is the same true of the Wild Hunt?"

Rustling sounded, and the other two warriors emerged from the bushes. I tensed, but they made no move to attack us. Side by side, they appeared close to identical, save for the patch the man on the left wore over his eye.

"Glad you could join us." Puck appeared in front of them in a swirl of leaves. "Would one of you like to be of more help than your reticent friend?"

"We will ride on the longest night," said the warrior on the right-hand side. "The Hunt will ride again."

"Great," Ivy said in an undertone. "They've all been smoking the same crap."

"Maybe one of the Vale outcasts cast some kind of spell on them." I returned my attention to the warrior who lay beneath the point of Ivy's blade. "Look, do you not remember summoning the Scourge? You slaughtered a dozen half-faeries and joined forces with the Aes Sidhe to summon him, but he escaped your grasp. I thought you came here to hunt him down."

When the horseman said nothing, Ivy said, "Don't you remember the second invasion? When Fionn betrayed you?"

"The Huntsman did nothing but open our eyes to the truth," he said.

So he did remember. "He's gone. So is Etaina. Who are you taking orders from now?"

Their addled state suggested someone else had put the idea of this "longest night" bollocks into their heads, but it was beyond me to figure out who might have been powerful enough to warp the minds of the Wild Hunt. Not the Unseelie Queen, surely... right?

"We will ride on the longest night," said the warrior.

"Oh, for fuck's sake." Ivy shifted the point of her blade, drawing a line of crimson across his throat. "We want the name of the Scourge. You must have needed it for the ritual, so I know you have it."

"The name will not help you, mortal," said the one-eyed warrior, advancing on Ivy from behind. "You cannot speak the tongue of the Ancients without tearing your fragile mind to pieces."

"I beg to differ." Ivy lifted her blade and spoke a word.

The Invocation rippled through the air, driving the other two warriors to their knees. My own legs buckled beneath me as the magic pushed my shoulders downwards, but I forced my head upright in time to see Ivy's blade pointing at the prone warrior's neck again.

"The name," she snarled. "Give me the name."

He spat out a string of syllables, the crimson stain deepening as Ivy's blade cut deeper until he fell silent.

The other two warriors forced themselves upright, but Puck's bear-form reared up in front of them while I turned the Morrigan's death stare in their direction. "Word of advice? Run while you can."

They did so, abandoning their fallen ally as they jogged round the corner and out of sight.

Ivy let out a low whistle. "Damn, that's strong."

"Speak for yourself." My gaze dropped to the dead warrior, whose neck gaped open, revealing white bone beneath glistening crimson. Ivy's talisman had done what even iron couldn't achieve. "Did you catch the name?"

She inclined her head. "Yeah. Let's go and snag us a god."

7

First things first, we had to get the hell out of the Vale. Leaving the dead warrior in the undergrowth, I went in search of his steed. Ivy followed, blood sliding from the end of her blade and splattering the grey leaves underfoot.

"That wasn't smart," Puck told her. "He'd have been more useful alive."

"We got what we needed." She shook more crimson droplets from her blade, looking up and down the path. "Where are those horses?"

"I'll find them." Ivy took the lead around a corner, where we found two jet-black horses sniffing around the undergrowth. "See?"

An echoing growl rang down the path, and the hairs on my arms stood on end.

"That's our cue to leave." Approaching at a soft tread, Puck reached out a stealthy hand and took the nearest horse's reins. It whinnied, ears pricked, but he murmured something softly, and the beast calmed in an instant.

"I hope you know the way back to Faerie." He gave it a stroke and then moved onto the next one.

"How'd you get it to listen to you?" Ivy asked.

"Even wild beasts of the Hunt are predictable in some ways." He lithely climbed onto the second horse's back and then met my eyes, as if waiting for instructions.

Some undefinable emotion twisted inside me at the knowledge that he trusted me to get us out. "You'll have to stay close behind me, both of you. Ivy, make sure you ask the Vale to send us back to Faerie, not the mortal realm. We need to find the others."

Not that I was overly keen to risk the Unseelie Queen's wrath again, but the sooner we handed the Scourge's name to our allies, the better.

"Got it." Ivy gave the second horse a wary look. "I can't believe I've been coming to the Vale for years, and I never thought of borrowing one of their horses to get out. Granted, they're known for being temperamental."

"Puck's the one who has a way with animals." I walked into the lead, picturing Faerie in my mind's eye. "Ready?"

Another, louder growl came from behind us, and then a huge ogre, its skin the colour of stone mottled with moss and lichen, lumbered into our path. Ivy was ready with her blade, dealing a vicious slash to the beast's thigh. Pivoting, she drove her next blow into the ogre's throat, splattering the path with blood. It fell in a heap onto the ground, while Ivy's mouth twisted in distaste. "Better run before it attracts the death fae."

As if on cue, the sound of eerie howling echoed behind us. Hellhounds, perhaps. Whatever it was, it spooked both horses into breaking into a fast gallop. I brought out my wings to follow, while Ivy sprinted after us, swearing under her breath. "Slow down."

"Get on the horse," Puck yelled from the back of his own steed. "And hang on tight!"

Ivy clambered onto the horse from behind, while I hurried onward with my wings beating fast. *Get us out of here. Get us back to Faerie.*

The Vale vanished from sight, to be replaced by the path between the Courts. I came to a halt, but the horses kept galloping onward in a panic. Puck's bird form took flight and leapt clear, but Ivy remained pressed flat against her horse's back while it veered out of control.

Puck flew towards her and shifted to human form to speak to the horse. Calming at once, it veered to a halt and deposited Ivy into a spiky bush.

As Puck returned to my side, I rolled my eyes at him. "You told it to do that on purpose, didn't you?"

"She yanked you out of your body, Holly."

"I'm flattered." I found myself fighting a grin as Ivy detached herself from the pile of thorny branches, scrambling to find her sword. "Nice bit of improvisation there."

"Only for you, Holly." He laughed under his breath as Ivy's feet tangled in the bush and she tripped over with a loud curse.

The sound of someone clearing their throat drew our eyes to the nearby trees, where Hazel stood watching us. "I wondered where you'd gone. Ilsa said you got kicked out of Summer."

"We went to the Vale," I said. "And we have the Scourge's name."

"Yes, we do." Ivy stomped out of the bushes, wearing

an aggrieved expression. "You couldn't pay me to ride one of those bloody horses again. Where's Lord Raivan?"

"With them." Hazel indicated the path to the Summer Court, where I glimpsed at least a dozen horses bearing Sidhe riders. "The Erlking agreed to send help. The others are talking to Lord Torin, but they'll be along soon."

"Lord Torin is the prick who threw us out," I said. "He'd better thank us for getting the god's name."

"How'd you pull that one off?" Hazel asked. "I thought you were going to Winter, not the Vale."

"As I tried to tell you, the Unseelie Queen wasn't willing to agree to my bargain, and she wouldn't give us the name without asking for a price we were unwilling to pay," I said. "Luckily for all of us, the Wild Hunt's warriors relinquished the name when we cornered them in the Vale."

Ilsa walked out of a nearby patch of trees, followed by River, Morgan, and Pepper. I cast a wary eye over the Sidhe, spying Lord Torin among them. He didn't seem to have noticed us yet, but Puck inched closer to me at the sight of him.

"We have the name," Hazel announced to Ilsa and the others.

"Whoa, you got the name from the Wild Hunt?" Ilsa's brow furrowed in confusion. "Or did Winter have a change of heart?"

"Ivy and I cornered the Hunt's warriors in the Vale." My gaze landed on Ivy, who'd gone to talk to a dark-haired Summer Sidhe. "Who's she talking to?"

"That's Lord Raivan," said Hazel. "He has the dubious honour of dealing with all mortal-related matters. Pity for him. He'll want this over with, so I expect he'll swallow his pride and agree to join us as soon as we have the trap ready for the Scourge."

"When will that be, exactly?" I asked.

"Soon," Ilsa said. "The mages might have been stalling, but the necromancers have been preparing for a while. All I need to do is give them the word."

"Wait, they have?" I asked. "I thought summoning the god was a last resort."

"The guild's been prepared for a similar disaster ever since the last one," Ilsa said. "It shouldn't take long for us to mobilise them to take action. Ivy and I will go back, along with anyone else who wants to help the guild, but the rest of you might as well stay here. With the way time works in Faerie, it won't take a minute for us to be ready."

"Is it even the same day back in the mortal realm as it was when we left?" Probably not, but it didn't necessarily matter. "We'll wait, then."

With Pepper in the lead, Ilsa, Morgan, and Ivy vanished through the Ley Line, while River remained with the Summer Sidhe. Hazel, meanwhile, seemed to have no intention of leaving Puck and me in peace.

"More of the Sidhe volunteered than I expected." She cast a critical eye over the assembled horses. "The Seelie King didn't come with them because his advisors said it was too risky. Seems overly cautious, if you ask me."

"I have to disagree there," Puck said. "I'm going to see what the other Sidhe think of all this."

He shifted into a bird and flew away, while I studied the gathering Sidhe, unable to ignore the sense of foreboding which had lingered ever since our bizarre encounter with the Wild Hunt in the Vale. We had everything we needed to summon and banish the Scourge, so why did I feel like we were walking in the wrong direction? Maybe it was the odd behaviour of the Wild Hunt's warriors, or my suspicion that the Unseelie Queen hadn't been trying to find them at all. She must know our plan, given that I'd sent my request for the god's name straight to her, but what would she possibly have to gain from letting her enemies walk free?

I paced in tense circles while we waited for the others' return. Fortunately, Ilsa had been right, because scarcely ten minutes passed before she and Morgan returned via the Ley Line.

"Ivy's with the Council," Ilsa said as Morgan restrained Pepper from running into the undergrowth. "She's bringing them to the location for the summoning. We'll meet them there."

"Cool." Hazel went to tell the Summer Sidhe, as well as River, who stood in conversation with Lord Torin. I wondered if *he* particularly cared that his dad had kicked me out of the Summer Court. Maybe he hadn't seen, but my sense of unease persisted.

I approached Ilsa and Morgan, lowering my voice so the Sidhe wouldn't overhear. "You should know... there was something seriously weird about how the Wild Hunt were acting when we cornered them in the Vale."

"Weird how?" Ilsa asked. "I never asked—did you leave the other warriors alive? Ivy said she killed one of them."

"She did, but they weren't fighting to kill the way they were before," I said. "They didn't seem to care about the Scourge at all. They acted as if they weren't *trying* to find him."

Her eyes rounded. "You think they let you win? They let you take the god's name on purpose?"

"They didn't want us to know, but they didn't go out of their way to keep us from pressing our advantage," I said. "The two survivors ran away into the forest. Maybe we should have finished them off, but they were acting like they were under some weird kind of enchantment."

"Ilsa," River called out. "We're ready."

"Got it." Ilsa beckoned to Morgan and Pepper. "We're shortcutting straight to the area in the mortal realm where we'll be doing the summoning."

"Not on the Ley Line?" I asked.

"Definitely not." Hazel bounded over to join us again. "We picked somewhere it's safe to summon a god without terrifying a bunch of human bystanders."

Puck flew to land beside me. "Ready?"

Not really. We had few options and even fewer chances to be rid of the Scourge, so I hastened to get out of Lord Torin's line of sight and followed Ilsa and her siblings through the Ley Line.

We all vanished in a flash, landing in an open field draped in heather and gorse. The Sidhe's horses galloped across the open landscape, while the humans followed on foot.

This place looks familiar. I recognised the nearby patch of forest and the hill leading down to a cluster of stone buildings that formed a small village. Foxwood, our former home.

"You never mentioned we'd be so close to the gate to Faerie," I said to Hazel.

"No need to sound so accusing." She pointed at a spot on a distant hillside. "The circle is going to be set up way over there, nowhere near the gate."

All the same, I suppressed the urge to scan the woodland nearby for the route which had once led our families into the heart of Faerie. The two gates had become one, while a simple stone cottage had replaced the two large houses which had belonged to the Summer and Winter Gatekeepers. Hazel, Ilsa, and Morgan's mother now lived in Thomas Lynn's former home. I wondered if they'd told *her* they'd be summoning a god on her doorstep.

My doubts multiplied in the back of my mind as I followed the others towards a group of cloaked individuals standing on the grassy hillside. The Sidhe had reached them first, their horses gathering in a semicircle and dwarfing the cluster of humans.

"This is a wide-open space," I said to Hazel. "Anyone might see us."

"Relax," Hazel said. "There's one village out here, and if they see anything weird, they're used to supernaturals."

"You'd better be right." As we drew closer, I glimpsed several candles set up at the necromancers' feet. "There's a ton of people over there. Did the necromancers leave anyone in Edinburgh at all?"

"We need as many fighters on the ground as possible in case this goes sideways," said Ilsa. "Just a precaution, nothing more."

"You worry too much." Hazel strode ahead, while I shook my head after her.

"Can you please suggest to your sister that her over-confidence might get someone killed?" I said to Ilsa. "This feels too… I won't say *easy*, but don't you feel it too?"

"Holly," said Ilsa. "I get why you're concerned, but the Scourge shouldn't be able to escape our trap. Not before we bring him down, anyway."

"'Shouldn't' isn't definite enough for my liking." If the

Scourge escaped, the Sidhe might be able to chase him down but not without him unleashing havoc in the process. No contingency plan could account for the unpredictability of one of the Ancients.

Puck fell into step with me as we neared the circle. While Ivy and Ilsa made their way to the gathering necromancers at the front of their circle, we joined the necromancers, mages, and witches who'd been called here as backup.

"Everyone ready?" Ivy's voice rang out. "I'll speak the god's name."

"First, we'll light the candles," Ilsa added from beside her. "Let's go."

Twelve blue lights ignited at the necromancers' command, their leaping flames linking to form a solid barrier around the circle. My heart leapt into my throat.

Puck edged closer. "Holly, are you okay?"

My breath quickened. "This is a mistake."

Ivy spoke the Scourge's name, and the word rattled in the air like the tolling of a bell. At once, the smoke within the circle began to swirl, resembling a tornado caught in a glass. The crushing dread intensified as a vaguely humanoid shape appeared within the smoke.

What the hell is wrong with me? I didn't have any reason to fear the Scourge more than any of the other terrors I'd faced today, but the dread felt like a giant foot crushing my rib cage. I gripped the iron knife at my waist to anchor myself in reality, but my very senses rebelled when I tried to look upon the Scourge. Like the inhumanly stunning forms of the Sidhe, the god defied ordinary description. I had the vague impression of large wings like the Morrigan's etched against the grey smoke within the circle, but the only other feature I could make out was a pair of pit-like dark eyes like swirling torrents of darkness.

The smoke cleared a fraction, while his form became more distinct, like the outline of a vast, towering figure. Most likely, he possessed some kind of glamour which warped our senses until we believed he appeared vaguely humanoid—which meant what he truly looked like was even more grotesque.

"You dare to try to summon me?" the Scourge's voice boomed out. *"You dare to entrap me in this pitiful cage?"*

"We're here to banish you," said Ivy.

She and Ilsa spoke several words in an echoing Invocation, and the Sidhe's voices echoed in unison. A rift opened in the air behind the creature, similar to the one which had appeared when the Wild Hunt had called forth the beast from the depths of whatever realm he inhabited.

The Scourge didn't move, instead letting out a terrifying rumbling noise which might have been a laugh. *"You fail to understand, mortal. I am part of this realm now. I can roam at will, as I did before your traitorous ancestors barred my kin and me from this world and confined us to our prison."*

"He can't be banished," I whispered. "Not even with his name."

The crushing dread bit deeper, reflected in those pitch-dark eyes, which shone darker even than the gaping rift behind him.

Ilsa raised the Gatekeeper's book in her hands, its light illuminating her pale face as she spoke. "I banish you."

The god's name left her mouth, and the Scourge recoiled briefly. Then he surged forward, and all twelve candles' lights burned out in a flash. Shouts and exclamations rose among the mages and necromancers, while the Scourge flew into the air, wings extending like some ghastly imitation of an angel.

"You will pay for attempting to banish me, mortal."

A bolt of darkness like shadowy lightning crackled from his hands, straight at Ilsa. A scream lodged in my throat, but I was too far away to reach her before the dark energy struck.

River shoved Ilsa out of the way, the darkness crashing into him like a hammer's blow, and panic erupted. The candles, rendered obsolete, were trampled flat as everyone ran in all directions, some attempting to strike the god, others simply fleeing for their lives. I could hear the Sidhe shouting Invocations, words which sealed the rift, but it was too late to force the Scourge back into his own realm.

Moving so fast he appeared little more than a blur, the beast appeared above the Sidhe with his dark wings extended. Spear-sharp bolts of darkness struck from his hands, knocking several Sidhe off their horses and causing a second wave of panic to slam into the crowd. I found myself shoved back, losing sight of Puck, and when I looked around for my allies, I spotted a cloud of darkness creeping uphill towards us. Death fae, perhaps drawn to the bloodshed—hellhounds and sluagh, death stealers and other beasts.

The Sidhe had scattered, the Scourge's most recent attack having left a sizzling burned patch on the hillside, so we had nothing between us and the death fae. A hellhound lumbered towards me, but Puck blocked its path, shifting into his giant bear form and ripping out its throat.

My hands shifted to claws, biting into a death stealer, while I glimpsed Ivy slaughtering another hellhound while Hazel fought with twin iron blades in her hands. Mages fought with fire and lightning, witches flung spells like fireworks, and several confused minutes of fighting passed before I became aware that the god's devastating strike on the Sidhe had been his last. Instead, when I next glanced up at the sky, the Scourge had vanished from sight.

I cut down a death stealer that tried to wrap a tentacle around my neck. "Where the hell is that god?"

"He's gone." Ivy felled another hellhound with a swing of her blade. "He flew away."

"What?" A buzzing sensation in my pocket made me jump violently. My phone. Who was calling me at a time like this?

The buzzing continued, throwing off my aim. I one-handedly fumbled to turn it off and spied two messages, both unread. The first, sent more than half an hour ago, said, *This is a mistake - Janet Lynn.*

The second simply said, *I told you so.*

8

"She knew," I said to the Lynn siblings. "Janet knew."

None of them argued. They'd gathered in the infirmary at the necromancer guild—not an ideal place for a private chat, but Ilsa refused to leave River's bedside, and her siblings had needed to be patched up too. More than half the beds in the wide stone room were occupied, while harried nurses ran back and forth carrying bandages and healing spells. The guild, I'd swiftly learned, didn't have nearly enough medical staff on standby to deal with the aftermath of a rampaging god, and everyone was paying too little attention to notice that Hazel and I had sneaked into the ward.

They also hadn't figured out what was wrong with River. The Scourge's lightning attack hadn't left much in the way of physical wounds, but he lay in a state of unconsciousness and hadn't moved an inch since the battle. Ilsa sat on a chair next to his bed, her eyes glassy and her expression grim.

Even Hazel didn't have any glib comments to make. "Did all of us get the same messages? Because in the last one, Janet sounded like she was taunting us."

"She sounds like a fucking troll," Morgan said. "She'd better hope we *don't* find her."

"One of us should text her back," I said. "If she's a genuine person, then there's got to be a reason she knew summoning the god wouldn't work. Let alone how she found out our plan in the first place."

"I can think of one reason," said Morgan. "She's working with the enemy."

"I didn't get the impression the Scourge had friends." Allies, though? It'd be just our luck to find that he and Janet had been conspirators all along. "Least of all human ones."

Morgan shook his head. "I'm going to find Lloyd."

Hazel pulled out her phone. "I'll text her back and ask how she knew our plan. Maybe she's a member of the guild."

"There's no spies in the guild, Hazel." Ilsa said thickly, her eyes red-rimmed. "It's more likely to be someone from Faerie."

"Except you can't send text messages from Faerie," I put in. "And the timing seems suspect too. How did she know to send the warning at that precise moment?"

"You think I know?" said Hazel. "Here's my reply. *How do you know, smartarse? Got a better idea?*"

"Doubt she'll share it with us." Morgan was right—she was screwing with us on purpose. If she knew the Scourge would easily escape our trap, why hadn't she shown her face sooner? For that matter, how did she even have all our mobile phone numbers? I could count the number of people in my contacts on both hands.

"You thought the plan would work, too, remember?" Hazel reached for her phone again as a buzzing noise sounded. "Damn, that was fast."

"She replied?"

"Yeah." She held up her phone so we could read Janet's response.

Yes, I do, as it happens. Come and find me in Carterhaugh.

"Carterhaugh?" I asked.

Ilsa's brow wrinkled. "I think I've heard the name."

"She wants us to come to her, not the other way around," I said. "I bet it's a trap."

"Might be." Hazel's eyes widened. "Ah… we have company."

All eyes turned towards the door as Lady Montgomery entered the infirmary, making a beeline for our corner when her gaze landed on her son. My breath stuck in my throat as the boss turned towards us, her expression flinty. "What happened to River?"

"The god—struck him down." Ilsa choked on the words. "I don't know why he's unconscious. There's no obvious physical wounds or anything—"

A faint glow lit Lady Montgomery's eyes before vanishing so swiftly I might have imagined it. "His spirit is damaged. Badly."

Ilsa's eyes brimmed over. "I didn't—I didn't check."

Understanding dawned. Lady Montgomery must have used her spirit sight to look for damage that wasn't visible to the naked eye. I could theoretically do the same, if I shifted into the Morrigan, but I didn't need to look directly to know it was bad news.

"He won't last more than a day." Lady Montgomery's voice was deceptively soft, her words falling like stones into a valley.

Tears spilled from Ilsa's eyes, and she reached for River's hand, gripping it in hers. "Can't I do anything for him?"

"Does the book have any advice?" Hazel fished the Gatekeeper's talisman from Ilsa's unresisting grip and flipped it open. "It's blank."

"Give it here." Ilsa lunged over and retrieved the book, her eyes roving the pages. "There's got to be a way to undo the damage. Can't we get a vampire to help?"

"Vampires can only take energy from other people, not give it back," said Lady Montgomery, in the same horribly calm tone. "There is nothing to do but quicken his end."

Nothing to do. I'd never *liked* River, whose righteous attitude had always rubbed me up the wrong way. But he didn't deserve to die like this, and Ilsa didn't deserve to lose him.

Lady Montgomery's face might as well have been chiselled from granite. All the air seemed to leave the ward as she extended her hands over her son's body.

"What are you doing?" Ilsa choked.

"It's kinder to end his suffering," she said softly. "For all of us."

"Wait." I lurched forward, shadows creeping over my fingertips. "Let me look at him. I—I have to shift first."

"Let her." Ilsa leapt to her feet, the talisman falling to the floor as she scrambled to prevent Lady Montgomery from grabbing me.

I'd never shifted so fast. In a blink, my claws came out, my wings extended, and the spirit sight slid into view.

Glowing lights appeared before my eyes, floating in a haze of grey, and when River's spirit came into focus, the damage became obvious.

His spirit had been slashed to ribbons as if incorporeal claws had ripped into him. I suspected that only being a necromancer had kept him alive for this long, because if his body had been in that state, he'd have died in an instant. There wasn't a necromancer equivalent of a healing spell, as far as I knew, but the shadows in my hands stirred, reminding me of the power in my grasp.

Power that could be used to heal as well as destroy.

I reached out and touched his glowing spirit, my shadows creeping over and filling in the gaps where the Scourge's attack had fractured his spirit. The gaping wounds vanished, one by one, as my shadows healed them, flooding River's spirit and leaving nothing but a faint glow in their wake.

Is that enough? I needed to use my actual eyes to know for sure, so I blinked back to reality and found myself nose to nose with Lady Montgomery. Entirely too late, it hit me that I'd shifted into a fearsome bird-woman in the middle of the infirmary, and everyone who wasn't unconscious in a bed had retreated against the walls or fled the room.

My hands shook as I shifted back into my human form, while Ilsa sank back into a seat, looking as though she might faint. My voice still sounded like the Morrigan's when I spoke. "He—he should be okay now, I think."

Lady Montgomery's expression turned from granite to steel. "What did you do?"

"I healed him." I swallowed against my dry throat. "I

wasn't certain it would work, but the Morrigan—she can heal souls as well as remove them. I—"

Her response cut through my explanation. "Get out."

Ilsa stirred. "Wait a minute."

"Get out." Lady Montgomery's words carried a deadly undercurrent, and my legs moved without conscious command. I walked past the stunned infirmary staff and petrified guild members, out into the lobby. I heard the infirmary door open behind me and Hazel's voice calling my name, but a roaring filled my ears. I quickened my pace until the cold air outside slapped me in the face.

I kept walking at a fast stride, my feet leading the way through Edinburgh's Old Town, my mind echoing with disconnected thoughts that didn't go beyond the urge to move, to leave behind the anger and fear until I found solid ground.

When I came to a halt, I found myself outside Puck's office. I stared at the door for a numb instant, not wanting to face him, unable to turn away.

Fluttering sounded at my shoulder, and Puck landed at my side. "I was waiting for you outside, Holly. Are you okay?"

My tongue felt stiff, as if it didn't belong to me. "It's… River."

His gaze lowered. "I'm sorry."

"No… he's not dead." I swallowed hard. "But I'm pretty sure I just got banned from the necromancer guild, if not sentenced to death."

Confusion flickered in his eyes. "Why?"

"I brought River back to life," I said, the words hanging between us for an instant. "I healed him, the same way I did to you."

He sucked in a breath. "What? You healed me, I know, but you didn't…"

"You would have died." I couldn't meet his eyes. "You were almost gone. River was, too, and his mother… let's just say she's less than thrilled that I broke the laws of the guild right in front of her."

"The laws of—" He broke off. "I've read the damn rule book, and it doesn't say anything about not bringing people back from the brink of death. You didn't even use necromancy."

"I shifted into a giant bird-woman in the infirmary. I'm pretty sure that's against the regulations."

He stared, his jaw twitching as if suppressing the urge to laugh. "I can make the boss see sense if you like."

"Don't." I barred his path. "Haven't we made enough enemies for one day?"

Getting kicked out of both Courts *and* the necromancer guild had to be some kind of record, but it was admitting to bringing Puck back from death that threatened to unravel the last shreds of control I possessed. If he'd been in River's place—if the strike had been fatal—what would I have done to get him back?

"You made the right call," he said. "You did."

"You don't even like River," I pointed out. "He left you as the Aes Sidhe's prisoner, remember?"

"I might have done the same in his place, considering he had no reason to trust me at the time," he said. "How'd your cousin react?"

"Ilsa? She's too shaken up to challenge her boss. I don't know or care what Hazel thinks, frankly, and Morgan left before the boss showed up."

"Ilsa will stand up for you when she gets over the

shock." He took a step closer, halving the distance between us. "Trust me."

When his hands found mine, I became aware of how badly I was shaking, from a combination of adrenaline from the battle, my flight from the guild, and the drain of using the Morrigan's magic. His grip steadied me, his arms wrapping around my back. Instinct drove me to seek his warmth, to lean into his embrace as his mouth pressed against mine.

"What the *fuck*," Roseanne yelled from the doorway. "I've been worried sick about you, and you're out here acting like a couple of Sidhe at an orgy."

"Whoa." I took a step back from Puck, startled at her outburst. "I'm sorry. I got delayed at the guild. River… he was injured."

"You're not hurt?" She grabbed my arm without waiting for a reply and all but dragged me into the office. "Hawk will heal you."

"I'm not hurt, but I got lucky."

"Good," Hawk said from behind the desk, where a brand-new computer sat in a tangle of wires. It looked as though he and Roseanne had been busy while we were in Faerie. "So, the mages' big idea went tits-up?"

"It was my idea, actually." I crossed the office, ducked into the living room at the back, and sought out an armchair to collapse into. Leaning back, I spoke to the ceiling. "I'm not sure where it went wrong, but the Scourge refused to be contained and went on the rampage, striking down anyone in his path."

"Bastard." Roseanne came into the living room and flopped onto the sofa.

"You're just inviting yourself into our house now?" Hawk walked in, followed by Puck. "Both of you?"

"You seem to have appointed Roseanne as your assistant anyway," I said. "Question is, what the hell do we do now?"

"Tell me what actually happened, for a start," said Hawk. "I heard the guild sent half its members up north to some undisclosed location. The mages too."

"They set up a circle to summon the Scourge away from any potential collateral damage," I said. "The summoning worked, but the Scourge broke the circle, and all hell broke loose."

"How'd you escape?" he asked. "Did you fight the god yourself?"

"No, he just threw lightning bolts at the Sidhe and nearly killed River. Then death fae attacked us, and he vanished at some point in the chaos."

"River?" he asked. "You mean the guild leader's son, right?"

"Yes," I said. "He wouldn't have survived if he hadn't been a top-tier necromancer, but the attack caused so much damage to his spirit that his mother was about to put him out of his misery when I stepped in. Unfortunately, healing him meant shifting into the Morrigan. It didn't go over well."

Puck swore under his breath. "Like I said, you made the right call, Holly. The Scourge, though... nobody saw where he went. I certainly didn't, anyway."

"Where the hell are the Sidhe?" I asked. "Did they go back to Faerie after the battle? I didn't see."

"Yes, and they took Ivy with them," said Puck.

"Great," I said. "She can get them to explain where we went wrong, because I haven't a damn clue."

Roseanne made a small noise. "If the Scourge is in this realm, might he come back to the city?"

"He might." I sank back against the cushions. "I should have known. I had a bad feeling when we got the name from the Wild Hunt so easily… and frankly, I'm starting to wish *they'd* finished him off."

Hawk pulled a face. "How did the Scourge end up being banished in the first place?"

"No clue," I said. "Might have been when the Sidhe initially kicked their gods out into the Vale, which was before most of the current Sidhe were born."

Except possibly the Wild Hunt, but after we'd left one of them dead in the Vale, I doubted the others would be happy to trade information with us.

"How inconvenient," said Hawk. "Sorry to dampen the mood even further, but I'm not going to be cooking tonight. I have a date instead."

I lifted my head. "With Leyton?"

"Sure," he said. "Live while you can and all that."

"Not for much longer at this rate," Roseanne muttered.

"That's bleak," said Hawk. "Don't you dare say she has a point, Holly."

I sensed Puck watching me, too, but I didn't have a word of reassurance in me. The Scourge was a seemingly invincible force of destruction, Janet Lynn had sent us taunting messages that explained nothing, and all I'd been able to do was get myself exiled from both Courts *and* shunned by the guild. Now our only option might be to go gallivanting off to this Carterhaugh place right after we'd pissed off the Ancient and let him escape again.

"The Scourge has spared us for this long." Puck crossed the room. "I'm going to wash this mud off me. Holly, the guest room upstairs is free if you want to clean up while you're here."

I looked down at my mud-stained jeans and jacket, becoming conscious of the trail of dirt and blood I'd left behind me. "Shit. I'm sorry I got mud all over your sofa, Hawk."

"It's fine. I grabbed some cleaning spells from the market," he said. "You survived a battle with a *god,* Holly. I can deal with cleaning up the mess you left behind."

"Not sure the guild can say the same." I closed my mouth before I said anything I'd regret. "I appreciate the offer, but I should head home."

Rosanne sprang to her feet. "I'm not going to get in your way, you know."

"That's not... I'd like to be alone."

I was lying, and the others knew it, too, but Puck nodded. "Sure. Let me know if you need anything."

For once, Hawk didn't crack any jokes. Perhaps something in my expression warned him it was a bad idea. While no traces of the Morrigan's shadows remained behind, it was hard to forget the look of horror on Lady Montgomery's face when she'd ordered me to leave. And the unforgiving way Lord Torin had condemned me. Maybe to some, I'd always be a monster, but I'd carried that reputation long before I'd had the claws and wings to back it up.

Besides, a monster might be exactly the person needed to win this.

My hands curled into fists. I'd brought River back

from the brink of death. I'd halted the Wild Hunt. I'd slain a god beyond the gates of Death. The Morrigan's magic answered to me, and with it in my hands, I'd find a way to end this, even if it meant slaughtering the Scourge and risking the Sidhe going to war over his lifeblood.

9

I woke with my head resting on the arm of the sofa in my own living room, unable to remember falling asleep. Roseanne had curled up on the end of the sofa too. I cast my mind around, recalling taking a long shower and making dinner, and then… nothing.

Puck walked into the room, an apologetic look on his face, which startled me upright. "What… how did you get into the house?"

"Your cousin invited herself in, so I followed to make sure she didn't startle you too much," he said. "You were dead to the world."

"Which cousin?" When I laid eyes on Hazel roaming around the kitchen, I jumped to my feet. "What the hell are *you* doing here?"

"Waiting for you to wake up," she said. "Ilsa and Morgan already said yes."

"To what?" How in hell had she got into my *house?* "You know I could report you to the police for breaking and entering, don't you?"

"If you'd answered any of my messages, I wouldn't have needed to." She waved my mobile phone in my face. "Or plugged in your phone."

"I fell asleep." I snatched the phone from her hand and plugged it into the charger on the wall. "What exactly is this big idea of yours?"

"Finding Janet Lynn."

"What?" I sat back down. "You figured out where Carterhaugh is?"

Puck frowned. "Carterhaugh?"

Hazel perched on the arm of a chair. "I asked Darrow if he'd heard of the name, and he told me the Aes Sidhe once had a secret path that led into the mortal realm, which came out near a town called Carterhaugh. I'm willing to bet several fortunes that Thomas Lynn was originally snatched from there, and so were the other mortals Etaina took as her sacrifices."

My hands curled into fists. "So it's back to her again."

It made sense that Etaina had established an easy route to steal mortals to sacrifice to the Scourge, but why would this Janet Lynn want us to meet her in the same place?

"Yeah, lucky us," said Hazel. "Janet sent a few more snarky replies to my messages, but I think we'll have to locate the town ourselves."

"I don't know the location," Puck said. "Only the name."

"Ilsa has some ideas about how we can find it," said Hazel. "If you come with me to the guild, she'll tell us."

I gave her a look. "I'm banned from the guild, Hazel."

"Not in so many words," she said. "Maybe you should keep your distance from the boss, though."

I scowled. "Did you seriously start pressuring Ilsa to

track down Janet Lynn right after she almost lost her boyfriend?"

"She's fine," said Hazel. "She was in shock yesterday, but she agrees that our best bet is to track down Janet and find out what she knows. Preferably *before* the god comes back for more."

I had to admit she had a point… and besides, part of me was curious to see the place where Thomas Lynn had been snatched all those years ago. "Fine, but I'm not going to the guild. We'll meet somewhere else."

"Cassandra's Café?"

"That'll do."

In typical Hazel fashion, she refused to leave the house while I went upstairs to get changed and make myself presentable. When I returned to the living room, however, it was to find Puck had left.

"He went back to his office." Hazel eyed Roseanne's sleeping form on the sofa. "Will she be all right if you leave her here alone?"

"Sure." I grabbed my jacket and boots. I hadn't done more than give them a quick wipe to get the mud off, but if we were about to head off on another ill-advised jaunt, there was no point in dressing my best. "Where'd you find Puck, anyway? He said he followed you in, but what was he even doing here?"

"No idea." Her eyes sparkled with mischief. "He appeared out of nowhere when I knocked on your door. I *did* think I saw a black bird sitting on the fence when I walked into half-blood territory…" She trailed off suggestively, but I didn't take her bait.

"He must have been keen to get away from you." My

gaze lingered on Roseanne for a moment before I made for the door.

———

Hazel and I met the others at Cassandra's Café, a supernatural-run establishment on the same street as the necromancer guild. Ilsa claimed that Lady Montgomery wasn't likely to be looking for me, since she'd departed to speak to the senior necromancers as soon as she was certain that River had recovered from his wounds and they'd spent the night arguing about how to strengthen the city's defences in case the Scourge came back.

"It's weird that he didn't," I remarked. "He must have been miles away before we summoned him into our trap. I wonder what he was doing?"

"Do you really want to know how creepy death gods spend their leisure time?" Morgan sat across the table next to Ilsa, while Hazel shovelled bacon into her mouth at my side. I didn't have much of an appetite anyway, but the sight of her eating was mildly nauseating. Especially when every time the door opened, I expected someone from the guild to walk in and spot us. I had little doubt that word of me shifting into the Morrigan in the infirmary had spread like wildfire through the guild, even if the details of how I'd saved River's life weren't widely known.

"Have you spoken to all the Aes Sidhe you have contact with?" I asked Hazel. "To see if they know where Carterhaugh is?"

"Darrow has no idea whereabouts the town is located,"

said Hazel indistinctly. "He said most of the other Aes Sidhe stayed in Faerie after the Court fell apart."

"The half-Sidhe who lived there must have moved to this realm," I said. "Puck and his friend Hawk did, and so did a few others who moved to half-blood territory."

"I doubt Etaina would have told the half-Sidhe the location of the route into the mortal realm," Ilsa said. "The sacrifices to the Scourge stopped after she captured Thomas Lynn, and that was hundreds of years ago in mortal years. None of the half-Sidhe can possibly be that old."

"Fair point," I said. "Can't you look at a map or run a search on the internet?"

"I tried and didn't get very far," said Ilsa. "If it's anything like Foxwood or similar places, it'll be hidden on regular maps."

"Typical." Supernatural communities had been concealed from sight by necessity in the old world, but more than two decades had passed since the faerie inva-sion had exposed the hidden world for all to see, and you'd think someone would have updated the maps at some point.

"Ilsa will add that to her endless to-do list when we get back," said Hazel. "I know the way to the Court of the Aes Sidhe, though. Or what's left of it. It's likely to be deserted, so we can scour the place for this hidden passage into the mortal realm."

"You seriously want to go back to Faerie?" The one Court I hadn't been kicked out of had been left in ruins after Etaina's death, but its former inhabitants had left, and for all we knew, the Aes Sidhe's hidden route into Carterhaugh remained intact. While I didn't relish the idea, going to Faerie was marginally more practical than flying around the fae-infested wilderness of the Highlands looking for a village hidden from human eyes.

"I did wonder if we might find anything useful in the Aes Sidhe's home," said Ilsa. "None of us has ever been there except Hazel, but Thomas Lynn lived with them for years. I wonder if he left anything behind."

Thomas had spent longer than a mortal life span in Etaina's company. Seven years he'd been taken for the first time around, but he'd returned to the mortal realm after escaping Etaina's clutches and stayed there until he'd learned the hard way that the vow he'd sworn to serve Faerie had passed to the rest of his family. While his twin daughters had been taken—one to Summer, one to Winter—Thomas himself had been dragged back to the Court of the Aes Sidhe to exist in limbo for centuries, his newfound immortally sustained by the blood of the gods.

"Like a twin sister?" Hazel put her plate aside. "I joke, but it'd explain how Janet knows so much."

"No… there are other Lynns," said Ilsa. "Distant relatives."

Like Ivy. After Thomas's second disappearance, his wife had remarried and had other children, and Ivy Lane claimed she was a distant relation of ours via that family line.

"That side of the family has no magic, though," I said. "Not even the Sight. How can one of them possibly know how to deal with the Scourge?"

"That's why we need to see her in person." Hazel stood decisively. "I'll take us to the Court of the Aes Sidhe."

"And what if there are surviving rebels lurking in

there?" asked Morgan. "They want the Gatekeepers dead, in case you've forgotten."

"We'll handle them," said Hazel. "We should go right away, before Janet changes her mind."

"Hang on," said Ilsa. "I'll need to tell the guild. So will Morgan, if he's coming with us."

Everyone looked at Morgan. He rolled his eyes. "Fine, fine. We Lynns have to stick together."

"Exactly." Hazel checked her phone. "Janet isn't going to send me directions, I don't think. She's ignored my last six messages."

"Then we'll go to her." Morgan cracked his knuckles. "Load up on iron in case she turns out to be fae in disguise."

Wouldn't that be typical. "I need to tell Roseanne. She won't be thrilled with me for running off again so soon."

"Bet she'd be even less thrilled if the Scourge comes back," said Hazel.

True. We'd had a lucky escape, and the Scourge's absence after yesterday's brutal attack baffled me more than a little. Not that I'd let an opportunity slip away, so I resigned myself to leaving my teenage death fae house-mate behind for yet another excursion to Faerie.

Ilsa and Morgan made for the guild across the street, while Hazel and I headed in the opposite direction. Neither of us spoke to one another, which was more than fine by me. When we neared half-blood territory, Hazel veered away. "I'm going to find Darrow. He knows the Court better than I do."

"Glad someone does," I responded. "I'll meet you at the Ley Line."

I quickened my pace, wishing I hadn't slept for so long,

even though I'd needed it. Who knew how long a reprieve the Scourge would allow us before he attacked again?

At home, I found another note from Roseanne saying she'd gone to Puck and Hawk's office. I'd expected as much, so I took the opportunity to change into my sturdiest clothing and restock my weapons.

When I exited half-blood territory again, I spied Hazel approaching the Ley Line, accompanied by Darrow, her boyfriend. The silver-haired half-faerie had the tall, lean build typical of half-faeries, with eyes which looked more aquamarine than Summer-green. I'd never really spoken to him before, and he'd always struck me as mildly antisocial, but he studied me with a hint of curiosity in his expression. "You're Holly, correct?"

"Yeah," I said. "I'm just heading to Puck's office to tell the others where I'm going."

"Who?" Darrow's eyes narrowed. "Not him?"

I spun on my heel to see Puck approaching, and from the way he and Darrow glared at one another, they'd met beforehand.

"Trickster," said Darrow. "So you did escape the Court."

"Darrow." Puck gave a mocking bow. "Etaina's favourite pet. How's the life of freedom treating you?"

Darrow's jaw tightened. "That's a fine insult coming from someone who spends more time as a vicious beast than a human."

Puck's teeth formed a humourless grin. "Vicious, you say? Would you like to see for yourself?"

"Puck," I said warningly, while Hazel looked on with a mixture of incredulity and fascination. "Darrow's supposed to be helping us find the Court of the Aes Sidhe. I'd rather you didn't skewer him before we leave."

"He's welcome to try," said Darrow.

Hazel took a step closer to her boyfriend. "I didn't know you'd met before."

"Everyone in the Court knows of Etaina's most treasured possession," said Puck. "Though I heard he turned out to be quite a disappointment in the end."

"You heard?" said Darrow. "I suppose you missed the battle, since you ran at the first sign of trouble. How typical."

"Better to run than to turn traitor," said Puck.

"Okay, that's enough." Hazel, for once, intervened before they came to blows. "Holly, why don't you escort your *friend* back home?"

"I heard you planned to visit my former Court," Puck said. "I thought it wise to give you my assistance, since there's a good chance the territory isn't entirely abandoned."

I suppressed a groan. A pair of bickering half-faeries were not what our latest trip into Faerie needed. "Look, someone needs to tell Roseanne."

"I heard." Roseanne bounded over and joined Puck. "I'm coming too."

"No," I said flatly. "We don't know what we'll find in the realm of the Aes Sidhe."

"This isn't about the Aes Sidhe," she said. "This is about finding that god and getting rid of him. I'm not going to stay behind as bait for the Wild Hunt."

"You aren't going to be bait," I told her. "The Wild Hunt's survivors didn't mention the mortal realm at all."

"They gave you the god's name for a reason," she said.

"They wanted you to summon him, didn't they? Or they didn't care if you were killed in the process."

Roseanne was smarter than I'd given her credit for, and for all I knew, maybe she would be safer with me than if she stayed behind. "Perhaps, but we have no idea what we might run into."

"I'm not useless, you know." She lifted her chin. "I can fight."

"I never said you couldn't." I guessed she resented being left out of yesterday's battle, but River's brush with death made me glad she hadn't been around to witness the god's attack.

"Then prove it." She folded her arms. "It seems like all you do lately is leave me behind."

Did she have to start this argument in front of Hazel and the others? "You know Faerie and the way it warps time, don't you? We shouldn't be gone for more than a day or two."

"I didn't survive being held captive in Fionn's castle to hide in my room and wait for the Wild Hunt to find me again."

I sometimes forgot the horrors she'd already witnessed. I'd taken her in to give her somewhere safe to stay, but leaving her alone in the house with the Wild Hunt at large was no different than the way my mother had left me to fend for myself for weeks at a time while she was in Faerie.

"Fine," I said, "but if I tell you to run away and save yourself, then do it. No arguments."

Her face broke into a grin. "Sure. I'll go and tell Hawk."

"So will I." The approval in Puck's voice was enough to dispel my lingering worries for Roseanne, who skipped ahead of him as if I'd offered to take her to Disneyland and not Faerie.

"Wow," said Hazel. "So much excitement, and we haven't even got to Faerie yet."

"If you can't keep your boyfriend under control in Faerie, then we won't last five minutes without being caught by the Sidhe," I told her.

"If the trickster behaves himself," Darrow said, "then there'll be nothing to worry about."

"What is your problem with him?" I frowned at the silver-haired half-Sidhe. "I thought you weren't loyal to Etaina any more than Puck was. It shouldn't matter what kind of rivalry you had when you lived in the Court of the Aes Sidhe."

"The trickster is disloyal by nature," he said. "We can't trust him."

"He doesn't want an angry death god wreaking havoc on this realm any more than the rest of us do," I said. "He knows the way to the Court of the Aes Sidhe too."

"So do I," said Darrow. "Bringing him is a mistake."

To my relief, I spotted Ilsa approaching, along with Morgan and Pepper. Turning my back on Darrow, I went to meet my other cousins. "The guild's okay with you leaving?"

"I wouldn't use the word 'okay,' but the boss has other things to occupy her attention," Ilsa replied.

"Let me guess—she's stuck River behind bulletproof glass," I said.

Ilsa managed a smile which looked more like a grimace. "Surprisingly not, but she's ordered him to stay at the guild and not go out on missions for a few days."

Sensing the need for a change of subject, I asked, "Did Ivy ever come back from Summer?"

"Haven't a clue," said Ilsa. "Ah… is Roseanne coming with you?"

"She invited herself along, and so did Puck." I kept an eye out to make sure Darrow didn't start another fight, but he simply watched Puck and Roseanne with narrowed eyes as they joined us again.

"We're all here?" said Hazel, snapping her fingers. "Ready?"

"Sure." Morgan coaxed Pepper over to the Ley Line. "Let's move."

In a flash, we landed on the path between the Courts, where Puck shifted into a bird to fly into Summer territory and look out for any signs of the Sidhe lurking nearby.

He landed beside me and shifted into a human again. "The route into Summer is clear, but there's no guarantee that the Sidhe won't sense our presence."

"We won't be in Court territory for long," said Hazel. "Unless someone wants to put a glamour on Holly?"

"Not just me." I turned to Roseanne. "They aren't fans of the Morrigan, as I found out at Lord Torin's house."

She lowered her gaze. "I can shift into a crow, but you…"

Puck cleared his throat. "It's up to you."

"Fine," I said, before anyone could argue. "Turn me into a bird."

This time I didn't flinch when he took my hand, but alarm zinged through my veins when his magic sizzled along my skin. Black feathers sprouted from my skin, while my limbs became flimsy claws, my wings beating hard to keep my balance as I shrank to the size of a bird. Roseanne and Puck both shifted into birds, too, landing on either side of me.

"We have our own murder of crows," Hazel remarked. "Let's go to Summer."

Darrow led the way into the trees at the edge of the borderlands, skirting the vibrant meadow of yellow flowers near the forest. As a bird, the magic of Summer didn't feel quite as stifling, but it came as a relief to get out of the direct sunlight when we reached a tangle of trees and a path that ran downhill.

"The Sidhe don't come down here," said Hazel. "Not often, anyway."

Roseanne turned into a human again, while I perched on a branch and tried not to ruffle my feathers too much as I waited for Puck to change me back. His magic encased me, and despite my best efforts to preserve my dignity, the instant I grew to the size of a person, I toppled forwards into a pile of leaves. Startled by the noise, Pepper broke into a run.

"Steady on," said Morgan, hurrying to keep pace with the puppy as he followed the steep path downhill.

Leaping to my feet, I joined the others in heading deeper into the woods. I swiftly lost track of the winding route, which led in the opposite direction to the borderlands but didn't look much like Summer either. The trees grew close and tangled, while the sound of running water filled the background until we reached a long river with fast-flowing waters coloured a deep crimson.

"The Blood River," said Hazel in explanation. "It runs through the heart of Summer and it's—"

"And it's red with the blood of the Erlking's enemies, I

know," I said. "I'm not entirely uneducated on the other Courts."

"The blood of *all* his enemies?" asked Morgan. "The guy hasn't been on the throne for that long."

"I assume it's the blood of all the Summer Court's enemies, which is a lot of people." Hazel walked at Darrow's side, a number of iron knives at her waist to match my own. "I think I recognise this place, but I was riding a unicorn at the time. Wonder if it's still out here?"

"A *unicorn?*" said Roseanne.

"Yeah, Thomas Lynn called upon a unicorn to help us escape," said Hazel. "We're close, I think."

The trees thinned out, to be replaced with briars and thornbushes. Roseanne stayed close behind me as we came to a long stone wall which stretched between the trees. Moss coated the grey stone, and I wouldn't have recognised it as the entryway to a Court if Hazel hadn't pointed out the wide hole in the wall leading into an earthen tunnel.

"Here we are," said Hazel. "That wall was originally sealed with an Invocation which only a Gatekeeper could undo."

"Doesn't look like anyone's been back since." Puck peered through the door-sized hole in the wall, his mouth set in a grim line. "Home sweet home."

10

Beyond the opening in the wall, an earthen passage extended to left and right, intersecting with other tunnels like a rabbit's warren. Doors fitted into the tunnel itself reminded me of the Aes Sidhe's temporary lair, but this one seemed a lot bigger, its earthen floor well-trodden and its doors partly open as though abandoned in a hurry.

Puck took the left passageway and walked ahead on light feet, the tension in his shoulders the only sign of his unease at being in his former home. The tunnels contained no windows or doors, instead lit by clusters of luminous toadstools sprouting from the walls and ceilings. Our footsteps echoed in the silence, emphasising the cavernous nature of the tunnels, yet the lack of daylight already bothered me.

Behind me, Hazel addressed Darrow. "Whereabouts might Etaina have hidden a secret passage into the mortal realm?"

"Not in the same place she kept Thomas Lynn,"

Darrow replied. "With her gone, I imagine it'll be easier for us to find. Etaina's quarters are this way."

"I already searched them thoroughly," Hazel said. "Suppose it's worth another look around, though."

Our winding route took us past an alcove containing a wooden door which stood slightly ajar. Behind the door, a noise sounded, indistinct but unmistakeable. We weren't alone.

The Morrigan's magic stirred beneath my skin as Darrow nudged the door open, revealing a large chamber formed of trees which appeared to grow from the very walls themselves. Thick trunks formed pillars while their arching branches covered the ceiling, and clouds of fire-flies cast circling lights on several transparent, shadowy forms below.

Wraiths. Some of the Aes Sidhe who'd been killed in the battle must have returned to haunt their former homes. Darrow's hands ignited with vibrant green Summer magic, while Ilsa's talisman glowed in her hands.

Shadows darkened my palms as Roseanne moved to my side, her mouth set in anger. Her claws might have trouble making a dent in the wraiths, but no physical weapons would be able to harm them either. Puck took flight as a bird and darted among the wraiths, while my shadows met them blow for blow, and Darrow and Ilsa directed bolts of magic at the wraiths' indistinct forms. One of them shattered like broken glass, while another hid behind a trunk-like pillar.

"Pitiful," said Darrow. "Who were you, cowards who fled the battlefield?"

"They can't talk, Darrow," Hazel said teasingly. "More's the pity. They might be able to give us directions."

One of the remaining wraiths gave a lunge at Roseanne. My claw got in the way, hooking into its fragile form, and it wriggled and writhed like a trapped bird. Instinct urged me to sink my teeth in the way I'd done to the being I'd devoured at the gates of Death, but the others' presence stayed my hand, and I flung the wraith into the path of Ilsa's talisman instead.

The last wraith exploded into fragments, leaving us alone in the empty chamber. Puck shifted into human form and gave the vast room a cursory glance before leaving, while I wondered if Etaina herself had stood on the raised platform at the front to give speeches to her soldiers.

"This way." Puck beckoned us down another tunnel. We walked a short distance before he pushed open a wooden door on our right.

An empty office greeted us on the other side. Cabinets and shelves filled the space, along with a shallow hole in the ground which looked like a badly thought-out escape tunnel.

"Etaina's lair," said Hazel. "That hole used to be where she kept the blood of one of the Ancients. It was how she made those pens her soldiers used for inking those blood magic runes onto their skin."

She'd kept a puddle of blood in her office? No wonder she'd needed to brainwash her soldiers using glamour to ensure they didn't turn against her.

"These?" Puck withdrew a pen from his pocket. "I found this in the Aes Sidhe's lair in the borderlands, and I assumed they came back and pillaged the place after the battle."

"And you took them for yourself, did you?" Darrow said.

"Not for me." He pocketed the pen again. "I can't write in the glyphs necessary to use blood magic, so they're no more use than weapons made of sand. I assumed Etaina taught only the best and most loyal of her soldiers how to use them, but I may be mistaken on the matter."

Darrow's jaw tensed as he registered the insult, but he simply said, "There's nothing to be found in here."

As Puck made to follow him out of the office, I snagged his arm. "Puck, cut it out. Whatever rivalry you two had is not more important than finding what we came here for."

"Hardly rivalry," he said in an undertone. "I don't trust someone who was so deep in Etaina's counsel."

"Can you save your argument for later, then?" I released him and walked down the winding tunnel, keeping my eyes open for any more wraiths.

Darrow took the lead, occasionally pushing open a door to reveal an empty room. No secret passages to the mortal realm appeared, though.

"The door might be hidden near where I met Thomas Lynn," Hazel said when I made a comment to that effect. "Granted, you'd think he'd have noticed it was there…"

"Or we're wasting our time," Morgan said.

"We're not wasting any time," Hazel said. "This place is in some kind of temporal stasis compared to the rest of Faerie, and we could spend a year here and not lose any time in the mortal realm."

"Does that apply with Etaina no longer around, though?" I asked.

Nobody had an answer. As we carried on walking, the repetitive nature of the stifling tunnels began to grate on me. No wonder Puck had leapt at the chance to get out, even if it meant becoming a spy. It sounded as though Darrow had done something similar, so their argument made no sense to me, considering they were supposed to be on the same side.

"Here." Hazel nudged another door open, revealing a narrow room. "This is where I met Thomas Lynn. Etaina locked me up with him, so I kicked him in the face and legged it."

"Of course you did." I rolled my eyes, while Hazel darted into the room.

An exclamation followed. "Hey! Look what I found."

Everyone crowded the doorway to see, while Hazel held up a gleaming golden harp with a triumphant expression on her face.

"That's Thomas's?" I already knew the answer. "You might want to be careful with that."

Typically, Hazel ignored the warning and plucked at the strings one-handedly, and everyone covered their ears as a resonant note echoed throughout the tunnel like a cat being strangled. "There's no magic in this, I don't think. It's a regular harp, not a talisman."

"If anyone didn't know we were in here, they will now," said Ilsa. "Morgan, don't get any ideas. We're here to look for a way to the mortal realm, not to loot the place."

"I'm not looting anywhere," he protested, tugging at Pepper's lead as the puppy moved into the room, growling. "What's the problem?"

"Maybe he smells a threat." Hazel's gaze snapped up. "Wait a second. I wonder if he can sniff out the exit?"

"To Faerie, maybe, but Thomas was locked up here for

years without any route home," I pointed out. "I'm guessing the door was abandoned a few centuries back too."

"So most of the Aes Sidhe weren't aware of its existence," said Puck. "She wouldn't have wanted them knowing they might be able to escape."

Darrow's gaze flickered towards him, but no insult underlaid Puck's tone this time around. "I travelled back and forth from Faerie but not via the mortal realm. Etaina told nobody of this supposed hidden doorway. I learned of its existence via rumour and conjecture."

Typical of Etaina. The vast majority of her Court had consisted of brainwashed soldiers who'd ultimately been willing to sacrifice their lives for her on the battlefield. The few who'd survived the battle with the former Seelie Queen had retained their loyalty even in the wake of her death, but I hadn't understood the depths of their devotion until I'd walked through these stifling, echoing tunnels. This was Etaina's domain, and yet despite controlling every aspect of her subjects' lives, she'd still used glamour to ensure nobody ever turned on her.

Glamour. I came to a halt. "Is the exit hidden by glamour, do you think?"

"All the glamour in here should have unravelled with Etaina's death," said Puck. "If she were a regular Sidhe, anyway, but given the strength of her talents... perhaps it didn't."

Darrow's jaw tensed when Puck's gaze travelled towards him, but all he said was, "Her glamour was seamless, so if we can't pinpoint the general location of the exit, we'll end up going in circles."

Pepper growled again, and Puck moved to his side,

crouching down. "Cu sidhe are good at sniffing out boundaries between realms. He might be able to detect the door if we tell him it's hidden by glamour."

He murmured into the puppy's ear, and Pepper barked once before breaking into a trot.

"Slow down." Morgan kept a firm grip on the lead as the puppy dragged him around one corner then another, until my head spun and I'd long since lost track of the route back.

"Are you sure he knows where he's going?" Hazel asked. "He didn't just smell a tasty snack?"

"Bloody hope not." Morgan almost tripped over Pepper when he came to a sudden halt near a blank stretch of wall. The puppy rose on his hind legs, pawing at the solid earth.

Darrow stepped closer and splayed his hands against the wall. "I can sense glamour here."

A brief flare of green light ignited his palms and filled the tunnel, but no door materialised.

"There's nothing there," said Hazel.

"Yes, there is." Roseanne dropped to a crouch, surprising all of us. "Look."

I peered at the lowest part of the wall. The faintest symbol was scrawled onto the earth, glimmering with a familiar sheen. "That's a blood magic glyph. Nice job, Roseanne."

Her eyes lit up. "Can you read it?"

"No." I turned to Hazel. "Didn't you open the door to Faerie in a similar way?"

"Yeah, but with the curse broken, I'm not sure I can safely speak an Invocation." She gestured to Ilsa. "You can try."

"Sure." Ilsa stepped forward and muttered a word. *Open.*

A wooden door sprang into existence, causing Darrow to take a sharp step backwards. Morgan jumped, while everyone else wore expressions of stunned surprise. Hazel broke into a grin. "There we go."

Darrow pushed the door inward, and we peered at a large chamber which resembled the one where we'd found the wraiths, with giant trees growing from floor to ceiling and their branches arching overhead. A large chair sat beside a small, empty pool similar to the one in Etaina's office.

"Old throne room, maybe," Darrow murmured. "I never knew this was here. Etaina must have abandoned this part of the Court a long time ago."

"Or maybe she used to come in here to get away from the rest of us," Puck said. "Perhaps to meet with lovers... unless you fulfilled that role yourself."

Darrow's hand curled into a fist. "Don't be absurd. She adopted me as her child."

"Enough." Ilsa stepped into the lead and crossed the hall. "There's another door over here."

Sure enough, a wooden door lay on the opposite side of the room, nestled between thick branches which melded with the earthen wall. Ilsa pushed on the handle, but it didn't give.

"Speak the magic word again," Hazel said.

Ilsa rolled her eyes. "I don't like using that language when one of the gods is on the loose, but I guess he's not likely to drop by here."

All the same, the mortal realm lay on the other side of that door, which meant we'd need to be prepared for the possibility of running into the Scourge again, especially if Janet turned out not to be what she seemed. Time would start passing normally again, too, if it hadn't already.

"Go on," said Morgan. "It's our only way out, right? We're right behind you."

Ilsa nodded. Then she spoke the word—*open*—and the door swung outward. A thick forest lay on the other side, wreathed in darkness that rivalled the tunnels.

"That's not Faerie, is it?" Hazel extended a hand through the open door and caught the end of a drooping branch. "I don't think it is, but it's hard to tell."

"Put that thing away." Ilsa indicated the harp Hazel held in her other hand. "We don't need to advertise our presence in a fae-infested forest."

"Yes, Mother." Hazel tucked the harp into her jacket pocket before stepping through the door.

We left the realm of the Aes Sidhe behind, and the instant the last of our group had stepped through the door, we found our way back had disappeared as if it had never existed.

"Shit." I spun on my heel, but nothing but trees surrounded us on all sides. Not a single door to be seen. "Better hope we don't need to go back anytime soon."

The forest was dark enough that I'd have had trouble pinpointing the door even if it'd still been present. Barely a ribbon of sunlight snaked through the thick canopy, while the trees were as ancient and tangled as the ones in the far reaches of Faerie.

"It's not nighttime, is it?" said Morgan. "We weren't in Faerie for that long."

"No." Ilsa studied the path ahead of us. "If we're on the Ley Line, then the forest must be in a liminal space. That was probably how Etaina lured humans into her trap. Once they wandered into the woods, they couldn't find the way out again."

A liminal space could stretch for miles, which meant it might take us hours or more to find our actual destination. I couldn't imagine anyone living this deep in the woods, either, though whether Janet Lynn was a regular human remained to be seen.

"Pepper, can you sniff the way out?" Morgan asked.

Pepper let out a whine and hid behind Morgan's feet.

"Guess not," said Hazel. "Better start walking before something comes and eats us."

Nobody objected. My cousins used their phones to light the way ahead, while I settled for relying on the rare strips of sunlight to figure out the route. The forest was certainly cold enough to belong to the mortal realm, with frost on the branches and shrivelled leaves scattered on the ground. Roseanne walked at my side, while Darrow and Hazel strode into the lead, Puck flew above Ilsa's head in front of me, and Morgan and Pepper brought up the rear. The puppy didn't seem to like the forest at all, whining softly as we walked.

A familiar blue light drifted over my shoulder as Ilsa pulled out her talisman and held it up to her face.

"If there are any dead in here, you just put a beacon on our heads," I reminded her.

"I know." The light illuminated the surrounding trees, while Ilsa's gaze roved up and down the pages. "I wondered if the book might know more about our location."

"I thought the book only knew about Death." Her talisman had had some glaring holes in its knowledge concerning the Gatekeeper's curse, too, and it hadn't even known about the Aes Sidhe and their role in our family's history. For hundreds of years, everyone had assumed that it'd been one of the monarchs of Summer or Winter who'd originally captured Thomas Lynn. Instead, Etaina had been the one to lay the trap, and when the Aes Sidhe had cut ties with Summer, they'd taken him with them while his descendants remained locked into a vow to the Courts instead. Hazel had unearthed the truth when she'd encountered him in the Court of the Aes Sidhe, but she'd been willing to forgive him for being willing to do anything to escape being sacrificed to the Scourge.

As for me? If Thomas had survived the battle, I'd have had a harder time forgiving his choice. The former Erlking had been happy to sacrifice the freedom of generations of Lynns in order to secure his own power, and for all I knew, Thomas had been exactly the same. He'd spent centuries living in the Court of the Aes Sidhe, and while he'd been unable to leave, he'd also experienced none of the hardships he'd foisted upon his descendants.

As we rounded a corner, the light from Ilsa's talisman vanished and left nothing but darkness behind. I heard the others swearing and tripping over branches as their lights winked out, while I slowed my pace, unable to even see my hands in front of my face.

"Shit," Ilsa muttered from nearby. "I can't even see my talisman."

"You do still have it, don't you?" I felt my way to her side by following her voice, but abruptly, the ground gave way underfoot.

Ilsa's yell mingled with mine as we toppled downhill, branches and tangling plants scraping at our limbs until we landed in a heap at the foot of a slope. When I looked up, the eerie darkness had vanished as suddenly as it'd arrived, but nothing but thick oak trees surrounded us. The others were nowhere to be seen.

"Damn." Ilsa disentangled herself from a long briar, peering up the slope we'd fallen down. "Where'd Hazel and the others go?"

"Roseanne?" I called out.

No reply. If she hadn't heard me, then we'd fallen farther than I'd thought… or the others had been taken somewhere else entirely. I tried to climb up the slope again, but thick mud lay beneath the coating of leaves and slowed me down. Even so, I didn't see so much as a hint of any of our companions.

"Hazel?" Ilsa called out. "Are you out there?"

Silence. My heart pounded in my ears, and I swore under my breath. "The forest sent them elsewhere."

"It's like Faerie," said Ilsa. "I should have expected some manner of trickery. We'll find them, Holly."

"Easy for you to say." My phone was a cheap piece of crap which didn't have a built-in torch function, which meant I had to rely on her talisman as a proper light to see our surroundings, let alone find our missing companions.

Roseanne. Dammit. I should have known bringing her with me had been a bad idea, but she'd insisted, and I'd caved in because my need to prove I wasn't like my mother had outweighed the obvious fact that we hadn't known what we were getting into.

When I saw the sympathy in Ilsa's expression, a bolt of disconnected anger shot up my spine.

"We'll find her, Holly," she said.

"We'd better." I tried to keep my tone even, but the

worries remained lodged in my chest like a festering wound, and I wanted nothing more than to turn my back on both Ilsa and that bloody talisman of hers. The mere sight of its glow was a screaming reminder that the Gatekeeper's book had catalysed at least half the current problems in my life. My mother's obsession with the talisman had brought about her own doom, while Ilsa had snatched it from my family's fingertips and had ultimately ended up keeping her Gatekeeper's status while the rest of us had lost out. *How convenient for her.*

Wait. Where had that thought come from? I'd once desperately wanted the Gatekeeper's book in order to use its magic to defeat my mother's wraith, but those days were long gone. Where had this sudden rush of bitter, angry thoughts come from? I turned to Ilsa, only to see an emotion on her face that I hadn't expected. Fear.

"Holly." She took a step back. "Get away from me."

"Huh?" Confusion replaced my growing unease. "What's the problem?"

"I can see you looking at my talisman," she said. "You've always wanted it for your own, haven't you?"

"No," I said. "I don't want it."

"Bullshit." She wrapped her arms around the Gatekeeper's book, holding it tightly against her chest. "You think I've forgotten what you and your mother did? You're both the same."

My anger returned, tempered by the knowledge that whatever was influencing her cruel words was the same as the force urging me to abandon her in the forest, and that it didn't come from her. "I'm not like my mother."

"Isn't that the tragedy?" She took a step closer to me,

the fear in her eyes turning to malice. "You couldn't even manage to be a real villain."

"Ilsa," I said. "Look, you do remember I saved your boyfriend's life yesterday, don't you? I wouldn't have done that if I'd secretly coveted your talisman. This is some trickery on behalf of the forest. Faerie magic, no doubt."

Her gaze clouded, and she shook her head fiercely. "You're a manipulator, just like her."

My mother's face appeared in my mind's eye, her expression mocking. Yes, I'd failed at living up to her in every possible way, but I'd also outlived her. And while I'd always thought I'd never tell another soul of the events which had led up to her death, I'd confided in Puck. At the thought, the image of his face replaced my mother's. *Puck.* Where was he? And Roseanne?

What if she was alone, unable to fight off the insidious effects of the forest's magic?

My pace quickened, but the sound of hasty footsteps tailed me.

"Holly." Ilsa caught up to me, breathing hard. "Shit. I can sense it now. The forest, I mean. It's screwing with my thoughts."

"You don't say." I pushed down the urge to reprimand her for not seeing the obvious. "It did the same to me."

"Yeah." Her gaze travelled over the surrounding forest. "Holly, I didn't mean to make you feel like I don't appreciate what you did for River. Honestly, I don't even know how I'll ever repay you."

"Debts are for Sidhe, not us mere humans."

She lifted her head, and a flicker of a smile stirred on her face. "True."

A scream cut through the trees. *Roseanne.* At once, I broke into a run, Ilsa's footsteps pounding behind me.

"I bet the forest is meddling with the others' minds, too," Ilsa gasped out. "We have to set them free if we want to stand a chance in hell of getting out of here."

I veered around a corner and into a clearing, where Roseanne cowered between two giant furred beasts. I recognised Puck's bear-like monster form, but the other beast appeared to be identical to him. Had the forest conjured up an illusion? Wait—the shimmering around the beast on the right gave it away as a glamour, and its aquamarine eyes were familiar. *Darrow? What is he doing?*

"Roseanne, get out of there!" I called to her.

The beasts let out identical roars. Roseanne flung herself flat a second before the two beasts locked claws and fell into a snarling, bloody heap.

"Stop it!" Ilsa yelled. "Stop fighting. Darrow—Puck— the forest is manipulating you."

Both of the beasts ignored her, while Roseanne crawled on her front until she reached my side. Lifting her head, she regarded me with accusing eyes. "You left me behind."

"I didn't do it on purpose," I said. "What happened to those two?"

"I don't know." She scrambled upright. "It was too dark to see anyone, so I walked for a bit until the light came back. You were gone, and I didn't know where to find you."

A bone-shaking crunch sounded as the two beasts collided with a tree and sent several branches crashing to earth. Crap. I had to stop them before they did permanent damage to each other. "Roseanne, stay back. I'll stop them."

"I knew it," Roseanne said. "You wanted to find *him*, didn't you? You don't care about me."

"I do," I insisted, "but they're going to kill one another if I don't stop them. Can you hide in those bushes over there until I get them to shift back?"

"No, thanks," she said. "I'm done with you."

The forest is meddling with her thoughts. Her rejection stung all the same, and horror sprang up when she stalked away into the undergrowth alone.

"Don't run off!" I winced as one of the bear-like beasts dealt a vicious blow to the other, and blood sprayed across the leaf-strewn ground. How could I choose between keeping Roseanne safe and stopping Darrow and Puck from tearing one another to shreds?

"I'll find her!" Ilsa called over her shoulder, running in pursuit of Roseanne. "Trust me."

That was a lot to ask after the forest's magic had come close to turning us against one another, but before I could reply, the two brawling beasts crashed to the ground again, clawing at each other.

"Cut that out!" I yelled at them. "The forest is messing with both of you."

Unfortunately, they hadn't been close friends to begin with, and neither paid me any attention as I tried to find an opening to stop them from gouging each other's eyes out.

Shadows swept over my arms, protecting me as I flung myself at one of the beasts from the side. The momentum caused him to roll onto his back, and when he lifted his furred head, I recognised his vibrant green eyes as Puck's.

"Stop!" I shouted in his face. "The forest is trying to make you forget why we're here. You came to help me, remember?"

The beast's claw slammed into me, and I flew backwards into a tree. Winded, I dropped to my knees, while Puck let out a furious roar in Darrow's direction and then ran away into the bushes. *What is he doing?*

Biting back a wince, I pushed to my feet and hurried in pursuit. A growl at my heels alerted me to Darrow's pursuit, and he overtook me in seconds while I struggled through the undergrowth. Briars snagged my sleeves and ripped my jeans, and when the ground gave way to a sharp cliff, I veered right over the edge. For the second time that day, I found myself tumbling downward until I landed in an undignified heap. Raucous laughter echoed somewhere above, and I lifted my head to look for the source.

Hazel perched in a tree nearby, her mouth twisted in a sneer. "Have a nice trip?"

"What are you doing up there?" I climbed to my feet, my body aching all over.

"Looking for my siblings," she said. "Not you."

Great. The forest is manipulating her too. "Ilsa is chasing Roseanne, but I didn't see where she went. Have you seen a giant bear anywhere?"

"Puck turned into a giant bear?" She laughed. "Has he forgotten how to turn back?"

"If he has, so has Darrow." I did my best to ignore her derisive tone. "The forest is screwing with all of us, Hazel."

She snorted. "Maybe it put him in touch with his

animal side. I wouldn't blame him for going to extreme lengths to avoid you."

"Did you not hear the part about your boyfriend being a bear too?" I asked. "Have you seen him?"

"I don't give a shit, Holly." She sneered at me. "Maybe I'm sick of you all. Especially you. You brought us here, didn't you?"

"No, you did." The childish retaliation sprang from my tongue as if we'd been transported straight into our teenage rivalry days. "This whole excursion was your idea. Now we're stuck in this fucking forest while a murderous god is on the loose."

I'd had bloody enough. Roseanne had gone off somewhere, Puck had forgotten himself, and whether the forest's magic was responsible or not, the impulse to take out some of my frustration on the person who'd been responsible for the shithole we'd landed in was too much to resist.

Hazel sprang out of the tree and landed in a crouch. "Let's finish this. Gatekeeper against Gatekeeper."

No, urged a voice in the back of my mind. "No. We have to find Janet Lynn. Remember?"

"Coward." She drew two iron knives, which gleamed wickedly in the sunlight streaming through the canopy.

My hands shifted to claws. "I'm no coward, but I won't waste my time on you when the others are in danger."

The blades spun in Hazel's hands. I dodged both strikes, but she laughed and struck again. I knew she wasn't in her right mind, but she was fighting to kill, and my pride refused to let me back away. With the side of my claw, I knocked one of the knives from her grip, but the second grazed my arm deeply enough to tear a hole in my shirt. She'd *stabbed* me.

A loud rustle of branches made both of us briefly pause, and a huge bear-like shape came crashing through the bushes. Both of us hastened to get out of the giant beast's path, while Hazel stared at it, her expression shifting to horror.

"Darrow?" she whispered.

I backed away from her while I had the chance, my arm bleeding from the long gash her knife had ripped in my sleeve. I'd come here expecting to face any number of foes but not my own allies. Not my cousins, or my friends. I broke into a run, knowing I was too late to catch up to—

A root tripped me up, and for the third time that day, I fell sprawling. Then I looked up into the vibrant green eyes of Puck's bear form.

"Hey." My heart beat in my throat. "Remember me?"

His gaze carried no signs of recognition whatsoever. Puck reared up on his hind legs, and his claws swiped at my throat.

11

I rolled to the side to avoid Puck's claws, unwilling to deal a potentially fatal blow in retaliation. Puck was already bleeding from several deep scratches, presumably inflicted by Darrow, and I backed up against the nearest tree as he turned towards me again. "Puck, you can shift back to human form. Can't you remember how?"

He growled, low and threatening. I met his stare head-on, but a voice in the back of my mind whispered that I was better at inciting anger than at stopping it and that Puck was too far under the forest's spell for me to bring him back. He stalked towards me, one paw after the other, and it took all I had to hold my ground and meet his gaze.

"You can transform into a bear, a bird, a briar, and a leaping flame." I felt ridiculous talking to a giant bear as if he could understand me, but I was all out of any better ideas. "But you can't turn into any person except for yourself."

His paw caught my legs, sending me sprawling onto my back. The movement jarred my injured arm, and within seconds, he had me pinned down beneath the weight of his bear form. Clutching my arm, I gritted my teeth and glared straight into his eyes. "Not cool, Puck. You promised to help me."

For a heartbeat, I expected his jaws to close on my skull. Instead, the weight of the beast's paws lifted from my body, and Puck—the *real* Puck—staggered away from me on human feet.

"Puck?" I raised myself onto my uninjured elbow. "Are you okay?"

"Holly." He leaned over me, worry shining in his eyes as his hand brushed my arm. "Did I do that to you?"

"Hazel stabbed me," I said. "If you want to turn her into a toadstool, then feel free to. Once we get out of here."

Puck's arms came around me, and I leaned into his embrace, ignoring the pain in favour of the overwhelming sense of relief. *He's okay. I'm okay.*

"Holly!" Hazel's voice came from startlingly close by.

Puck was on his feet in a second, shifting into a bear again as he positioned himself between Hazel and me.

"Whoa." I leapt up, a fresh spike of pain jarring my arm. "Puck, shift back. Unless you're about to stab me again, Hazel."

"No." Hazel bit her lower lip. "I think the forest is screwing with us all."

"About time you figured it out." I scanned the path behind her. "Where's Darrow?"

"Back there," she said. "I saw Morgan, but he ran off, yelling about ghosts."

"And—Roseanne?" I asked. "Ilsa was chasing her the last time I saw them both."

Darrow emerged from the bushes, back in his human form and as bedraggled and bloodstained as the rest of us. I tensed when Puck moved towards him, but he shifted into a human again instead of lunging at Darrow.

"You nearly took my eye out, trickster," Darrow said.

"Don't start." I made to block Puck from starting another fight, but a distinct shout had all of us looking for the source.

"Get out of my head!" Morgan came stumbling out of the trees, punching wildly at thin air. His feet tangled in the undergrowth, and he tripped and fell into Hazel. She gave her brother a push, while I heard a familiar shriek in the background.

"Roseanne?" I ran towards the noise, at the same time as Pepper came out of the bushes after Morgan. When I stepped aside to avoid tripping over the puppy, Ilsa emerged next, holding a struggling Roseanne in her arms.

"Holly, help me out here." Roseanne lay draped over her shoulder, her feet kicking at Ilsa's chest. "She won't believe the forest is manipulating her, but she might listen to you."

"Roseanne?" I reached out a tentative hand towards her, but she wriggled free of Ilsa's grip and dropped to her feet on the forest floor. "Roseanne, don't run off again."

She made for the bushes, dodging Ilsa's attempts to grab her. "I want out of this forest. You shouldn't have brought me here."

A pang hit my chest. "You chose to come here, Roseanne. I wanted you to stay safe, but you convinced me to let you fight with me. You insisted you were strong enough to face everything we ran into."

She turned back to me, her expression confused. "I didn't... did I?"

"We're going to get out of here, but you'll need to trust me first," I told her. "Nobody else is going to run off. Right?"

"No," Ilsa said. "Including Morgan... Morgan, what are you doing?"

Morgan swayed towards the trees, his hands swatting at thin air, while Pepper ran in agitated circles around him. "Get outta my head!"

"Who's in your head, Morgan?" Ilsa asked him.

Morgan seemed to notice he wasn't alone for the first time. "Am I the only person who hears that damned voice?"

"What voice?" asked Hazel. "A human voice?"

Ilsa's eyes widened. "Is someone trying to psychically contact you?"

"Psychic?" Hazel stepped closer to her brother. "Is the voice coming from inside the forest?"

Morgan rotated on the spot, pointing into the trees. "Somewhere over there, I think."

"Then we'll find the source." Hazel walked behind her brother as he and Pepper took the lead.

For the lack of any better options, the rest of us followed them, treading carefully so as not to fall into another trap. At first, nothing about the forest appeared to change. Then the trees gradually thinned out, and bright sunlight streamed through the canopy.

"I can see the sky," Ilsa murmured.

"Same." Roseanne lifted her head, relief sweeping across her face. "We're nearly out."

Within a minute or two, I glimpsed a stone building visible between the trees. A small cottage, and outside, a woman stood facing the trees as though waiting for us. Her brown hair hung loosely to her shoulders, and she was dressed in a flowery dress whose colours were faded with time and wear.

In silence, our group left the woods, taking in the sight of the modest stone cottage and a pool of clear water behind the woman. Fields bordered the garden on its other sides, and I glimpsed a cluster of other stone buildings among the hills and fields. *Carterhaugh.*

I studied the stranger, noting her familiar brown eyes. "You're Janet Lynn, aren't you?"

"Yes," she said. "I am."

"Here." Hazel flung Thomas's harp at the woman, who caught the golden instrument by her fingertips. "You're welcome to keep this."

"Was that your idea of a game?" Morgan demanded. "You lured us into your forest and let us wander around for Sidhe-knows-how-long when we have more important shit to do. We might have died."

"Exactly." Ilsa's voice was quiet, less heated, but she must have been thinking of River's close call. Perhaps Janet hadn't intended for us to try to summon the god, but if she'd managed to send a warning by text message, there was no reason she couldn't have come to see us in person.

"It was not my intention," Janet said. "I cannot leave this place, and it's taken me this long to be able to contact you. The pond will heal your injures."

"The what?" said Hazel.

"I'm guessing that pond?" Puck indicated the small pool, whose waters glittered in the sunlight.

"You have the blood of one of the Ancients *here?*" Ilsa's eyes rounded. "In the mortal realm?"

"I believe the pond once belonged to Etaina," said Janet. "See to your injuries, and then I'll answer all the questions you might have."

Without another word, she strode towards the cottage, entering via the red-painted front door. Pepper dragged Morgan in the direction of the pool and began to gleefully splash around in the shallows, while Hazel reached out a hand and immersed it in the clear water. "This feels like the pond that used to be in our garden."

"So it's not a trap?" Morgan refused to go into the water himself, but Hazel reached out and grabbed Darrow's arm to pull him closer. He did not look thrilled at the notion of sticking his head into the water, but after a brief second of immersion, the deep cut left by Puck's claws had vanished entirely.

When the cut on my arm gave a sharp throb, I took my own turn to approach the clear water. Crouching on the bank, I immersed my injured arm up to the elbow. Rivulets of blood mingled with the water, and I watched them swirl out of sight until the pain faded. *Ancients' blood.* For beings so hard to kill, they sure seemed to spill a lot of blood at the Sidhe's hands.

Roseanne waited for me on the bank and eyed the blood dripping from my sleeve. "Did someone stab you?"

"Hazel," I said. "Under the effects of the forest's magic."

"I think I bit Ilsa," she mumbled. "She probably thinks I'm a wild beast now."

"Nah, I'm sure she doesn't," I said. "The forest was screwing with our heads. I bet it was Etaina's doing. Go and talk to her if you're worried."

Roseanne hesitantly shuffled towards Ilsa, while my gaze travelled over the others. Puck and Darrow were studiously ignoring one another, which wasn't surprising, given that they'd come close to tearing one another to shreds back in the forest, while Hazel hovered nearby, furtively glancing at me without speaking.

Given how she was incapable of being quiet for more than a few minutes, it came as no surprise when she approached me and cleared her throat. "I don't really want you dead."

"Could have fooled me."

"It was the forest," she said. "It put a spell on us."

"I know it did." I rubbed my damp arms, shivering in the chill breeze. "Etaina left a souvenir behind, I guess."

"Or her." Hazel indicated the seemingly tranquil-looking cottage. "I don't trust her."

"Who, Janet?" I was inclined to agree, though. What kind of person made their home on the doorstep of a cursed forest, even a distant descendent of the Lynn family?

"I don't trust her either," Morgan said. "She led us straight into a trap. She might look human, but she acts like one of the Sidhe."

"We've come all this way to find her," Ilsa said. "Let's face it, we're short on any better ideas, and we need to get rid of that god."

"Yes," said Darrow. "We do. That's why we're here."

"She said she could help us," Hazel said. "Let's see what Janet Lynn has to say for herself."

Hazel and Darrow entered the house first, followed by Ilsa, Morgan, and Pepper. Roseanne, Puck, and I approached more warily. I knew from growing up in the Winter Gatekeeper's home that outside appearances could be deceiving, but unlike the forest, the house seemed to have normal dimensions. One room dominated the ground floor, filled with a mismatch of well-worn furniture, while a fire burned in the old-fashioned grate. A large rug was spread across the wooden floor.

Since there wasn't enough room for everyone to sit down on chairs, we all gathered on the rug and sat cross-legged. Pepper began to chew on the throw draped across one of the armchairs, but Janet didn't pay any attention to him, instead offering us all cups of tea. Common sense told me not to accept any food or drink from someone so close to the Sidhe, but I warmed my hands on the mug she gave me as I studied Janet's profile. I saw the family resemblance in her features, but she looked nothing like Thomas at all.

"You were his wife," I said to her. "Weren't you? You're the mother of the two original Gatekeepers."

She inclined her head. "Yes. And you are Holly Lynn, the former Winter Gatekeeper."

Hazel sucked in a breath. "I thought you were human."

"I am," she said. "This was the house Thomas and I originally lived in, before we moved to Foxwood."

"So you *are* immortal," said Hazel.

My eye twitched. "Give her the chance to explain without interrupting."

Janet took a seat in one of the moth-eaten armchairs while the rest of us clustered around her like children gathering to hear a story. Janet wrapped long fingers around her teacup, her gaze fixed at a point somewhere in the distance.

"Thomas and I met in this very forest," she said. "I'd been warned against coming to Carterhaugh, but I was a rebellious youth, and I was intrigued by the rumours of a strange man who was said to roam the woods."

"I *have* heard the story before," said Hazel. "You came here anyway—ow!"

Ilsa, who'd jabbed her in the back from behind, said, "Go on."

"You likely already know the essential details of what transpired between us," said Janet. "Thomas and I courted for a while, but during those visits to the forest, he failed to mention that he was bound to another. Etaina of the Aes Sidhe had held him as her servant for seven years, and he'd willingly signed himself into service to her in order to forestall the death that he knew awaited any mortal who fell under her spell. Eventually, he warned me that the seven years he'd bargained for were almost over. Then he disappeared without a trace."

"He came back, though, right?" Hazel shuffled forward to avoid another prod from her sister.

"While Thomas was gone..." Janet began, her mouth creasing into a frown. "I discovered I was pregnant with twins. I went to the forest in an attempt to find him again, and when he tracked me down, he told me that he was scheduled to die that night. Unless, that is, I helped him escape being sacrificed."

"Thought so," said Hazel. "Where'd the unicorn come into it?"

"Hazel," said Ilsa. "Quiet."

Janet lifted her head, her gaze distant. "That night, on

Halloween, the Wild Hunt rode through the skies, carrying the souls of the dead to the next world... and they took their sacrifice to the one known as the Scourge."

I suppressed a flinch at the name. "The same god who's hunting us now. Was he always called that?"

"Aside from his true name... yes." She looked around at us, her eyes deep with sadness. "Thomas rode with the Hunt, and as planned, I followed with the intention of rescuing him from their clutches. I thought I succeeded when I pulled him off the horse, but what I didn't know was that he'd already made another vow to secure his freedom."

"The *Wild Hunt* were the Sidhe who rode that night?" Hazel said. "Not the Courts?"

"They rode with the Aes Sidhe," I murmured. "I bet Etaina had the Hunt handle the actual sacrifice rather than dirtying her own hands."

"We thought we were free," Janet said. "But when our children were grown..."

"They came back," said Morgan. "We know the rest. The Courts took your children, and Etaina dragged Thomas into the Aes Sidhe's home."

"She took you, too," said Ilsa. "Didn't she?"

Janet inclined her head. I'd known Etaina had taken Thomas for a second time, and that since she'd been unable to destroy him, she'd kept him as her prisoner. What he'd neglected to mention was that his wife had also been taken—and, like him, she must have bathed in the blood of the Ancients and been reborn as an immortal.

"How did you get away, then?" I asked. "You weren't around during the battle, were you?"

"Thomas helped me escape several years after our capture," she explained. "He expected to spend the rest of his days in the realm of the Aes Sidhe, but when Etaina was away on a mission, he seized the chance to track down the door leading back to Carterhaugh. No doubt she punished him harshly for aiding my escape, since he refused to join me. As soon as I found my way out of the forest, I fled Scotland immediately and settled down anonymously elsewhere."

"So how'd you end up back here?" Morgan asked.

"This was our home," she said simply. "Thomas and I lived here for several years after his initial escape, but we ultimately decided that we had no desire to raise our children so close to the faerie realm."

"So you picked Foxwood instead?" asked Hazel. "Did you not know your new home was practically on Faerie's doorstep too?"

"We did not." Her mouth pressed into a thin line. "Thomas might have, but it would have made no difference. They were always going to find us again."

"You know he's dead, don't you?" asked Hazel. "Thomas gave his life to destroy Etaina, and we—the Gatekeepers—gave up our magic in the process. Except… well." She cut off when Ilsa drove an elbow into her ribs, no doubt to stop her from blabbing about the Gatekeeper of Death—a late addition to the family that Janet might not even be aware of.

"Yes," Janet said. "I know he is dead."

"Why didn't you come and help in the battle?" I asked. "Don't you have magic of your own?"

"I am no fighter," she said. "I might be immortal, but I have never trained with the Sidhe. In the years I spent with them, Etaina all but ignored me. It was Thomas she wanted. When I returned to this realm, my children had aged and had had children of their own. I had no place among them."

"Where did you go?" asked Ilsa.

"I travelled," she said. "For a long while, I wandered wherever took my desire, until my path brought me back here. To Carterhaugh."

"You said you can't leave," Hazel said. "Why?"

"Because this is the only place that *they* cannot find me."

"The Scourge?" I asked. "Or the Wild Hunt?"

"Both," she said. "The town is unmarked on any map, while the presence of the forest masks any other magic in the area."

Morgan, ever inclined to ask the important questions, spoke up. "How the hell did you get a mobile phone, then?"

"She lives in the mortal realm," Ilsa reminded her. "She might be hundreds of years old, but she hasn't been living in a cave all this time."

"He has a point," Hazel said in an undertone. "Why'd she pick that way to contact us? How'd she get our numbers?"

Janet's attention turned in her direction. "I have always made a point of keeping an eye on my descendants. All the Gatekeepers lived in Foxwood until recently, and when you left, I approached the one person who remained behind."

"Our *mother?*" Morgan said incredulously. "She gave you our phone numbers?"

"Did she even know who you were?" Ilsa asked.

"I mentioned my connection to your family."

Hazel fidgeted. "You took the time to find *her,* but you couldn't be arsed to come and help us deal with the god in person?"

Janet shook her head. "I acquired the means of contacting you prior to the Scourge's escape. All of you were easy enough to find… except for the former Winter Gatekeeper, that is."

"You mean me," I said when the others glanced in my direction. "Who'd you ask?"

"A half-Sidhe of your acquaintance with ties to the Aes Sidhe." When my gaze went to Puck, she added, "This was several months ago."

"Brook, maybe." I'd given my number to Blaine, his predecessor, before his death, so perhaps Brook had been desperate enough to get rid of the weirdo who'd shown up on his doorstep that he'd gone through his mentor's contacts. Who even knew what story she'd given him? She was no regular human, and she was definitely more devious than she appeared. In the forest, she'd used some kind of psychic link to communicate with Morgan directly, yet she'd intentionally chosen a means of sending a message which would reach all of us at once for maximum impact.

Come to think of it, if she had psychic abilities, that made her a necromancer, albeit an untrained one. Was that why she thought the Scourge might come after her?

Another question occurred to me. "Janet, you said the Wild Hunt carried Thomas to be sacrificed on behalf of Etaina. Were they working directly for her, not Summer or Winter?"

"No," she said. "The Hunt's purpose was to carry the

dead to the next world, which included sacrifices such as Etaina's."

I frowned. "And the Courts let her get away with it?"

The Aes Sidhe hadn't been in hiding at the time, so the Summer Court must have known perfectly well that Etaina was sacrificing humans to the gods every seven years. Of course they hadn't stopped her, though, not when the victims were mortals who didn't matter. Even the former Erlking hadn't tried to intervene until Etaina had attempted to steal his throne and his talisman.

My hands curled into fists when Janet didn't respond. "So Etaina was allowed to learn blood magic from the Wild Hunt and sacrifice humans all she liked, but it wasn't until she threatened the Courts' supremacy that they stood up to her."

"Sounds about right." Hazel's expression mirrored my own anger. "The Wild Hunt were happy to work for her too. What did it matter to them whether the souls were human or not?"

"Why?" Roseanne burst out. It was the first time she'd spoken since we'd entered the cottage. "Why did the god want human souls?"

"In exchange for favours," I said. "Right?"

"Precisely," said Janet. "Like many of the Ancients, the Scourge primarily feeds on souls. To Etaina, sacrificing humans was more preferable than giving him her own people's souls."

"Obviously," Hazel said. "That would have made her unpopular."

"She wasn't the only one," said Janet. "The Ancients had long since been exiled even then, yet many of the Sidhe retained connections with their predecessors."

"The other Sidhe made sacrifices to the gods in order to access their magic without risking their return," I said. "Do I have that right?"

"Etaina wasn't the first." Ilsa had gone pale. "They've done this to humans for years. Centuries."

"Yes, but not always humans," said Janet. "The original sacrifices to the Scourge were the souls of the Sidhe."

12

All of us stared at Janet for a long, stunned moment.

"Excuse me?" said Hazel. "You're saying the Wild Hunt used to feed the *Sidhe's* souls to the Ancients?"

"The realm to which they banished the Ancients is the closest the Sidhe possess to an afterlife," she said. "The Wild Hunt were designated as carriers of the dead, delivering the Sidhe's departed souls to the afterlife before they turned into wraiths and became a menace to the Courts."

My heart missed a beat. *So it* was *the afterlife that Ilsa opened when she banished the wraith in the Death Kingdom.* At one time, the souls of Sidhe had passed into that realm the same way the souls of humans and other mortals travelled beyond the gates of Death. What did that say for the cauldron of resurrection, though?

"Let me get this straight," I said. "The Sidhe banished the gods to their *own* afterlife and then panicked when the same gods started devouring any souls that travelled there? Was *that* why they forged the cauldron?"

"I cannot say for sure," said Janet. "However, the Sidhe wanted to bargain with the Ancients without sacrificing their own, and so they took up the habit of capturing mortals instead."

"The Sidhe made a bargain and then wriggled out of it," Hazel said. "How like them."

"The Scourge has a very good reason to be furious with the generations of Sidhe who escaped the sacrifices he believes they owed him," Janet said. "Yet the roots of his fury result from the immortality the Sidhe stole from the Ancients' own hands."

"By making the cauldron," I said. "But—Etaina had an immortality source, too, didn't she?"

"Yes, she did," said Janet. "Not as strong as the cauldron, but Etaina claimed her choice was intentional. She told me that the Sidhe were never supposed to be reborn from death indefinitely. That honour was reserved for the Ancients and their direct descendants alone."

My heart missed a beat. "She did?"

Darrow leaned forward, his brow pinching. "Are you telling the truth?"

"I cannot lie," Janet said. "The Lady of Light told me herself, and no doubt she told Thomas too. She never expected either of us to escape her realm, after all."

From the stunned surprise on Puck's and Darrow's faces, Etaina hadn't breathed a word to anyone else in her Court. Then again, why would she? I'd have bet she made liberal use of the immortality source herself, but she hadn't shared it with the rest of her Court.

"No true immortals in Faerie," said Hazel. "Except the Ancients' direct descendants… meaning who?"

"The death fae," I said. "The Morrigan and the banshees. They die and are instantly reborn without the need for a cauldron."

"Is that why the Unseelie Queen hates the Morrigan?" Hazel asked. "She knows the Morrigan is a true immortal while she's only a pretender?"

Roseanne shifted uncomfortably, and I gave her a reassuring look. Being half-human made her as mortal as I was, but the Morrigan truly *was* a direct descendent of the gods she resembled so closely. In fact, I'd have bet the Sidhe had been jealous of her ability to revive from Death and had sought to recreate the same kind of magic themselves in the only way possible: by killing an Ancient and using the magic in their blood for their own.

"So the Sidhe have spent the past thousand years or more lying to themselves?" asked Morgan. "Kind of impressive for people who supposedly can't lie."

"Pretty much." It didn't explain why the Morrigan had disappeared, though, unless the Unseelie Queen's jealousy had finally pushed her over the edge.

"You said the Sidhe who die without their souls being taken to the next world eventually turn into wraiths?" said Ilsa. "I thought it was only the Sidhe who died in the Vale who were cut off from the afterlife."

"No." Janet's expression turned pensive. "The Sidhe are not meant to endure past their deaths. While they might initially resemble their living selves, without anyone to take them to the afterlife, they will inevitably forget themselves and turn into wraiths."

"You mean without the Wild Hunt." Yet the Hunt had

betrayed the Courts and helped Fionn's coup. "Some of the Unseelie Court's members were weirdly insistent on telling their Queen that they needed to re-establish the Wild Hunt. Was that why? They knew—or suspected—that they'd be doomed to turn into wraiths upon their deaths?"

"Perhaps." Janet studied me as though wondering how I'd come to hear a conversation that wasn't meant for human ears. "I have never met the monarchs of Summer or Winter, but I have long suspected many other Sidhe were secretly aware of the fate that once awaited them after death."

"What about the ones who aren't?" asked Hazel. "Has anyone tried telling them *why* recreating the cauldron is a bad idea? They'll probably sentence us to death if we tell them the truth ourselves, but someone has to."

"No thanks," said Morgan.

"If they never make a new cauldron, the Sidhe will keep getting stuck in limbo after they die," I said. "They'll all become wraiths. Right?"

Janet inclined her head. "It was easy for them to ignore the issue as long as the cauldron existed, but without it, more and more wraiths are showing up in Faerie. If they keep up their warring ways, then the situation will only get worse."

Damn. Everyone thought the Sidhe's current dilemma stemmed from the destruction of their source of immortality, but they'd written their own fates by creating the cauldron solely to prevent their souls being devoured by the very gods they'd banished from their realm to begin with.

As for Thomas Lynn? He'd ended their temporary

habit of sacrificing mortals instead, and I was starting to agree with Hazel that he'd faced a terrible choice and picked the only way out that would spare as many people as possible from the backlash.

"What I'd like to know is how the Sidhe banished the gods to begin with," I said. "Specifically, the Scourge. That was what you wanted us to talk to you about, right? You said you knew how to get rid of him."

"No human can banish the Scourge," she said. "If the ritual used to summon him enabled the god to roam freely between the realms, then even the Sidhe will be unable to repeat the feat of their predecessors."

"So you called us here to say it was impossible to get rid of him?" Hazel said incredulously.

"There is a good reason Etaina of the Aes Sidhe never directly summoned the Ancients into this realm," she said. "Some say the Sidhe were wrong to exile their predecessors, but others might claim that their actions were necessary in order for any other forms of life to have a chance at survival. Each of the Ancients possesses a different gift, but the Scourge is among the strongest of a particular group known to some as the Furies. Their strength is fuelled from the dead, and their talent for manipulating souls proved alluring to the Sidhe. After all, there is one element of their lives over which they have no control… death."

"Is the Scourge stronger than the Devourer?" Ilsa asked. "The god whose power resided in the old Erlking's talisman? Because the Erlking's staff was so lethal that he destroyed anything living that went near him, and he was forced to exile himself from his own Court. The Scourge doesn't seem to have power on that scale."

"There are different kinds of power," said Janet. "Some Ancients' strength is limited. Others are virtually without limit, and the Scourge gains power from each soul he devours. If the Sidhe had not stopped making sacrifices, he might have eventually been able to escape his imprisonment without being summoned at all."

My throat went dry. "The Wild Hunt planned to kill the Scourge. Would they have succeeded?"

"I cannot say for sure," she said. "I learned everything I know of the Wild Hunt from being an observer in the Court of the Aes Sidhe, and I have not laid eyes on them in a long time. I do know that they once escorted the dead into the afterlife, directly to the Scourge himself. For that reason, there is a chance they know how to banish him."

"So the message you sent was a ruse." Morgan rose to his feet. "You want us to find the Wild Hunt? Holly already did that."

"Yes, I did," I said. "That's where I got the Scourge's name. You might have warned me."

"I wasn't aware of where you got the name, but I suspected that summoning the Scourge using an Invocation would be the Sidhe's first move," she said. "Most of them are too young to remember how the Scourge was banished initially, but the Wild Hunt are almost as old as the gods themselves. How many of their number survived?"

"Two, as far as I know," I said. "There were three, but we killed one of them in order to get the god's name. The other two deserved the same fate, frankly, considering they murdered over a dozen innocent half-faeries while trying to summon that god in the first place."

"They summoned the god?" Janet's eyes widened. "The Wild Hunt summoned the Scourge?"

"I thought you knew," I said. "They planned to slaughter him in order to remake the cauldron."

"Last time we saw them, they seemed to have abandoned that goal," Puck said. "They gave us the god's name, but I'm guessing they knew the summoning wouldn't work."

I hadn't known at the time that the Wild Hunt had once delivered the dead into the Scourge's hands. *Did* they know how to permanently get rid of him? If so, why had they stopped their hunt in favour of roaming around the Vale making cryptic remarks?

"The Hunt's former leader was killed a few years ago," Ilsa said. "I think they lost their way for a bit after that, but it's entirely possible the survivors were born after the gods' initial banishment and didn't know their own history."

"I never had the impression the Hunt frequently added to their numbers," said Janet. "From what Etaina told me, the Wild Hunt were older even than the Court's most ancient monarchs."

Like the Unseelie Queen. If *she* knew how to get rid of the Scourge, then all the snow in the Winter Court would melt into a puddle before she gave that information to me. Still, if the Wild Hunt had been born in an era long before the other Sidhe in Faerie, it explained why their betrayal had shaken the Courts to their foundations. While it was possible that the trouble had started when Fionn had taken over the Wild Hunt, they might have been corrupted for far longer than that.

The Sidhe believed they had always lived forever, but

that wasn't true. Not at all. In a way, I'd been right about the Morrigan too. She'd slipped her chains and travelled into the faeries' afterlife after giving me her magic, and I was willing to bet that the botched ritual and the Scourge's rebirth had caused her to end up stuck somewhere on the other side.

"So we're fucked," Morgan said. "Unless we convince the Wild Hunt to tell us how to get rid of the Scourge, then he's here for the duration."

"Or we banish him ourselves," Ilsa said. "I've seen the Sidhe's afterlife with my own eyes. It can be opened with an Invocation… but it'd require more people than the dozen or so who tried to banish the Scourge last time."

"You tried to banish him?" Janet asked. "With the aid of the Sidhe?"

"A few," Ilsa said. "I can open the Sidhe's afterlife myself, but it comes as a huge risk to my own life."

"How is that possible?" Janet's brow puckered as she looked upon Ilsa. "You weren't one of the Gatekeepers, were you?"

"I have this." Ilsa reached into her pocket and pulled out her talisman. "I'm the Gatekeeper of Death. The magic of an Ancient who once served an ancestor of mine is in this book, and since he had no connection with the original Gatekeeper or with Thomas Lynn, I didn't lose my magic when the others did."

"Technically," I said, before I could stop myself, "the Ancient originally served my side of the family, before the talisman changed hands. It's been around for a while."

Ilsa shot me a scowl, perhaps recalling our spat in the forest, but Janet's expression flickered with interest. "The Ancient served you?"

"Not me, but a past Winter Gatekeeper," I said. "The Ancient took the form of a raven called Arden who worked for both sides of the family until his death."

Janet extended a hand. "May I look at that, Ilsa?"

Ilsa held out the book to show her, but she didn't relinquish her grip on her talisman. "The book only shows its contents to me, nobody else."

Janet examined the book's leathery cover and yellowed pages for a long moment then lowered her hand, and Ilsa pocketed her talisman with visible relief on her face. "Perhaps you can find a way to use that talisman to banish the Scourge, but if so, its powers are not within my knowledge."

"Great," said Morgan. "So we have to risk Ilsa's life or go looking for those dickheads again. Unless you'd like to tell us something that's actually *useful?*"

"I have told you everything I know," said Janet. "If you wish to return to Edinburgh, then the Ley Line is not far from here."

I glanced out the window. The sky had begun to darken, and since our only route home was via Faerie, we'd better hope the Courts hadn't noticed our presence there earlier. "All right. If that's really all you have to say…"

"It is." She rose from her seat and watched the rest of us straighten upright, not speaking.

Turning my back on the others, I took the lead out of the cottage door and came to a halt beside the pool of water. A moment later, Puck's reflection appeared beside mine. In the background, I heard Ilsa and Hazel talking to Janet, but I had little interest in hearing tales of her time in Etaina's lands.

"What a waste of bloody time," I muttered.

"I wouldn't say that." Puck moved closer to my side. "It was worth trying out all our options."

"Worth nearly dying in the forest?"

"No, of course not." Our hands were inches apart, and our rippling reflections on the water closed the distance, seeming to merge together. "I was afraid I'd brought about your death myself when I was trapped in the form of a beast, unable to escape."

I lifted my head to look at his real face, not his reflection. "The forest lied. Whatever it made you think, it wasn't true."

"I know," he said softly. "I know."

We stood there for a moment, poised on another threshold. Something had shifted between us in that forest, in the moment I'd waited for death at his own hands and instead found he'd remembered himself in time to stop his claws from ripping out my throat. When self-preservation should have won, but it hadn't.

Out of the corner of my eye, I glimpsed a dark blot above our reflections in the water. A winged shape blurred the water's surface, distant at first, but a chill of recognition struck me.

The Scourge had found us.

13

The dark shape drew closer, blurring on the surface of the water. Puck and I both stepped away from the pond, a chill breeze ruffling its surface.

"Warn the others," I told him. "I'll distract the Scourge myself."

"Holly—" He cut off in a curse as the dark shape grew larger, its shadow casting the cottage in darkness. As he ran towards the open door, darkness folded over my skin, wings sprouted from my shoulders, and I launched myself into the air.

Had the Scourge been following us all along? Or had Janet somehow lured him here? I wouldn't have thought she'd want to risk her own safety, but I'd long suspected her seeming powerlessness was an act. Beating my wings, I caught up to the shimmering humanoid shape in the air. The beast flickered around the edges like a picture taken slightly out of focus.

"*You again,*" said the Scourge. "*The false harbinger.*"

"That's me." I could hear the others moving around below us, but I didn't dare take my eyes off the god's blurred form. The image of him knocking River down with a bolt of darkness replayed in my mind, and fear threatened to drag me down to earth again. "What do you want with us?"

"Nothing more than what I am owed, mortal."

"What—the souls you were denied after Thomas Lynn wriggled out of being sacrificed?" Was Janet his target? It seemed impossible that he hadn't known she was here until now, but even the Sidhe had overlooked her hiding place.

"I desire more than the souls of mortals, but if you insist upon standing in my way..."

The god raised a clawed hand, a bolt of darkness forming. I shot upward like a bullet, and the attack grazed my wing, scattering feathers in its wake. I caught my balance, my heart pounding. The Scourge had spared us at the site of the summoning, but this time, he'd hunted us down himself, and I could only assume he'd come to finish the job.

I can't let that happen. I'd consumed the soul of one god already, and while the Scourge was indisputably far stronger than the being that I'd faced in Death, I was all out of any better ideas.

Descending towards his shadowy form, I reached out —but my claws passed straight through him as though he didn't exist. A moment later, pain exploded in my skull, blurring my vision and causing me to drop several feet in the air.

"You dare to touch me, pretender?"

The spasm of agony fled as swiftly as it had arrived, leaving a throbbing headache in its wake. "What the—?"

The Scourge took aim with a handful of darkness, but a black shape darted past his line of sight, causing his attack to crash into the forest instead. The crunch of branches and leaves falling echoed from below as a second crow joined the first. *Puck. Roseanne. Dammit.*

The Scourge swiped at the two small birds, and I regained height, alarm blaring through me.

"Hey!" I shouted at him. "What are you playing at? Why'd you run away last time?"

The Scourge moved towards me in a blur, his clawed hand easily knocking mine aside and seizing my throat. His other claw swatted at the two birds, while I struggled, unable to breathe. My vision wavered, and the image of the Morrigan appeared in my mind's eye. If I died, would I go to the humans' Death, or Faerie's—the same realm to which the Morrigan was bound?

Would dying enable me to bring her back? It was one silver lining, I supposed, but even the Morrigan might not be able to stand up to the true god of death.

The Scourge's grip tightened, his voice a low whisper in my ear. *"All will be revealed on the longest night, and all that was broken will be set right."*

Pain split my mind in two, and I tumbled head over heels before slamming into bitter darkness.

———

I expected to wake up as a ghost. Instead, I surfaced from the pool in Janet's garden, coughing and spluttering, drenched but alive. My vision wavered as I lifted my head, seeing Puck hurrying towards me. "Holly!"

I dragged myself to the bank. "Where'd the Scourge go?"

"He flew off," said Roseanne. "Soon as he dropped you."

"What?" I tilted my head to look up at the sky and saw the faintest shadow of a winged form disappearing into the clouds. Shakily, I climbed to my feet, seeing that Ilsa, Hazel, Darrow, Morgan, and Pepper had all come outside while Janet watched from the doorway of the cottage.

"How did he find us?" I directed my question more at Janet than the others. "I thought you were hidden from him. Does the Scourge know where you live?"

"I'd say yes." Morgan gave Janet a distrustful look. "He must have known *we* were here, at the very least."

"The god is enraged," she said. "He has likely been tracking you since you summoned and angered him. Until now, he has not been able to find my location."

"You think he'll come back for you?" If so, then we'd brought him here ourselves. *But why did he leave?*

"I think this house is no longer a safe haven for any of us," Janet said. "You always intended to leave, did you not?"

"We have to," I said. "The Scourge… before he dropped me, he said something weird."

"Said what?" Ilsa asked.

I repeated his words: "*All will be revealed on the longest night, and all that was broken will be set right.*"

"Sounds like a faerie riddle to me," Hazel remarked. "The longest night… that rings a bell."

"The winter solstice," Janet said.

A chill raced down my spine. "Is that significant? To the gods, I mean? I know it's the night when Winter fae are at their strongest."

"On the longest night of the year, the faerie and mortal realms overlap," said Janet. "The Scourge received his sacrifices on a similar night."

"The Wild Hunt mentioned it too." A suspicion struck me like a thunderclap. "They can't be working together."

"It certainly would not be the first time," said Janet. "I will make my preparations to leave before the Ancient returns."

"Or you can actually help us," said Morgan.

Her expression clouded. "I am no fighter, let alone against a being that cannot be destroyed by mortal hands."

"You drew us here," said Hazel. "You brought this on yourself."

I wasn't sure I agreed, but I'd come here hoping for a solution and instead narrowly escaped death at the god's hands. "Where's the quickest route to the Ley Line? I'm not going back into that forest."

Janet pointed towards a field to the left of her cottage. "A short distance away. Do be careful."

She didn't need to tell us twice. While she retreated into her home, we left the back garden via a creaky metal gate and made our way across the hillside separating the stone cottage from the rest of the village.

When we veered into the neighbouring field, it didn't take long before we came across the Ley Line's shimmering presence. Had Janet and Thomas truly believed that they were leaving Faerie behind when they'd moved to Foxwood? The curse upon our family had once prevented any of us from moving away from the Ley Line at all, so perhaps that had influenced their decision. After all, in the end, there'd been no escaping the Sidhe.

"C'mon, Pepper," Morgan said to the puppy. "I know you don't want to go back to Faerie, but if we don't, we'll have to walk back to Edinburgh on foot or get lost in that bloody forest again."

The puppy whined and tugged on the lead, dragging Morgan across the hillside and forcing the rest of us to hurry after him.

"What's wrong with him?" asked Ilsa.

"I don't think he trusts that forest," Morgan said. "Neither do I—or *her*, either."

"Janet ought to have known bringing us here would paint a target on her own head," Hazel said. "Serves her right for refusing to meet us in Edinburgh instead."

"The Scourge couldn't detect her because of the forest's magic," said Darrow. "We came to her cottage via the forest, so how did the god know we were there?"

"Good point," I said. "Perhaps he was watching from the skies, but I don't trust her either. She's not a regular human anymore, is she?"

"No," said Puck. "She isn't."

"She's psychic, for a start," Morgan said. "And she wasn't as nice and mild-mannered as she acted in person when she was battering away at the inside of my skull."

"Psychic," said Ilsa. "Does that mean she's a necromancer?"

"Wouldn't surprise me," said Hazel. "It'd explain how we ended up with necromancer ancestry in our family as well."

Psychics were among the rarest type of necromancer, and Morgan had found himself the target of murderous ghosts as a result of his own talents. According to Ilsa, one of the Ancients had had no physical body but could possess the living via a psychic link, killing off his hosts when he was finished with them. Did the Scourge have the same talents? Surely not—he'd have demonstrated by now—and yet the strange pain which had split my head in two before he'd thrown me out of the sky hadn't been caused by any physical wound.

"C'mon." Morgan pulled on Pepper's lead so that he came to a halt. "Everyone get closer."

We did so, crowding around him as the Ley Line glowed brighter. At once, the countryside disappeared, and we landed on the leaf-strewn path of Faerie.

Quietness surrounded us, and I looked up and down the path, my spine prickling. We weren't alone.

Dread gripped me, followed by exasperation when Lord Lyle stepped out of the nearby bushes. "Must you insist upon constantly trespassing where you are not welcome, mortal?"

"This is neutral ground," I pointed out. "I'm not in Summer or Winter, and nobody kicked me out of the borderlands."

He shouldn't know I'd been chased out of Summer, but the Unseelie Queen had clearly been sending him to spy on me for a while. Did she know we'd gone back to the former home of the Aes Sidhe? She couldn't possibly know Janet Lynn had survived, surely, but I'd learned not to underestimate her spies.

"I heard that your attempt to entrap the Scourge was unsuccessful," he said.

"No thanks to the generosity of the Winter Queen."

His eyes flared bright blue, but he made no move to

strike me down. "She was right to turn down your request. Many of Summer's Sidhe were injured during the attack."

"Doesn't say much for your faith in your own army." I knew it wasn't wise to goad him, but I was soaking wet, exhausted, and through playing nice with the Sidhe. "I don't suppose she'd like to enlighten me on how she and the other Sidhe banished the Scourge the first time around? You should ask her to tell you the story, you know. I'd be interested to hear how she spins it."

Lord Lyle's jaw tensed. "You are lucky the harbinger's magic protects you, human."

"Tell me something I don't know." I glimpsed the others giving me warning looks, but I ignored them and kept my attention on the Winter Sidhe. "She's deceiving you, Lord Lyle. She's hidden the truth from your Court for her entire reign, and she was born in an era before most of you were ever heard of. Were you aware that the Sidhe once sacrificed each other's souls to the gods for favours?"

"I would advise you not to make such an accusation in front of my queen," he said. "Your lies will not poison our Court any longer."

"I'm telling the truth," I said. "Have you even asked your queen how her search for the Wild Hunt is going? Because from what I heard, she's made no real effort to find them at all. I'll give you this information for free, though—I have reason to believe they're planning to return to the mortal realm on the winter solstice, and it just so happens that the Scourge mentioned he has plans for that night as well."

"Lies," he said. "You intend to incite war in the Courts."

"I intend to warn you," I corrected. "Whatever the Scourge is planning will affect the Courts too. He wants revenge for the souls you denied him, and it wouldn't surprise me if your queen was near the top of his list."

He raised a hand. "Leave."

The word he spoke rang out with the power of an Invocation, and light dazzled my eyes. The next thing we knew, our group landed on the dark street of Edinburgh under the shadow cast by a streetlamp.

"You know," said Hazel, "you're never allowed to lecture me about disrespecting the Sidhe again, Holly."

"Did you not hear a word Janet Lynn said?" I asked. "She *is* deceiving him and the other members of the Winter Court. The Unseelie Queen trusts Lord Lyle marginally more than the others, though, and if he warns her of the Scourge's plan, she's more likely to listen to him than the rest of us."

"Assuming she doesn't have her own agenda," Ilsa said. "Which she does."

"True," I said. "The god isn't on her side, so we have that in our favour, but she's unlikely to give two shits if a few humans end up dying before she makes a move against him."

"And the sky is blue," said Hazel. "What does it matter what the Winter Queen does?"

"She left the Wild Hunt to roam around the Vale," I pointed out. "Didn't they once make sacrifices to the Scourge themselves?"

The others all stared at me, even Puck.

"You think the Wild Hunt is working *with* the god?" asked Hazel. "After they tried to kill him?"

"They both mentioned the longest night, the solstice," I said. "How far away is that?"

"It's this week… and that's assuming we didn't lose any more days in Faerie," said Ilsa.

"We did," said Hazel. "Look at the sky. It's dark. We've lost more than a few hours, at least."

"Damn," said Ilsa. "The boss *might* be awake at this hour, but I think we'll have to wait until morning to give the necromancers an update."

"What do we tell the Council of Twelve?" asked Hazel. "That we wasted our time?"

"We didn't," I said. "We found out the Scourge has justifiable reasons to hate the Sidhe and that he plans to act on the solstice, when the barriers between realms are thin."

"What, you think he's going to declare war on Faerie?" asked Morgan.

"He can't take on both Courts at once," Ilsa said, but she didn't sound certain. "They'd slaughter him first."

"He's a death god," I said. "I bet he's like the Morrigan and is reborn every time he dies, and as long as he exists, the Sidhe will never stop trying to find a way to bring back their immortality. Even if they do manage to banish him, he'll lurk in the realm of the dead, waiting to feast on their souls."

"Serve them right for exiling their gods to begin with," said Morgan. "Besides, don't we *want* them to banish him?"

"His old home is also where the Morrigan is hiding," I said. "Maybe we should have summoned her after all."

"Why?" asked Hazel. "To get rid of the Scourge? Do you think *she* knows how to banish him?"

"Possibly, but the Morrigan is supposed to be reborn after her death," I said. "I bet when the Wild Hunt did that ritual the first time around, it somehow brought out that creature I found lurking in Death *and* caused the Morrigan to get stuck in limbo. She's related to the Scourge, though, so it's not unreasonable to expect her to know his weaknesses."

Roseanne shuddered. "Ugh. I don't want to be related to that thing."

"Neither do I, believe me." *Could* we summon the Morrigan? Convincing the guild to agree after the incident with the Scourge would be a tall order, though for all I knew, she planned to return on the solstice as well. It'd be like a family reunion in a way. "We have until the solstice to stop whatever the Scourge is planning. The council needs to know, even if we can't give a definite explanation of what he's doing."

"I'll tell anyone at the guild who's awake," said Ilsa. "Hazel?"

"I'll go back to the hotel and knock on a few doors," she said. "Coming, Darrow?"

He gave Puck the merest glare before turning away and leaving with Hazel. Puck watched his fellow half-Aes Sidhe, his expression stony, but he said nothing. An improvement on them trying to kill one another, if nothing else.

"We're going back to the guild." Ilsa beckoned to Morgan, who tugged on Pepper's lead to stop him chewing on a patch of grass.

"Sure," I said. "Let me know if I'm invited to another urgent meeting… unless Lady Montgomery put a price on my head, that is."

"I bet she's forgiven you by now," said Ilsa. "I'll text you, okay?"

"Sure." I waved goodbye to her and then turned to Puck. "You're going to update Hawk?"

"I want to update him too." Roseanne winked at me and bounded down the road.

I rolled my eyes after her. "She's keen to get away from us, isn't she?"

"I'm not complaining." He drew me into an embrace, the sudden warmth startling but not unpleasant. "You scared the crap out of me at least twice today, so I think I deserve to look after you for a bit."

"Do you think I need looking after?" I found myself fighting a smile, all the same. "Scaring the crap out of people is kind of my thing."

"Ah, but I don't usually scare easy." He kissed me softly on the lips. "Come on, before you catch your death of cold."

We walked the rest of the way back to the office and caught up to Roseanne at the door.

"I don't think Hawk's in," she said.

Puck unlocked the door himself. "Bet he's on another date with Leyton."

"So nobody's going to cook for us." Roseanne gave a sigh. "We're going to starve."

"I'll order takeout," said Puck. "You go and warm up, Holly. I'll be back in five minutes."

"Will you now?"

Instead of answering, he took flight as a bird and left me blinking after him. While Roseanne happily sprawled on the sofa, I removed my soaking-wet jacket and shoes before heading up to the guest room to have a warm shower. Not that it'd help much if I didn't have a change of clothes with me, but I hadn't thought to stop at my own house on the way. I draped my jacket on the radiator instead, but I'd barely turned on the shower when a soft knock came on the guest room door. Puck was already back, which shouldn't have surprised me, given that flying across the city as a bird was bound to save on time.

The shower's water was cold, so I left it to warm up while I crossed the room to the door, conscious of the way my wet jeans and T-shirt clung to my skin.

"I brought some spare clothes," Puck's voice said from the other side.

"You did what?" I yanked the door open. "You flew back to my house?"

In answer, Puck sauntered into the room and dropped a handful of clothes on the bed. "You shouldn't have to go back outside into the freezing cold after diving into that pond."

"The pond saved my life." I drew my arms to my chest, feeling oddly self-conscious, when he sat down on the bed. "What are you doing?"

Puck looked up at me, his green eyes bright. "Let me know if I'm overstepping."

"You're not stepping anywhere. You're sitting down."

On my bed, to be precise. Or *a* bed, anyway. Puck tilted his head questioningly. "Do you want me to continue sitting down? Or lying down, perhaps?"

"No, thanks." The heat of the shower beckoned. "I'd prefer you to be in here. With me."

He moved in a blur, our lips meeting in a breathless kiss, his heated gaze warming me until the chill was a distant memory. His hands tugged at my clothes, which I removed in short order, peeling the damp fabric from my skin. He swore softly, half in English, half in the language of the fae.

I smiled against his mouth. "I understand the faerie tongue, you know."

"I know." Mischief glimmered in his eyes as he removed his own clothes with deft hands, pausing between breathless kisses to extract a condom from his pocket.

"I see you came prepared." Thanks to my knowledge of magical herbs, I could brew a contraceptive potion if necessary, but at the moment, I didn't want to think about the future, only the present. No guy had ever touched me like this, tender yet fierce, planting swift kisses on my lips as we explored one another's bodies.

I caught Puck's free hand and pulled him underneath the shower, warm water spraying over both our heads. His hands continued to roam south until he found me slick and ready for him, and his devilish fingers sought out the places which urged pleasure from me and weakened my knees.

He paused for a brief second to slide on the condom before he thrust inside me, drawing a gasp from my mouth. We moved against each other, our mutual pleasure mounting, the spray of water muffling the sound of my stifled cry as I came.

In that moment, there was only him and me and a new determination not to let anything take this away from me, even Death itself.

14

A message from Ilsa hit my phone the following morning. As we'd established yesterday—when Puck and I had both remembered to check the date—the solstice was in two days' time, which gave us entirely too little time to make a plan. Especially when we didn't even know what, precisely, to expect from the Wild Hunt on the longest night.

Puck watched me across the kitchen table as I put down my piece of burnt toast to check my messages. *Meeting with the council at 10,* the text from Ilsa read.

"There's a meeting in less than an hour," I told Puck. "With both the guild and the Council of Twelve, I assume."

Did that mean Lady Montgomery had forgiven me for breaking the guild's laws when I'd revived River from the dead? I assumed they weren't about to arrest me, because Ilsa would have forewarned me, but not knowing what to expect from the boss made me edgy.

"Let me guess, the council wants to give you an

earful?" Roseanne scraped at the bottom of her cereal bowl for the last dregs of milk.

"Or they want to hear my side of the story about yesterday," I said. "I don't know how much detail Ilsa gave them on our quest to find Janet."

"Is it even their business?" Puck asked. "She told us more about the Sidhe than the Scourge."

"Yeah, I bet the Sidhe will be mad if you tell the whole world they aren't real immortals," Roseanne said. "Let alone that they've been cheating death for centuries to avoid their souls being eaten by the gods they banished with their own hands."

"Lord Lyle didn't believe me when I told him," I said. "Most of the Sidhe wouldn't, in fact."

The ones who knew the truth had spent centuries rewriting their own history in order to pretend that they'd always been eternal, so I didn't care if they got mad at me for telling tales.

"You don't have to tell the council about Janet's link to your family," said Puck. "It's up to you."

"Not really," I said. "You know Hazel and Morgan can't keep their mouths shut, and even Ilsa will tell the council if she thinks it makes sense."

"Want me to walk you to the meeting, then?" he asked.

"Nah, I'm good." I got to my feet. "You wait for Hawk to come back so you can give him an update on yesterday."

Roseanne grinned at me. "Including what you and Puck were up to last night?"

I gave her an eye roll. Keeping secrets from an inquisitive teenage death fae was impossible, and besides, she'd been trying to bring Puck and me together from the moment she'd picked up on the mutual interest between us.

Roseanne had come a long way since I'd found her in that cage in the redcaps' lair, that was for sure.

———

Today's meeting was held at the headquarters of Edinburgh's mages, and the number of people seated at the long table in the meeting room filled me with apprehension. I sat down beside Ilsa, not knowing if she'd shared the details of our meeting with Janet Lynn with anyone yet. She'd have told River, of course, and Morgan would have told Lloyd and half the necromancers, but that didn't mean Lord Addison and his colleagues deserved to know.

It seemed our visit to Janet Lynn wasn't the first item on the agenda, however. An argument broke out between Lord Addison and Lady Montgomery, who I gathered wasn't thrilled at the mages for leaving the necromancers and the witches to clean up the aftermath of the Scourge's attack. No surprise, given that mages who'd actually accompanied us to the failed summoning hadn't been much help when the Scourge had turned against us.

Sitting next to his mother, River didn't look at all like he'd been near death not so long ago. Lady Montgomery didn't make eye contact with me, but the memory of her fury as she'd driven me out of the infirmary wouldn't fade for a while. Once she'd exhausted her disappointment in the mages, Lord Colton moved to the next subject of the meeting. "It is my understanding that the former Gatekeepers recently paid a visit to an informant south of the city. Am I to understand you have information to share?"

Farther down the table, Ivy's expression turned intrigued at the word "informant," though now that I thought about it, it made sense for the others not to have mentioned Janet by name.

Most of what she'd told us had been relevant to our family alone, and none of the mages' business.

"Our informant told us that the Scourge is too strong for any of us to banish him," said Ilsa. "The only individuals who might stand a chance are those who lived in the time when he was originally banished from this realm. Therein lies our dilemma."

"Meaning the Sidhe who were alive in the time of the gods," Ivy supplied. "Do any of them still exist?"

"The Wild Hunt might have lived that long," Hazel said. "Other than that, I have no idea."

"I can corner them again," Ivy said. "I bet *they* knew this would happen."

I had to agree, but that didn't mean they'd be willing to share anything more, especially if they'd allied with the same god they'd summoned to kill.

"The Wild Hunt?" asked Lord Addison. "The ones who summoned the god might know how to get rid of him?"

"I doubt they'll give the information voluntarily." Ivy rested a hand on her sword's hilt at her waist. "But if they knew how to summon him, it's a safe bet they know how to do the reverse. I can persuade them to give us the information like I did with the god's name."

"The god's name didn't work," said Lord Addison.

"Because we didn't know who we were dealing with," I said. "The Wild Hunt used to ferry the dead to the same realm in which the Scourge was once confined. The Scourge once fed on the souls of Sidhe and mortals alike, and even the Sidhe weren't able to permanently be rid of him."

I might want to keep our meeting with Janet private, but I didn't care if the Sidhe's secrets went public. If everyone called them out on their lies, they wouldn't be able to silence all of us.

"How delightful," said Drake, who sat beside Lord Colton. "Is that why the Sidhe were so intent on cheating death?"

"I bet it is." Ivy's eyes gleamed with understanding. "They purposely made the cauldron to avoid their own souls being devoured. The bloody hypocrites."

"They're also the ones who banished the Scourge in the first place," Hazel said. "Which means they aren't likely to want to do the same again."

"So we cannot count on their cooperation," said Lord Colton. "The Wild Hunt, on the other hand… are you sure you can convince them to give you the right information?"

"At this point, I don't have any better ideas," said Ivy. "They're roaming around the Vale blathering about riding on the longest night. I still haven't figured out what they meant."

"The Winter Solstice," I said. "That's the longest night of the year—and I think the Scourge is planning something for that night too."

"I was not aware of this." Lord Colton turned towards me. "When did the Scourge mention the longest night?"

"He followed us to our informant and attacked us," Hazel said. "Holly chased him off."

So much for keeping her mouth shut. "I didn't chase him off. He thought he'd killed me, so he fled the same way he did the last time."

"Did he now?" Lord Addison gave me a piercing stare. "You didn't mention setting up a meeting with the Scourge. Did you offer him a deal?"

"We didn't meet with him; he ambushed us," said Hazel. "Holly distracted his attention from the rest of us and got herself thrown in a pond in the process."

Thanks for that, Hazel. At least she hadn't mentioned the qualities of the pond's waters, because the last thing we needed was everyone to find out there was another source of the Ancients' blood in this realm.

"I didn't make any kind of deal with him." I addressed the whole table. "The Scourge fled, presumably for the same reason he disappeared after the failed summoning. He doesn't see us mere mortals as significant enough to bother with unless we directly provoke him. We're little more than ants to him."

"How pleasant," Ivy said. "But you said he's planning something on the solstice?"

"He didn't give any details," I said. "That said, the Wild Hunt implied they were going to ride again on the longest night, so it's entirely possible they know what his plan might be."

"Then we must ask them," said Lord Colton. "There is no other option."

"The Council of Twelve's original purpose was to protect us from the Ancients," said a blond mage sitting next to Lord Addison. "Didn't they bind Fionn, originally, and some of the other Ancients too? I know that many would prefer for that information to remain hidden, but I saw the records myself."

An uncomfortable silence swept the room, though I had no idea what he was talking about.

"Binding Fionn," said Ivy, "is what caused the deaths of the former Council of Twelve and led to those same records disappearing for over two decades."

"Precisely," said Lord Colton. "Besides, Fionn was ultimately able to subvert the binding and escape. Binding spells of that nature—aside from being illegal—are not a permanent way to defeat a god, even a self-styled one like Fionn."

"Absolutely not," said Lady Montgomery. "The binding spell is a sacrificial ritual which involves slaughtering innocent lives. I will never allow such a spell to be used in any circumstances in this city."

Whoa. I'd never even heard of a spell powerful enough to bind a god, but it made sense that it would come with a heavy cost. The discussion returned to the Wild Hunt, with Ivy agreeing to lead the mission to question the surviving warriors in the Vale, before the meeting came to a swift end.

I intended to wait for Ivy outside, but Lady Montgomery beckoned me aside as I left the meeting room. "Holly Lynn. May I talk to you?"

My heart leapt in my chest. She hadn't decided to haul me back to the guild for a trial, had she? "Yes, but I'll be going to the Vale with Ivy in a bit."

"I know," she said. "I should have thanked you for saving my son's life."

Relief swept over me, tempered by wariness. "Is there something else you wanted to talk about?"

"Ilsa told me of your meeting with Janet Lynn."

"She did?" I knew that Ilsa trusted Lady Montgomery far more than she did the mages, but there was still a chance it might have ended badly. "Yeah, I hoped Janet might be able to tell us more about how to get rid of the Scourge, but it didn't work out that way."

"She gave you the truth of the Sidhe's lies, did she not?" she asked.

"Yes, but even if some of *them* know how to banish the Scourge, I doubt they're willing to share with us."

"You are likely correct," she said. "I have not entered the Sidhe's realm since the birth of my son, but I highly doubt they have changed much in the interim."

It surprised me that she'd been to Faerie at all, though intellectually I'd known she must have spent some time there with the man who'd fathered her child. How Lord Torin had ended up having an affair with the straight-laced leader of the necromancer guild was a complete mystery to me, and given that Lord Torin himself had thrown me out of his home not long ago, I didn't blame her for not wanting to stay in Faerie.

"I'm not exactly welcome in the Courts at the moment," I said. "I hope Ivy and I will have more luck getting through to the Wild Hunt."

"As do I," she said. "However, I must focus upon the mortal realm and my guild. The god is a menace to all of us, whether or not the Sidhe acknowledge their role in his presence here, and it displeases me to rely upon the same individuals who put my guild under siege."

"If we had another option on the table, I'd take it." The Sidhe wouldn't be fans of us consulting the Wild Hunt either, but Lady Montgomery had a point in that the mortal realm's safety ought to be our priority. The Sidhe, as they'd demonstrated time and time again, looked out for their own and nobody else. None of *them* had shown up to the meeting, despite their involvement in our disastrous attempt to restrain the Scourge. If they threw a temper tantrum when they found out we'd been hunting their outcasts, it was not my problem.

"Lady Montgomery." Another necromancer accosted her, so I took that as my cue to leave the mages' headquarters.

I crossed the lobby floor to the exit and caught up to Ivy near the gates. She gave me a sideways look. "Is it true?"

"Is what true?"

"That Janet Lynn is an immortal human."

"Thomas was the same," I said. "Etaina didn't mess around with her eternal bargains."

"Your family has no end of surprises," Ivy remarked. "What kind of magic user is Janet Lynn?"

"She has some level of psychic abilities," I said. "Why?"

"A necromancer, then," she said. "I wondered if she might be fae, given her knowledge of the Sidhe."

"She learned everything she told us from Etaina," I said. "Thomas helped her escape a few centuries ago, and she's been on the run ever since. I bet you're descended from her side of the family."

"Maybe," she said. "I don't know if I have any relatives left, but they'd be pretty distant. Most of my family was killed in the invasion."

"I don't have any family either," I said. "I mean, except my cousins. No close family."

"You aren't close?" she asked. "I'm surprised."

My mouth parted. Now I thought about it, while I'd never seen eye to eye with the other Lynns, I had trouble imagining going back to the distance we'd maintained in the past. The notion weirded me out, so I sought a change of subject. "Is it true that the original council bound Fionn using a spell?"

Ivy inclined her head. "Right after the invasion, they imprisoned him in a liminal space using a little-known binding ritual. It was never going to last forever, and the spell broke when one of Fionn's admirers stumbled across his body."

"What kind of ritual is it?" I asked. "I have trouble imagining *any* supernatural council willingly permitting human lives to be ritualistically sacrificed."

"Desperate times called for a little innovation," she said. "I'm not sure the council knew what they were getting into, but the ritual requires the use of Winter and Summer magic as well as a huge surge of energy. The Ley Line was all kinds of fucked up already."

"No kidding," I said. "What we need is a permanent way to banish him back to the realm he came from, not imprison him in this one. The Wild Hunt must know how to do it, since they used to travel into that realm all the time."

"And feed souls to the god," she said. "I've never really regretted destroying the cauldron, but I kind of understand why the Sidhe wanted to be spared that fate. Even if they did bring it on themselves."

My gaze snapped to her face. "You destroyed the cauldron? I thought Fionn did."

"I broke it using an Invocation while trying to kill the Huntsman," she said. "I let the Sidhe believe he did it himself, since it was his own damn fault for capturing me to begin with. He had this plan to make an army…"

"Roseanne told me."

"I suppose she did," said Ivy. "I'm glad she's taken a liking to you. I was worried about her, to be honest. After I killed Fionn, I told her that she'd have the chance to start over, but I wish I hadn't left her to fend for herself."

"She wants to join the necromancers, I think." I slowed my pace as we reached the end of the road. "We're going to talk to the Wild Hunt, then?"

"Yeah, but I need to discuss the specifics with Vance and the others first, *without* Lord Addison hanging around. I don't trust that guy."

"Nor me." My phone started buzzing in my pocket. Puck was calling me. "Hang on, I need to take this call."

"Hey," Puck said when I answered. "I have a slight problem over here. Hawk and Leyton are missing."

15

"Missing?" I echoed. "What do you mean, missing? Didn't Hawk stay over at Leyton's house?"

"Hawk never came back last night, and he wasn't answering his messages, so I went to Leyton's house to check he was okay," he said. "They aren't at home. Either of them."

"So they went for a walk?" I suggested. "I know this is a bad time for wandering off without telling anyone, but the world might end any day now. Let them have their moment."

"Come and meet me on half-blood territory, and you'll see what I mean."

He ended the call. Unease trickled down my spine, and I turned to Ivy. "I'd better go."

I broke into a fast stride and quickened my pace until I reached half-blood territory. Puck waited outside Leyton's house, his gaze shadowed with worry.

"The door was unlocked," he said. "Pretty sure they

wouldn't have both forgotten to lock up before they went out."

"Ah, shit." I followed him down the hallway and into the living room where we'd once spent a great deal of time trying to evict a ghost from the cloakroom. Nothing appeared to have been moved, but the unlocked door was suspicious enough on its own.

"I searched half-blood territory for both of them and dropped by Brook's house," said Puck. "He said he hadn't seen either of them since yesterday evening, when Hawk first came to visit Leyton."

"What about his neighbours?"

"They haven't seen him either," he said. "I might be overreacting, but given what happened the last time Hawk disappeared when the Wild Hunt were up to no good…"

"No, I understand," I said. "Is Roseanne back at the office?"

"She went back to your house," he said. "I can ask her to help us search, but frankly, I don't know where to start if they aren't on half-blood territory."

"I guess she can fly around and look, but it'll be easier if I went to the guild to ask Jas for a tracking spell. I'm sure she'll have one going spare."

I'd done the same when Roseanne had been taken, and the timing was concerning enough that I wanted to confirm that Hawk and Leyton were safe.

"If it's not too much trouble," he said. "I know Hawk can be a pain in the arse, but he's my best friend."

"I just spent a few days in the company of my cousins," I reminded him. "It's no bother."

Puck stepped forward and kissed me on the mouth.

"I'll stay here and keep an eye out, and I'll text you if I find him."

"Sure." Once again, I found myself trekking towards Edinburgh's Old Town, this time avoiding the mages' headquarters and making for the necromancer guild instead. Updating Puck on the details of the council meeting would have to wait, though I didn't yet know when Ivy would be ready to go into Faerie. I could spare a few minutes to help Puck in the meantime.

As I turned into the guild's cobbled street, Lloyd walked past, holding Pepper's lead. "Hey, Holly. Survived Faerie, did you?"

"Just about," I said. "Ah—is Jas around?"

"She's on a mission," said Lloyd. "You're not going to drag *her* off to meet your distant relatives next, are you?"

"No, I need a tracking spell," I said. "A couple of half-faerie friends of mine vanished from their house overnight. Might be a false alarm, but given the timing…"

"If you want to borrow the puppy again, then you'll have to go through Morgan," he said. "The poor thing's been hysterical ever since you brought him home."

I grimaced. "Sorry."

"Apologise to him, not me."

Pepper seemed more interested in the contents of a discarded takeout container than in me, but I obliged and said, "Sorry we keep dragging you to Faerie, Pepper."

Lloyd snorted. "If you want to find Jas, she and Keir went over to the Royal Mile, looking for a runaway ghost. You should be able to catch them."

"Thanks." I broke into a fast stride, crossing my fingers that Hawk and Leyton *hadn't* been taken to Faerie, if just to spare the poor puppy another trip through the Ley Line to bring them home. Given the note on which I'd left Lord Lyle, I wouldn't be surprised if he waited to arrest me on the spot if I showed up in Faerie again—but where else might Hawk and Leyton have disappeared to?

I crossed Waverley Bridge past the abandoned train station and spotted Keir and Jas pursuing a dark shadowy form across the road. *That's no ghost. It's a wraith.*

Catching up to the wraith, Jas set off an explosive spell that knocked it into Keir's path. The vampire seized the creature from behind, but it slid out of his grip before he could drain it. Instead, he conjured up a handful of necromantic energy and hurled it at the wraith, which exploded into nothingness.

I strode towards them. "Made a new friend, did you?"

Jas raised a hand in greeting. "We unearthed this guy sniffing around Keir's friend's car shop. They seem to be getting bolder."

"Are there more wraiths than before?" I asked, completely out of the loop on the current ghost situation in the city. "Lloyd said you were after a regular ghost."

"It's nothing compared to the madness a few weeks ago," said Jas. "The annoying part is these amateur witches keep using glyphs to hide the ghosts from sight or amplify their magic, which makes them harder to get rid of."

"Like the one in those catacombs?" I caught Keir's eye, and he gave me a frown.

"Exactly like that," Jas said. "The glyphs themselves are pretty basic. It's the ghosts who turn out to be wraiths who are more of a nuisance."

"Yes, they are," said Keir. "Especially when our best wraith-hunter keeps disappearing for days at a time."

Oops. "Were you trying to use your vampire ability to drain that wraith?"

"Unsuccessfully," he said. "What are you doing here?"

"I need to borrow a tracking spell," I said. "Puck's friend Hawk and the guy he's seeing disappeared without a trace, and… and the last time Hawk disappeared, it was the Wild Hunt who took him. As a sacrifice."

"You mean you need to *buy* a tracking spell?" Keir said. "Everyone keeps hitting Jas up for free spells."

Jas poked him in the arm. "When I hear the word 'sacrifice,' I'm inclined to want to make an exception. What do the Wild Hunt need more half-faeries for, though? They already freed the god."

"That's what I want to know," I said. "It might not be them, but it's better to be safe than sorry."

Jas dug in her pocket and pulled out a handful of bracelets. "There'll be a tracking spell in here somewhere."

While she sifted through the bracelets and examined each one, Keir said, "Are they attempting another ritual, do you think?"

"Haven't a clue. You'd think one death god would be enough." Then again, who knew what they might be planning on the solstice? "Also, can one of you convince Morgan to loan us the puppy if they turn out to be in Faerie?"

"Don't you have another way into Faerie?" Keir asked.

Not if I want to bring several people along with me. "There's River, but I can't imagine his mother is letting him out of her sight these days."

"No, she isn't," said Jas. "I heard what you did, Holly. You saved his life."

I made a noncommittal noise, sensing Keir's suspicious stare. He'd commented that my soul looked different after I'd taken on the Morrigan's powers—and as a vampire, he would know—but I'd rather not tell everyone I'd also used the same magic to return River from the brink of death.

"You did." Jas tugged out another handful of bracelets from a different pocket. "At the meeting, you said the Scourge is intentionally avoiding a direct attack on us unless we provoke him. You think that's true?"

"That or saving his worst for last." Since the vampire kept watching me, I turned my attention towards him. "I don't have experience of any of the other Ancients, but I get the impression he's not overly concerned with humans, whatever his goal. Do they all see us that way?"

Jas's grip on the bracelets slipped, but she caught them before they hit the ground. "Depends. Sounds like the Scourge has a good reason to be pissed off at the Sidhe, though."

Keir gave a shrug. "Then let them fight it out."

"It's not that simple," I said. "Our realms are interconnected, and on the solstice, they'll be closer than ever. The Sidhe have been fighting the gods for millennia, and somehow we humans always end up in the crosshairs."

"Funny that," said Jas. "Aren't the Sidhe descended from the Ancients anyway?"

"Yes, they are," I said. "There aren't many left who are closely related to them, except the Morrigan."

"She's the one who loaned you her magic, right?"

"Right." I expected a comment from the vampire, but Keir's expression cleared as if I'd answered an unspoken question.

"The vampires are all descended from one of the

Ancients, too," he said. "So are the shifters, while the witch covens and necromancers have ties with the gods going back thousands of years."

"Wait, they do?" I looked to Jas for confirmation. "Is that why your witch spells look so similar to the Ancients' glyphs?"

"One of the reasons." Jas extracted a bracelet, examined it, and held it out to me. "Like you said, our realms are interconnected. The Sidhe might try to deny it, but it's true."

"Exactly." I pocketed the spell. "Thanks for this."

"Anytime."

I veered back across Waverley Bridge, over the abandoned train tracks where wild fae lurked in tangles of briars, until I reached the other side and broke into a fast stride past the worn stone buildings. There was still the slightest chance that Hawk and Leyton's disappearance might be nothing to worry about, but I didn't blame Puck for being concerned about a potential repeat of the Wild Hunt's last sacrificial ritual. Even though it made little sense. They already had what they wanted, didn't they?

Upon returning to half-blood territory, I found Puck and Roseanne waiting for me near Leyton's house.

"I can't believe you didn't tell me!" Roseanne gave me a scowl. "That Hawk and Leyton are missing, I mean."

"I didn't realise for a while," Puck said. "I thought they went out. It wasn't until this morning that I came here and found Leyton's front door unlocked."

I dug out the tracking spell. "This will help us find them."

"Good." Roseanne bounded over to the door to Leyton's house, while Puck and I followed her. Upon entering the living room, I offered Puck the bracelet-shaped spell.

"Thanks." He took the spell from me. "This won't show us if they're in Faerie, though, right?"

"No, but if you see him being carried through the Ley Line..." I trailed off, unable to forget seeing Roseanne suffer that very same fate.

His mouth pressed into a line. "Yeah. I figured. Okay, let's do this."

Puck laid the bracelet down on the floor. As the spell ignited under his hands, the bracelet expanded and formed a large circle. Puck placed his hands in the centre and fixed his gaze on the carpet, and while I couldn't see what the spell showed him, he grew pale. After a few seconds, the light faded, and the circle collapsed into dust.

Puck sprang to his feet. "Damn."

My heart sank. "Did someone take them through the Ley Line?"

"Possibly," he said. "It was confusing. I think they were blindfolded, because I couldn't properly see who grabbed me. I didn't see much except darkness and then one bright flash—that must have been the Ley Line. Nothing else is that bright."

"They covered their tracks again," I said. "Remember when the Wild Hunt used those glyphs to block the sight of their murder victims?"

"If the Wild Hunt have Hawk and Leyton, then we haven't any time to waste," he said. "What if they're planning on summoning *another* god?"

"I can't figure out why they would, but it's anyone's guess what they're planning for the solstice." I followed him out of Leyton's house, and the three of us made our way across half-blood territory. "Ivy is going to track down the Wild Hunt, and I was planning to go with her anyway."

"The mages agreed to let you ask the Wild Hunt how to banish the Scourge?" he asked.

"They didn't have any better suggestions." I didn't have Ivy's number, so I fired off a message to Ilsa asking if Ivy was ready to leave yet.

Ilsa's reply came when we reached the gate at the far end of half-blood territory. *Ivy is on her way to the Ley Line. Be careful, won't you?*

Will do. After I hit Send, I turned to Roseanne. "I can't let you come with me this time. You need to stay well out of the Wild Hunt's way if they're looking for sacrifices again."

"To hell with that," she said. "I'm not scared of them."

"You should be." I didn't want to push her away, but this was not the time for any foolish bravado. "We already have two people to rescue, and if we get tied up in Faerie, then the solstice will be here before we know it."

"Isn't that a good reason to bring me with you?"

I spotted Ivy approaching out of the corner of my eye. "You can try convincing her instead of me and see how that works out."

Roseanne pulled a face. "That's mean."

"You know, she wanted to talk to me about you," I said. "Ivy, I mean. She was worried how things would turn out the last time she left you."

"She what?" said Roseanne. "I thought she hated me."

"That's not the impression I got," I said. "She's not the biggest fan of faeries in general, I don't think, but she regretted leaving you to fend for yourself."

"I did all right, you know." She glanced sideways at me. "But... but I'm glad I have you."

"So am I." Ah, screw it. Maybe we needed one more person to back us up when we went to find the Wild Hunt after all. Turning my back on Roseanne seemed to invite more trouble than the alternative. The way Puck was grinning at both of us cemented my choice.

Ivy crossed the road to meet us. "Ready? What was that phone call about earlier?"

"Two half-faerie friends of ours went missing," I explained. "One of them was taken by the Wild Hunt during their first ritual attempt, so we think they might be up to their old tricks."

"Fuckers," said Ivy. "Is Roseanne coming as well?"

"Up to you."

"Hey, I'm not about to stand in her way." Ivy trod towards the spot where the Ley Line's shimmering outline cut through the road. "I know the Wild Hunt is hiding in the Vale, but the Sidhe wanted an update from me too. Where do you want to go first?"

"They definitely won't want to see *me*," I said. "We'll go straight to the Vale."

"All right." Ivy stepped onto the Ley Line and vanished from sight.

"Can you bring us through too?" asked Roseanne.

"Good question," I said. "You might need to shift and hang onto me."

Puck shot me a faint smile. "I should have figured you were planning revenge for the times I carried you around as a crow."

"At least you can shift back of your own accord." I let

the Morrigan's shadows overtake my human form, and Puck and Roseanne both shifted into crows.

A bird perched on each of my shoulders as I launched myself after Ivy. A brief spasm of fear shook me when the Ley Line turned transparent and the tangled paths of the realms converged, but the birds clinging to each shoulder kept me grounded. I focused on the silvery path of the Vale and landed beside Ivy.

"Never thought I'd be glad to see the old bird walking free again," she remarked, while I gladly shifted back into my human form again.

"Don't speak too soon." The Morrigan herself might be hiding in the faeries' afterlife, but if the Scourge's plan involved that realm in any way, I couldn't guarantee she wouldn't return at the worst possible moment. And there was no guarantee that she'd choose to fight on our side. "Okay, Vale. Take us to the Wild Hunt."

Puck and Roseanne flew as crows while Ivy and I walked down the path, silently repeating our request to the Vale to take us directly to our targets. Within less than a minute, Ivy came to a sudden halt. Two horses roamed near the path, but not a single horseman was in sight.

"Weird." She strode over to the horses, which both whinnied and backed away from her.

"Hang on." Puck turned into his human form and hastened to calm them down. "Can you find your masters?"

"Aren't they here?" Ivy said.

The horses continued to back away, and Puck's steady gaze clouded. "I think they're back in Faerie."

"Shit." Ivy's gaze travelled over the horses. "I have to ride that thing again?"

"It's quicker than walking, isn't it?" Not that I was particularly keen to go anywhere near the Courts. "Do you think they're in the borderlands?"

"They're not welcome there, but I don't see them showing their faces in the Courts." Ivy resignedly climbed onto a horse, while Puck mounted the other. Roseanne perched on my shoulder as I shifted into the Morrigan again, concentrating on the boundaries between realms.

Take us to Faerie. Take us to the Wild Hunt.

The Vale's path turned transparent, and our group stepped out onto the path between the Courts. A tall, forbidding figure watched us, dressed in the finery of the Winter Court. Lady Rive, Lord Lyle's less pleasant companion. *Oh, fuck.*

"Again, you trespass in these lands, mortal," she said.

"I'm not on your territory." Rustling sounded when Puck and Ivy dismounted their horses, which promptly galloped away into the borderlands. "The Wild Hunt is somewhere in Faerie, and they took two of our friends with them."

"Lies," said Lady Rive. "We caught the Wild Hunt's traitors ourselves and brought them before the Unseelie Queen to be trialled for the crimes they committed."

My heart missed a beat. "You caught them?"

"Seriously?" Ivy said. "They didn't have any half-faeries with them?"

If the Unseelie Queen had already arrested the Wild Hunt's two surviving warriors, then where had Hawk and Leyton disappeared to? Had someone else taken them?

"No," she said. "We captured them from the Vale despite Lord Lyle's absence—which is entirely your fault, mortal."

"Absence?" I echoed.

Her eyes were as cold as shards of ice. "Lord Lyle is currently incarcerated in the dungeons for repeating your poisonous lies to his Queen."

"She locked Lord Lyle in jail?" He'd passed on my warning after all, and the Unseelie Queen had responded by locking him away. Damn her.

"Yes," she said. "She did, and so you must suffer the same fate."

Puck tensed, while Ivy drew her sword. Roseanne, still in the form of a bird, took flight, scattering feathers in her wake. Panic brewing inside me, I backed up to Puck's side. "Take her and run."

Lady Rive would think I meant Ivy, but Ivy wasn't the most vulnerable of our group. I would never let the Unseelie Queen get her hands on Roseanne, and besides, Hawk and Leyton weren't with the Wild Hunt at all. If Puck wanted to find them, he'd have to leave me behind while I dealt with Her Majesty. While she could certainly do some serious damage to me, the Morrigan's powers ought to spare me the worst of it. Roseanne wouldn't have that advantage, and Hawk and Leyton might not have enough time to waste.

Puck shook his head fiercely. "I won't abandon you."

"I'll be okay." I gave a squeeze of his hand, and he blinked in surprise at the gesture. "Find Hawk and Leyton. I'll be back as soon as I can."

He inclined his head. "Okay. I'll find them."

Puck disappeared in a flutter of feathers, while Lady Rive beckoned me after her. "I wouldn't advise you to run, mortal… or fly either."

"I never wanted to make an enemy of your Court," I

said. "I told Lord Lyle the truth about the Sidhe's involvement in the gods' exile and the reason for the Scourge's anger. I'd be doing none of us any favours if I let everyone bury that information again."

"That is not for you to decide, mortal."

That's the problem. Nobody is allowed to question anything around here.

"You should ask the Unseelie Queen what she hasn't told you," I said. "For one thing, did you know the Morrigan is a relation of the very same god who is on the loose in the mortal realm? Or that the souls of your own people were once fed to the Scourge after his exile?"

"What are you talking about?" she said. "If you think you can infect my mind with the same lies you used on Lord Lyle, then you are mistaken."

"They aren't lies." I followed her past the snow-laden trees and gleaming white lawns until the tunnel entrance to the Winter Court appeared before us. "I'll tell Her Majesty, then."

The two ogres outside parted to let us in. The Queen must have expected me to show up, but what had tipped her off? Had she somehow been involved in Hawk and Leyton's disappearance? There seemed little point in the Unseelie Queen capturing two half-bloods, but I wouldn't rule anything out.

I entered the cave, where the Unseelie Queen sat on her throne, hard lines of anger etched into her stunning face. "You again."

"I heard you caught the Wild Hunt and that you wanted to speak to me." My voice echoed, and it struck me that there was nobody in here but the two of us and Lady Rive. The usual band of mortals did not stand in the corner, no hobgoblins served refreshments, and aside from her throne, the only thing that stood out to me was —*oh, crap.*

A familiar set of chains lay at her feet, coiled in front of the throne like a metallic serpent. I took a step back, dread trickling down my spine.

"You cost me one of my best soldiers and advisors, mortal," she said. "You warped his mind with your lies."

My heartbeat thundered so loudly I half expected to hear its echo in the empty cave. "Every word I said to him was the truth as I knew it."

"Nothing but lies," she said. "The Wild Hunt is the same. Liars, every one of them."

"The Wild Hunt is under someone's influence, and I don't think it's yours." Panic tangled the words in my mind, and I'd never felt so vulnerable before her. Iron couldn't kill me, but it'd brought down the Morrigan and rendered her unable to use her own magical abilities. "The Hunt used to escort the dead into the afterlife, but their purpose was corrupted long before Fionn turned out to be an impostor. The Scourge was devouring the souls of the dead, and that was why you made the cauldron—"

"Enough!" she snapped. "I will not listen to another word of these lies. Chain her."

My hands fisted. "Will you keep me in iron while your own realm burns to the ground and while the Scourge wreaks his revenge on Faerie?"

"Threats do not frighten me, mortal."

"I'm not threatening you. I'm warning you." A pleading note entered my voice. "I have the Morrigan's magic. I can help fight the Scourge if he comes here, but not if I'm chained in iron. And he *will* come, eventually. You must know that. He plans to act on the winter solstice."

"We brought the gods low once before, mortal," she said. "I have no fear of them. Take her away."

Her ogres lumbered forward, closing in on either side of me. The Morrigan's magic reacted at once, and my claws shot out, ripping at their throats in unison. Wings sprouted from my back, and I launched myself at the exit —but not before the chains struck me like a whip, twisting like serpents across my back until they bound my wrists and ankles.

I hit the ground, my knees buckling, my body turning human again as the Morrigan's magic was crushed beneath the iron's weight.

The Unseelie Queen looked down at me with pitiless eyes. "Perhaps this will teach you a lesson, human."

16

The chains weighed me down like the tug of a great current, preventing me from so much as lifting my head as the ogres dragged me out of the cave and down a tunnel which plunged below the earth until all the natural light disappeared. The lamps lining the corridor were my only guiding point as they dragged me along until we came to a blank stretch of earthen wall.

Part of the wall pulled back like a curtain, for long enough for the ogres to throw me into the cell, chains and all. I hit the ground with a crash which jarred all the bones in my body, and when I recovered enough to lift my head, an even more unwelcome sight greeted me. Two large men dressed in armour had jumped to their feet when I'd landed in their cell, and one wore a ragged patch over his missing eye.

She'd thrown me into a cell with the horsemen.

I struggled onto my knees, but the chains prevented me from doing much more than falling back into an awkward sprawl. The one-eyed horseman glared down at me, and while I assumed the Unseelie Queen had taken his weapons away, his hands were thick enough to close around my throat.

I shuffled back against the wall, dragging the chains with me, and watched both him and his companion. "Look, I don't want to be in here any more than you do."

"You killed one of our own, mortal," growled the one-eyed horseman. "I told you she wasn't to be trusted."

"That wasn't my idea," I said. "Ivy was the one who stabbed your friend."

"The faerie killer." His remaining eye narrowed. "The same who slaughtered the Huntsman, Fionn."

"You mean the impostor." What the hell. If I was going to die in here, I might as well satisfy my curiosity. "You said Fionn opened your eyes to the truth. Did *he* know that the cauldron was a creation of the Sidhe's to prevent their souls from being devoured by the Scourge?"

The other horseman joined the first, their looming figures seeming to fill the entire cell. "You speak of secrets which are not yours to know, mortal."

"Ah, but it's the truth, isn't it?" I gave him a challenging stare. "The Sidhe made you swear to keep their secrets, but a long time ago, you used to escort the dead to the afterlife, *not* the cauldron. To the realm where the gods were banished."

"Our purpose was corrupted," said the horseman.

"You said that before," I said. "Was that what you meant? You were bound to ferry the dead to the afterlife, but the Sidhe forced you to stop? Strange, that, because before you summoned the Scourge, you claimed that you wanted to slaughter him to remake the cauldron yourselves."

"No," said the one-eyed horseman. "That is not our goal."

"It used to be," I said. "You can't lie, can you? And if you can, you went to a lot of trouble to summon the Scourge back to this realm only to abandon that goal altogether."

Why would they get this far, sacrifice so many lives, and then just… give up?

"Our purpose was corrupted," said the other horseman. "We were misled."

"By whom?" I studied their faces. "I take it you don't mean Fionn?"

"He opened our eyes to—"

"To the truth, I know." What did that mean? All he'd done was lie and cheat and slaughter and even kick off an unnecessary war with the mortal realm. Unless the Hunt hated the Sidhe more than they did him, of course. "You know Fionn wasn't even his real name, don't you? He stole it from the original Huntsman along with his title. He even stole from the Unseelie Queen herself."

"Fionn was first to challenge *her*," spat the one-eyed horseman. "And for that we will always revere him."

"Was *she* the one who bound you?" It was the only explanation I could think of, though I'd always thought of the Wild Hunt as a separate entity from the rest of the Courts. If the Unseelie Queen had bound them, then it all but confirmed she'd played a major role in the gods' banishment and the cover-up as well as the creation of the cauldron. In fact, she might well be one of the only surviving Sidhe from that era now that Etaina and the former Seelie Queen were dead. The old Erlking too. Too bad she'd locked me up rather than admit the truth to anyone else.

"No longer," said the one-eyed horseman. "Soon, we ride."

"On the longest night, like you said," I said. "You'll have a hard job riding anywhere from inside a cell."

"The Hunt will ride, with or without us," said his companion.

That didn't sound ominous at all. "The Scourge said the same."

He's giving them orders. How, I hadn't a clue. If he had some kind of psychic influence upon them, then it shouldn't be able to reach us down in the dungeons, but I knew not to underestimate a creature as ancient and incomprehensible as the Scourge. Besides, the Scourge had as many grievances with the Unseelie Queen and the Courts as the Wild Hunt did, and if he came here, then blood and death would follow. As long as I remained imprisoned in chains, I wouldn't be able to do a damned thing to stop him.

"We will ride," repeated the one-eyed horseman. "Perhaps you will ride, too, mortal."

"Does that mean you're sparing my life?"

The second horseman beckoned to his companion, and they began to converse in low voices, speaking in some variation of the faerie tongue I didn't understand. Whoever wrought their influence upon the pair of them, these weren't the same horsemen who'd fought alongside the Aes Sidhe and sacrificed lives to summon the gods. They were strangers who answered to an unseen higher power, and I'd almost rather be stuck in a cell with the Unseelie Queen than with them.

I cleared my throat. "How will you know it's the solstice? It's not like there's a clock or anything in here."

The second horseman eyed me. "When it is time, we will know."

Because *that* made sense. "Why have a Wild Hunt at all if you no longer carry the dead to the afterlife? I mean, it's not like the Scourge wants to go back, does he?"

The one-eyed horsemen gave me a withering look. "You understand nothing, mortal."

"I get that a lot," I said. "I thought it was Etaina you used to ride for."

His face spasmed with anger. "Do not speak the name of the Lady of Light."

"Don't you remember that the Scourge devoured her soul himself?" I went on. "What makes you think your fates will be any different?"

"The Lady of Light was unjustly cast out by Summer and Winter," snarled his companion. "She was betrayed."

"She did a fair bit of betrayal herself," I said. "And so did you, if you kept working with the Aes Sidhe for the centuries after the Courts cast them out."

"We did not," said the one-eyed horseman. "Thanks to *her.* After their banishment, she saw to it that we were never able to enter the Court of the Aes Sidhe again."

Holy shit. No wonder the Wild Hunt had been absent during the battle, if the Unseelie Queen had forbidden them from going near the Aes Sidhe or their leader for centuries. I almost understood why they'd sided with Fionn, but that didn't mean I'd let them get away with murdering any more innocent people.

With the iron chains weighing down my limbs, though, I couldn't even reach my magic. I was unable to do more than squirm until my wrists ached and blood dampened the skin beneath the iron. At least my humanity prevented death by iron poisoning, but the Wild Hunt warriors didn't seem that bothered by its presence either.

I leaned against the wall, panting. "Why does iron have little effect on you compared to the Sidhe?"

I didn't expect a reply, but the one-eyed horseman growled, "We are hard to kill."

"But not eternal," I said, thinking of how Ivy had skewered one of them using her talisman. They weren't indestructible, and if it came down to it, I might be able to turn the iron chains into a weapon against them. "The Morrigan loaned me her powers so I could use them to destroy you, did you know?"

The longest night was drawing closer, and I'd rather provoke them into a fight which might draw the Unseelie Queen's attention than sit here and wait for the Scourge to attack the Court first.

"You have no magic now," he said. "You are less than nothing."

"Doesn't say much for the pair of you that she locked us up together, then."

I expected that to hit a nerve, but I didn't quite manage to raise my chained hands in time to block him. The one-eyed horseman backhanded me so hard I tasted blood, and I spat a mouthful of crimson at his feet.

"Do you expect the Scourge to come and rescue you?" I asked. "Isn't it more likely that he'll leave you to rot?"

The second warrior joined the first. "No. The ride will begin soon."

"With just the two of you?" I didn't know if there'd been any other survivors from the original Wild Hunt, but Lady Rive and Lord Lyle had admitted that they'd needed to re-form the Hunt from scratch. Their Queen had refused to listen to them, and if she was the one to whom the Hunt had originally sworn, it explained why they would have needed her permission. Yet the Unseelie Queen had never forgiven the Hunt's betrayal, and she'd never let them walk free again.

If I kill them, there's a good chance their ghosts will end up escaping the dungeon. She won't want that.

It wasn't much of a plan, but I was all out of any better ideas. Short of stalling until the Scourge showed up—but that might be too late for all of us.

"Enough of your mockery, mortal," said the one-eyed horseman. "Perhaps we will feed your soul to the Scourge first."

"No thanks," I said. "He used to devour the souls of the Sidhe before they started feeding on mortals, didn't he? Bet he's mad at the Sidhe for wriggling out of that one."

"Not for long," said the one-eyed horseman. "When he comes here, he will regain the strength long denied him."

Crap. Now that I thought about it, who knew how much stronger the Scourge might grow if he came to Faerie and devoured the souls of the Sidhe? He must be at his weakest right now, but the Sidhe had once feared him so badly that they'd concocted the lie of the cauldron's eternal existence in order to spare any other Sidhe that fate.

If the Scourge returned to Faerie, we'd all pay the price for the Sidhe's reckless arrogance.

As the thought crossed my mind, a blood-chilling howl sounded from above. I knew the call of a hellhound, but I couldn't recall ever hearing one this close to the Unseelie Queen's domain. The two horsemen turned to the blank stretch of earthen wall which had once been the door, but it remained opaque.

"Was that you?" I asked. "Did you call them?"

"Not us," he said. "Perhaps it is time."

My blood went cold. Where the hell was the Unseelie Queen? How could she have let *hellhounds* into the Court?

A cold breeze hit all three of us, and the wall folded back abruptly, revealing none other than Her Majesty herself. Dark blood stained her formerly immaculate clothing, along with greenish stains which resembled hellhound poison. If she'd fought the hellhounds herself, how had they made it this far into her domain?

"Which of you summoned hellhounds into my palace?" she demanded.

"We did not call them here," said the one-eyed horseman.

"Don't look at me." I held up my chained hands. "If the Scourge is here, though, you're in danger. You have to—"

Streams of icy magic shot from her hands. I threw myself flat to avoid being hit in the face, but the ice spread across my bound hands and my back, while the horsemen both stiffened on the spot.

Another howl echoed, much closer. She spun away, a snarl on her lips. "Guards! Watch them."

As she swept off, I saw the outline of an ogre

approaching, and panic rose inside me like a geyser. I tried to lift my head, but my neck and back were frozen stiff. The ice spread over the backs of my arms and legs, but… hang on a moment. The iron had prevented the ice from touching my wrists and ankles, and iron neutralised faerie magic.

With a jerk of my wrists, I swung the chains outward. As they clattered against the floor, I flicked my wrists again, trying to divert the chains to hit the ice covering my back. On the third attempt, the iron struck my skull so hard I saw stars, but the ice on my neck cracked in the same instant and enabled me to lift my head. The ogre lumbered into view, the opening in the earthen wall tantalisingly close.

Another swing of the chains shattered the ice covering the back of my legs. Straightening upright, I shuffled forwards, my ankles and wrists still cuffed but most of the ice gone.

"Get back, mortal," the ogre growled.

"Nah." The chains clinked together as I raised my hands. "Move it."

The ogre charged. I swung the chains, catching him in the kneecaps. While my escape was painfully slow, ogres weren't known for their speed, and the two horseman-shaped ice sculptures prevented him from turning around fast enough to catch me. Another swing of my chains knocked the ogre on the skull, causing him to slump to the ground.

Thanking my sensible thinking that I'd memorised the route into the prison during my years in the Winter Court, I lurched out of the cell and began a painfully slow shuffle towards the way out. Twice, I had to hide behind corners to avoid guards, but they were more likely to be looking for runaway hellhounds than escaped prisoners.

I found a hellhound corpse lying in the tunnel leading to the main cave, and when footsteps came from ahead, I ducked behind the stinking carcass to hide myself from sight. Not hard, because the hellhound was the size of a tank. They had no shortage of death energy to feed on here in Winter, after all.

After the guard had passed, I launched into a galloping shuffle again, the uphill climb even more painful under the weight of my chains, but a combination of desperation and adrenaline spurred me on until I reached the tunnel opening to the throne room.

Inside the cave, pandemonium reigned. Hellhounds trampled over the floor, cracking stalagmites and crashing into stalactites. Blood and poison smeared their paths, and I was halfway across the room before one of the Sidhe spotted me.

"It's her!"

I swung the chains at him and sent him recoiling from the deadly iron before resuming my shuffle towards the exit. The ogre guards were too occupied with fighting the hellhounds to notice my escape, and whenever someone tried to grab me, a swift strike of iron chains knocked them back.

"Thanks for this," I puffed out, shuffling over the threshold. Mud and blood churned the path, while more hellhounds ran amok through the snowy fields surrounding the Court's centre.

As for me, I couldn't do anything but keep moving, ignoring the pain in my wrists and ankles until I reached the sloping path leading out of the Winter Court. Abandoning all dignity, I sank into a sitting position and slid downhill like a child riding a sledge.

I came to a halt in front of none other than Ivy Lane, who held the reins of a struggling Pepper in one hand.

"You look like shit," she said.

17

Of all the people I might have expected to come to my rescue, Ivy Lane was not one of them. "What are you doing here?"

"Rescuing you, apparently." She eyed the iron chains. "Good timing, by the looks of things."

I frowned at her. "You didn't send those hellhounds… did you?"

"Yes, I did. You're welcome."

Pepper whined and shuffled away from the chains. He didn't like iron any more than the other fae did, but I was surprised Ivy had managed to bring him with her at all after our traumatic experience in the forest.

I held up my wrists. "Can you please get these off me?"

"On it." Ivy drew her sword before bringing it down in a sweeping slash which broke through the iron as though it was paper. She then crouched and did the same to my ankles, and I gladly kicked away the chains, wincing as the bloody skin of my wrists became evident. "Those are the Morrigan's chains, aren't they?"

"I bet the Unseelie Queen was so proud of herself for thinking of that one." I grimaced, stretching out my sore muscles. "Since when could you order hellhounds to do as you ask?"

"For a while, but I never managed to figure out whether it's because I killed Fionn or because my talisman belongs to one of the Ancients," she replied. "It comes in handy, though. I'd wager you can probably do the same. Anyway, we have a situation back home. Let's move."

One step through the Ley Line brought us to Edinburgh again. I'd barely had time to catch my balance before Ivy began to walk away, still holding Pepper's lead.

"Hang on!" I hurried across the road, each step causing my sore ankles to protest. "Slow down. It's not the solstice yet, is it?"

"That's tonight," she said. "Don't look so alarmed. I doubt the Unseelie Queen will have trouble with a few hellhounds."

"I thought the Scourge sent them, but if we still have time, can I at least grab some weapons before we run into battle?" Where were we even going? Ivy had marched straight past half-blood territory without stopping, and it was only now that I remembered the utter shit show we'd left behind. "Hang on! Where's Puck? And Roseanne?"

"That," she said, "is our situation. He's gone, and so are a few other rather important individuals, including the head of the local Mage Lords."

"Gone? What do you mean, gone?" My legs burned from the exertion, but I didn't slow down. "The head of the mages—you mean Lord Addison? Did someone capture him? Because it wasn't the Wild Hunt."

"He vanished shortly after the last meeting," she said.

"Several of his advisors did, too, and when I asked around, I heard several stories of them being seen vanishing into the spirit line which leads north of the city. This happened while we were in Faerie, so I didn't find out until I got back."

Why had the head of Edinburgh's mages left at a time like this? Maybe he was doing a runner. He'd all but tried to foist responsibility upon anyone but himself, after all, so it made sense for him to take the coward's way out.

"Weird," I said. "Wait, what does this have to do with Puck? Did he go with them?"

"No," she said. "Ilsa said she saw two crows flying through the spirit line and assumed they followed him."

"Two crows?" No way. "Roseanne went with him too? Why didn't you stop her?"

"Did you expect her to listen to me?" She shook her head. "They were looking for your missing friends, right?"

"Right—" I broke off, coming to another horrified realisation. "The Wild Hunt never took Hawk and Leyton captive. They don't plan to do another ritual, but... someone took them. Is that summoning circle up north still there?"

"What's left of it." Ivy's mouth pressed into a grim line. "I don't know for sure that's where those mages were going, but it's an isolated enough location to make a second attempt to summon the god."

"And bind him?" I guessed. "Is that why Lord Addison brought it up at the meeting? But—that's sacrificial magic."

Ivy flashed me a sideways look. "It also requires one Summer faerie and one from Winter."

Hawk and Leyton. "Fuck." I broke into a fast stride, ignoring the pain in my ankles and the blood encrusting my wrists where the chains had held me. "Who else went after them? The necromancers?"

"No." She overtook me with ease, her talisman gleaming at her waist. "When I returned from Faerie, Vance and the others had only just figured out the mages had gone missing. Ilsa mentioned that she'd seen your friends following them, but she didn't know why."

Puck and Roseanne had gone to confront the mages before they summoned the Scourge again... and before they tried to bind him by sacrificing Hawk and Leyton's lives. "We used a tracking spell, and it seemed to show them being taken through the Ley Line, but they were blindfolded."

"The spirit line probably looks the same when viewed through a blindfold." Ivy veered around the corner, and I followed fast on her heels until we came to the street where the necromancer guild was located.

Pepper broke into a sprint when he saw Morgan outside the guild, hiding himself behind his ankles.

"Finally." Morgan took Pepper's lead from Ivy. "I should start charging you for borrowing him, you know."

"Holly!" Ilsa hurried over to us. "You're bleeding."

"The Unseelie Queen bound me in iron chains and threw me in a cell with the two horsemen," I said. "Ivy didn't give me any time to recover before dropping another bombshell on me."

"Here." Jas reached out and pressed a spell into my hands. "Healing spell. I can't believe you walked all the way here right after you got out of Faerie."

"I had to." Behind her, Ivy conversed with River and Hazel. "Since the mages went north to summon the Scourge again in order to use an illegal binding ritual."

"You're shitting me," said Hazel. "Is that why Puck went after them?"

"And he took Roseanne with him," I said. "Why didn't anyone else follow them?"

"Hey, don't look at me," she said. "I heard the mages sneaked through the spirit line, and I assumed they were doing a runner. Or maybe going to fight the Scourge alone again, which they're welcome to try if it takes his eyes off the rest of us."

"What binding ritual is this?" Morgan asked.

"A dangerous one." I turned on the healing charm, and the pain in my wrists and ankles vanished at once. "Which requires lives to be sacrificed."

River gaped at me. "Lord Addison thinks he can conduct a binding spell using sacrificial magic to confine the Scourge? Was that why he brought it up at the meeting?"

"Yes, and he went through the spirit line." I looked up at the guild's exterior, which concealed the invisible current of energy flowing through its path. "I assume they're going to the site of the failed summoning the other day."

"Using the spirit line is much faster than walking on foot." Ilsa's mouth pinched with worry. "We have to go after them."

"I know the way," said Jas. "Who's coming with me?"

"I'll go and find Vance," said Ivy. "I bet Drake and Isabel will want to come too."

"Isabel was the one who helped me learn blood magic,"

Jas explained to me. "She also gave me the information on those glyphs… and you know, she never trusted Lord Addison."

"Neither did I." Keir joined his girlfriend. "I'm not surprised he turned out to be another fuckhead Mage Lord who thought he could fight the gods and win."

"We don't have any time to waste," I said. "Puck and Roseanne have been gone a while already, right?"

"I'll come with you," Ilsa offered. "River…"

"I'll tell the boss," he said. "Then we'll catch you up. Just—please, be careful, Ilsa."

"I will." She embraced him, briefly. "You be careful, too, okay?"

"Follow me," Jas said over her shoulder, as she and Keir took the lead down the cobbled street.

My cousins and I followed her to the end of the road and turned left, but I didn't see the shimmering outline of the spirit line travelling north from the guild until we stood directly on top of it. Worry fluttered in my chest. While the healing spell had soothed my aching wrists, I didn't feel the usual presence of the Morrigan's magic under my skin. No doubt being chained up had stifled it, but what if it didn't come back before we reached the mages?

Then we'll have to make do. They already have Hawk and Leyton, and Puck and Roseanne need your help.

The spirit line blurred our surroundings, and the street was replaced by a long path with a giant oak tree sprawling in its centre. Jas stepped around the tree's roots and headed north, while I fell into step with Ilsa, who kept one hand on the Gatekeeper's book in her pocket.

"I talked to the Wild Hunt," I said. "The Unseelie

Queen decided to throw me into the same jail cell as the pair of them, so we got to have a nice chat."

"She did what?" She swivelled to face me. "Did you kill them?"

"She turned them into ice statues before I needed to," I said. "But that isn't the important part."

I gave her an abbreviated summary of the discussion we'd had in the jail, while the others listened in as we made our way north. It didn't seem to surprise anyone that the Unseelie Queen had been the one who'd bound the Wild Hunt and that they'd seen Fionn as their saviour even when he'd betrayed the very oaths they'd sworn to the Courts.

"She forbade them from ever returning to see Etaina," I added. "That said, they aren't acting on their hatred of the Unseelie Queen at the moment. The Scourge is in the driver's seat, and they'll do anything he tells them to."

"The Scourge plans for the Hunt to ride on the solstice," Ilsa said. "To what end?"

"To attack the Courts and devour as many souls as he can." I grimaced. "The Scourge gains strength from each one he devours, and right now he's at his weakest after centuries of being deprived of the Sidhe's immortal souls."

"I'd rather not see what he looks like at full power, then, thanks," said Morgan.

"I bet that's another reason the Sidhe stopped sending their souls to the afterlife," Hazel said. "They were unintentionally fuelling their enemies' forces."

"I think not wanting to be eaten is enough of a motivator," I said. "Fionn took advantage of their fear, but it was the Unseelie Queen who fuelled the Wild Hunt's betrayal by forcing them to break contact with Etaina and the Aes

Sidhe. The worst part is that I know she can probably fix this single-handedly, but she'd rather jail her most loyal Sidhe followers than face the truth."

"Serves her right if the Scourge *does* eat her soul, then," Morgan said.

"I don't disagree, but imagine how strong the Scourge will be after he's devoured the Unseelie Queen." Ilsa walked on, while the blurry path beneath our feet remained uniform with no indication of how much ground we'd covered.

Were we too late to stop the ritual? The mages would need to summon the Scourge before they could bind him, and there were countless ways that the first part alone could go horribly wrong. Like the last time, for instance.

"The Wild Hunt is working with the Scourge now?" Jas asked. "Is that what you're saying?"

"The Scourge is controlling their actions," I said. "Exerting influence over them, perhaps via a psychic link or something similar."

"Psychic?" Morgan said. "Weird. He never came after me."

"Be glad he didn't," said Hazel. "Come on, you aren't jealous of the Wild Hunt for having their minds invaded by a creepy god, are you?"

"And the mages are going to summon him again?" Jas said incredulously. "After the last time?"

"The solstice is tonight," I said. "They don't have many options. They're desperate."

Another minute or so passed until Jas brought us to a stop by holding out an arm. "We're close, I think."

"How can you see where we're going?" My own spirit sight wasn't turned on, and I still didn't sense any traces of the Morrigan's magic. I'd better hope the mages hadn't managed to summon the Scourge yet.

"I can see through the spirit line, too," Ilsa said. "We'll be right out in the open as soon as we step off the path, so we might want to employ stealth spells if we have them."

"I have some," said Jas. "Anyone need some explosive spells too?"

"Me," I said. "The Unseelie Queen stole my weapons, and I didn't have time to grab any spares."

Which put me at a major disadvantage if the Morrigan's magic didn't switch back on soon. Talk about bad timing.

"Here." Jas handed out a number of bracelet-shaped spells among our group. "These are mostly flash-bang spells designed to wound, not kill. We don't want anyone caught up in the crossfire by accident, and they won't have any effect on the god."

"All right." I slid the bracelets onto both wrists, glad I'd healed my wounds but wishing I'd had time to grab a knife or two. I'd become too reliant on the Morrigan's magic. "What kind of magic do the Mage Lords have, do you know?"

I was pretty sure I'd never actually fought one in open combat, since most people who pissed off the Mage Lords were arrested before they had the chance to put up a fight.

"Lord Addison is an air mage," Jas said. "Not sure about the others, but we're aiming to subdue them without dealing any fatal wounds. Mostly to cover our own backs."

"I personally don't give a shit," Keir said. "They deserve what they get."

Jas veered off the path. "Shit, I can see some kind of light over there. It's starting."

When the rest of us hurried after her, a rainy field replaced the foggy path beneath our feet. I recognised our surroundings at once, though we'd emerged on the opposite side of the hillside to the area where the circle of candles had been set up for a second time.

A small group of cloaked figures stood in a huddle in front of the candles, while two figures sat back-to-back nearby, their hands bound with ropes and their eyes covered with strips of fabric. *Hawk and Leyton.*

The mages outnumbered our small group, but they couldn't all be mages either. The candles needed a necromancer to light them. Was someone from the guild helping them? And just where were Puck and Roseanne?

Our group crept across the hillside, using the thickets of heather to stay hidden. A commotion rose from among the mages when two of the cloaked figures wrestled a third onto the grass, shoving him past the candles and into the circle. The figure's hood fell back, revealing a teenage boy with red hair who looked pale and terrified.

"A necromancer," Ilsa whispered in my ear. "He's a novice. They must have convinced him to come and help them."

Cold fear clenched a fist in my chest. The ritual required a surge of energy to activate… like the death of a necromancer. The image of a similar circle, which I'd set up in a desperate attempt to contain my mother's wraith, appeared in my mind's eye.

A flutter of wings dragged my gaze away from the circle, and two crows landed a short distance away. *Puck and Roseanne.* Did they have a plan? I didn't know if they could see us hiding in the bushes, but if we gave the game away, we'd lose the element of surprise.

"Ilsa," I breathed. "When do we move?"

"Wait for my signal," she returned. "We have one chance to ambush them."

Since the mages had the advantage in numbers, we'd need to use everything we had. I scanned the bushes, seeing Morgan struggling to restrain Pepper from leaping forwards. Hazel, Jas, and Keir were nowhere to be seen, perhaps using Jas's stealth spells to hide themselves. I'd already forgotten which of the many spells I wore on my wrists was for what purpose, but the Morrigan's magic remained dormant.

When the twelve candles flared up in a flash of light, my heart leapt into my throat, but they all went out a second later. A smile touched Ilsa's lips, clueing me in to the fact that she must have used necromancy from a distance. An unexpected laugh rose in my throat at the perplexed expressions on the mages' faces, but sooner or later, they'd figure out they had company.

"Light them again," Lord Addison snapped at someone on his right. "I told you doing this in the rain was a mistake."

"Do you want that god coming anywhere near the city?" said the blond mage I'd seen sitting beside him in the council meetings. "I don't think so."

"Light the candles and then speak the name," Lord Addison commanded, addressing a shorter figure wearing a coat which looked several sizes too big for him. "Quickly."

Ilsa sucked in a breath. "They want that guy to say the Scourge's name."

"But—it'll kill him." No human could speak the language of the gods and survive. Lord Addison truly was the scum of the earth. "Ready when you are."

Ilsa gave a faint nod and pulled out her talisman in a vibrant flare of light which caused the mages to turn towards our hiding place. An instant later, several witch spells went off in a series of flashes from all sides of the circle. I glimpsed Jas, Keir, and Hazel moving towards the mages from three different directions, while Morgan let Pepper off his lead in a barking frenzy.

While the mages were distracted, Puck and Roseanne took flight and landed next to Hawk and Leyton. I kept one eye on them as I climbed the hillside, pulling a bracelet off my wrist. The moment one of the mages spotted me, I gave the bracelet a twist. A blinding flash of light sent the mage scrambling to cover his eyes, and I darted around him, willing the Morrigan's shadows to rise over my hands.

Nothing happened. *Crap.* Worse, one of the mages raised both hands, and the drizzling rain became a deluge that soaked us through in an instant. I struggled through the blinding rain, my feet skidding in the mud-soaked grass. The circle had all but disappeared, the candles buried and drenched, but the mages had gained the upper hand. Flashes of witch spells continued to flare up, but the relentless rain didn't cease, and I glimpsed Roseanne shift back into her human form, coughing and spluttering.

I hurried to catch up to her, spotting Puck undoing the ropes binding Hawk and Leyton's hands and feet. I slid with every step but pressed on, pushing a mass of soaking-wet hair out of my eyes. Puck caught my gaze and spoke, but his words were lost in a roar as a current of wind swept towards us.

I braced myself, but the attack hit the mages instead of us, briefly lifting the torrential rain. As the haze cleared, I saw Lord Colton approaching, along with Ivy and some of the other council members. Backup had arrived.

Lord Colton raised his hands and sent another blast of air at the bedraggled mages on the hillside, causing several of them to slip over in the mud.

"Bloody hell," said Drake. "I can hardly use my fire magic in this rain. Hey, where do you think you're going?"

Lord Colton veered around, facing a group of mages who were attempting to flee. "Don't be a fool, Lord Addison."

"You are misguided, Lord Colton," said the considerably bedraggled Head Mage. "We cannot rely on the Sidhe to help us. Someone has to make the sacrifice."

"So you've decided that killing innocent people is the best way to defend your own?" said Lord Colton.

"Or don't you see us as human?" Roseanne suggested, looking at the Mage Lord in open defiance. "You think half-faeries will happily be your sacrificial lambs, do you?"

"What about the person you 'volunteered' to help you summon the Scourge?" I added. "Did you tell him that speaking an Ancient's name means an instant, painful death?"

The short figure in the oversized cloak detached himself from the rest of the mages. "What?"

"You think your band of amateur witches and necromancers is going to be any use when the god turns on you?" Drake said. "Word of advice? Stand down."

"You know what punishment awaits you," added Lord Colton. "You wrote some of the laws yourselves."

"I will not regret doing what I had to," said the blond mage next to Lord Addison. "The Council of Twelve's allegiance with the faeries has brought nothing but misfortune upon us all."

"I have already told you that the original Council of Twelve bound Fionn and paid with their lives," said Lord Colton. "It was our decision not to repeat their mistakes."

"Then you should have given your lives instead," said Lord Addison. "Rather than expecting the Sidhe to come and save us. It was they who angered the gods and set them against us."

A breeze drifted across us, driving the rain sideways. All eyes went to the mages, but none of them had moved. Instead, a familiar winged shape appeared on the horizon, dark and indistinct.

Lord Addison made a disbelieving sound. "Impossible. We never did the summoning."

"The Scourge can fly, Lord Addison, remember?" I called to him. "I bet he saw your amateur summoning circle and came to take a look for himself."

The winged shape neared. Instinct screamed at me to run for the spirit line again, but how many other chances would we have to banish the Scourge before the longest night began?

I focused on the shadows beneath my skin, and this time, they answered. Darkness spread up my arms, and my hands became curved claws.

"Holly!" Puck shouted my name, but when the Scourge descended, I broke into a run.

Wings spread behind my shoulders, carrying me into

the air. The Scourge seemed to have been expecting me, as he waited for me to rise to his level before speaking. "You are vexing, mortal. You should have stayed dead."

A horrible pressure crashed into my skull like a vice had clamped onto my head. Agony exploded behind my eyes, and my vision doubled. The Scourge's laugh rang through my skull, while my wings collapsed, and my body tumbled towards the hillside.

A haze of darkness overtook my vision.

18

The pain in my skull gradually faded, making me aware of the cold dampness soaking into my back and legs. When I opened my eyes, alertness hit me like a train. In the sky, several winged shapes soared above the rolling hills, crashing into one another like trains colliding, and one of them exhaled a stream of fire which lit up the rainy sky.

Are those... dragons?

A pair of warm hands touched my shoulders. "Good," Puck's voice said near my ear. "You're awake."

I struggled into an upright position, finding myself lying in a swampy patch of rain-drenched mud halfway down the hillside. "What the hell is going on up there?"

"Trouble," he said. "I wanted to get you out of here, but it's hard to run for cover when the enemy is in the sky."

"They're fighting the god." My gaze followed another stream of fire as it disappeared into the clouds.

"Don't worry, they're on our side," he said. "The Council called them in for backup, I think."

"They're dragon shifters?" They must be. Several large reptiles circled the Scourge, vast wings beating, while a handful of figures remained below. I could see Ivy running across the hilltop, her blade unable to reach her target while he was up in the air. "Where's Roseanne?"

"I sent her back to Edinburgh with Hawk and Leyton."

"Good." I heard someone whisper my name and turned sharply, spying Hazel beckoning frantically at me from a nearby patch of trees. Ilsa and Morgan were visible among the bushes behind her. "C'mon. Let's get out of here before the Scourge sees us."

With Puck on my heels, I hurried over to join the others in the shelter of the trees.

"Holly." Ilsa looked visibly relieved, clutching her talisman in one hand. "I saw you fall out of the sky, but we couldn't get near you. If those dragon shifters hadn't shown up, I'm pretty sure the Scourge would have killed all of us."

"What happened back there?" Hazel asked.

"I think the Scourge used his psychic ability on me," I said. "Knocked me straight out."

"Fucker," said Morgan. "Unless one of you has enough stealth spells for all of us, we'll never make it back to the spirit line without him divebombing us from the sky. Jas and the other necromancers managed to run back to the guild for reinforcements. They took Pepper with them, fortunately."

Roseanne, Hawk and Leyton had escaped, too, but we'd be hard-pressed to avoid the god's attention now there were so few of us left. If not for those dragon shifters, he'd have finished me off there and then.

"There's always the gate," Hazel said. "We're not far from the forest."

"We're *in* the forest," Ilsa said. "Part of it, anyway. We can walk to the Ley Line from here, but do you really want to drag Mum into this?"

The forest. The site of the original Gatekeepers' route into Faerie.

"Pretty sure she's already seen everything," Morgan said. "An aerial battle between a god and a bunch of dragon shifters is hard to miss."

"I think Faerie is a safer bet, personally," said Hazel. "I think I remember the way."

Puck gave me a puzzled look. "Where?"

"The gate to Faerie," I said. "We used to live in a liminal space on the Ley Line, but the gate moved back to the mortal realm after the curse broke."

"Mum's gonna be pissed at us," said Morgan.

"Nah, she won't be." Hazel took the lead through a tangle of briars. "Though I'd like to ask her why she gave my phone number to Janet Lynn."

We made our way through the forest, the sounds of the dragon shifters clashing with the Scourge fading into the background. The village of Foxwood lay somewhere on the other side of the woods, and I hoped the god's attention was too focused on his other adversaries to notice the community of vulnerable humans nearby.

Hazel's steps slowed after a few minutes. "Do you hear that?"

I listened out, and the murmur of voices drifted from elsewhere in the trees. "We're not alone in here."

Ilsa kept her talisman close at hand, while Hazel gripped an iron knife. We walked on until we reached a clearing where several cloaked figures lay tangled in a large net that stretched between several trees. All were soaking wet and covered in mud, yet I instantly recognised Lord Addison among them.

When the Head Mage saw us, his eyes widened. "Get me out of here at once!"

"Who threw you in a net?" asked Morgan.

"Whoever it was, I want to thank them." Hazel snickered. "What did you do, try to run away? Don't you know there are monsters in the forest?"

Lord Addison's blond friend glared at us through the net. "This isn't the work of wild animals. A faerie set this trap."

"She was human," said one of the other mages in a muffled voice. "That woman we saw. She laughed at us."

"Do you think it was Mum?" Ilsa whispered to her siblings, both of whom smirked. "I guess she had some traps set up for any faeries who tried to sneak up on her."

"If you ask me, she did you a favour," Hazel told the mages. "Considering your other options were to go through the gate into Faerie or get caught in a battle between dragons and gods."

"We could have prevented this," said Lord Addison. "You will regret spurning our offer of help."

"Don't you start," I said. "You tried to sacrifice innocent lives to summon and bind the god. There was no chance it wouldn't backfire on you."

"We cannot defeat the Scourge in battle," he said. "Binding the beast was our only chance at survival."

"Did you not hear the part where the last binding spell didn't work?" Ilsa asked him. "Even if you'd succeeded, the Scourge's allies would have undone the binding and rendered your actions obsolete. Assuming your own allies didn't flee when they realised speaking an Invocation would cost their lives."

"Exactly." Hazel gave the mages a blistering look. "Anyway, if you don't mind, we have somewhere else to be. Have fun hanging in there until someone remembers to look for you… or the god finds you first."

"Wait!" Lord Addison's tone turned frantic, but we were already walking away from the clearing, leaving the mages behind.

As the captives loudly voiced their displeasure, Ilsa tutted. "They'll bring the god on our tail at this rate."

"We're not far from the gate." Hazel stomped through the undergrowth, hacking at briars with her knife. "I wonder if that's where Mum went?"

"Hope not, since she doesn't have any magic." Ilsa fell into step with her sister, while Morgan, Puck, and I followed behind them.

Within a few minutes, the gate came into view. Nestled between two trees, it was formed of thorny branches instead of metal, a faint glow outlining its edges.

"Ready?" Hazel reached out and pushed the gate open, revealing a leaf-dappled path on the other side. She walked through without hesitation, and the sight of the sunbeams reflecting on the bright leaves told me we were closer to Summer than Winter.

While the heat soothed my cold skin, Puck's hiss of alarm drew me to a halt. A contingent of warriors melted out of the trees around us, some on horseback, some on foot, and all armed to the teeth. The Summer Sidhe turned towards us, all dressed in varying shades of green and gold, their vibrant finery a stark contrast to our battered, mud-stained clothes.

"Ah," said Hazel. "Hi."

"Sorry for trespassing," Ilsa said. "I didn't know the gate would bring us so close to Summer."

"Gatekeeper." A male Sidhe spoke, silver-haired and sharp-featured. "Three Gatekeepers, in fact."

"That's us," Hazel said. "Sorry we crashed the party, Lord Raivan. Where're you all going?"

"What brings you here?" Lord Raivan asked, ignoring her own question. "Do you come to ask for another favour?"

"The Scourge is attacking the mortal realm on the other side of the gate," Hazel said. "We figured we'd be less likely to get our souls ripped out if we came here instead."

"So you wish for us to fight for you again?" asked Lord Raivan. "You might have the favour of the Erlking, but he will not have us sacrifice our lives needlessly."

"The Scourge is coming here," said Hazel. "He wants you dead, all of you. Right, Holly?"

Thanks, Hazel. "There's a strong chance he'll come here," I said. "He has allies imprisoned in Winter, but I'm sure Summer won't escape his notice either."

"This is not your first time trespassing on our territory, harbinger." Lord Torin stepped forwards, his eyes narrowing at me. At the sight of River's father, Puck moved closer to my side, his shoulders tensing.

"We're not asking you to fight for us," said Hazel. "But you need to be prepared. The Scourge can devour the souls of Sidhe as well as humans, and he gets a hell of a lot more power from eating one of you than a mortal."

"I don't think you're defusing the situation here," Ilsa muttered to her sister.

"Then we would request that you explain yourselves to the Erlking," said Lord Raivan. "All of you."

Shit. We didn't have time to get delayed in Summer, but if we fled back through the gate, we'd end up in the vicinity of the Scourge again. Was that any worse than being locked up in the Unseelie Queen's dungeon? Debatable, but now that we'd drawn Summer's attention, it was only a matter of time before Winter found out too.

"All right," Hazel said. "I'll speak to the Erlking."

"The hell we will," Morgan muttered. "What're they all doing here, anyway? They look as if they're going to war."

"Precisely," Hazel whispered. "The Erlking will have an explanation, I guarantee it."

"This way." Lord Raivan beckoned to our group, and the other Sidhe parted to allow us to walk through the clearing.

I moved closer to my cousin. "Hazel, the last time I went near a faerie monarch, I ended up in a cell with two mass murderers."

"The Erlking is fair," she whispered back. "I've told him everything so far."

"Not the latest, though," I said in a low voice. "Like how the Sidhe were never meant to be immortal. Think he'll be happy to hear that?"

"He's young by Sidhe standards," she said. "Plus he's more reasonable than that Winter Queen of yours."

With a dozen Sidhe on either side of us, we didn't have many options, and since the Summer Sidhe hadn't outright attacked any of us, I caught Puck's eye and nodded.

"Are you sure?" he whispered.

"We can always shift and fly out again if we need to."

All the same, I stayed close to Puck as we crossed the clearing and entered a patch of woodland. When the trees thinned out, we found ourselves in a familiar bright meadow.

Two figures waited on the grass. One was undeniably the Erlking, and the other... the other was Flora Lynn.

"Mum?" Ilsa said in disbelief. "What are you doing here?"

"What else?" Flora watched her children approach with an impassive expression. "Getting you out of trouble."

The resemblance between Flora and Janet Lynn was striking close up. I hadn't seen my aunt in a long while, and I'd forgotten she had the same brown eyes my cousins and I all shared now that the traces of Summer and Winter magic had vanished from our family. She and Hazel had the same tall, strong frame, while her face showed no fear at standing beside the most powerful Sidhe in Summer.

The Erlking himself looked younger than I expected, though with the Sidhe, appearance wasn't necessarily a reliable indicator of age. A crown sat atop his blue-black hair, his ebony skin glowed faintly, and his green-and-gold armour was more practical than I might have expected of a monarch who typically took a back seat on the battlefield. His Summer-green eyes travelled across my cousins before focusing on me. "So, you are the Winter Gatekeeper."

"The former Gatekeeper," I corrected automatically, my heart jumping into my throat. "Your Majesty."

"And the Summer Gatekeeper's cousin." His gaze went to Hazel. "I see the resemblance. Is there a reason you used the old gate to travel to my Court?"

"I didn't know it came directly to Summer." The urge to explain myself fought with the instincts telling me to get the pleasantries out of the way. "We were fleeing the Scourge. I believe your warriors are familiar with him."

"Yes, they are," he said. "I saw him myself during the battle in which the former Seelie Queen met her end, though at the time, he was unable to leave his own realm."

"He's angry," said Hazel. "The Mage Lords tried to summon and bind him, but he launched an attack on the mortal realm. We think he's coming here too. Well, Holly does."

"He all but stated his intention," I said. "Is that why your warriors are assembling?"

"I though it wise to prepare for any eventuality, given the recent stirrings in Winter." The Erlking gave me a considering look. "I heard you were involved yourself, in fact. Might you explain yourself?"

I glanced at the others, and Ilsa gave me an encouraging nod. If I didn't at least try to explain myself, then I'd only have myself to blame if I wound up back in the dungeon. Puck remained visibly on edge, but he'd come this far without anyone chasing him off, for what it was worth.

"I intended to inform the Unseelie Queen of my belief that the Scourge planned to attack the Courts," I said. "Instead of listening, she locked me in her dungeon with two members of the former Wild Hunt."

"You need not fear punishment from me, Holly Lynn,"

he said. "I simply want an understanding of your perspective."

He was young, for a Sidhe, and new to the throne. He might not have been born in the time of the gods, but he'd come into leadership after the destruction of the cauldron, which meant he didn't necessarily expect immortality to return the way some of the other Sidhe did. For that reason alone, I might stand a fighting chance of convincing him to listen to me.

I gave the Erlking an abbreviated explanation of everything I knew of the Scourge, starting from the original Wild Hunt's role in escorting the dead to the afterlife, the creation of the cauldron, the Hunt's subsequent binding to the Unseelie Queen, and how Fionn's betrayal had exposed her lies. I added a little about their ties to the Aes Sidhe and Etaina, though I refrained from bringing up Puck's name or his role as trickster. However, I did add that the Scourge seemed to be exerting his influence on the two surviving Wild Hunt members.

The Erlking's mouth parted as though he wanted to interrupt a few times, but he didn't. If he disbelieved me, then I was dead—if not at his hands, then at the hands of the Unseelie Queen or the Scourge himself. Even Hazel refrained from making any comments, while the Erlking was silent for a long moment after I'd finished speaking.

"My predecessor often spoke of the wrongs his generation of Sidhe did to their predecessors," said the Erlking. "As for the Wild Hunt, they operated chiefly from the Winter Court, so I was unaware that the gods were banished to the very realm to which the Wild Hunt once carried the dead. Nor did I know the reasons for the cauldron's creation."

"I don't know if it's possible to banish him again in the same manner," I said. "The Wild Hunt originally planned to slaughter him and remake the cauldron themselves, but the Scourge's influence hit them as soon as he escaped. Now, they're talking about riding on the solstice…"

"You told the Unseelie Queen this?"

"I tried," I said. "She refused to give anything away about her own role in the Wild Hunt's binding and the cauldron's creation, though I'm certain they originally swore to her alone. I also know some of the other Winter Sidhe wanted to nominate a replacement for Fionn and re-form the Hunt, but she's denied them every time."

"To my knowledge, that is true," said the Erkling. "I have tried to contact her on the subject several times, but she has neglected to respond to me."

"I'm not surprised," I said. "Maybe she's reluctant to make the same mistake again, but if there isn't someone to take the dead to the next world, then all Sidhe in Faerie who die will eventually become wraiths."

"Who told you that?" he asked.

"Janet Lynn?" said Flora, startling me, mostly because I'd forgotten the older Lynn was present. "I gather she had access to information known only to the Sidhe."

"You met her," said Morgan in accusing tones. "And gave her our phone numbers too."

"She claimed she was a distant relation," said my aunt. "She wanted the means of getting in touch with you if necessary, and I saw enough of a resemblance in her face to assume she was telling the truth."

"Your family is full of surprises," said the Erkling. "I confess, I did not expect another ancestor of yours to resurface, much less one who spent time in the company of Etaina of the Aes Sidhe."

"You told him?" Hazel asked her mother. "I thought she didn't want the Sidhe to know she was still alive."

The Erlking focused his attention on Hazel. "I do not fault you for being reluctant to share Janet Lynn's existence with me, given her narrow escape from the Lady of Light. That said, we have a dilemma as to how to break the news to the other Sidhe. It was incredibly difficult for many of them to accept the loss of my predecessor."

No kidding. Hazel had had to endure weeks of assassination attempts when she'd been helping the Court to choose the former Erlking's replacement, and some Sidhe had been convinced that he'd never died at all or that he would be reborn. Some refused to believe the cauldron was truly gone. Yet keeping the truth from them as the Unseelie Queen had would only enable schemers like Fionn to take advantage of them.

The Erlking's gaze travelled over to Puck. "Trickster, is it?"

"Some call me that, yes." Puck's tones were carefully neutral. "To most, I am known as Puck."

"I heard you formerly held a position in the Court of the Aes Sidhe," he said. "May I ask to whom you now owe your allegiance?"

"My allegiance?" said Puck. "I belong to no Court, but I owe my allegiance to Holly Lynn, and I believe that following her advice will give us the best chance of survival."

My heart missed a beat, and I struggled to hide my surprise when the Erlking turned back to me. "Might you tell me what advice he is referring to?"

I drew in a breath. "The Scourge plans to act on the longest night, when the boundaries between realms are thin, and that might be our last chance to stop him. I know the Unseelie Queen won't listen to me, but I would very much appreciate it if you would offer us your help, if you are able."

He gave a gesture behind him, and several other Sidhe appeared as if they'd been hiding in plain sight all along. "I will talk to my council, but we will make our discussion brief. You may converse with your allies in the meantime."

The other Sidhe closed in to speak to him, while Hazel strode over to join them. Ilsa and Morgan approached their mother, while I stood beside Puck, trying to ignore the dread gnawing at my innards.

Even with the Erlking's help, did any of us stand a chance of bringing down the Scourge when the Sidhe who'd lived in the time of the Ancients refused to share any of their own knowledge? And if the Scourge was killed, would that then lead to the creation of another cauldron as the Wild Hunt had once planned?

Even if it did, what choice did we have? If the Scourge was allowed to gain the upper hand, each soul he consumed would make him harder to defeat. Spilling his lifeblood would create a new set of problems for the Sidhe, but it was better than the alternative. Wasn't it?

My mother wouldn't have hesitated to strike him down, but maybe that was why the notion bothered me so much. I could picture all too clearly how she'd have used the god's downfall to consolidate her own power, yet when I tried to imagine my own future on the other side of this war, I saw nothing but fog, thick as the deepest layer of Death.

Maybe that was why she'd thrived, while I'd failed over and over. When you were handed the tools of a villain, trying to be heroic was an exercise in futility.

Ilsa waved a hand in front of my face. "Are you okay, Holly?"

"If we kill the Scourge, what if the Unseelie Queen uses his lifeblood to make a new cauldron?" I whispered. "We'd be back to square one, and it'll be as if nothing we did ever mattered."

"That isn't true," she said. "We broke the curse and freed all future generations of our family from enslavement to the Courts."

"For now." I knew it was my old pessimism talking, but I couldn't shake the feeling that whatever the outcome, the Unseelie Queen would be let off lightly for deceiving everyone. And even after the curse had broken, she'd seized every available opportunity to sink her claws in me.

"We're going to win this," Ilsa said. "Whatever the Sidhe end up doing, we're going to survive. We're Lynns. It's what we do."

"Survival isn't enough," I said quietly. "Survival isn't living. I should know."

I'd been surviving for long enough that even the brief happy moments I'd had with Puck and Roseanne had felt like they were stolen from someone else's life. Would it be worth enduring the war to know the Sidhe would go on living a lie and the Unseelie Queen would continue to exert her tyranny over them?

"That's not what I meant," Ilsa said. "We never thought we'd break the curse, either, remember? If we'd stuck to that assumption and hadn't tried to beat the odds, then we'd still be trapped. Or worse."

My mother's face came to mind. When she'd failed to break the curse, she'd seen death as her only way out and had been willing to go out in a blaze of glory. Or villainy, depending on your viewpoint. I wasn't her, and I wasn't the Morrigan either. I'd have to choose my own way out of this.

"Holly." Puck's lips brushed my ear. "The Summer Court sent an emissary to Winter. Would you mind if I followed them?"

"Yes!" I jerked back to scowl at him. "Puck, they want us dead."

"They won't see me," he said. "I want to know what Her Majesty says to them. I'll stay hidden."

"You'd better." I'd have liked to know what the Unseelie Queen had to say, too, and her attention would doubtless be focused on her unexpected visitors. "Be careful."

I briefly squeezed Puck's hand, and he vanished in a shower of feathers.

"He's not going to spy on the Winter Queen?" Hazel walked over to me. "The Erlking's risking getting on her bad side by sending a message at all."

"Why does he want to talk to her?" I asked. "The Queen's already pissed off because Ivy sent a hellhound attack as a diversion so I could break out of jail."

"Ivy did what?" Hazel blinked at me. "Wow. That might play in our favour, though. I reckon the Unseelie Queen knows full well what's at stake, and she's under pressure to make the right choice."

"Do you trust her, though?" I asked. "Does the Erlking honestly want to form an alliance with Winter against the Scourge?"

"Makes sense," Hazel said. "The Courts have a common enemy."

"Yes—me, if we're not careful," I said. "The Unseelie Queen won't lock up the Erlking for repeating my so-called lies, but I'll bet she'll find some way to blame it on my bad influence."

"She can't keep the truth hidden for much longer," said Hazel. "Especially with those Wild Hunt members in her jail and hellhounds attacking her territory. If she isn't careful, she'll lose her grip on her own forces."

"She even jailed Lord Lyle for repeating what I told him, so she's down one soldier," I said. "But she's held onto power for long enough that she must have a contingency plan."

"I don't know about you, but I don't want to end up facing an angry faerie queen as well as a god," Morgan said.

"We need her," said Ilsa. "I know she's a little unhinged, to say the least, but she's the one who bound the original Wild Hunt, and she doesn't want her Court to fall any more than the Erlking wants to lose Summer."

A bright flash drew our eyes to the Erlking, who extended a hand to catch a piece of parchment which fluttered out of the air. He unfolded the parchment then read the words written on it. "The Unseelie Queen has accepted our offer. We will meet her warriors on neutral ground."

She said yes? I had no doubts she was still scheming, but

it was a huge deal for her to agree to meet with the Erlking in person.

I only hoped that this meeting between Sidhe monarchs didn't end as badly as the last one.

19

"Neutral territory" turned out to be a clearing in the borderlands, surrounded by oak trees. The Erlking's procession made their way through the woods, accompanied by the Lynns. I watched for Puck, but I assumed he'd stayed in the form of a crow to keep an eye on Winter's forces.

Please say he hasn't been caught. I didn't trust the Unseelie Queen an inch, despite her apparent change of heart. At least the King of Summer hadn't come to meet her alone, with at least a dozen armed Sidhe gathering around him while we waited for the Unseelie contingent to arrive. Minutes trickled by, and in the mortal realm, that might mean hours had passed. The sun set early in December too. When did the longest night officially begin? Might we already be too late?

We can't fight the Scourge without the Sidhe. Like it or not, we needed the Courts' help.

Rustling in the bushes indicated more new arrivals—human ones. Ivy and River came to join us, and I caught enough of their whispered words to Ilsa and Hazel to guess that the Scourge had escaped their grasp once again.

Then all eyes turned to the far end of the clearing as the trees peeled back like curtains, and a large procession came into view, clad in white and blue and silver. The Unseelie Sidhe had arrived. I recognised Lady Rive among them—and Lord Lyle. Why had the Unseelie Queen freed him? Did that mean she finally believed me? I didn't dare get my hopes up, and yet I had to wonder if the urgency of the situation had finally sunk in.

Once they'd filled one side of the clearing, the Unseelie Sidhe parted to allow their Queen to walk through to the front. Instead of her usual dress, she wore armour made of a deep silvery metal which moulded to her tall, lean form. Blue jewels studded the circlet on her head, while her curls were carefully tied back, out of the way of her vision. She was stunning yet utterly merciless, and fear squeezed my chest when her vibrant eyes sought me out among her enemies.

"Erlking," said the Unseelie Queen. "I am told you have a proposition for my Court."

"You would be correct," said the Erlking. "We face an enemy the likes of which the Courts have not faced in a thousand years or more. The Scourge. This is not the first time you have encountered this being, is it?"

"No," said the Unseelie Queen. "I also know your Court encountered him recently and failed to bring him down."

A ripple of anger passed among the Summer Sidhe, and the Erlking raised a hand to calm them. "The Scourge is a unique foe that we can only overcome with our fellow Sidhe as our allies and not our enemies. I would offer you an alliance with the Summer Court so that we may put our collective forces together to bring down our enemy."

"I will not wage an unnecessary war," the Unseelie Queen said. "I would rather direct my efforts towards defending my territory, not sending troops into battle in the defence of helpless mortals."

"That's nice," Hazel muttered, quietly enough that only Ilsa, Morgan, and I could hear. "I can see why you two are such good friends, Holly."

"If we do not bring down this beast before he reaches Faerie, then the outcome will be catastrophic," said the Erlking. "The Scourge intends to strike on the solstice, gathering strength by devouring the souls of any who oppose him. We have little time to delay before we risk him bringing about our end."

"Who informed you of this?" the Unseelie Queen's gaze bit into me. "If you are basing your strategies upon the lies of the former Gatekeepers, then you are wasting your time."

"Have you not seen the evidence with your own eyes?" said the Erlking. "Or heard it with your own ears? The former Wild Hunt, who were once loyal to your Court, are tied directly to the god himself."

"Do not speak to me of them." Her voice echoed like the tolling of a bell. "You dare to bring a mortal traitor to our gathering and speak of unity? Was it you who aided in her escape from my Court?"

"Actually, it was me," Ivy said loudly. "Holly risked her life to warn you of the Scourge's intentions, and you locked her in the dungeon. I figured it was only fair to give her a shot at warning Summer too."

That wasn't *quite* how it'd happened, but the Seelie

Sidhe drew their weapons the instant the Unseelie all turned towards Ivy and me.

"Traitors," said the Unseelie Queen. "You conspire with the false Wild Hunt yourself."

"I would not allow anyone who conspired against any of the Sidhe into my Court," said the Erlking. "The Scourge will not discriminate between each Court. We are stronger if we stand together, and stronger still if we share information. Let us strike the Scourge down and split the remains between us."

My blood chilled as the Unseelie Queen's piercing blue eyes roved over the Erlking. "You wish to remake the cauldron?"

"Is that not your own desire?" said the Erlking. "Creating the cauldron requires the blood of an Ancient, and one might call it serendipitous that the Scourge has crossed our paths in our time of need. If we slay him and use his lifeblood to reforge the cauldron, then we may truly begin a new era in Faerie."

This is wrong. Yes, the destruction of the cauldron and the Wild Hunt's betrayal had wrought havoc in Faerie, but the vows the Hunt had sworn to the Unseelie Queen had been founded on a lie at the very start.

The Unseelie Queen cast a glance around at her fellow Winter Sidhe. "The cauldron would not be of much use on its own. There would need to be a replacement for the Wild Hunt to carry the souls of our people to be reborn. Someone who would not turn against us."

"That is within your power, is it not?" said the Erlking. "The former Wild Hunt were a force set apart from the Courts. Their vows were shrouded in secrecy, but they were sworn to you alone, correct?"

Murmurs rose among the other Sidhe, and I found myself wondering how many of the Winter Court's members actually knew the nature of the Wild Hunt's original vow. The fact that the Unseelie Queen hadn't shared that knowledge ought to be a screaming red flag. Given the former Erlking's isolated nature prior to his unexpected death, he'd have had little opportunity to pass on the knowledge to his successor, but the Unseelie Queen had no such excuse.

"The Wild Hunt served all Sidhe, from both Winter and Summer," said the Unseelie Queen. "Yet they betrayed us both for a false Queen who was cast out from your Court. Who is to say the same will not happen again?"

More angry mutters came from the Summer Sidhe. The Erlking's expression, however, remained calm. "Etaina of the Aes Sidhe was a traitor to Summer and Winter alike. As I have not lived for as long as you have, I would gladly invite you to share your years of experience with me, so that we may construct a vow that would not give the new Wild Hunt any opportunities for betrayal."

"And the cauldron?" The Unseelie Queen's features might as well have been chiselled out of ice. "What if one Court were to steal it for their own use?"

"Did the same ever occur beforehand?" he asked. "Not to my knowledge, though I was not alive in the time of its creation."

"The cauldron has always existed," one of the other Sidhe said. "Has it not?"

"I assume the cauldron had a beginning, like we all did." The Erlking directed his words at the Unseelie Queen. "Unless it simply sprang up out of the ground?"

The Sidhe stirred, uneasy, while even the Unseelie

Queen's composure wavered as anger flickered in her eyes. Clever. The Erlking was publicly exposing the gaps in her story, but he was also offering her everything she'd ever wanted. A chance to remake the cauldron *and* the Wild Hunt and turn back the clocks, as if to pretend that Fionn's betrayal and the breaking of the first cauldron had never happened.

Except some of the Sidhe wouldn't forget. And neither would we.

"This does not seem a fair trade," said the Unseelie Queen. "You place the burden on me to share all my knowledge with you, yet you offer nothing of equal value in return."

"Is the blood of an Ancient not of equal value?" he said. "If we bring down the Scourge and spill his lifeblood, then we need not fear death any longer. When we win, those who give their lives in battle will be reborn from the blood of the false god who sought to destroy us."

The Unseelie Queen paused for a moment, as if considering his words. Was she actually going to agree? I should have expected the only way to convince her to join with Summer would be to offer her the one thing both Courts wanted badly enough to place their rivalries aside for a short time—yet my instincts rebelled against letting them rebuild the very system which had nearly led to our ruin.

Even if the Hunt rose again with a new leader, how could they ever fully be trusted, given the Unseelie Queen's penchant for manipulation? She'd do her best to turn the situation in her favour, and even if she agreed to his offer, she would only share information with the Erlking that she deemed convenient.

On the other hand, if they didn't make an alliance, the Scourge would win.

The Unseelie Queen answered. "I will consider your offer."

"I apologise for my haste," said the Erlking. "But the Scourge's attack is imminent."

"The Scourge will certainly strike, but we will not wait on ground that is not our own," she replied. "We will weather the storm within our own territory."

My hands curled into fists. Would nothing stir her to action? I opened my mouth to speak, but a flash of feathers drew my eye, swirling between the Erlking and the Unseelie Queen. *Puck.*

Straightening upright in human form, he bowed. "Pardon my interruption, but you should know that the dead are rising in your Court."

The Unseelie Queen's mouth twisted. "What have you done, trickster?"

In the background, a howl sounded. *Hellhounds.* This time, I knew Ivy wasn't responsible. The Scourge's army was stirring, and it seemed he did indeed have allies in Faerie.

"Prepare," said the Unseelie Queen to her warriors. "Be ready to fight."

My heart sank as she turned away from the Erlking, as did her soldiers. Hurrying towards Puck, I called to the Unseelie Queen. "Wait a moment."

She whirled on me. "You presume to talk to me, mortal, after your treachery?"

"Listen to me for a second, please," I said. "The Wild Hunt are connected to the Scourge. He's exerting some kind of psychic influence over them, and they might even be communicating from within your Court—"

"The god has spoken to you?" she said. "Is that how you escaped?"

"No. I'm not—"

The ground heaved underfoot, the jolting vibration cutting off my words. Trees trembled, and the grass gave way as several grotesque skeletal shapes dragged themselves out of the earth. Some resembled humanoid figures, while others were shorter, like goblins or piskies. Others still were much larger, lumbering like ogres or trolls, except with little flesh on their twisted bones. *Undead... undead fae.*

The Unseelie Queen's expression turned blank as she looked upon the rising dead, but the wideness of her eyes betrayed her genuine shock. In her own Court, she held control over both living and dead, but the unnatural sight of the dead rising had stunned Sidhe from both Summer and Winter alike.

The stench of rot rolled through the air, while the dead fell upon the living. Recovering from their shock, the Sidhe struck back against their attackers, blades cleaving through bones, but more undead surged out of the forest while hellhounds howled in the background.

"This is the rest of the Hunt," I murmured, though the noise meant nobody heard me. "I guess this was where the Scourge's army was hiding."

All the dead in Faerie had risen, or so it seemed. Swords, spears, and knives struck, streams of arrows flew, and Puck leapt across the clearing, his bear form crushing bones and his flames setting them alight. Yet when I called for the Morrigan's magic, not so much as a faint shadow stirred beneath my skin. *Not again.*

"We're being overrun!" Ilsa fought her way over to me, her talisman glowing in her hand. "They're not ghosts; they're zombies. I can't banish them."

"Typical." Morgan kicked an undead goblin's head clean off. "I'd have brought a shit-ton of salt if I'd known we were going to end up having to deal with zombies."

"Want to sneak back to the guild and grab some supplies?" Hazel tossed the decapitated skeleton of some small fae beast over her shoulder. "Honestly, I don't think there's anything we can do here. Not until we kill the beast that raised them."

"The Scourge." Fear flooded me as the sound of beating hooves echoed like a death knell in the background.

The Hunt was riding. The longest night had begun.

20

The echo of pounding hooves grew louder, and all eyes turned to the sky as a cloud of darkness gathered over the forest, resolving into the shapes of horses riding on a wave of shadows.

"Where are they going?" Ilsa stood on tiptoe. "Shit. Isn't that the path which links to the Ley Line?"

"The Scourge isn't here yet," I said. "He must still be in the mortal realm... and I bet they're going to meet him there."

We moved through the clearing, heading towards the nebulous cloud of shadows. The Morrigan's magic remained worryingly absent, but I didn't have time to hesitate. The first time I'd fought the Hunt, I'd had nothing but an iron knife in my hand, and I'd still stabbed one of the horsemen in the eye and freed Roseanne from his clutches. For her sake, I needed to stop them.

River and Ivy fought their way across the clearing to join us, their talismans making quick work of any undead who got in our way. When the cloud of darkness abruptly vanished, Hazel swore. "They've gone to find their boss."

"Fuckers." Ivy flicked her sword, severing the skeletal arm of a lumbering ogre. "Bet they won't stay away for long. They wouldn't have raised the dead otherwise."

Our group ran out of the trees onto the path between the Courts, where an odd shimmering overlaid the air. The Ley Line flickered, showing glimpses of other paths, some I recognised and some I didn't. This time, I hadn't needed to tap into the Morrigan's magic to be able to see the way the realms interlinked.

"Stay close behind me." Ivy stepped through the Ley Line, and between one blink and the next, we found ourselves in Edinburgh again.

A dark cloud greeted us, smothering the sky overhead, while low-level fog swept through the street. A cacophony of discordant noise filled the background, the beating of hooves mingling with cries and howls.

"I think the Hunt woke up all the dead in the city," Ilsa remarked. "Damn, that's loud."

"No kidding." Morgan had gone pale, pressing his hands to his ears.

Crap. If the Morrigan's magic didn't switch back on soon, I'd better hope I didn't need to deal with any ghosts. Not that they were the biggest issue here.

Ilsa walked towards the gate to half-blood territory, her book in one hand and an iron blade in the other. "The guild... shit, it's right on top of that spirit line. I wonder if the Scourge is still up north?"

"Is that where they're going?" The dark cloud swirled around the sky, hovering above the Ley Line to the north of our location.

"The Scourge was still fighting the dragons last I saw," Ivy put in. "They really gave him a hard time, in fact."

"Yes, but hours have passed since then," Ilsa said. "I hope everyone at the guild is okay."

"We'll find them." River took a decisive lead, and we walked past half-blood territory.

The cloud of darkness receded with every step we took, wheeling northward and over the Firth of Forth. Then a blur of feathers descended from the sky, turning from a crow into a human. Roseanne flung herself at me so hard that I stumbled back a step.

"What the hell did you run off to Faerie for?" she said. "I thought they captured you again!"

"We got dragged into a meeting between Courts," I said. "Which almost ended in their first peaceful agreement in centuries, except the Hunt interrupted by filling the Courts with zombies."

"Zombies? In *Faerie?*"

"I know, right?" Ivy said. "We tried to rally the Sidhe to kill the Scourge before he reached their realm. They almost reached a deal, but they're too busy defending their Courts to help us now."

"The Scourge had his hands full dealing with those dragons," said Puck.

But can they win? Keir had mentioned that all the shifters were descended from the gods themselves, and the dragons had the advantage of being able to fight in the air, but hours had passed since we'd left through the gate into Faerie.

"Anyone want to chase the Hunt?" Ivy walked on, her hand on the hilt of her blade. "I *might* be able to catch them up if I leave my body behind and travel on the spirit line."

"Same, but if my spirit ends up trapped up north, then I won't be much use here in Edinburgh," Ilsa said. "It'd help if we all had wings."

"One of us does." Hazel winked at me.

"Yeah, slight problem." I drew in a breath. "The Scourge hit me with some kind of psychic attack earlier, and I haven't been able to access the Morrigan's magic since then."

Roseanne wheeled to face me. "Seriously?"

"Guess we're going to have to follow the Hunt on foot," said Hazel. "I hope the god finds Lord Addison and his cronies. That'll keep the Hunt busy for a bit."

"Where is he?" Ivy said. "I saw him running away when the Scourge showed up, but I was a bit distracted by the fire-breathing lizards."

"Our mother was resourceful enough to put a trap in the forest for any trespassers who went near Faerie's gate," said Hazel. "They're currently stuck in a net. Serve them right, if you ask me."

"Damn right," Morgan said. "The council can go in and fetch them later. I doubt they're going anywhere."

No doubt the mages would pick being jailed over being killed by the Scourge or captured by the Sidhe, especially when Faerie was currently under siege from the dead. Then again, so was the mortal realm. Clouds of ghosts drifted past as we moved, occasionally crowding around Ilsa and forcing her to use her talisman to repel them.

"Not sure banishing anyone would do much good," she remarked. "If Death is as screwed up as the land of the living."

"I'd check, but… well." If there was another god lurking in the afterlife, someone else would have to deal with it. "The Hunt's moving fast."

The cloud had vanished from sight by now. How long would it take them to reach the Scourge? When they did, would they return to the city via the same route, or would they hitch a ride on the spirit line on top of the guild? My mind swirled with thoughts as we hurried into Edinburgh's Old Town, where Ivy parted ways with us.

"I'm going to find Vance and see if he can use his teleporting ability to get up north," she said. "Quicker than walking."

"Is that his mage power? Teleporting?"

"Displacing, if you want the technical term," Ivy said. "He can move things around, including himself, but bringing other people along for the ride is trickier. We'll have to go after him alone."

"Be careful," said Ilsa. "Right—let's tell the guild why the city is flooded with ghosts."

She and River approached the oak doors of the necromancer guild, with Morgan close behind them.

Hazel caught my eye. "Coming? We Lynns should stick together."

I hovered on the balls of my feet for a moment. Lady Montgomery might have apologised for kicking me out of the guild, but I didn't exactly feel welcome there. I didn't want the guild to be trampled by the Wild Hunt, though, either. As the doors opened, I followed the others into the guild's lobby, which was packed with cloaked necromancers. Jas, Keir and Lloyd were among them, and Lady Montgomery stood in the centre. Upon seeing our entry, the guild's leader arched a brow at us. "I assume one of you has an explanation?"

River cleared his throat. "The Wild Hunt is riding north, and their presence has disturbed the dead in both this realm and in Faerie. I believe the Hunt's intention is to join the Scourge before returning to strike the city."

"They're travelling via the spirit lines," I added. "That means there's a chance they might use the one on top of the guild to return."

"I am aware of the disturbance on the spirit lines," said Lady Montgomery. "But I will not abandon the guild. We have fought the Ancients before, and we will survive this attack too."

I'd expected her refusal to leave, but would the guild's defences be enough? The building was covered in iron wards, but it'd been designed to keep out the dead and the fae, not the Ancients.

"I don't dispute your skills," I said, "but the Scourge has influence over the dead, and he seems to have psychic abilities too."

Mackie shuffled closer to Morgan, who slid his hand into Lloyd's. The guild had only two psychics, but who knew what other damage the Hunt might do to the necro-mancers?

"Am I to understand that the Sidhe will not be joining us?" asked Lady Montgomery.

"The Hunt interrupted our meeting," said Ilsa. "The Sidhe were too preoccupied fighting the dead to accom-pany us back to the mortal realm."

"Unsurprising," said Lady Montgomery. "The Sidhe are not known for their commitment."

A murmur rose among the crowd at the implied

acknowledgement of her prior relationship with Lord Torin. River lowered his gaze, but his mother looked upon the others without any trace of embarrassment. "I will not give the Hunt the satisfaction of surrender," she said. "I will defend this place with my life."

"As will I," said River. "If they travel via the spirit line, then it might be possible for us to reach them before they return to the city."

"Exactly," Ilsa said. "I'll gladly volunteer."

"Sounds good," Hazel said. "If you guys head them off, they might decide the guild isn't worth bothering with and ride straight past."

"Doubt we'll be that lucky," Morgan muttered. I was inclined to agree.

Lady Montgomery moved among the necromancers, giving orders. Sensing that non-guild members wouldn't be included, I made for the exit behind Hazel. Puck and Roseanne must have slipped outside at some point, if they'd ever come in, but before I reached the doors, Jas and Keir approached me.

"Is Ivy back yet?" asked Jas.

"She went to find the rest of the council," I said. "But if some of them are still up north…"

"Isabel and the witches are still in Edinburgh," said Jas. "We're going to tell them our plan."

Upon leaving the guild, I found no signs of Puck or Roseanne outside, but a group of people had gathered near Cassandra's Café. Hazel waved at them. "Hey, Isabel."

One of the witches detached herself from the group and made her way towards us. I recognised Isabel from when I'd seen her in council meetings, though she'd swapped out her bright attire for something more subdued. When she lifted her hand in a wave, I glimpsed swirling marks inked onto her warm-brown skin. Blood magic.

"I know the Wild Hunt is on their way south," Isabel said before Jas could speak. "Ivy told me, but she ran off to tell the other mages without explaining anything else. I gathered everyone I could, but what exactly are we fighting?"

"Death fae," said Jas. "With the Scourge in the lead. We're gonna divert them away from the guild. Have you met Holly yet?"

"Not in person." Isabel gave me a smile. "I've heard a lot about you, though."

Uncertain whether she meant that in a positive way or otherwise, I said, "If it was you who helped translate those symbols for me a while ago, then thank you."

"It was." She cocked a brow. "Wow, even the half-faeries are here."

"Are they?" I rotated on my heel, seeing Puck and Roseanne leading a group of half-faeries into the street. They must have flown off for reinforcements while we'd been at the guild. Even Darrow had joined them, though he studiously ignored Puck.

"Where have you been?" Hazel asked Darrow. "I thought you'd have come to Faerie when you found out we were there."

"I wasn't in the city at the time," he said in apologetic tones. "I went to look for… well, for Janet Lynn. Call it a hunch, but I thought she might be up to some trickery tonight. Her house is empty, though. Abandoned."

"She'll be in hiding, if she has any sense," said Hazel.

"I have my doubts," said Darrow. "No, she's bound to

show her face at some point, but I'm more concerned about whose side she intends to fight on."

"Assuming she doesn't hide like the Courts," I said. "Has an immortal ever turned out to be reliable?"

"That's a bit harsh on the Erlking," said Hazel. "Poor guy didn't expect a zombie invasion to ruin his day."

"Zombies?" Darrow said. "In—"

"Yes, in Faerie," Puck interjected. "Keep up."

"Don't start fighting again," I warned. "We don't have long before the Hunt returns to attack the city."

"About that," said Hawk, pointing up at the sky. "Is that them?"

I lifted my gaze and saw a dark cloud masking the horizon. The Hunt's numbers had swelled during its brief absence, forming a mass of darkness which entirely blotted out the sky to the north. The Hunt was here, and its target was the necromancer guild. From the outside, the building looked as solid as ever, wards shimmering with glyphs against the iron-laced brick walls… but could they stand up to the power of the Scourge?

Puck moved closer to me, while Roseanne grabbed my arm. "They're here."

"Back to the guild!" Hazel ran to the oak doors, while the others snapped into action, forming groups and handing out spells.

"Holly," said Puck. "You don't have your magic…"

"If you're going to tell me to stay at the guild, forget it," I said. "I can't fight from the spirit realm like the necromancers."

"Same," said Roseanne.

"Roseanne…" I broke off. "The Wild Hunt might target you again. You know that, right?"

"Then they can find me in the guild as easily as outside." She gave me a defiant look. "I'm not running."

As Hazel pushed open the guild's doors, I could see the necromancers in the lobby readying themselves to fight. Some of them sat or stood in silence, their eyes closed or staring into the distance. They'd gone to fight in the spirit realm, with the risk of never being able to return.

"We'll hold the fort here," Ilsa told us from near the door. "We'll be okay."

"You bet." Morgan lifted his gaze to the ceiling. "I'll see if I can reach the Hunt psychically and give them a shock."

"Shut them out if they start to get too violent," Hazel warned him. "None of you even think about dying, got it?"

"Got it." Ilsa gave her sister a nod, and Hazel ran to join Darrow again.

I, meanwhile, hesitated on the threshold. I couldn't help Ilsa and the others if the Morrigan's magic was out of my reach, but I refused to remain under shelter while they risked their lives and souls. Above our heads, the sky darkened, but it was impossible to make out any distinct forms amid the clouds from this angle. Where was the Scourge?

Roseanne made a choked noise. In the same instant, a pressure on my skull made my vision double. I braced myself for another psychic assault, but instead, shadows rushed to the surface of my hands. I stared disbelievingly at the darkness flickering over my skin.

It's back. My magic is back. Darkness roared in my veins, urging me to shift, to fly.

Roseanne's grip on my arm tightened. "They're trying to call us to them. Don't let them, Holly!"

"Shit!" I came back to my senses, but the shadows continued to flicker up and down my arms, urging me to take flight and join the Hunt.

If I shifted into the Morrigan, I might be able to find the Scourge before he caught up to my friends, but if the Hunt's pull was this strong when I was in my human form, it might be unmanageable once I gave myself over to the Morrigan's magic. Roseanne's death grip on my arm reminded me what else I stood to lose, and I had the horrible feeling that even if she hid in an underground bunker, the Wild Hunt's call would still find her. The Hunt's magic trailed like smoke over the city, reaching into every nook and cranny to tease out anyone who might join their ranks.

Roseanne held my arm, whimpering, while Puck's eyes shone with concern. "Is the Hunt affecting you both?"

My decision snapped into place. "Puck, take Roseanne and run. Hold onto her, and don't let her get away no matter how hard she struggles. This is likely to be my only chance to get close to the Scourge."

"You're shitting me," he said. "Holly, you can't join them."

"The Hunt's magic is already trying to draw me in," I said. "So why not let the Scourge think he's won?"

"You might lose yourself in the process." Puck swore under his breath. "Please don't die, Holly."

"I won't." I embraced him, then Roseanne, before I gently pried her grip loose from my arm.

The Morrigan's magic washed over me, and Roseanne cried out my name as wings sprouted from my back and the tide of shadow drew me upward and towards the oncoming darkness.

21

Within seconds, thick shadows surrounded me, blotting out the world below. The Hunt's magic continued to surge inside me, but I fought its efforts to overpower my thoughts even as I let myself shift fully into the Morrigan.

In the haze of darkness, shapes flickered before my eyes, clawed and fanged beasts, stunning banshees, slavering hellhounds, and creepy sluaghs. The pounding of hooves surrounded me on all sides, and I veered to the side as a sleek horse almost ran me down. The two surviving horsemen rode down the path, and to my utter confusion, they both laughed. The light, happy sound merged with the cries of joy emanating from the rest of the Hunt.

"You came to join us after all, false harbinger," said the one-eyed horseman. "You are part of the Hunt now."

Not bloody likely. "Where's the boss?"

"He will come," said the other horseman. "We ride for him, and we ride to victory."

Or devastation. Then again, to the Scourge and the rest of the Hunt, the two were one and the same. The horsemen appeared too far under his spell to realise I was in control of my own mind, so I seized my chance to ask a couple of questions. "Did he give any specific instructions? I mean, how long do we ride for? Until the end of the spirit line, wherever that leads?"

"We go where his magic leads us," said the one-eyed warrior. "Ride with us, mortal."

No, thanks. I let their horses overtake me and began to fly north, in the opposite direction to the tide of darkness flowing towards the guild. Wings brushed mine, and shadowy shapes slowed me down, but I kept moving against the Hunt until a light pierced the darkness.

I flew towards the light, disconcerted to suddenly be able to see the spirit line's path beneath me. The Hunt continued to move south, but they avoided this particular section of the path, and it immediately became obvious why. Two winged shapes crashed into one another in midair, one covered in bright-red scales and the other formed of rippling shadows.

The Scourge. He'd tried join the Hunt, but the dragon shifters had no intention of letting him get away. Blood dripped onto the path as the Scourge flew at the dragon shifter, their teeth and claws clashing as they disappeared into the clouds once again.

"Holly!" Ivy ran below me, her sword blazing in her hand. "There you are."

I swooped down to land at her side. "How on earth did you get here?"

"I went north just as the Hunt started to move south,"

she said. "Figured I'd take down as many of them as possible in the process."

"The rest of the Hunt is already heading to Edinburgh," I said. "Have the dragon shifters been fighting the whole time? They must be exhausted."

"They are." Worry pinched her forehead. "Worse, the Scourge has been getting stronger ever since the Hunt started moving."

"Damn," I said. "The guild is straight in the middle of their route, and the necromancers are preparing to fight on the spot."

"They didn't evacuate?" Ivy said.

"Have you *met* Lady Montgomery?"

"Actually, no," she said. "I've seen her in council meetings, but I can't say we've talked."

A bright flash made us both look at the sky. The Scourge's magic struck the dragon in a bolt of darkness, and the shifter let out an agonised screech. My heart lurched as the dragon toppled out of the air, tumbling head over heels and crashing onto the transparent path of the spirit line. An instant later, the dragon's reptilian form shifted into a woman with flame-red hair.

"Fuck." Ivy ran up to the prone dragon shifter, while another winged lizard launched across the sky in pursuit of the Scourge.

The god, however, had other ideas. In a wave of shadow, he vanished amid the surging cloud of the Hunt and joined the pounding of hooves heading to the south. He hadn't even noticed Ivy or me. *He's going to Edinburgh.*

"Ivy!" I staggered when the second dragon wheeled around in the air and drove a gust of wind across the path before landing next to the fallen dragon shifter.

The second dragon turned into a red-haired woman who looked similar to her companion and crouched beside her. "Ember. Shit. Please don't be dead."

The first dragon shifter stirred, lifting her head. "I'm okay, Cori."

"Get her off the path," Ivy warned her, waving her sword in the air. "Where the hell did that god go?"

I pointed over my shoulder. "He joined the Hunt. Let's move."

Ivy broke into a sprint, while I gave a brief scan for any more low-flying dragons before launching into flight. As soon as I started flying south, the rush of intoxicating darkness tried to draw me into its depths again. I kept an eye on Ivy while I flew, fighting the urge to let the Hunt's magic overtake my thoughts, to become nothing but instinct and let the inevitable tide carry me away.

Despite the tug of its magic, the Hunt's progress seemed much faster now that I flew with the darkness instead of against it. I lost sight of Ivy amid the surge of spirits and death fae, but when a large tree loomed ahead, a thrill of horror hit me. We were almost at the guild, which meant the Scourge had already found my allies.

The shadows veered to either side of the tree without touching it, but a transparent barrier met them on the other side. Lady Montgomery, Ilsa, River, Jas, Keir, and countless other necromancers floated in a wide circle that surrounded the area of the spirit line which overlapped with the guild, their hands igniting with necromantic power.

The entire shadowy mass of the Hunt had come to a complete halt, entrapped within the barrier formed by the circle of necromancers. *Whoa.*

"How dare you?" the Scourge's booming voice rang out, the god's blurry winged shape appearing amid the darkness. *"You will pay dearly for interrupting our Hunt, mortals."*

"We will not have you enter our home," said Lady Montgomery.

Dread pulsed inside me, mingling with admiration and shock. The guild's leader faced the god without fear, while the other necromancers added their strength to hers. Fear pounded in my chest, and when I tried to close in·behind the Scourge, an invisible force prevented me from moving. I made an attempt to catch Ilsa's eye, but it was impossible for her to spot me amid the giant mass of shadow crammed inside the circle.

"You, a mere human, dare to challenge me?" the Scourge said.

"Yes," said Lady Montgomery. "There are defences built in our walls which are more than sufficient to keep out your kind, and I would invite you not to test them."

"I think you misunderstand what I am, human."

The shadows around me began to swirl like a whirlpool of darkness, and the thrumming magic which had urged me to join the Hunt altered imperceptibly. Piece by piece, the joy fuelling the Hunt twisted and changed, turning to raw anger, and a thousand battle cries rose amid the shadows.

It took everything I had not to join the rush in as the whirlpool became a tidal wave that crashed upon the guild's forces in a deafening roar. As it struck, the spirit line turned transparent, revealing the wave of magic breaking upon the city and sending pieces of brick and glass and shattered roof tile scattering into the streets. I glimpsed humans running for their lives as the magical backlash flared outward—yet the necromancer guild remained intact, and so did the transparent circle that surrounded it.

Lady Montgomery. The darkness cleared, showing her ghostly form standing with her arms braced as if to hold back a heavy weight, her power fuelling the magical force field around the guild. The spirit line flickered into view again, revealing the giant oak tree behind the necromancers' circle, radiating a vibrant green glow as bright as anything in Faerie. The same green glow had spread below the feet of the necromancers in the circle, fixating on Jas in particular. When she lifted her head, I glimpsed shimmering green runes glowing on her arms and neck. She'd used blood magic to form some kind of defensive shield which strengthened the necromancers' barrier.

Yet the Scourge was not to be defeated. He roared, his winged form rising above the necromancers. A second wave of darkness rose among the Hunt, and this time when it crashed upon the guild, the transparent circle shattered like glass.

Darkness clouded my vision as the Hunt moved in a surge, while I fought to keep myself from being swept away with them. Panic flared beneath my skin, struggling with the shadows for dominance. *They can't have destroyed the guild. They can't have.*

I beat my wings, the dark haze over my vision lifting to show me the spirit line's winding path. The Hunt overtook me, moving south, and when I spun around to look at the guild, I saw nothing but the brightness of the green glow surrounding the tree. The necromancers had vanished. But did that mean the guild had been destroyed?

Heart thumping, I flew out of the spirit line to look at the city below. *No way.* The Hunt had vanished, bypassing the guild altogether and leaving the building intact. The necromancers' circle may have broken, but they'd held their ground in every way that mattered.

A commotion rose from the streets below, and I glanced down, seeing several people pointing up at me from between the ancient stone buildings. Shit, they must think I was part of the Hunt. Hastily, I flew lower and landed in an alley before shifting back into a human again.

Breaking into a sprint, I made for the guild. My legs shook with adrenaline. The magic of the Hunt continued to stir beneath the surface of my blood, but it wasn't as strong as before. Rounding the corner, I found Isabel helping several injured witches move to shelter.

"Isabel!" Ivy came into view, her sword dripping with blood. "Ah—Holly. Didn't recognise you without the beak."

Right... "Glad you got out of the spirit line. I got stuck in the necromancers' trap."

"They really went all out." She reached Isabel, and they embraced. "Are you okay?"

"You're the one who went chasing after a god, Ivy," said Isabel. "Again."

"Have you seen Vance?" Ivy asked.

"In about ten different places." Hazel ran over to join us. "Bloody teleporting mages... you okay, Holly?"

"Barely. You?" My cousin didn't look injured, but she'd had limited chances to get close to the Hunt from on the ground. So had Darrow and the other half-faeries. Except... "Wait, where are Puck and Roseanne?"

"I don't know." Her expression shadowed. "Last I saw, he was trying to get her away from the Hunt's spell."

A cry rang out from the guild. I turned that way, as did Hazel, no doubt thinking of Ilsa and Morgan. Without saying a word, we hurried over to the doors, which had opened, revealing a commotion in the lobby. A number of figures lay prone on the floor, unmoving, and a large crowd gathered in the centre.

Amid the crowd, Lady Montgomery lay on her back, her cloak spread-eagled around her. River leaned over his mother, shaking her shoulder, but she didn't stir. Ilsa crouched at his side, her expression hollow. Jas had buried her face in Keir's shoulder, while Morgan and Lloyd looked on in stunned disbelief. Being necromancers, they knew the instant someone's spirit had vanished from this realm.

Lady Montgomery had given everything to protect the guild. Including, it seemed, her life.

I backed out of the guild, reluctant to intrude on their grief, my head spinning. The Hunt had gone for now, but the guild might not survive a second attack. Would the Scourge's anger at the Sidhe win out, or would he come straight back here to finish the job?

A crow swooped down in front of me and transformed into Puck. "Holly. I'm sorry… they took her."

Horror hit me. "Not Roseanne?"

"I tried to stop them." He held up his arms, which were marked with vicious scratches. "Almost got her away from them too. Then *he* took her."

"The Scourge."

Puck lowered his hands, his expression bleak. "I'm sorry, Holly."

"It wasn't your fault." I looked up at the spirit line and the darkness heading south of the city. "I'll find her."

He didn't stop me as I shifted into the Morrigan and launched myself into the sky once again, heading south in pursuit of the retreating cloud of darkness. It wasn't long before the thrumming magic infiltrated me again but less intensely this time, as if the Scourge's fury at the guild thwarting him had cast a pall over the thrill of the hunt.

That was why he took Roseanne. As revenge.

I flew onward, over the city and then the countryside until I merged with the shadows. When the Scourge didn't appear, I kept driving forward as fast as my wings allowed. Beat by beat, I overtook the Hunt's riders until the two horsemen appeared within my line of sight.

Atop one of the horses sat Roseanne, who clung to the steed for dear life, her head bowed.

I flew lower, intending to grab her, but the Scourge's booming voice echoed from nearby. *"I sense an intruder who does not wish to be part of the Hunt."*

Ah, shit.

In two wingbeats, the Scourge's winged form appeared, barring me from reaching the horses as they carried Roseanne away. *"It was you who stopped me from breaching the guild, mortal."*

"No, it wasn't," I told him. "It was the necromancers. Shame on you for not being able to beat a bunch of humans, right?"

I expected him to focus his anger upon me, but he didn't move to strike me. *"Why do you fight your instincts, mortal? Why not ride with us?"*

"You captured Roseanne." I kept one eye on the darkness, but the horses were getting farther and farther ahead of us by a second. "You killed innocent people."

"Innocence. Such a human perspective."

"I *am* one," I reminded him. "Also, you're planning to start a war, aren't you? What do you plan to do when the night is over? Retire to the countryside in peace? I doubt it."

"The night is far from over," he said. *"We will grow stronger, much stronger, and then we will return and raze that necromancer guild to the ground. You will join us, or you will die."*

Stronger. That meant they were going after the Sidhe next. If the god devoured the faeries' souls, the Hunt would have more than enough strength to bring down the guild, and everyone would pay the price for it.

Rage and helplessness collided inside me. *Roseanne.* Dammit. I had to divert the Scourge away from the Sidhe, but the instant I moved against him, I'd risk Roseanne's life.

The Scourge raised a hand, and the Hunt changed direction, the darkness veering eastward along another spirit line. The tide of shadow swept the horses along with it, and Roseanne lifted her head when she passed by, her gaze meeting mine for a brief instant. Her expression pleaded with me to let her go, to make the ruthless choice and abandon her to the Hunt so I could return to my allies and stop the Scourge.

My mother wouldn't have hesitated to sacrifice Roseanne for the greater good. Then again, she would never have become attached to a teenage half-fae to begin with. To her, like the Sidhe, love was a weakness, and so was pain.

"I'll join you," I said. "Just—don't hurt Roseanne."

"Good," the Scourge said, his chilling tone raising the hairs on my arms. Shadows swept around me, and the Morrigan's magic reawakened in my veins as the Hunt called me into its midst once more.

The power flowed beneath my skin, urging me onward, until I lost track of my surroundings and my sense of identity threatened to disappear into a haze of shadows and flight.

No. I can't. If I become one with the Hunt... then everything is lost.

A horse rode past me, and I focused on my other senses to ground myself. I saw Roseanne clinging to the horse's back, tears stark on her face. When she neared me, she whispered, "You should have left me behind."

I gave the faintest shake of my head. "No."

Pain seized me at the sight of the heartbreak in her eyes, and I clung to that pain until it formed a barrier against the wave of joy and destruction which fuelled the Hunt. A tear fell from my eye, then another, while we veered towards the brightness of the Ley Line.

We flew onward, towards Faerie… and the end.

22

The Hunt rode on. The Ley Line beckoned, and so did the realm of Faerie on the other side... except a person stood on the Ley Line, right in the path of the Hunt. An unassuming feminine figure raised her head and looked directly at the oncoming Scourge. Janet Lynn.

My ancestor opened her mouth and *screamed.* The noise rippled through the air and sent the entire Hunt reeling. While the audible assault was bad enough, I could *feel* the scream under my skin, clashing with the Hunt's magic until the urge to join the revelry released me from its grasp.

As the Hunt reeled back from Janet's scream, I seized the chance to approach the horsemen from behind. Before they could react, I grabbed Roseanne by the hand, pulling her off the horse and into my arms. She clung to me tightly as we ran through the chaos the Hunt had dissolved into, its shadowy magic merging with the brightness of the Ley Line and turning our surroundings into a blur. I couldn't even tell whether we were in the mortal realm or in Faerie until I spotted an armoured Sidhe warrior swinging a blade at an oncoming skeleton.

Lord Lyle sliced off the zombie's head and stared at me, his usually impeccable face streaked with dirt and grime. "What are you doing here, mortal?"

"I could ask the same of you." I walked towards him, Roseanne clinging to my arm. "Janet Lynn stopped the Hunt before they reached Faerie, but the Scourge is right behind her."

I gestured over my shoulder at the rippling Ley Line, where darkness and light merged together. The boundaries between realms were thinner than ever, and Janet's psychic assault wouldn't be able to hold the Scourge off forever.

Lord Lyle lowered his blade. "You should leave, mortal. If the beast comes here, he will not be able to breach our Court."

"Why, what's the Unseelie Queen doing?" I asked. "Does she think she can beat him?"

His gaze travelled past me. "My queen went off alone, to the Death Kingdom. She ordered the rest of us not to follow her."

"She went *where*?" I'd assumed she'd have holed herself up in the most secure place in her Court if she didn't want to fight on the front lines, but sneaking off to the Morrigan's home seemed out of character, to say the least. "Why?"

"She gave no details."

Roseanne spoke up, her voice hoarse. "Either she's running away, or she has a plan."

If the latter was the case, I intended to find out what it

was. The Unseelie Queen had been there for the first Hunt's creation, and she surely understood the gods more than anyone else in the Courts. Yet despite how close she and the Erlking had come to joining forces against the Scourge, she'd chosen to run off alone and leave her people to weather the assault without their Queen.

Lord Lyle's brow furrowed. "She mentioned the Morrigan."

"She's back?" Roseanne's voice rose in surprise.

"I doubt it." She'd have come to take her magic back from me if she'd returned. "But I bet there's a reason the Unseelie Queen ran off to her home."

With my mind made up, I turned towards the forest.

"What are you doing?" asked Roseanne. "You're not going after the Unseelie Queen?"

"She doesn't get to run away in the middle of a battle." Besides, I'd be a fool not to track down the one person who might know how to stop the Scourge's rampage. Now that I had the Morrigan's magic back, she couldn't hurt me. *I hope not, anyway.*

"Stay close to me," I added to Roseanne. "If the Hunt tries to drag you away again, I won't let them."

Roseanne swore under her breath. "I shouldn't... you shouldn't have taken the risk for my sake."

"What's done is done," I said. "Let's see where Her Majesty is hiding. Are you coming, Lord Lyle?"

"She forbade me from following her."

"You can find a way around that, I'm sure," I said. "She didn't forbid *me* from finding her, and if you follow me, you aren't technically breaking your word."

His mouth pressed into a disapproving line, and when

Roseanne and I headed off the path and towards the Death Kingdom, I glimpsed him following us silently.

The entire Death Kingdom seemed oddly quiet compared to the chaos in the borderlands. Maybe most of the death fae had left to join the Hunt, from the wailing banshees to the lumbering ogres and shrieking redcaps. Unless the Unseelie Queen had terrorised them into hiding.

It wasn't until we neared the Morrigan's lair that we found signs of her presence. The moat had entirely frozen over, corpses and all, and a thick layer of ice gleamed over the crimson waters. Despite being frozen, the smell of decay remained, so I held my breath as I approached the bridge across the moat.

Roseanne's nails dug into my arm. "There's someone in the cave."

"The Unseelie Queen." I gave Lord Lyle a distrustful look. "Roseanne, you should stay back. She has a grudge against your mother for working with Fionn, and I'm not sure she's entirely in her right mind at the moment."

Roseanne's face spasmed with fear, but then she shook her head. "No. I'm not going to be afraid of her."

I opened my mouth to object, but the steely look in her eyes gave me pause. I'd protected her from the Unseelie Queen from the moment she'd expressed an interest in having her very own harbinger, but Roseanne had never made that choice for herself. "All right, but stay close to me."

I made sure to keep myself positioned so that I'd be able to shield her if necessary while we crossed the bridge. Then, holding my breath, I entered the cave.

The Unseelie Queen crouched near the Morrigan's

throne, almost unrecognisable at first glance. Blood and viscera covered her armoured clothing and matted her hair, making her look more like one of the corpses in the moat than the Queen of the Unseelie. Yet her talisman's gleam betrayed her identity, and a similar glow surrounded the contents of a sizeable bowl on the ground behind her.

Not a bowl. A cauldron, brimming with a substance that flickered with blue light. The blood of the gods.

"You—" I broke off. "You *already* remade the cauldron."

"Really, Holly Lynn." The Unseelie Queen rose to her feet. "I'm disappointed in you. You should have guessed."

I should have. She'd agreed to the Erlking's requests too easily, and it would have been simple for her to break their agreement if her Court already had its own cauldron.

"Who gave you the blood?" I asked. "The Scourge is still alive."

"Put your mind to it, and you'll figure it out, I'm sure." She leaned over the cauldron again, the glow casting her face in an eerie light.

Confusion gave way to certainty. "Janet. *You* sent her to distract the Hunt, didn't you?"

How long had they been in contact? Janet had never set foot in the Winter Court, or so I'd thought, but I couldn't believe I'd never considered the possibility of her allying with Winter. Admittedly, she'd shared the truth of the Unseelie Queen's deception on her entire Court, but had that been an attempt to gain my trust while she secretly conspired with the Sidhe?

"Correct, mortal," said the Unseelie Queen.

What the hell, Janet? When she'd brought the Hunt to a

standstill, I'd wondered if I'd been wrong to distrust her, but I'd little expected anything like this. Questions collided in my skull, and the Unseelie Queen's smirk made me want to smash the cauldron over her head. Its metal sheen hinted at a substance not found anywhere on Earth, though, and it'd take more than physical force to break a magical object of that calibre.

"I thought you hated the Aes Sidhe," I said, more to wipe the smile off her face than anything else. "Janet belonged to them once. You must know that."

"Janet Lynn was never a member of their Court," she said. "Besides, the help she gave me was valuable enough that I was willing to overlook her unfortunate history. Soon, everything will be as it once was, and the Hunt will return to its true purpose with a new leader."

"And who would that be?" I sensed Roseanne trembling behind me, but the Unseelie Queen hadn't acknowledged her presence at all. Her attention was entirely on the cauldron. "I'm guessing you won't let Summer join in, despite what you told the Erlking. No doubt you enjoyed pretending to be in a position of weakness."

"The new Erlking is a child compared to me," said the Unseelie Queen. "After the countless wars I have lived through, I do not fear the threat of a lone god, and I will not consent to allow the original purpose of the Wild Hunt to be warped by the foolish ideas the Erlking has gained from taking counsel from mortals and other weaklings."

My hands curled into fists. Her duplicity didn't surprise me, but her strategy relied upon being able to name a replacement for the original Huntsman who would take on the job of transporting souls into the cauldron. Someone she'd be able to exert absolute control over.

"Unless you take on the title of Huntsman yourself, Your Majesty, then there is no way for you to prevent a repeat of Fionn's betrayal," I said. "When you deal in duplicity, you reap what you sow."

"Oh, but there are ways to bend anyone to my will." A light gleamed in her eyes as she looked me up and down. "How useful it will be to have a harbinger as my Huntsman, I wonder?"

I took a step back. "Oh, no. Don't you even think about it."

"A mortal was not my first choice for the job, I confess," she went on, "but you are more than a regular human. I suspect the magic you stole will extend your life span, and if not, then I can always remove it myself and pick a new host."

Shadows swept up my arms, and claws flickered into view. "You want to chain me like you did the Morrigan. Are you so afraid of me that you're willing to commit to making the exact same mistakes again?"

"I fear nothing, mortal," she said. "I am tempted to have you swear a vow that will contain that sharp tongue of yours, but it does add a certain element of intrigue to our dealings, not unlike the letters I exchanged with the Morrigan."

"You're out of your mind." No shit, Holly. She was so scared of change that she wanted *me* to work for her again. "The fact that there was a cauldron in the first place was doomed to end in failure. Even Janet knows that."

"You know nothing of the cauldron, foolish girl," she said softly. "The cauldron was always part of my deal with the Hunt, but initially, only a select few were chosen to be reborn after death and the rest were delivered to the abyss. The traitorous Huntsman warped the cauldron's purpose so he could use it to build an army of his own."

So only a handful of the Sidhe got to be immortal. I bet she included herself in that number.

"That changes nothing," I said. "I know you sacrificed souls to the gods of death in exchange for favours. The Scourge told me himself that once he starts killing your people and devouring their souls, he'll only grow more powerful and more difficult to destroy. Do you want that?"

"The Scourge is inconsequential," she said. "My people outnumber him by far, and he will fall long before he breaches the walls of my Court. If Summer wishes to sacrifice their armies on the battlefield, however, then I will not stand in their way."

"You have no honour." The Erlking had tried to make a fair deal with her, and she'd repaid him by spurning his offer and hoarding the cauldron for her Court alone. No, for her*self* alone. I was willing to bet most of the other Winter Sidhe wouldn't get a look-in.

As the only survivor of the original rulers, the Unseelie Queen was a stark example of the rot at the heart of the Courts. Etaina had perished, along with the former Erlking and his Queen, but as long as the Unseelie Queen remained on Winter's throne, the whole of Faerie would remain entrenched in corruption. She would happily burn down the rest of the Courts in order to preserve her power.

The Unseelie Queen gave me a mirthless smile. "The Morrigan said something of the sort, once."

The truth hit me like a thunderclap. "*You* made the Morrigan disappear."

Of course she had. The two had hated one another from the outset, and even with the queen of the death fae in chains, the Unseelie Queen had felt threatened by her mere presence in the Winter Court. But I'd have bet Her Majesty hadn't foreseen the Morrigan passing her magic on to another person before she'd left this realm. As a result, she wanted me bound to her or else rendered harmless, just to ensure none remained who might challenge her rule.

"The Morrigan threatened me, did you know?" the Unseelie Queen said. "If you ever read the letters that she had you bring me, you'd know that she sought to unseat me from my throne. I should have known she'd find a way to wriggle out of true death."

"She was supposed to be one of the only true immortals in Faerie," I replied. "Because she's related to the Ancients. You, however, are nothing more than a thief."

Anger spasmed across her face, forcing me to avert my gaze from her warping features. "You *will* bind yourself to me, or you will die and forfeit your magic to another. I wonder if that half-blood hiding behind you would like to take your place?"

Roseanne flinched. As I moved to shield her, however, Lord Lyle appeared from the cave's shadows. "I cannot allow this."

The Unseelie Queen's gaze fixed on him. "You would defend a human over your queen?"

"I am bound to defend Holly with my life, since she saved mine."

My mouth dropped open for a second. I'd never asked

him to repay the favour, but the fact remained that I *had* saved his life and that a bond existed between us. One which, perhaps, would not allow his Queen to set him against me.

"I knew I should never have given you a second chance." She rose fluidly to her full height, her talisman glittering in her hands, and brought the blade down on her soldier.

Lord Lyle blocked her strike with the side of his own sword, but when she raised her hand to send a bolt of deadly magic at him, a blur of dark feathers flew into her arm, knocking off her aim. The Unseelie Queen sent a shard of icy blue magic at the cave wall instead, blasting a fist-sized hole in the packed earth.

Fragments of soil rained down as the blast reverberated through the cave. I watched the crow soar around the room, my mind flickering back to the Morrigan—but then it landed and turned into Puck.

"Trickster!" The Unseelie Queen lunged at him with wild eyes, but he shifted forms from a bird to a bear to a leaping flame that danced overhead and dodged her attempts to grab him.

Bolts of magic blasted from her palm, but he flickered out of the way, and her attacks blew several holes into the roof of the cave. Blinding sunlight streamed in, and earth continued to rain down on our heads, splashing into the cauldron.

Puck turned into a human and gave a mocking bow. "You should know, Your Majesty, that the enemy approaches. The Wild Hunt rides again, and it will not be long before they see the damage you have caused."

Another handful of soil struck the cauldron's surface.

Shooting a bitter glare at all four of us, the Unseelie Queen vanished from sight, and so did the cauldron.

"Damn." I stared at Puck. "When did you get here?"

"Not long after you did," he replied. "I was following the Hunt when Janet unleashed her attack, and I used the chaos as a cover to get into Faerie. I saw you and Roseanne leave for the Death Kingdom, but I wanted to keep a close eye on the Hunt."

"So Janet's diversion didn't last?"

"It did." Mischief glimmered in his eyes. "I simply wanted to make Her Majesty squirm."

I looked at the spot where she'd vanished and then grimaced when a chunk of soil fell onto my head. "Wherever she went, this place isn't going to stay intact for long."

Lord Lyle left the cave and began to cross the bridge, so I ushered Roseanne after him. "Do you know where she went? Back to the Winter Court?"

"Unlikely," he said. "She will want to keep the cauldron hidden from the rest of the Court until the last possible moment."

"I'm not binding myself to her." I followed him across the bridge. "I am *not* being the new Huntsman."

"*That* was what she wanted?" Puck asked.

"Only if Holly agreed to bind herself to the Unseelie Queen," Roseanne cut in. "Which is ridiculous. Oh, and the Unseelie Queen is the one who sent away the Morrigan too."

"Of course she did." Puck stayed close behind me as we reached the end of the bridge and retraced our path through the Death Kingdom. "Where'd she get the blood for the cauldron, anyway?"

"Janet gave it to her." The pond near her house must have been more potent than she'd claimed. We never should have taken our eyes off her. "Don't ask me how long she and the Winter Queen have been in touch, because I haven't a clue."

We continued through the woods, which remained eerily empty. Had all the dead in the Courts joined the Hunt? Or had the Unseelie Queen driven off everyone living or dead who got in her way? The sounds of fighting echoed in the distance, but they sounded disjointed, their location hard to pin down.

Where the hell had the Unseelie Queen gone? To confront the Scourge? Or to place the cauldron in the same spot as the last one, on the path of the dead? What would be the point, if the Hunt now served the enemy? Questions swirled in my head as we walked onward until the sight of two figures on horseback brought us to a stop.

The one-eyed horseman spotted me first, his remaining eye simmering with anger. "There you are, mortal."

"I didn't know you were looking for me," I said. "I thought you were happily riding with the Hunt."

Unfortunately, I could guess what had riled him up. With the breaking of the Scourge's hold on the Hunt, their anger at me had returned in full force.

The one-eyed horseman rode forward, his companion at his side, and both of them drew their blades. "We will end this, mortal."

"You changed your tune pretty fast." I called on the Morrigan's magic and shifted into her giant bird form, relieved to no longer feel the pull of the Hunt beneath my skin. "Roseanne—run."

The horsemen rode forward, whipping their blades out. I caught each blade in a clawed hand and tried to twist them out of their owners' grips, but their superior strength won out and forced me to let go. I spun around instead, directing the full force of the Morrigan's deadly stare at both of them.

The two horses reared back, and both warriors jumped clear, landing on the frosted earth. Even without their steeds, they stood a good six feet and a half each, their heavy armour making them seem twice as large as Lord Lyle. The Winter Sidhe ran at one of the warriors, and their blades clashed with a deafening clang. Puck and Roseanne both shifted into crows and flew around to distract him, but the other horseman kept his remaining eye fixed on me. "You are not the harbinger. You are an impostor."

"So was your beloved Huntsman," I responded. "What's the matter? Can't think for yourselves without the Scourge controlling you?"

The one-eyed horseman charged at me. Puck shifted into a bear and slammed into the ground in front of him, while I took advantage of the pause to unleash my claws. A snarl of frustration escaped me when his armour got in the way of dealing killing blow.

The one-eyed horseman moved in a blur, the side of his blade slamming into my shoulder. Pain shot up my arm, but it would have been a lot worse without the Morrigan's thick feathers to cushion the blow. As he raised the sword again, Roseanne dove at his face and dug her claws into his remaining eye.

The warrior roared in anger, batting blindly at his face with his free hand. He swatted Roseanne aside, and we traded blows, fast and brutal, my claws colliding with his sword.

Behind me, Lord Lyle shouted a warning from where he lay sprawled in the bushes. He was bleeding from several wounds, while his opponent gained on me from behind.

Puck intercepted the second warrior, turning into a beast resembling a wild boar and tackling him, armour and all. I winced at the painful crash when he landed on top of the warrior's heavy armour, but Lord Lyle took advantage of the distraction to recover and kick the blade out of the horseman's hand.

Then Puck's teeth came down and ripped out his opponent's throat.

His one-eyed companion bellowed in rage, swatting Roseanne out of his face once again. I went on the attack, but a familiar tugging sensation surged through the magic in my veins. The call of the Hunt.

Shit. The Scourge must have recovered. The one-eyed horseman hesitated for a brief moment, and that was all the time I needed. I lunged forward and stabbed him in his one remaining eye, my claw piercing through to the bone beneath.

The warrior staggered backwards, carrying me with him, and I grimaced when I crashed on top of his heavy armour. Yanking my claw out of his eye, I stabbed him in the throat for good measure. He gave a gargling cry then moved no more.

Drained, I staggered to my feet, my claws disappearing. I wiped my hands on my knees, trying my best to ignore the tantalising call of the magic beneath my skin. I was in no shape to slay a god, but how had he stopped Janet's attack?

"Holly." Puck caught my arm, urgency in his tone. "We have company."

I rotated on the spot as Ivy ran into the clearing, followed by Ilsa and her siblings.

"Holly." Ivy eyed the two horsemen's corpses. "Nice job."

"What are you doing here?" I took a halting step forward. "Where's Janet?"

"I don't know." Ilsa's expression clouded. "We were chasing the rest of the Hunt, but they've scattered."

"Not for long." I held up my arms, indicating the shadows flickering under my skin. "The Scourge is calling me again, but something's different. I don't know—"

"Holly." Roseanne pointed into the sky. "What's going on over there?"

A dark cloud gathered over the forest. Our group moved in that direction warily, and I kept one eye on Roseanne to make sure the Hunt didn't claim her again.

Puck wiped the horseman's blood from his face. "It might interest you all to know that the Unseelie Queen has her own agenda."

"You might say that," I said. "Guess who had a secret cauldron that Janet helped her fill with the blood of the gods?"

"She made another cauldron?" Ivy said. "Fucking hell. I *thought* one of the Sidhe would have tried, but the Scourge is going to be even madder than he already is."

"Janet helped her?" Hazel said. "I thought she was on our side."

"Supposedly, the Unseelie Queen offered her a better

deal." I moved towards the cloud of darkness, fighting the tug beneath my sin.

Then a crack of lightning split the sky, and a body fell downward, tumbling head over heels until it crashed through the forest canopy. *Janet.*

The god descended, wreathed in darkness, wings outstretched across the sky. The Scourge had returned to claim what was left of his army.

23

At the Scourge's arrival, darkness stirred above the treetops, circling the humanoid winged form of the god.

"Come, Hunt," he called out. *"We will ride once more, and we will smite these Courts where they stand."*

Dark spears of lightning shot from his hands, and trees trembled below the regrouping forces of the Hunt. Shadows stirred beneath my skin and urged me back to his side, but I kept my gaze on the spot where Janet had fallen. It might be too late for her, but her voice had bought us time. Admittedly, she'd also helped the Unseelie Queen, but I'd rather the Scourge didn't choose hers as his first immortal soul to devour.

"Where are you going?" Ilsa hissed. "Don't let him control you."

"I'm not," I whispered. "Janet... whether she's alive or not, we can't let him take her soul."

Her eyes widened in understanding, and our group silently moved into the woods. The trees gave us some cover, but we'd have to be careful not to get in the way of one of the Scourge's lightning-bolt attacks. I veered around a fallen tree, keeping an eye on the swirling clouds of darkness gathering above the forest. We passed several exhausted-looking Sidhe who'd been fighting the dead, most of whom paid us little attention, until Morgan let out a yelp that made Hazel tread on his foot. "Quiet."

"I heard her," he muttered. "Janet. That way."

I followed his lead, and a short distance away, we found Janet sprawled in a thorny bush. Her limbs were splayed at odd angles, and blood streaked her face, yet the Scourge hadn't ripped out her soul. She was still breathing, albeit close enough to death to make shadows stir beneath my skin, urging me to heal her wounds.

"Don't." Her eyes flickered open. "Holly."

"Why?" I whispered. "Why did you do it?"

I wasn't entirely sure what I was asking. Yes, I'd have liked to know why she'd helped the Unseelie Queen, but she hadn't needed to take part in the battle at all. She might have hidden away, concealed herself in the forest as she had before, until the danger had passed.

"I..." She coughed, blood bubbling from the corner of her mouth. "I always regretted not fighting at his side... at Thomas's side... one last time."

"Don't try to speak," Ilsa said. "We can get help."

She made a choked noise. "Thomas's last words to me... he told me never to come to Faerie again. I treated his command as if I'd sworn a vow, but I suppose I must break my word after all."

"Hang on." My hands found the fraying threads of her soul.

"Don't repair me," she said. "I have lived too long… far too long."

A gust of wind struck the trees behind us, and the Scourge descended, wings spreading beyond his shoulders like a ghastly rendition of an angel. *"Did you think you could escape, mortal? You promised to ride with me in exchange for her safety."*

He lifted a hand, revealing a struggling Roseanne dangling from his grip, and fury jolted me upright. "I didn't swear a vow to you, and if I did, I wasn't the one who broke my word. Those riders of yours deserted the Hunt and tried to kill me."

"You are a conundrum," said the Scourge. *"You are my kin, and yet you insist on acting like my enemy."*

"Your kin?" Was that why he'd spared me so far—the presence of the Morrigan's magic? "Yeah, no. The woman who gave birth to me once said the same, but she means nothing to me, and neither do you. Family doesn't stem from blood or magical bonds."

My gaze went to Roseanne, who said, "Damn right. Let me go." She yelled and squirmed, but she couldn't break free of the god's grip.

"This is pointless," I shouted up at him. "You do realise that if everyone in the Courts is dead, there won't be anything to rule over but ruins, don't you?"

"It is no less than what they did to the Ancients."

"I know that." How could I make this unfeeling being see that perpetuating the same cycle wouldn't lead anywhere? "The first Sidhe, that is. They're long gone, and the one person who I know *was* alive to take part in the slaughter of your fellow Ancients is currently on the path of the dead, hiding a replacement for the cauldron of resurrection."

"What do you say, mortal?" He flew closer to me, Roseanne dangling perilously from his clawed hands. *"What web of lies do you weave?"*

"She isn't lying." Janet stirred, coughing. "She tells the truth."

What is she playing at this time? She didn't need to alert the Scourge to her survival, not when he might still devour her soul. Besides, she'd given the Unseelie Queen the blood of the gods with her own hands.

"The Unseelie Queen remade the cauldron," I told the Scourge. "She had it forged in secret while the rest of her Court was unaware. She intends to remake the Wild Hunt to serve herself alone—after she has slain you, of course."

The Scourge released Roseanne. She tumbled over with a cry, shifting into a bird mid-fall. While Puck moved forward to catch her, the Scourge released a howl of anger which reverberated throughout the growing cloud of darkness comprising the Hunt.

Evidently, I'd hit a nerve. It was a wild gamble to make, but I couldn't think of a better way to stop the Scourge's rampage than to pit him against the Unseelie Queen and hope they finished one another off.

"Where is she?" he roared. *"Where is the traitorous Sidhe?"*

"I don't know," I said, "but if I had to guess, she's in the same place the cauldron used to lie, at the end of the path of the dead."

If she wasn't, at least we'd bought ourselves time. The Scourge spun around, becoming one with the cloud of darkness, which swept away over the treetops and out of sight.

Meanwhile, I turned back to Janet Lynn. She lay silently in the bushes, her mouth parted, eyes partly open yet lifeless.

"She's gone." Ivy limped to my side, her blade dangling from her hands. "She put up a hell of a fight, though."

Shit. Had I doomed us all by not reviving Janet when I'd had the chance? She'd asked me not to, but she was the only person who'd come close to stopping the Scourge in his tracks. A faint glow surrounded her body, and I took an instinctive step back.

As I watched, a transparent figure rose from the bushes, looking down at her broken body in puzzlement. "This is… strange."

"Do you still have your psychic abilities?" Some necromancers did keep their abilities after death, until they passed beyond the gates, at least. And since this realm didn't *have* any gates of Death, I could only assume she'd stick around for the duration. I bloody well hoped she would, anyway.

"Yes," said Janet, "but I don't know how long I can stay."

"Stick close to me," I said. "You don't want the Scourge to catch you."

She shuddered. "No. I don't."

"We're chasing him down?" Ivy hefted her sword. "Please tell me you and your cousin have a plan."

"You mean Ilsa?" I looked over my shoulder, but she'd disappeared from sight.

"Yeah," Ivy said. "She ran off a minute ago and took her talisman with her."

"If she's planning something, she didn't tell me what it was." I left Janet's body behind and retreated from the forest, my gaze on the shifting cloud of darkness. "We'll find her. Maybe I can take the Scourge down from behind while he's distracted by Her Majesty."

"I tried," said Ivy. "I stabbed him at least a dozen times, but he didn't go down. Better hope the Unseelie Queen can take him on."

"Not sure it'd be much better if she won, to be honest." For the lack of any better options, I followed the retreating cloud of darkness through the trees, Janet's ghost floating alongside me.

Ilsa must have found a shortcut, because I saw no signs of her on our way through the forest to the path of the dead. Silence followed us, while Janet drifted in the lead, transparent against the trees. With the absence of the Wild Hunt's magic tugging at me, exhaustion began to creep in, while I had serious trouble seeing a way out of this shit show which didn't end with us all dead. If Ivy's talisman hadn't been able to bring about the Scourge's end, would even the Unseelie Queen be able to thwart him? If she did, I doubted her victory would lead to any improvements in Faerie *or* the mortal realm.

This fight was between the Sidhe and the gods now, though, with the rest of us nothing more than collateral damage.

Soon enough, the path of the dead appeared beneath our feet, its packed earth trampled flat by countless hooves and its winding route stretching into the distance. We walked until the shadowy mass of the Wild Hunt came to a halt at the path's end, swirling above a glimmering light. I'd been right, and the Unseelie Queen had laid the cauldron in its former resting place. She stood bathed in its glow, her expression betraying no surprise that she'd been found.

"Scourge," she said. "Have you come to return home?"

The Scourge's black lightning shattered against an unseen barrier which surrounded both the Unseelie Queen and the cauldron. Words whipped from her mouth, having no effect on their target as the Hunt's darkness swirled around the Scourge and formed a shield against whatever Invocation she'd used.

"You dare to use my own tongue against me?" he roared.

As the two struggled against one another, unable to break each other's defences, I spotted Ilsa crouching out of sight behind a nearby bush, gripping her talisman. Yet she didn't dare move closer to the battle, where the Unseelie Queen held the Scourge's entire army at bay with the force of her power.

Words rang out in the Unseelie Queen's resonant voice, and a great swathe of darkness opened within the air in a deep slash that cut across the area above the path. *The afterlife.* The Unseelie Queen had opened the god's own realm, but as long as the Scourge remained at full strength, she wouldn't be able to banish him. Would she?

"You will not banish me." Behind the god, the Hunt's magic rose in a tidal wave, breaking against the Unseelie Queen's barrier.

Janet drifted closer to the battling immortals, moving too fast for me to utter a warning. I realised what she was about to do a second before she began to scream.

She might no longer be breathing, but her scream reverberated painfully against my eardrums and caused the Scourge's shadowy barrier to shatter like glass. The

Hunt broke apart, reeling away from the sound of her cry, leaving their master alone.

Wait. Janet's psychic attack had done more than drive back his army. It'd also temporarily broken the link between the Scourge and his followers. A knowing smile spread across the Unseelie Queen's face before she raised a hand and beckoned the army of the dead to swarm over to her side.

To the cauldron.

The shadowy army reformed, surging forward, and this time no invisible barrier blocked them from reaching the Unseelie Queen. Yet they didn't attack her, instead moving around the cauldron, drawn towards its life-giving waters. She'd single-handedly stolen the god's army from under his nose.

The Scourge gave a cry of pure rage, but his army no longer answered to his call. One by one, the dead sank beneath the surface of the fluid substance within the cauldron. And one by one, they rose.

No longer were they the insubstantial shadows of the dead and the damned. The creatures which stepped out of the cauldron were more akin to Sidhe, creatures of unimaginable beauty and terrible power yet cloaked in the same darkness that had surrounded them when they'd served the Scourge. The god roared his displeasure as his former soldiers emerged from the cauldron and joined the Unseelie Queen's side.

"The Scourge seeks to take your newfound life from you," the Unseelie Queen told the newly reborn warriors. "Stop him."

The army charged at the Scourge, some running, others sprouting wings like fallen angels and launching into flight. The god fired bolts of darkness from both hands, but for every soldier he felled, another rose to take their place. As the weight of a dozen winged creatures dragged the Scourge out of the air, the Unseelie Queen laughed, high and cold.

"I have no need of my old Court any longer," she said, her voice echoing as if speaking to Faerie as a whole. "I will reforge this realm anew."

The god released a horrible scream, his winged form hardly visible beneath the confusing mass of creatures holding him captive. Shadowy yet graceful, and… falling to pieces?

One by one, the immortals stumbled back, legs crumbling, their beautiful features tarnished as their skin peeled from the bones. More swiftly replaced them, but their newly reborn immortal bodies were mutating before our eyes. Rotting flesh replaced smooth skin, brittle bones snapped, and life faded from their eyes. The Unseelie Queen's bright-blue eyes widened in horror as the army—some still rising from the cauldron's depths—turned to little more than lumbering zombies.

Before the Scourge could throw off his weakening foes, however, Ivy's blade speared him from behind. As if waiting for her signal, Ilsa leapt out of her hiding place and shouted, "Go back to the realm of shadows, Scourge."

A bolt of bright blue energy arced from her talisman and crashed into the Scourge, pushing him towards the rift the Unseelie Queen had opened.

Countless zombie-like creatures battered at the god as he beat his wings in an attempt to free himself, but Ivy gave another swing of her blade and knocked him closer to the darkness of his own realm. A second blast from

Ilsa's talisman sent him tumbling through the rift and out of sight.

The Unseelie Queen, however, had bigger problems. The remainder of the Scourge's forces continued to enter the cauldron, but they lasted little more than a few seconds before their flesh rotted and their skin peeled from their bones.

I rounded on Janet, who hovered at my side. "That was you, wasn't it?"

"It was." A faint smile touched her transparent features. "The blood in the pool at my house was potent, but it was easy to corrupt. The true lifeblood of an Ancient can only be drawn at the moment of death, the instant their soul is severed."

She tricked the Unseelie Queen. She'd known precisely what the Queen of Winter had wanted, and Her Majesty's eagerness to avoid letting the rest of her Court in on her plans had spelled her own doom.

As her fledgling army collapsed, however, the dark slash in the air shimmered around the edges for a moment before the Scourge clawed his way out once more. *Crap.* If anyone dealt a killing blow to him, they'd be able to refill the cauldron after all. This wasn't over yet, and while the Scourge was visibly weakened from his wounds, he wasn't defeated. One wing emerged from the rift, then the other.

Hooves pounded on the path, and a number of Sidhe ran or rode into view, others emerging from the trees in front of the Scourge. The god freed himself from the void, but Janet let out another deafening scream. The Scourge fell back as though he'd been hit by a truck, and I took my chance to strike.

Shifting into the Morrigan, I launched into flight before tackling the god head-on, my claws hooking into him. If I ripped out his soul before someone dealt a fatal blow to his body, then no blood would be spilled and the Sidhe would lose their chance at victory.

"Don't you dare, mortal!" The Unseelie Queen flung a shard of ice straight at the Scourge, only for her attack to shatter against Ivy's sword.

I dug my claws in deeper, ripping into the Scourge's spirit. With a wrenching sensation, his soul came loose, snagging on my curved claw. Keeping a firm hold on the nebulous form of the god's spirit, I gave another firm tug. The god's winged body tumbled headfirst out of the air, and when the Scourge's ghostly form left his body, the Unseelie Queen sent another icy attack at him—or rather, at me.

When I dodged, the Scourge's ghost slipped out of my grip, but Janet's ghostly arms locked around his wings from behind. The god's body lay facedown, unmoving, as Janet held onto his ghost, dragging him through the rift. He gave a desperate lunge, but she screamed—the sound cut off—and they both vanished.

Janet's last scream rang out, turning into a cry of victory, before all fell silent. For a moment, everyone stared into the rift. Then a large feathery shape emerged from the void.

The Morrigan's wings stretched out, her feathers as black as pitch, and her eyes gleamed with mischief as she landed near the cauldron.

"You!" The Unseelie Queen pointed at the Morrigan, her hands aglow with magic. "You should have stayed where I put you."

The Morrigan gave a wave of her clawed hand. "You didn't think I would survive when you banished me, did you? You hoped the gods would devour me, and they might have—had the Scourge not escaped when he did."

The Scourge's body lay unmoving on the ground. Could the blood spilling from his wounds be called "lifeblood" if his soul and body had split without a fatal blow being dealt? Surely not, but we had bigger problems. As the two angry queens faced off against another, another shadow appeared against the gaping hole in the air. Magic rippled around the Scourge's winged form as his grasping hands once again tried to pull himself out. *Damn, he's persistent.* When his soul and his body had split, he'd taken his magic with him into the void, but if he was able to return to his body, then there was still the possibility of a fatal blow creating a new source of lifeblood.

"I close the rift!" Ilsa ran forwards, her talisman glowing in her hands. "Close!"

Her cry rang out in the language of the gods and was echoed by a dozen Sidhe as well as Ivy. The rift shimmered at the edges and began to close, but not fast enough. A haze of shadows folded outward, and the Scourge's spirit emerged from the rift, unnoticed by the Unseelie Queen or the Morrigan.

If a human's soul was severed from their body, they were dead. A god, though? Janet had vanished into the void, and I was the only one left who might be able to stop him from returning to life.

I launched into flight, hooked my claw into the Scourge's soul, and held tight. His winged form vibrated with mocking laughter. *"You cannot banish me, mortal."*

"I can do worse." I drew back and flung the Scourge's spirit into the cauldron.

His spirit sank beneath the bubbling, glowing surface and into the mist. The warring faerie queens looked away from one another for long enough to see the Scourge emerge from the cauldron, the liquid-like substance trickling off his ghostly form. A solid body formed around him, tall and Sidhe-like—yet he'd hardly taken a step before he began to crumble to pieces.

"No!" The god's voice was strident, pleading, but it was too late. Skin peeled from bone, and the rotting skeleton which had once been an Ancient fell to the ground, his blood no more potent than the cursed substance rippling in the cauldron.

The Morrigan watched him fall with satisfaction. "Good."

"Good?" The Unseelie Queen jabbed a finger at me. "She ruined our last chance to get genuine lifeblood, and Janet Lynn lied to my face."

"If she hadn't, you'd be dead," I told her. "Be glad of it."

The Unseelie Queen unleashed an inhuman roar, shards of icy magic shooting from her fingertips. The Morrigan vanished into shadows, but she wasn't the target. The attack slammed into the cauldron, causing it to shatter, and I flew high to avoid being hit by the cursed liquid as the thousand pieces of metal which had formed the new cauldron scattered into the clearing.

The Morrigan reappeared from the darkness, laughing softly. "How tragic, to see your new cauldron reduced to a failure."

"Janet was working with you instead, wasn't she?" I addressed the queen of the death fae. "What I'd like to know is this: did the Unseelie Queen banish you, or did you leave of your own accord?"

"A very good question," she said. "I saw her actions coming, so I took precautions."

"You might have mentioned you knew Janet Lynn." She might even have known Thomas, too, though she'd been chained down during the last battle and hadn't been able to intervene. "Did you expect the Wild Hunt's ritual to succeed?"

"I gave you everything you needed to win, didn't I?" she croaked. "Even against a god."

"Only to free yourself."

Which had, no doubt, been the point. She'd been chained in iron as a punishment for her former alliance with Fionn, and while she'd spent every waking moment contriving a way out, ultimately, she'd realised that the only way to ensure her freedom was to let the Unseelie Queen think she had the upper hand. She'd even gone as far as to allow herself to be banished into the void while the Scourge ran rampant, until a convenient time for her to return presented itself.

The Scourge had been a powerful adversary, but the Morrigan had no doubt been confident that the Sidhe would eventually bring him down. It probably didn't matter to her whether the cauldron was recreated or not, but she hadn't been able to resist the chance to join forces with Janet in order to thwart the Unseelie Queen's schemes and come out on top.

"You conniving snake," the Unseelie Queen said. "Was everything you did simply to free yourself of the bindings that you deserved to have placed upon you for serving the Huntsman?"

"If you were not so determined to gain supremacy over Death, then I would not have needed to set myself against you," said the Morrigan. "I *am* eternal, but you are not."

And me? I still had some of her magic, and now I knew why the Unseelie Queen had been so incensed when I'd shown up with the Morrigan's power at my fingertips after she'd thought she'd washed her hands of a dangerous enemy. Yet the Morrigan hadn't cared how I used her power. Everything she'd given me had been for her own gain.

She was one of the last true immortals, after all, and she wanted to stay that way. She wanted the Sidhe to bow to her rule. We might have beaten the Scourge, but the true victor had been the queen of the death fae. Of the furies.

The Unseelie Queen lowered her gaze, her posture slumping a little. "What do you want of me? You wish to rule the Winter Court in my place. Is that it?"

Can she do that? The Unseelie Queen had won the position by killing the competition, including her own sister. But the Morrigan had thwarted her on several levels, and many of the Sidhe might interpret that to mean she was more worthy of the Unseelie Queen's talisman and her crown. Yes, they might arrange some kind of duel to settle the matter, but no matter how many times she perished, the Morrigan would always come back.

The Sidhe watched both queens, while the remnants of the Wild Hunt began to creep into view again. Those who had yet to immerse themselves in the cauldron looked upon its ruins with a mixture of sadness and defiance.

When the Morrigan raised a claw, the dead halted. She

had command over them. They'd originally belonged to the Death Kingdom, after all.

A chuckle came from the Morrigan. "I will give you time to think over your decision, as I must attend to certain issues that I let slide in my absence. Feel free to send an emissary to negotiate the terms of surrender if you believe it would be too great a threat to your dignity to attend in person."

Anger flared in the Unseelie Queen's eyes, but before she could move an inch, the Morrigan took to the sky, carrying her army with her.

24

The rest of us watched the Morrigan leave, stunned silence reverberating from the shattered remains of the cauldron to the rest of my allies gathering on the path of the dead. The remainder of the Wild Hunt trailed in her wake. The Morrigan might not have the same influence over the dead as the Scourge did, but she had enough to gain control of his army. And if Winter fell under her control, too, Summer would be vulnerable to attack on two levels. No, I couldn't let her become the sole ruler of Faerie.

Yet the only magic I possessed was a reflection of her own. It wasn't enough to beat her.

Think, Holly. The Morrigan already assumed she'd won, but she'd left me with her magic without even asking what I'd used it for. I'd have bet she'd never in a million years have guessed I'd use her lethal power to heal others and not kill. To guide souls into the afterlife and not devour them.

To guide souls...

How had the Hunt originally been bound? Not via a psychic influence but a vow to escort the dead into the afterlife, sworn to the person they served.

I turned to the Unseelie Queen, whose head was bent over the remnants of the shattered cauldron. "Your Majesty."

The Unseelie Queen didn't respond to my words, but I pressed on. "I have a request."

She lifted her head. "Have you not taken enough from me, mortal?"

"I thought you wanted me to work for the Winter Court," I said. "You remember, don't you? You asked me to bind myself to you the way the original Wild Hunt did."

"You wish to become the Huntsman, then?" A scornful note entered her tone. "Or do you seek to mock me?"

"I'll only swear a vow to you if the terms are a little different from the ones the original Wild Hunt agreed to." I glanced over at the nearby Sidhe, who I knew could hear every word. "To ensure no duplicity is allowed. The Huntsman's task is to carry the dead to the afterlife, and they are sworn to no individual Sidhe or Court. Oh, and they are forbidden to use their magic for any other purpose. No declaring wars or killing for fun."

"A good start, mortal." The Erlking strode down the path, holding a rolled-up piece of parchment in his hand. "Whatever the Morrigan might have done, we all know there must be a new Wild Hunt. You have seen what damage the dead can do if they are allowed to roam this realm."

Murmurs travelled through the Sidhe scattered around the path, some of whom had come from Summer, some from Winter.

The Unseelie Queen regarded the Erlking with a haughty expression on her face. "So you seek to bind me into an agreement."

"The only person to be bound will be the Huntsman, if she opts into the position freely." He gestured towards me. "It certainly sounds as though she will."

"What are you doing?" Ilsa hissed from behind me. "You really want to do this?"

"Sure." I kept my voice low. "Provided they manage to come to an agreement without any loopholes, anyway."

The Erlking raised the parchment. "The vow we propose would bind the Huntsman to ferry the souls of the dead from every corner of Faerie into the next world and to otherwise be forbidden to enter the Courts. The Wild Hunt would be a neutral force, as they once were."

Had he guessed my plan? If he hadn't, then he'd evidently had people working on the terms of the new vow for a while. More of the Sidhe closed in around the Erlking and the Unseelie Queen, and they broke into a discussion of terms, most of which flew right over my head.

"Holly." Hazel caught up to her sister, confusion wrinkling her brow. "What are you doing?"

"I'll tell you later." It wouldn't kill her to be patient. The others' expressions ranged from baffled to resigned, but they'd all have to trust that I had a plan to get us out of this. We were down to our last option.

The Sidhe's discussion petered out, and an air of expectation settled in the air as the two monarchs turned towards me.

"Is the future Huntsman ready for us to perform the binding?" asked the Erlking.

"Yes." I shifted into the Morrigan's form, allowing her magic to overtake me until my vision turned the Sidhe to blurs of light. "I'm ready."

The Erlking and the Unseelie Queen both spoke an Invocation, the other Sidhe's voices chiming in unison. They spoke words of binding, words which locked around me like iron chains, melding into the very magic flowing in my veins. When their voices fell silent, I lifted my head. "Is it done?"

"It is done," said the Unseelie Queen. "You are now the Huntsman, Holly Lynn, and from now on, you will serve the dead alone. Not yourself and not us. You will never set foot or wing in the Courts again."

Luckily for all of us, my destination was not anywhere in the Courts. Without a word, I took flight over the tree-tops and soared towards the Death Kingdom.

Soon enough, I came upon the remains of the Morrigan's lair. The ceiling had been removed, opening her cave to the daylight for the first time since she'd been bound in iron. Perched on her throne, the Morrigan watched as I swooped over the bridge and landed in front of her.

"You," she said. "What do you want?"

"Is this a joke?" I demanded, brandishing my clawed hand. "You left me with your magic, and you didn't even think about what it would feel like to be stuck halfway between a death fae and a normal person? What the hell were you thinking?"

"Excuse me?" She rose from her throne, a scowl on her craggy face. "Do you mean to say you did not appreciate my gift?"

"It was supposed to be temporary." I glared at her, not needing to fake my anger. "You ran off to the afterlife and left me to deal with the chaos you left behind. The Unseelie Queen tried to have me executed, the Summer Court kicked me out, and now it turns out you only gave me your power as insurance in case you got stuck in the realm of the dead for longer than planned. You *used* me."

"I thought you would appreciate being able to draw on the power of death," she said. "Isn't this what you always wanted?"

"Are you kidding?" I glared at her. "Even the necromancers nearly locked me up for illegal magic when I raised someone from the dead."

"You did what?" The Morrigan left her throne, her clawed feet digging into the earthen floor. "You raised a human from death?"

"A half-Sidhe, technically, but yes, I used your magic to heal my fellow mortals." I emphasised the last word. "I guess that's not something you've ever considered using your power for, since you care only for yourself."

"I gifted you with a portion of my magic in order to defeat the horsemen," she said. "I did not intend for you to heal your friends and make a mockery of me."

Oh, I'd definitely hit a nerve. When I'd raised River from the dead, I'd been right in thinking I'd overstretched my limits, but not for the reasons I'd feared.

"Too bad," I said. "If you think I'm going to be like my mother, then you're mistaken."

"You ungrateful wretch." She drew herself up to her full height, wings stretching like pillars. "Perhaps I will rid you of the burden of carrying my magic, then."

"You're welcome to try." I smiled at her. "You know, I heard that your magic might even extend my life span. Was *that* an intended consequence? Or did you hope I'd perish before the ability ever proved advantageous to me? Because you might have given me the means of displacing you altogether, if that was what I wanted."

"Ingratitude," she said. "You are as much of a disappointment as my daughter."

I gave a laugh. "That wasn't the insult you thought it was. Your daughter is pretty fantastic."

The Morrigan's claws stabbed me in the chest—not just piercing the flesh but the spirit beneath and the shadowy magic tangled up inside me. Pain speared my body and soul, mingling with a rush of triumph as she wrenched the magic straight out of me. Shadows formed a blot in her clawed hand, merging with her feathery skin —along with the binding spell, which wove into her magic like a thread in a tapestry.

Despite the whiteness edging my vision, I saw the moment she felt the binding spell sink its claws in her. She let out a screeching cry, but the magic she'd taken back had already become hers, along with the vow making her the new Huntsman. The Morrigan's wings spread wide as she cried out in impotent rage, but even the loud fervour of her anger didn't quell the rising darkness dragging me to the ground.

My last thought was that it was ironic that I would be the first soul the new Huntsman carried with her to the afterlife.

———

As my vision returned, I drifted, my ghostly feet skimming the ground of the Morrigan's cave as she raged and stormed at the top of her lungs. I had no control over my motions, as if an unseen force pulled my spirit across the bridge and away from my body.

Ilsa appeared at the end of the bridge, grabbing my hands in hers before I could drift any further. "Whoa, there."

I looked down at her solid hands gripping my transparent ones. "What are you doing?"

"Saving your life," she said. "Relatively speaking. Just hang onto me until help arrives."

"I'm dead, Ilsa."

"Yes, you are," she said. "But the current master of Faerie's afterlife is a tiny bit distracted at the moment."

The Morrigan continued to scream and rage behind me, but the new vow decreed that she couldn't use her magic against another person, human or Sidhe. All she could do was throw an endless tantrum, unable to prevent Puck and Roseanne from flying over the bridge in the form of crows and landing in the ruins of the cave.

"Hold still," Ilsa said when I craned my neck to look at what they were doing. "They're bringing your body back, and I'm not letting your soul go drifting off in the meantime."

"You can't put my soul back into my body, Ilsa."

"No, but I can keep hold of it until you're healed."

I hadn't the energy to argue and simply drifted in front of Ilsa while Puck and Roseanne carried my body over the bridge. Puck's head was bowed, while Roseanne's eyes streamed with tears. When she saw my ghostly form hand in hand with Ilsa, she screamed, "Holly!"

I tried to wave, but Ilsa held me in a surprisingly strong grip for a living person holding a ghost. "Don't mind me. Ilsa says she has the situation in hand. Or both hands."

Puck couldn't see me, but Roseanne didn't look away as Ilsa tugged my ghostly form through the Death Kingdom. The journey passed in a blur, and only Ilsa's grip on my flagging spirit prevented me from drifting beyond reach. My awareness didn't return until we reached the path between the Courts and crossed the Ley Line into the mortal realm.

As the streets of Edinburgh came into view, I saw a crowd gathering around half-blood territory, watching the Ley Line. In addition to Hazel and Morgan, I recognised Darrow among them, as well as Brook and Leyton. Hawk strode over to meet Puck, who carried my limp body in his arms. "Is she—?"

"Not quite." Ilsa all but dragged my ghostly form towards Hawk, though nobody else appeared to be able to see me. "Trust me, she's alive, but she desperately needs a healer."

"Please help her," Roseanne sobbed. "Please."

Hawk's expression softened. "Of course I will, but I can't promise it will work."

The crowd parted around us, with Roseanne leading the way through the gate into half-blood territory. Ilsa held my ghostly hand, while Puck carried my body into the cottage after Roseanne. After he laid me down on the living room sofa, Hawk leaned over my body, his hands glowing with green healing magic.

"I don't think this is working," he said. "If she's already dead…"

Watching his hands moving over my body made me so dizzy that I had to look away. Instead, I watched Ilsa, who released one of my hands and pulled out the Gatekeeper's book. A glow suffused the talisman as she murmured under her breath. She wasn't using the same shadowy magic I'd used to heal Puck and River, but the sensation was similar, a transfer of energy which bolstered my own.

I closed my eyes to stem the dizziness, but a sudden jolt of dread prompted me to open them again. The gates of Death appeared before me, opening to reveal a faint glow as if someone waited beyond... someone reduced to nothing but magic and shadows.

No. She isn't there. Besides, I don't fear death. I don't fear joining her on the other side. She's gone.

I forced myself to turn away from the gates, but Ilsa's grip broke on mine, and I found myself tugged downward into the fog. I choked on nothing as breath returned to lungs which had no right to breathe, and my eyes opened to a kaleidoscope of light. The last thing I saw was Puck's face before darkness descended.

———

Consciousness returned, piece by piece. First came the cold, the sort of bone-deep chill that even the lingering traces of Hawk's healing magic couldn't dispel. Someone had pulled a blanket over me, but I trembled, my hands gripping my arms. *Alive. I'm alive.*

"Holly!" Roseanne squeaked. "You're awake."

"Don't throw yourself on her just yet," Puck said. "Ilsa said you'll feel like shit for a while, Holly."

"Great." My throat was dry, and I gratefully took the glass of water he offered me, my shaking hands making it hard not to spill any. "How long have I been out for?"

"A while," said Puck. "Ilsa told me that necromancers often get weird side effects from disconnecting from their bodies for a long time, but you were—"

"Dead." I swallowed hard. "I don't understand. Why bring me back?"

We'd lost so many people, yet out of everyone who'd died, *I'd* been spared. I placed the glass down before it fell from my clumsy fingers, my body trembling. Disregarding his own advice to Roseanne, Puck pulled me into his arms. I clung to him with both hands, sobbing like a child until exhaustion drew me into its embrace once more.

When I woke again, it was dark outside the window across the room. I glimpsed Puck's bright hair against the side of the sofa as he leaned back with his legs outstretched. Upon seeing that I was awake, he tilted his head back and smiled up at me. "Hey."

"Have you been here the entire time?" I looked down at him. "It can't be comfortable to sleep on the floor."

"I'm not asleep. Besides, Roseanne took the armchair."

I blinked across at the other side of the living room, where Roseanne had curled up like a cat in a nest of cushions, and then I drew my knees up to my chest. "Here, sit next to me."

He bounded onto the sofa in a smooth motion, and I shivered when he dislodged the blanket to join me underneath. His hands were freezing cold, but so were mine. We lay together for a few long moments, not speaking, sharing the little warmth we had.

"Your cousins have been calling every few hours," Puck said. "If you're awake in the morning, they'll be on the doorstop, no doubt."

"Don't they have more important things to do?"

He rested his head against the cushions. "You stopped the Morrigan becoming the ruler of Faerie *and* defeated the Scourge. I'd say that counts as pretty important, Holly."

"I don't want accolades."

If the Council of Twelve wanted to speak to me, I didn't need to hear their meaningless platitudes. I'd been nobody until I'd gained the Morrigan's magic, and now I had none at all.

After the way the Morrigan had used her so-called gift to manipulate me, you'd think I wouldn't miss having her magic, but I did. It hurt like hell. I might have given the power up willingly, but it was hard to ignore the gaping hole it'd left in its wake.

Puck wrapped both arms around me. When I tilted my head and saw the emotion shining in his eyes, I knew he understood. "Are you okay?"

"Honestly?" Was there a way to quantify the pain of losing something I should never have wanted in the first place? "No. But I will be."

As I'd expected, the following day brought a summons to the necromancer guild to meet with the Council of Twelve. I assumed the necromancers had yet to put a new leader in charge, but I couldn't begin to figure out how they'd go about replacing someone as established as Lady Montgomery. Her successor had a lot to live up to, that was for sure.

Puck and Roseanne walked with me to the guild,

where I met the other Lynns outside. Ilsa ran over to hug me. "How are you feeling?"

I hugged her back awkwardly. "Okay. More or less." I didn't elaborate, and luckily they didn't ask for more details.

"Hope you're up for a grilling by the Council," Hazel said. "Nah, it won't be that bad. They want to hear from all of us."

"Even me," Morgan said. "Yeah, I actually got an invitation this time. How about that?"

"I got you one, since you'd only try to eavesdrop anyway," Ilsa replied. "Anyway, I have to drop into the guild for a moment to listen to a quick announcement. You, too, Morgan. The rest of you can come in if you'd like—River won't mind."

A weird choice of wording considering River wasn't with them, but I suppressed my questions and followed Ilsa through the oak doors into the guild.

The guild's lobby was packed. In fact, it seemed as though every necromancer was present as countless cloaked figures descended the stairs and entered via the lower corridors. Morgan went to join Lloyd and Mackie, while Jas and Keir stood on their other side.

When the lobby was full, River strode to the front and raised a hand for silence. "I brought you here for a quick announcement. The Council has chosen me to succeed Lady Montgomery as the new head necromancer of this guild, and I am delighted to accept the position."

Oh. Of course he'd been chosen as the replacement. I had little doubt that River would do his best to live up to his mother's legacy.

"Secretive, aren't they?" Hazel whispered to me. "Ilsa didn't tell me either."

"Don't forget I've been out of the loop for the last few days," I whispered back.

"The guild has faced a lot of turmoil in recent days. I will not deny that fact," said River. "However, I hope that we can rebuild together while honouring everything my mother created. The city will have need of us in the coming weeks and months, but it is my hope that the guild will remain strong and resolute as we move forward."

He'd been well prepared, I'd give him that, with most of the crowd hanging onto his every word. To finish, River said, "I have been called to meet with the Council of Twelve, so I will give all novice and junior necromancers the rest of the morning free to do with as you like before you return to the usual rota."

"That'll make him popular," said Hazel in an under-tone. "Stops the novices getting under his feet, too, I bet."

"After the last few weeks, everyone needs some down-time," I said.

"Even us," said Hazel. "Not that it's exactly relaxing to listen to a bunch of entitled mages. What're the odds that they put someone worse than Lord Addison in charge next time?"

"Too high," Ilsa muttered. "That was why River had to step in as quickly as he did. Our guild needs to be at full power."

"Where is Lord Addison? Do you know?" I asked. "Did anyone ever get him and the others out of the forest?"

"He's in jail," said Ilsa. "It took a while for anyone to remember to go looking for them, but they never managed to escape the net. What with all the wild fae running around the woods, he and the others were scared out of their minds by the time anyone found them."

Hazel snickered. "Serve them right for underestimating our mum."

I'd been surprised to see Flora Lynn in Faerie, but it was even more disconcerting to see her in the meeting room with the Council of Twelve. Ilsa, Hazel, Morgan, and I joined them at the long table, where the same collection of mages, witches, and necromancers awaited.

This time, it was River who called the meeting to a start. "It's my honour to be at my first meeting as the head of the necromancer guild in Edinburgh. I have every intention to continue working with the Council of Twelve according to my mother's extensive preparations for the eventuality of her stepping down."

It made sense for Lady Montgomery to have been ready for her son to take her place in the event of her death, and I had little doubt River would do his best to live up to everything she'd achieved. The mages would have a much harder time rebuilding, with Lord Addison jailed and their reputation in tatters, but I didn't feel sorry for them in the slightest.

"That is good news," said Lord Colton. "We hope that the downfall of the Scourge has ended the current spate of attacks upon this city, but we would like for the rest of the Council to remain here to oversee the appointing of a new head mage."

"That would be appreciated," River said. "My mother had several recommendations to make, which I can send to the mages' guild in confidence if that would be acceptable."

All eyes went to Edinburgh's mages, who were a subdued group huddled at the far end of the table and who didn't seem to have nominated anyone in particular to speak for them.

"That is acceptable," one of them finally said.

As I'd predicted, the conversation soon turned to the Scourge's demise and the Morrigan's return, along with my success in thwarting her plan for domination over Faerie. While the council wanted to hear from everyone, they left me to explain those crucial last moments when I'd conceived of a plan to steal the Morrigan's newly won freedom from her own claws.

"Admirable," said Lord Colton. "So am I to understand that the Morrigan is no longer an equal to the Erlking and the Unseelie Queen?"

"It wouldn't surprise me if the Unseelie Queen didn't hold her title for much longer either," I said. "Her Court sees strength as a virtue, and she lost hers in front of an audience. She was also tricked by a mortal several times over, and it won't be long before they all find out she lied to everyone for centuries about her own role in the original Wild Hunt's role and the creation of the cauldron."

I wouldn't lie. I was a little worried the Unseelie Queen would take the loss out on the rest of her Court. Or on me. Without any magic, I was vulnerable to her whims, but I doubted the mortal realm would be her target. Still, it was the Morrigan who'd truly lost out. She could rage and scream all she liked, but a binding was set in stone, and she would carry the dead to the next world throughout all her immortal existence whether she wanted to or not.

As the meeting neared its end, River took charge again.

"When the Council of Twelve was originally set up, the Sidhe played more of a role in its decisions," he said. "We hoped to continue that tradition, but the turmoil in Faerie's leadership has made that somewhat difficult in recent years. However, we cannot deny that our realms have been intertwined for thousands of years and that we all have a lot we can teach one another. The necromancer guild, for one, would be happy to work with the half-Sidhe living in this city as well as those in the Courts."

"An alliance between faeries and necromancers?" I whispered to my cousins. "Are you sure they'll go for that?"

"You never know," Hazel muttered. "The Court being overrun by zombies might have changed some of their minds. Besides, River has a foot in both worlds."

True, but which world did I belong in? That remained to be seen.

When the meeting came to a close, I left the guild along with the others. Puck and Roseanne met me outside and accompanied me back to half-blood territory, where we found a familiar Sidhe waiting near the back gates.

"What does Lord Lyle want?" I remarked in an undertone. "To learn necromancy?"

Roseanne snorted. "When Summer freezes over."

"I wouldn't tempt fate." I approached Lord Lyle. "Has Her Majesty called for me, by any chance?"

"No," he said. "It is the new Huntsman who I have been sent to meet with."

An uneasy shiver ran over my skin. "I wasn't aware that you were carrying messages on her behalf."

"I am not, but the Unseelie Queen refused to meet with the Huntsman and asked me to go in her place."

"So… you want me to go with you to speak to the Morrigan?" Was he still afraid of her? Maybe. Even with her wings metaphorically clipped, she was still a force to be reckoned with.

"It won't take long," he said. "These days, even her own fellow death fae avoid her."

"Serves her right," I said. "You want to go now?"

"Seriously?" said Roseanne. "You don't have to do anything the Sidhe ask, you know."

"No, but I'd like to make sure the new Huntsman isn't shirking her duty." I'd also like to ensure that the vow was working as intended. "Provided Lord Lyle promises that I won't come to any harm."

"Nor me," Roseanne said. "I want to come with you."

"If you're sure." My gaze landed on Puck. "I know you're going to follow me anyway."

"Obviously." A smile played across his lips. "I wouldn't have it any other way."

Lord Lyle led the way to the Ley Line, where we disappeared in a flash and reappeared on the path between Courts. I didn't have my realm-crossing ability any longer, but that was the least of what I'd lost when I'd parted ways with the Morrigan's magic. Still, the pain had lessened in the days since my return, and in time, the sting would fade, if not entirely disappear.

"What's going on in Winter, then?" I asked Lord Lyle. "Is the Unseelie Queen doing well?"

"She's been locked up in her quarters ever since she returned from the path of the dead."

"So that's a 'no,' then."

It didn't come as a surprise, considering how thoroughly she'd been defeated. Not just by the Morrigan, but by me, a simple mortal who'd once been entirely at her mercy.

"She fears losing her throne," he said. "She fears irrelevance, and she fears exile. Specifically, being exiled to the Vale, where her sister's ghost still roams."

"Does everyone know she killed her sister, then?"

"It's never been a particularly well-kept secret." His tone sounded sad, rather than recriminating. "Not compared to her role in binding the Wild Hunt, at any rate."

"Guess not." I walked on through the frigid woodland, with Roseanne and Puck at my back. "Is it likely that someone will try to usurp her throne?"

"If she isn't careful, then it's almost a certainty," he said. "But the current law in the Winter Court is that only the wielder of the Unseelie Queen's talisman has the right to sit on the throne, and she guards it carefully. If she dies, however, she has no replacement named."

Most of the Sidhe's strongest weapons were forged from the gods' magic, but I didn't know if that was the case with hers. If someone killed her, though, there would be no returning from death.

The Morrigan would see to that.

"I'm glad the new cauldron turned out to be faulty," I said. "Janet was more scheming than I gave her credit for."

I got the sense she'd have been pleased with the ultimate outcome, and so would Thomas Lynn. Whether the Unseelie Queen remained on her throne or not, no Sidhe would be able to wrest control over the Wild Hunt with the Morrigan eternally bound as the new Huntsman.

When we crested a hill, I spied the Morrigan's domain. Her cave had disappeared, and someone had even cleared up the bodies from the moat. Instead, the goddess of Death sat atop her throne in the centre of an island formed of barren ground.

"Not much of an improvement, really." I turned to Roseanne. "Ready?"

Roseanne simply nodded, her face pale and her countenance wary. Puck, meanwhile, shifted into a crow and perched on a nearby branch to watch us descend the hill towards the bridge.

"Be careful what you say," said Lord Lyle. "Her initial temper tantrum lasted for over a day, and we were unable to see for the clouds for a long while."

"Soon she'll have her hands full escorting the dead who were killed in the battle." I led the way across the bridge to the island and then approached the Morrigan's throne.

When she spotted me, the Morrigan laughed. It was not a pleasant sound. "So you cheated death as surely as you cheated me."

"Hardly cheating, given that you rewrote the rules of the game at every opportunity," I replied. "Besides, if I'd been dead, I'd have come back here to haunt you."

"I would have taken you to the afterlife myself, you impertinent mortal." Her gaze went to Roseanne. "Is my daughter happy to follow you around like a lost sheep?"

"I'm joining the necromancers," she announced. "That's my plan. I don't need you."

"You can laugh all you like, but you lost," I added. "So you can stop throwing temper tantrums and start actually doing your job. There's an awful lot of dead who need to be cleaned up."

"We have given you this long to recover from your loss," said Lord Lyle, "but if you continue to neglect your new position, we will force the vow to stir you to action."

"I look forward to severing your soul and casting it into the void, Sidhe," she said.

When Lord Lyle flinched, I whispered, "The afterlife isn't that bad. She's the scariest thing in it, and she can't harm anyone anymore, not even ghosts."

"Was it worth it?" the Morrigan asked me. "Becoming a helpless human?"

"Helpless?" I shrugged one shoulder. "That's a relative term. Anyone can be brought low, and power doesn't equal freedom. You should know that."

Anger flared in her gaze, but she said nothing more. Instead, she launched into flight above her throne and flew until her winged shape disappeared from sight.

Upon returning to the path between the Courts, Roseanne and I parted ways with Lord Lyle, while Puck flew over and shifted into human form again.

"No trouble?" he said. "I saw the Morrigan flying off."

"She can't go far," I said. "She has to start doing her job, or the vow will kick in and make her life miserable."

"Oh, good," Hazel said, walking into view. "The Erlking wanted me to tell her to stop pissing about, and frankly, I'd rather eat dirt than set eyes on that evil old bird again."

"Do you always take your siblings with you when you meet the Erlking?" I asked, seeing Ilsa and Morgan behind her.

"No, but I had something we all wanted to discuss

with him," she said. "We wanted to talk to you too. I've had an idea."

I raised a brow. "Am I going to like it?"

"You might," she said. "Janet Lynn left her old house to us in her will, so I thought we could do something with it."

I tilted my head. "What do you mean by 'we'?"

"Darrow and I," she replied. "You're welcome to come and help, though."

"With what?" I asked. "Are you implying you and Darrow are moving to that creepy forest on the Aes Sidhe's doorstep? You really want rogue faeries in your house?"

"Half the country is overrun by rogue faeries," she pointed out. "Which is where I got the idea. Some humans have the Sight, but others can be trained to use it. I think I can help with that."

"You want to train humans to get the Sight?" What was she thinking? "By dragging them into Faerie?"

"Only if they volunteer," she said. "Lots of people want to learn to effectively fight against the faeries, and honestly, most mercenary guilds aren't any good. They can't even *see* what they're dealing with. I think there's a gap in the market."

"There is," said Morgan. "Also, I thought of a name. The Gatekeepers' Institute. What do you think?"

"I think it's a decent idea," I said. "If you want to hire me to work for you, though, I'm going to have to decline."

"Because you already have a job?" asked Hazel.

"Yes, as an employee of Goodfellow Detectives," said Puck. "If she says yes, of course."

"Let me think about that." I faked a thoughtful expression and then said, "All right."

"Thought so," said Hazel, her eyes gleaming with amusement. "And Ilsa is probably going to be promoted to the guild's senior necromancers any day now, if she hasn't already. Not to mention her PhD."

"And there's something else, too," said Ilsa.

"What?" Morgan squinted at her. Then Hazel gasped aloud when Ilsa raised her hand, revealing a ring on her finger. "You and River got engaged?"

"How did you hide that?" Hazel demanded. "You're as tricky as the Morrigan, you are."

"I wouldn't go that far." Ilsa grinned. "I thought I'd ask you for your opinion, though. Which name sounds better, Lynn-Montgomery or Montgomery-Lynn?"

"Why?" said Morgan. "You want to keep your surname?"

"Did any of you think I'd give up being a Lynn?" Ilsa said. "Definitely not."

As the Lynn siblings broke into a heated debate over names, I turned to Roseanne. "You can still join the necromancer guild when you're old enough. You don't have to work for Puck and Hawk."

"I can do both," she said. "You'll need more clients, though."

"It'll be easier without Faerie constantly knocking on our doors," I said. "We'll find a way."

Faerie was glamourous, but I was more than happy to keep both feet in the human world for the time being, building on the foundations of the new life I'd begun to lay down. Whatever else came my way, I wouldn't have to face it alone.

My cousins kept on arguing in a good-natured manner, while Roseanne and Puck walked on either side of me as we travelled through the Ley Line, towards the place where I belonged.

ABOUT THE AUTHOR

Emma is the New York Times and USA Today Bestselling author of the Changeling Chronicles urban fantasy series.

Emma spent her childhood creating imaginary worlds to compensate for a disappointingly average reality, so it was probably inevitable that she ended up writing fantasy novels. When she's not immersed in her own fictional universes, Emma can be found with her head in a book or wandering around the world in search of adventure.

Find out more about Emma's books at www.emmaladams.com.

www.ingramcontent.com/pod-product-compliance
Lightning Source LLC
Chambersburg PA
CBHW030806200726
48285CB00015B/1538